HISTORY MAPS: USER INTERFACE

Gill Kilner

Dedicated to my dear husband Mike, without whom this would not have been possible. And with grateful thanks to my children too, for their constant help and encouragement.

1

'Mum.'

We are driving through a busy junction. I am watching traffic with one part of my brain and lost in thoughts with another. Her sweet voice, from the back seat, calls me back.

'Why do those houses have really small doors?'

I know which ones she means, without needing to take my eyes off the road.

'Because they're hundreds of years old,' I reply.

'Were people really small, in those days?'

'Not really. People were almost as tall, in medieval times, as they are nowadays. They only started getting smaller when most of them had to work in factories and mines, more recently,' I tell her.

I am consciously modifying the terminology. She can understand factories and mills, but not, I think, the Industrial Revolution. It occurs to me that perhaps I should name it, to give her the chance to find out what it means if she wants to, but then she herself brings it back to the initial question of door sizes.

'So why the small doors?'

'I think it might be to do with the way houses were built, back then. An opening creates a weakness in the structure, so it made sense to keep them small. Maybe also because they wanted to try to keep the heat in and opening a big door would let it all out.'

Her next question is the one that makes me really ponder my reply.

'Were there just four families living here, then? Then more came and they built bigger houses, with bigger doors, because they knew better ways of building?'

We have stopped at a red light, thankfully, so that I can look around and think, try to take myself back in time, by about four or five hundred years and see how it must have been then, when the little cottages were new.

'No, I think there was a bigger settlement here, when those houses were built. Look at the pub next to us. Can you see how small its doors are? I think it's probably as old as the cottages and maybe even older. We'll look online, when we get home and see if we can find out anything more. That row of cottages, over there by the mills, looks old too, so I bet they were here then. And if there was a pub and cottages, there were probably farms and maybe even a market.'

'Why have a market here in this little place, when the big town is just up the road?'

The lights are changing. I am easing up my clutch and leaving space for the car beside me to switch lanes.

'Well, it's just up the road if you have a car, but do you know how long it would take to walk there?'

'Hmm...' In my rear view mirror, I can see her looking back in the direction of town, trying to gauge the distance, to make a guess. 'About half an hour?'

'I think, more like an hour. We'll look more closely on the way back. Maybe even park up and time ourselves walking it?' I can feel, rather than see, her nose wrinkling up behind me.

'Nah,' she says and we both laugh. 'Let's just guess. Or get Google Maps to tell us. What's your point, anyway? Too far to walk into town all the time?'

'Yes. It would take too long. I think they might have traded for most of what they needed there, in that settlement.'

'What's it called, anyway? And didn't they just make or get all of their own stuff? What would they be buying or selling?'

We are rapidly leaving what is now just a road junction, but would have once been a picturesque and possibly quite vibrant settlement in its own right, instead of the nodule on a major transport route to which it is now reduced.

I feel sad, not to be staying there and looking around, while Amy is interested.

I want to go back and properly explore that place with her, through which we usually only drive on the way to somewhere else, but I also feel a familiar reluctance to pull out of the relentless flow of traffic, especially spontaneously. I would slow someone down and make them wait and I could not see where to park. Even now, I cannot see anywhere to turn round, even if we did want to go back.

'I think it's called Bradley,' I reply. 'I ought to know, really, since it's only a few miles away from home, but I don't really think of it as a place.'

'I didn't really think of it as a place, either. Not until we started thinking about what used to be here. I do now, though.'

'As for buying and selling, I think they did start to specialise around that time, when those houses would have been built.'

'What do you mean by specialise?'

'Oh, so… up until then, probably nothing much was traded outside of the towns. Each farmstead and cottager would produce their own food and clothes and cut their own firewood and so on. But after The Plague…'

'The… *Plague*?' I laugh at the drama in her voice. The age she is – eleven – I cannot work out whether she is being sarcastic, when she does this. *Not that it matters.*

'Yeah, you know, the big illness lots of people died from, in the 1300s.'

'It's okay, Mum, I do know about The Plague.'

Sarcasm, then. I smile, with warm pride at her maturity

when, in my head, she is still about eight years old most of the time, or even younger, barely understanding words at all.

'Okay, so there were a lot fewer people, which meant it was harder for farmers and landowners to find people to do work for them. So, for the first time, they had to offer something more than just food and housing as payment. They had to actually pay them in money.'

'They didn't pay them in money, before that? Wow. I wouldn't work without being paid money for it. Not unless it was something I really enjoyed and I was just doing it for the fun of it.'

'I *know*! But *before* the Plague, I think that was all they needed and all they had. There wasn't much money around and, because there were so many people, they didn't mind working in exchange for food and a roof over their heads. Also, if you have no money, trading is harder, because you have to be able to offer something the other person wants.'

'Oh, so you have to have the thing they need? Like, if you need milk and they need bread, you have to swap bread for their milk?'

'That's it, exactly.' We have stopped at more traffic lights, so I turn around to engage in some eye contact, for this. I love the way her brain works and feel privileged, to be able to witness it developing.

'But if you don't have bread, they won't let you have their milk, because they want to save it, for someone else, who has bread?'

'Yep, so coins make everything so much easier, don't they? All those people dying from the plague raises the value of work, because there are fewer people around to do it. So the ones who are left actually have coins and can buy and sell, more quickly and efficiently. So that gives them more time to...'

'...to make things! Or, to make extra things. To sell things.'

'Yes, if you have some extra wool, you might make a few spare pairs of gloves, or hats. If you have leather, you might make some extra saddles and so on. Until gradually, people are specialising in whatever trade they're good at, or whatever trade they inherit from their parents.'

'Why don't we inherit trades from our parents now? You didn't, did you?'

She does not mean to upset me. I know this. And she has no idea about the hard swallow I do, to hide it from her. She is right, though. After twenty-one years of parenting and home educating, I have no trade now and possibly no universally recognised purpose to my existence. Except that *I* recognise the benefit, to Amy and her brother, of my focused attention and endless unconditional love and luckily, their dad does, too. But, to the wider society, a woman – even a mother – without a salaried job, is something of an aberration.

We are about two miles away from Bradley now, progressing through the mixture of little-used fields and suburban semi-detached and terraced houses, that fill so much of West Yorkshire in between the busier places. It is the scenery, on our route to activities and structured lessons.

I am coming up with an answer to her last question.

'Some people still do. Our milkman took over the round from his dad. Mr Leyland's son, Craig, is going into his accountancy firm...'

'*Eww*. Why?'

'Well, some people like accountancy!'

'It's just *maths*, isn't it? I don't know who would want to do *that* for a job...'

'Some people like it! Craig Leyland must. Anyway, we have more choices now, because of schooling.'

It is not until I say it, that I fully realise the truth of this and the possible hypocrisy, of *me* saying it. But I have to fully explain to her, as much as she wants to understand.

5

'I don't have schooling and I don't miss it,' is her retort. 'How does schooling help our choices? I've got loads of choices. I don't have to wear a uniform, or study when they tell me to, or keep quiet, or get up super early, or go to bed on time, or do what they tell me to do, all day long. It's the school kids who have fewer choices than *me*.'

'Yes, but they'll all take exams and get certificates that get them into university…'

'I don't want to go to university.'

'Well, you don't *now*, but you might, when you're eighteen, or older…'

'I won't.'

'Okay. But the point is, qualifications help employment, like money helps trade. They make it quicker and more efficient. Jobs have got more specialised…'

'Yeah, I know what that means, now. People just doing one thing and getting really good at it.'

'Yes. Jobs have got more specialised and the things we do have got more complicated. And there's a lot more choice, in terms of what we can do to make money, nowadays.'

'I wish I could see that village, Bradley, five hundred years ago,' she unexpectedly responds. I thought we had moved on, past that place, both physically and conversationally, but her wistful words return me to my earlier, myopic squint into the past.

And yes, like my daughter, I am madly curious to know how that place – and lots of others like it – must have looked, back then.

I want to see it, too. See it, walk through it, touch it, even smell it. I am feeling quite sad and frustrated, to know I will never be able to do that.

2

I am sitting at my desk, supposedly writing an article, but the view from my window keeps pulling my attention away from the work. It is a sunny morning in very early spring, the kind of soft sunlight that turns all the colours pastel and highlights the paler structures.

Ours is a hilltop house, overlooking the land of my ancestors, or at least it is the land on which several of the ancestors I know about lived and worked. A quirky variety of old and new industry and housing, nestling in the valleys between sheep farms that sit above tree-clad slopes.

The undulating, soothing green carpets of upland grass are what always catches my eye, but really, the space is dominated by buildings, especially when one is down amongst them. From above, it is more like a three-dimensional map, or even a model village, from which I often feel emotionally distant. Observing, rather than partaking.

I observe that the striking element of the buildings is their eclectic design and era. Victorian woollen mills, alien-seeming municipal concrete high-rise apartments, post-modern giant steel boxes of industrial units and then row upon row of old mill houses: shady and crowded, built only for the essential shelter – and never the indulgent pleasure – of their inhabitants.

There are trees on our hillside and trees on the opposite one, still sparse-leafed after a mild winter. My childhood memory is of fewer trees, our culture still then being intent on conquering, rather than hastily befriending, Mother Nature. I was a young adult by the time a critical mass had worked out the carbon-to-oxygen ratio and begun to plant more, in something of a panic, so now they are comparatively everywhere. At the centre of traffic islands, the sides of roads, in gardens and more extensively, on the steep hillsides. Anywhere there is financially viable space for them.

Someone posted a photograph of this view, from a hundred years earlier, to our local history Facebook group, which features a shocking absence of trees. The woodland on our opposite hillside, which I previously imagined to be always there, was absent. The elevation was starkly, embarrassingly naked and vulnerable, like the newly-shaven face of a formerly bearded man. It was the same shape as this hillside and in the right place, but it was inappropriately raw.

To most of my ancestors, trees were vital fuel and building material. Felling them would have been a necessary chore and a duty. Vast swathes of the English countryside were cleared of their ancient woodlands as a virtue, to make space for farming, so that humanity could proliferate. Cutting and burning were daily rituals, in a lifestyle from which they would have viewed our own with utter incredulity.

But prior to that, almost the whole area was forest. We are seventy miles north of Nottingham, but some parts of one of our local towns are named after Robin Hood, because he allegedly died here, on the then outskirts of Sherwood: his sprawling organic empire. The pre-industrial villages are all on the hill tops, near the moorland, where the wind blew more strongly and so the trees grew more sparsely. If I force myself to think about it – and in preference to writing the article in front of me, I do – I grasp something of the enormity of the task of taking down a tree with only pre-industrial tools. Suddenly, their avoidance of the more sheltered, thickly-wooded valleys becomes perfectly logical. Resources were scarce and expensive and if a community was to be settled, then crops had to be grown and access to other settlements made viable, for trading.

In more illiterate ages, the names of places would often have to serve as the main advertisement of its trade. From this village, one would know to travel north to Hipperholme to buy a horse, north-west to Wainstalls for a wagon, west to Heptonstall for a cow and east to Sheepridge to replenish one's flock. Slower, more expensive and therefore important journeys they would be, full of hazard.

I look at the view from my window, through imaginary overlays of history. The Victorian mills and mill houses in the valleys. The medieval farmsteads on the hills and the impenetrable, universal tangle of forest before. But the precise details of my overlay are guesswork and I really want to know for sure.

I am suddenly filled with a fervent desire for an online resource, for the pooling and easy, open access of such information: the gleanings and educated guesses of both professional and amateur historians. A website I could visit with Amy, to show her the way places would have looked at certain points in time. Somewhere to bring it all together, in a simple-to-use, familiar format, like Google's Street View.

I remember seeing a project for a London street presented in this way, so that people could navigate through and between the buildings by computer mouse. It brought that section of time and place alive, in a way that no body of text or two dimensional image ever could. I start wondering what was involved with that and what it would take, to extend the project to different time zones and places. I am beginning to imagine how it might work, when I am joined in the room by the rangy figure of my son Alf, who traverses the short space between door and sofa, in one fluid movement.

Just into his twenties, he is yet to fill out and still seems too long for conventional furniture. My heart lifts to see him again. But at the same time, I am slightly puzzled, because this is not his first visit of the day in which he has been restless, without explaining why, uncharacteristically treating me to some slightly impatient small talk about the weather and my plans for the day. I sense that this time, the mystery is about to be solved.

'So, what time are you likely to be finished in here? I'm not meaning to rush you or anything, but I wouldn't mind some time on the Playstation to have a look at the new game I got yesterday.'

His approach is casual as if he does not really care either way, but I know he hates asking for things, so must secretly be really keen to play. I look at the screen and out of the window again, conscious of the time I have wasted here, picturing and pondering, when I should have been working to meet my deadline for the article. I am working on a potentially mobile laptop, so I could easily yield the room to him and will. But I decide to briefly press-gang him into my fantasy first, before I let it go and knuckle down elsewhere.

'I'm nearly finished, but can I just ask you something?'

'Yeah.' It is said as part of an impatient, testosterone-fuelled heavy sigh. *He doesn't want me to ask him anything, he just wants to play his new game.*

Reducing the number of words I was going to say by a factor of at least ten, I settle for, 'Have you done any 3D buildings at college?'

'Huh? Why?' He is instantly suspicious, as if I am in the habit of coercing his input, which is possibly true from his perspective.

'I just wondered how easy it is to do them,' is my follow-through, which I should have known would make him even more impatient.

Another heavy sigh and a shake of his head, to dislodge the long fringe of hair from his eyes.

'It's as easy or hard as you make it, depending on the complexity, Mum. So are you done here?' His eye is actually fixed on the case of his new game on the shelf, so I admit defeat to myself and close my machine, gathering it up, with my teacup, to finish working in the kitchen. The TV is on, before I have stood up. My single-tracked boy is to be delayed no longer, in the pursuance of his chosen activity.

I am happy to find Hugh in the kitchen, eating and reading simultaneously, a presumably warm shaft of sunshine on his back. He smiles at me too and I am drawn in as usual by his cornflower blue, spectacled eyes under bushy brows. Intelligent eyes, full of thought and inquiry, instantly engaging with mine, as he switches his attention from the book to my face.

'How is the article coming along?' And then he replicates my answering grimace in sympathy and I know he is going to try to be both diplomatic and encouraging, because we do need the extra spare cash my articles bring. But he knows me well enough to fully comprehend how difficult I find it, to keep my mind on the task in hand.

I forestall him with a grin of rebellious hedonism and launch into: 'Anyway, I've had a brilliant idea,' and watch his face for the reaction, even though I can guess what it will be. Mock horror and a groan.

'Ugh. How much will it cost?' My last big, brilliant idea was an earth loo that was supposed to cost next to nothing and be built out of old pallets and other recycled wood, but which is still a dominant feature of our credit card bills, a whole year later. I am bemused and amazed that he indulges me in such things, as in so many other aspects of our relationship.

'Nothing,' I laugh a little at the exaggerated relaxing of his shoulders. 'I'm sure it can't be done, but wouldn't it be wonderful, if... well.' *How to explain it to him properly and succinctly?* I lift the kettle, to check it for water and fill it from the tap, to buy myself thinking time. 'Wouldn't it be wonderful, if... well, you know Google Street View? Wouldn't it be wonderful, if you could use that, to travel back through time?'

His scrunched face of intrigued bafflement encourages me to continue.

'So...' I am thinking as I talk and the idea starts to take shape a little. 'You could visit anywhere and use the Google Street View function to look around, as we do, but instead of it being only for the present, as it is now, it would work for the past, too?' He is still puzzled, so I rush to give words to the fast growing concept in my mind. 'So you could look at this street, for example, fifty years ago? And then a hundred years ago, and then three and five hundred and maybe even a thousand years ago? And you could use the function to mouse around the place, exploring and seeing how things were, then?'

Hugh smiles at this, eyebrows raised and eyes roving, as he envisages my plan in action and I can see that he gets it and loves it. I knew it would appeal to the historian in him, or at least to the computer programmer who once did a history degree in him. I love him for, amongst many other things, his willingness to meet me in my fantasies especially at such times, when many other cash-strapped spouses would be nagging about the looming deadline instead.

'It would be cool,' he says, eyes now half-closed, as he sinks further into it, and then suddenly open and looking directly at me again, his practical mind not able to resist being engaged. 'The university history departments would love it.'

'And, I thought, the local amateur history groups and societies. I'm on about three on Facebook and there are the old-fashioned, real life ones as well still, I think. If only it could actually happen.'

'It could. You could do it. I mean, it would be enormous, but you could try, or at least put the idea out there? It's such a good one that it ought to happen. It would be *so cool*.'

I smile at his enthusiasm. The idea's applicability is beyond doubt, but its development, beyond this initial fantasy concept stage, is unfeasibly unlikely. Especially as we do not run Google, or anything like it. In fact, we have the altogether more realistic and unexciting prospect of an unrelated article to finish. To even begin. Right now.

I slip into the chair beside him and open my laptop again. This time, I force myself to start typing.

3

It is about three years since my friend Ben left his chainsaw in our temporary care and we have barely heard from him since, because they have been so busy with their new public relations agency, in the city. But now, he has messaged, out of the blue, to tell me that they suddenly have a farm.

I am reading the message and my imagination is doing somersaults, as it tries to bridge the gap, between their previous life and this news. *Have they gone bankrupt? Come into money? Decided to commute into the city, instead of living there? Knowing Ben, anything is possible.*

In their relationship, Ben provides the sparky energy, of which he seems to have an abundant store. He talks and thinks fast: ideas constantly shooting from his brain. My favourite attribute of his is his permanently upbeat mood – he is the epitome of enthusiasm. His wife, Rachel, quietly does all of the family's background support, with a seemingly unflappable, enduring perseverance. If they were both water, Rachel would be a lake: serene and peaceful, while Ben would be the loud and foamy rapids, recklessly dashing to a dramatic waterfall.

And now he wants his chainsaw back, so they are coming to visit and are, in fact, about to arrive. Ben is spontaneous. He wants the chainsaw and he wants it now, but I expect they will probably stay for a drink, so I go to prepare the outside seating area. Cushions on chairs, the little camping stove and kettle. A parasol, which seems bizarre for February, but we are enjoying an unseasonal spell of warm sunshine. Mugs, drinks for the children. Some flapjacks.

I am setting this out, when they pull up and Ben jumps from the car, leaving Rachel to help the children. One of them, definitely her father's daughter, leaps out to join him, as soon as she is free from her seatbelt. I look from father to daughter and see the same dancing, adventurous eyes, looking back from both. The younger child, more like his mother in nature, hangs back, with justifiable shyness, given the length of time since they were last here. He probably does not remember the place at all.

I approach, with what I hope is a welcoming smile, social graces having been trained into me as a child. Even though my inner self feels as nervous as Rachel and her son seem to be, my exterior does not betray it.

Soon, we are all sitting comfortably and catching up on news. It transpires that my earlier guesses are both right, in a way. The agency is doing well enough for them to have employed staff and cut down their own working hours. I am really pleased to hear this, since I know they were nervous, about taking the risk of starting the business and moving to the city.

They are very different people to the couple I first knew. More relaxed and assured, but now with a shade of urgency about them, which seems to reflect urban confidence instead of their previous uncertainty. They look trendier, with more expensive clothes and hairstyles than before. It is nice to see, though a little bit alien, to me.

They are still, unmistakeably, Ben and Rachel. Ben is animated in face and body, talking rapidly and punctuating this with expansive hand movements. Rachel sits by, watching him and listening carefully. Ben is explaining about the farm, which has been purchased by his dad, but which they all plan to share. It sounds run-down, if not actually derelict, hence their need for the chainsaw and any other tools we have spare.

They are all excited to be leaving the city after three years, even though both Ben and Rachel will still have to commute to work, part-time, but Ben is saying that they will work from home for much of the time and only travel in, when it is absolutely essential. I glance to Rachel and guess this will be a huge relief for them both, but perhaps especially, for her.

I ask about the farm and its history and Ben's eyes light up even more, as he effortlessly switches the flow of his narrative to the building and its various historical features. This is accompanied by photos on his phone. I am shown a date, above a door, which clearly denotes the year 1782 and the barn interior, showing possibly original stable partitions. The whole thing seems remarkably undeveloped and therefore unspoiled.

There is a semi-derelict building across the yard, whose original purpose is uncertain and there are also the remains of something that might have been a row of farm cottages, a short distance away. Ben is frustrated.

'We can't work out what they were at all! Could have been anything.'

I smile and jump in to speak, while he draws breath. *You have to be quick, with Ben.*

'Don't you sometimes wish you could time travel back to the past and see how things used to be?'

'YES! That's exactly what I'd like! Oh it'd be *wonderful* if we could do that,' replies Ben straight away, in his broad Yorkshire accent, which I am pleasantly surprised he has managed to keep, after three years in the city. My own accent seems to change slightly, depending on who I am talking to.

'I've got this idea, actually,' I begin, hesitantly and Ben starts to listen, as intently as he has just been talking. Rachel simply switches her focus from Ben, onto me. I am a little nervous about sharing my concept, newborn and vulnerable as it feels to be, but I trust these people and always have. I also respect their views and know them to be a reliable sounding board, so I swallow and continue.

'You know Google Earth and Google Street View? I'd love for there to be a historical version of that, so that people can look back at certain time periods and see what was probably there.'

'GOD yes, that would be *perfect!*' Ben instantly and loudly enthuses. Rachel only nods, slowly. 'Tell us more,' he continues. 'How would it work? Who would build it? You could... no, no. You go on.'

I can see his mind racing off with his own ideas, but then hitting the boundary of decency, with the immediate recollection that the concept is mine and not his.

I press on, tentatively.

'I suppose the history experts will want to have some input and the historical knowledge will have to come from them.'

'The universities...' A rare interjection, from Rachel.

'Yes, I was thinking about the history departments and wondering if they might be interested. Also, the local history societies and the more casual Facebook groups. I'm sure every area has at least one, doesn't it?'

Ben nods and tells me, 'Yeah, we're on about three. At least.'

'Five,' corrects Rachel with quiet precision and lists them all, counting them off on her fingers.

A slurp of tea and I go on: 'I imagine it would grow quite gradually, but that several dates could be chosen for most areas and developed by committee or something.'

We all laugh at that, thinking the same thought, which is spoken out loud by Ben: 'Never happen, then,' and I become aware of that warm, bubbly feeling in my chest, of being amongst kindred spirits. I have missed these two and am very happy to see them again.

'Oh, I'd *love* that, though,' Ben again. 'Instead of wondering about those ruins, Rach, we could just log onto Google Maps

17

and go back two hundred years, to find out what they were.'

'Well, they probably couldn't be a hundred percent sure…' I feel I ought to caution, even though it is stating the obvious.

'I know,' says Ben. 'But they'll have a better idea than we ever could, won't they?' Then, with a snort, he sounds out one of my worst concerns about the idea so far. 'Would they ever agree, though? Seriously, I can imagine the debates dragging on for years. Have you ever seen two historians arguing? You could grow old and die before they've even got going!'

I suck in air and grimace my acknowledgement of this. He is right, of course, and it is only one of the countless, apparently insurmountable obstacles on the path, between where we now sit and the fantasy of this coming to fruition. *I'm being ridiculous to imagine it could ever actually happen. Getting above and ahead of myself.*

'It's a rubbish idea, really,' is what I say out loud. 'Would be a great resource, if it ever did come to pass, but there will be some very good reasons why it hasn't already and getting all of the historians to agree, would be among the least of them. When I start to think about it, realistically, it looks like a non-starter.'

They both silently contemplate this, then Rachel speaks up. When she speaks, it is usually well worth listening and Ben and I both play close attention now. The time she spends observing and listening instead of acting and talking seems to have made her wise, beyond her years.

'I think you should try, Zoe. Make a start. If you have the time and the enthusiasm, you should just begin working on it. Don't worry about the funding, or the organisation of it, too much just now and don't let yourself get overwhelmed, by the enormity of the task. Just put on some metaphorical blinkers and begin. Pretend to yourself that you've been commissioned to do it by Google, if that's what it takes, but don't be put off by the challenges, which will be huge. It really is a great idea and above all, it's *your* idea. So you should be the one who puts it into motion.'

The sunlight catches her ash blonde, shiny hair and for that moment, I see Rachel as an angel: so, calm, steady and supportive. I glance towards Ben and see the same rapturous expression on his face, as he contemplates his beloved that I probably had. I know I am also smiling broadly. I want to try to capture this moment in my memory and I have an absurd desire to see her words carved into stone, or something equally permanent, to keep me going, for the eternity I suspect this job might take.

They are both waiting for me to respond, so I do, still smiling.

'Thank you, Rachel. That means a lot to me. Such kind and necessary words! Do you know, I've spent the last few weeks veering madly from thinking it's such a great concept that it has to happen, come what may, to seeing it as a crazy, hopeless waste of time? I wouldn't have even thought about trying it, if you hadn't said that, but now, I think I *will* give it a go.' This feels momentous. A proper commitment, to do... at least *something*.

'Glad to hear it,' grins Rachel, giving up her chair to join the children, who have gone to play on our old trampoline.

'I think she's probably right,' says Ben as his wife goes out of earshot. 'You'll never know until you try and you *might* make it happen.'

'Hmm. To be honest, I wouldn't even know where to start, Ben.' I say, as I am relighting the camping stove, fuelling my old habit of tea as a conversational prop – a habit Ben always used to share. 'Where do you start, with something like that?' and almost as soon as I have said it, I am regretting the question.

I know that he will now fire out a list, containing about a dozen tasks for me and, so very easily, this ethereal, fledgling project could become his, instead of mine.

4

Before I sit and relax, I have to tidy the kitchen, empty and fill the dishwasher, wipe down the surfaces, bin any detritus. Further than that and, something I struggle to admit, I have to keep chanting the task in hand, to prevent myself from being distracted from it. It would be very easy for me to sit down and become immersed in my computer game, completely forgetting about the kitchen until bed time, when I know I will be too tired and leave it until morning. This is disastrous, when I prefer to begin a new day with a clean sheet, instead of still cleaning up after yesterday.

Only with middle age, have I learned to think about domesticity as meeting my own needs, rather than those of my family. The children do not mind a little mess, but I relax more easily when everything is back in its place. The computer game meets my need for escape: a press of the button and I am in the medieval age, playing God over a town of farmers, foresters, miners, herbalists and millers, in which my real life kitchen plays no part whatsoever. Even though my body is sitting in it, my mind is entirely in the game.

I have four villages, fully developed and a fifth, under construction. The footprint of the future houses is established, so that I know where to put the roads to the new village, but their build jobs are on pause until the resources are available. If I build too many houses, I will trigger a population explosion for which I do not have the food or fuel. So I must build them slowly, but not so slowly that I run out of people to do the necessary jobs of food and fuel gathering, while keeping enough spare to build the houses.

They need graveyards and churches, which literally tower over the houses and use disproportionate amounts of stone, but I must build them, or my people will be unhappy and then less productive. They walk faster and are therefore more productive on stone roads than on dirt ones, which are cheap, but will eventually slow the process of development. A ship arrives: I must exchange my surplus for whatever I am lacking and I have to take workers from the build jobs, to give them the task of transporting goods, to and from the harbour. I have a shortage of logs and must build more foresting zones, to supply my woodcutters, or some of my people might freeze to death next winter. Foresters need lots of space, but I can overlay them with gatherers and hunters, although not herbalists, who need old woodland and not the new growth the loggers will plant.

I play this game for probably more hours in the day than I care to count, such is the seduction of a virtual escape into the past, before society became as complicated as it currently is. But I imagine it always being preferable and easily compulsive, to play from the perspective of a god over any kind of collective situation, instead of as one of the teeming multitude who must personally experience every facet of the era. A virtual interaction is also more comfortable and physically less demanding than a physical one would be, but since time travel is currently impossible, this is my only substitute, for now.

Would I travel back to the medieval era, if I could? Yes, for a look around. I would love to visit the past like a tourist, maybe even to stay for a while, as long as I knew I would be able to return to now, the time of central heating, good plumbing, cars and the internet.

Playing this computer game gives me a burst of appreciation for those things, when my tiny avatars have to constantly chop wood, trudge around on foot and fetch water. Even my own grandmother spent most of her waking hours on the kind of domestic drudgery I no longer have to think about. Our cutlery, pans and crockery go straight into the dishwasher and our dirty clothes, made of fabrics that do not need ironing, to the automatic washing machine. Even if computers had been invented in my grandmother's day, she would have had no leisure time to spend on them. Instead, in the short time spent not working, she would read paper books and magazines, visit real shops and talk to real people.

I talk to real people too, but lots of the communication with them happens online, where I have long term friends I have never met face-to-face in the same physical place, some of whom live thousands of miles away. My own cousin lives thousands of miles away and we chat sometimes on Zoom, whereas my grandmother's brother moved to Canada, after which they could only communicate by letter through the post and she only saw him two or three times, in the rest of her life, when he came back to England on visits.

The unreality of my beloved game does irk me, sometimes. The sterile, mechanised algorithm, which reliably underpins it all, divorces me from any real insight into life at those times. I can see the kind of surroundings that might sometimes have been prevalent, but everything is uniform and pre-set: the buildings, trees and paving, all of a type and repeating identically and of course, there are no smells and the sounds are like the image blocks, tessellating in a coded format.

The real life sounds in my kitchen are only the background hum of the computer and the brrr and swish of the dishwasher, mingled with the distant chatter of Amy and her friend, drifting through from the dining room, where they are playing a board game together. I do not know what it was that managed to pull my attention out of my virtual world and into the physical one, but I get up and depress the switch on the electric kettle, whilst remembering the stove-top one, at my grandmother's house. Even the regular ritual of tea-making has become simple. *Maybe too simple.*

I go and look for Hugh, to see if he wants tea and find him at his desk, still working, even though it is Sunday. I put a hand on his back and feel the tension: something must be glitching with a database, probably an emergency situation. My offer is distractedly accepted and he only briefly glances away from the screen towards me, which he then continues to scan, with a frown.

I look at it and see a page full of tiny numbers, punctuated by only the occasional bunch of apparently random letters and I experience my usual wonderment, that he can make any sense of his job – that anyone could. The best thing I can do for him in the current situation, is to deliver the drink and then stay out of his way and let him work through the problem, without distractions. So I do that and go back to my game, with a familiar feeling of futility.

Hugh is saving a significant section of the global banking empire, even though he would laugh at the grandiosity of this description and hastily insist that he is a very tiny cog in a complicatedly colossal machine. Whilst I am supervising, merely supervising, the building of a virtual shop by virtual avatars which will impact nothing and nobody.

A heavy sigh and I puff out my cheeks, to blow out a slow and strong stream of air, thinking: *what do I really want to do?* And the History Maps idea comes straight back to me, even though I am automatically trying to dismiss it, at the same time.

Building those virtual houses would feel so much more fulfilling, if they had some actual basis in historical reality. Not just a vague, generic concept of reality, but a re-creation of the past for specific dates in specific places. I want to be able to show the village of Bradley to Amy, as it looked in 1800 or 1850 and as it probably looked, back in 1650, or even 1500. I want to see for myself too, and for anyone else who is interested to be able to do so.

Sipping my tea, I sink into a fantasy scenario, in which I

can envisage the development of this concept taking place. Sketches from historians, pulling together scraps of evidence. Myself in a research library, searching out old pictures and maps. And then people, a hastily amassed selection of random, sample people, wondering about the historical changes in their villages, their towns and cities and being able to use a device which will show them. A grandfather, showing his grandson the landscape of his childhood. A genealogist, being able to pinpoint the visual representation of some ancestor's house. An archaeologist, knowing where to start digging for more clues, to further populate even earlier versions of the maps.

The harsh reality of the question, *where do I start?* snaps me out of my warm and happy reverie, as I start to think about some of the practicalities involved. The first – and surely, the biggest – hurdle begins to take appalling shape in my mind.

I need to persuade someone at Google that this is a good idea, worth developing.

The very impractical thought of this sends me back to my game, as I automatically shy away from it, protecting myself from its impossible enormity. Within seconds, I am frowning at my inventory list, realising I need to build more cotton farms, weavers and tailors, to keep my villagers sufficiently warmly clothed for the winter. But the heavy-hearted, tight-stomached feeling of plunging disappointment remains, refusing to be masked or tricked into disappearing.

The bare truth of the situation cannot be understated and must be acknowledged, though it pricks my eyes with tears.

Nobody at Google would ever listen to me. Nobody there would ever know who I am, or be interested in a single word I might want to say to them. To anyone at Google, in a position of any degree of power or responsibility for anything even vaguely important, I am nothing and nobody. A middle-aged British housewife, one of about ten million, with a strange obsession with the Middle Ages. One of a multitude of random cranks and weirdos, against whom they will have systems and staff, to protect themselves.

I picture myself, trying to present the concept to them and force myself to acknowledge the ludicrousness of the mental images that ensue.

If I email the idea to them, nobody will read it or if they do, they will be someone with almost as little influence as I have, to act on it or even pass it on. If I try to call or, perish the thought, turn up there – where? *I don't even know that – to try to visit someone, I will be ignored at best and more likely, politely removed by security personnel. I have no power there and not the slightest realistic prospect of ever generating any, so the whole project is an absolute non-starter.*

My face is now wet, with tears of sadness and self-disgust. I am scathingly contemptuous of my former enthusiasm and the relatively late stage at which I am finally facing up to the truth of the situation.

If I had knuckled down to my studies and reached anything like what my parents used to bemoaningly refer to as my full potential, my situation might now be a little better. But I did not, which is both nobody's fault but my own (says the voice of my mother in my head) *and far too late to remedy. My position is such, that even if I dreamed up the best idea in the world, there is not a single thing I could do about it.*

So, it is better for me not to dream at all.

5

So far today, I have eaten four sweet pancakes stuffed with a mixture of bacon, onion, garlic and mashed potato, fried in butter – the pancakes and the mixture, but not together. Plus one piece of Amy's chocolate and now I cannot resist another, so I will have to buy another bar for her, eat the first half and then put it back into the fridge, to restore the status quo.

It is only nine-thirty in the morning and I officially do not eat breakfast, a hangover principle from my intermittent fasting phase, of several years ago. Not that this involves real hangovers, because I have yet to turn to drink, although I can easily see why people do.

My jeans feel tight and I have a strange, stitch-like pain in the right side of my waist.

Why am I eating so much? Best not to question it.

This is the whole point of overeating, to shut down the interrogating brain and silence the painful enquiries, by flattening them under a dollop of buttery, salty mashed potato, or similar.

I have played my medieval game for an hour, instead of emptying the dishwasher of last night's crockery, so it is still sitting there. I feel slightly sick when I try to bend over to empty it, so I go to find that extra piece of chocolate instead and wash it down with tea, though this tastes vile, as I have stopped taking it with milk, in an effort to be more healthy. I internally laugh, at the irony of this. "Sardonically" is the word of the day on my dictionary app, which popped up in my notifications a few seconds ago and it does seem appropriate, right now.

The choice of sweet pancakes, to eat with savoury filling, was born out of utter laziness. I could have made fresh, unsweetened batter from buckwheat flour, to prevent the bloating I get from wheat. I did consider doing so, but the wheaty, sweet ones were there in the packet, bought yesterday from the supermarket and such was my need, today, for a quick supply of copious amounts of dolloping food, that I used them anyway. It is a strange flavour combination and not altogether palatable, but it somehow hit the spot. As I ate them, I was thinking about the fast-food burger joints and their secret salt-sugar recipes of food-addiction doom.

I no longer smoke. I rarely drink alcohol and I have even temporarily given up caffeine because it stops me sleeping, so food is my only remaining substance of abuse for times of trouble.

Is this a time of trouble? Don't ask, don't think about it. Just eat. Alternate between sweet and savoury, to delay the full feeling and keep the numbness going.

There is something I must not feel, some thought or knowledge causing me upset, but for now, it is being pushed aside and away.

Outside the window, there is a high wind blowing. I can tell, without looking, because the windows have been whistling and the chimneys howling all night. This is not a new house, or a particularly well-maintained building. Replacement window frames would solve some of the noise, but we can never seem to afford to do that and it is not urgent, so not very high up on the list of priorities. Casting my eye over the view, I can see sunshine, illuminating fast-moving clouds. A cold and bright, early March day. Too windy for seed-planting, although I have a lot to plant this year.

Unlike Hugh, I do not like to be blown about, frozen or

drenched, when I am outside. I prefer hot, dry and peaceful days and the kind of weather in which irrigation is a more pressing problem than battening down the hatches. Hugh hates those days, because they overheat his body and burn his pale skin.

We are like the little wooden man and woman in an Alpine weather house. He comes out when it rains and I come out when it is dry. This thought makes me smile. Opposites attract and sometimes they fit together perfectly well: tears and laughter; leather and lace; bacon and maple syrup – which works far better than my pancake and might well now be the next thing I eat. But I can hear footsteps on the stairs and presently, Alf comes into the room and I am, magically, much happier.

Alf is, in my company, probably a typical twenty-one year old in the presence of his mother: sullen and undemonstrative, needing what he needs. This morning he will need, I know, strong coffee with two sugars and the creamy top of the milk, plus a generous serving of quiet company and not too much talking before he goes out for his bus to college.

With friends and other people his own age, or even people of any age who did not give birth to him, he is a different person entirely: accommodating, gregarious and charming. All heart-melting smiles and focused attention. I try to take it as a compliment, that he does not feel the need to make an effort with me. He knows I will still love him, whatever he is like.

By the time I have made his coffee, put it on his table and sat down with him, his laptop is open and he is typing at the speed which always amazes me. I do not know how anyone can think so fast, let alone type it, but Alf grew up with computers from day one. As soon as he was old enough to hit the space bar and stop the virtual train at a virtual station, they were his absolute favourite things, though I have learned not to frequently remind him of that.

He suddenly stops typing and starts peering at the screen,

his forehead pulled down in a frown and he is sort of flicking at the mouse with his hand.

He groans exasperatedly, the same agonized, angry noise he makes when his character dies on Overwatch or World of Warcraft, a low *'Ohh,'* going up a couple of tones to a much louder *'Ahh!'* and I cannot help tentatively leaning across, to look at what the problem might be.

What I see on his screen makes me blink and my mouth fall open. I close it, gulp, look at his face and back to the screen again.

It is a house, but not just any house. A half-timbered, overhung, sixteenth century, town house, with white plaster infill and clearly visible bressummer under the jetty. The close studding is eastern school and it is slowly rotating, as the deep brown colour of the wooden beams rapidly changes its hue, but only slightly, so that I wonder if it is happening at all, until I realise that his mouse button clicks, agitatedly, every time it happens.

'What... are you doing?' I finally manage to ask, through my utter bewilderment.

'I've got to get this *colour right*,' he answers, to my surprise, even though I can logically see it makes sense. The beams are still switching browns, with every mouse click. But I am still puzzled, by so many aspects of what I can see.

The building incongruously sits in mid-air. There is the equivalent of perhaps a foot of ground around it, but only white space under and around that. It turns slowly, as if it is on an invisible "lazy Susan", the pivoting table-top plinths that were all the rage in my own, young adulthood.

I am also amazed by his skill level. The building looks extremely realistic, to the extent that I wonder, at first, whether it is some kind of a three-dimensional photo or video of an actual structure and I am only sure it is not on closer, more careful inspection. Most startling of all is the fact that this is a historical building, which I would have expected to have been amongst the last of Alf's choices of subject, for any element of his graphic art course. So far, this has mostly consisted of intricately designed spaceships and alien body armour, all gothic gleaming pewter and black.

Realising I need to formulate the right question, if I am going to be relieved of any confusion at all, I try to reorient my brain and make it think logically.

'Okay,' I finally ask, after a few seconds which feels like a few minutes. 'Why have you created an image of a medieval house?' and I watch his face and wait, for him to register the question.

He frowns in a different way, irritated to be asked, on top of his irritation about the shades-of-brown decision.

'It's just an assignment...' he imparts, not giving his answer much thought. I do not suppose it would occur to him to wonder why I am asking, except that mothers always ask questions, just as tutors always issue assignments. It is merely another kind of hurdle to jump, on the running track of his life, on the way from annoyance to a stress-free, idyllic existence. I am simultaneously remembering asking him, about ten days ago, whether he had ever designed a three dimensional building and not receiving an answer at the time.

I give up on questions and resort to statements.

'I didn't know you could do this kind of thing,' and: 'It's very good,' which is something of an understatement. 'It must have taken a long time.'

The admiration or empathy – I do not know which – opens him up to the conversation a little more. He gives me a brief instance of eye contact, a flash of dark brown iris: what I used to call his chocolate-button eyes half a lifetime ago, though I can hardly presume to even think it, now.

'Yes, I've been rendering it for about eighteen hours, so far.'

Another bout of confusion for me, as I immediately think of actual plaster rendering, on actual buildings, before I remember that the term also now applies to the creation of computer graphic images. I cannot help feeling impressed, that he has devoted so many hours, to something that is not a computer game. But he is still about fourteen years old in my mind, so this is not justifiable.

I think of another question.

'Did everyone on your course get the same assignment?'

'Yes, there should be about forty-eight medieval houses rendered by now, when they're all put together.'

'They're all being put together?' I think I might be starting to dream again.

The skills and the people are right here in this town, pretty much under my nose – or at least, some of them are.

This is the first time I have even considered the mechanics behind the creation of a historical, virtual, three-dimensional map. Until this point, I have been assuming I would have to somehow magically persuade Google to take the whole thing on, from start to finish and, as I am no magician, this to be completely infeasible.

But right now, I can picture the combined efforts of Alf and his fellow students, forming... *something.* A tiny sample of the historical map I want to make, at least. In my mind's eye, I can see it taking shape and then, almost immediately, along comes pragmatism, to remind me that I have almost as little influence at Alf's college as I do at Google's headquarters, wherever they may be.

At least I know where the college is and how to get there. What I do not know is who to see, or what to say when I do, but hope is kindled within me once again and, instead of seeking more food, when Alf goes for his bus, I sit, with a pad and pen, to think and make some notes.

6

'An' that were Barrett's farm, that one down there wi' t'grey slate roof. Do you see? Wi' t'brick shed next to it?'

'Oh, yes...' I am peering in the direction my dad is pointing, trying to make out the building in question. We are standing in our garden on the hill, looking down into the valley, which is currently busy with newish suburban semis, but in my dad's memory is still the farmland pastures of his childhood adventures, seventy-plus years ago. Even I remember many more fields than can be seen now, too. But some of the houses had been built by the time I came along.

I love that so many of the old farm buildings are still there, even though very few of them are still being used for farming. My dad's integral knowledge of their history strengthens my emotional roots in this place, so that I can almost feel them extending down to the planetary core, like a physical link. It is a solid, safe feeling of belonging, for me, which might explain my fascination with the past in my home town.

He begins to reference some of his relatives.

'Me Uncle John and Auntie Barbara lived at that house, fourth one along after the telegraph pole...' and I am conscious of thinking of them as *his* relatives but not mine, even though biologically, they are mine too. I never knew them, but wish I had. The house that was theirs is an inner terrace, circa 1900, built to house a few of the many hundreds of mill workers needed in our town, at that time. It appears to be almost entirely surrounded by the millstone grit from which it is built, being one of a row of almost identical others.

It has no garden, just a small, flagged yard at the front, enclosed by a uniform stone wall: nowhere for children to play, although in the days of my dad's childhood and earlier – and my own, now that I think about it – the street was the playground. There was so much less traffic in those days and parents had fewer nightmares about potential predatory paedophiles, rightly or wrongly.

My dad echoes my thoughts.

'No gardens, but we didn't mind. Uncle John's house wa' very like ours. You know, t'one on Easterly Street they knocked down to build t'bypass.'

We contemplate the bypass in question, sweeping down the adjacent hill from the motorway on top of it, swathing the land like a ribbon, but buzzing with vehicles which look, from here, like toy cars. I can imagine Alfie playing with a miniature scene like it as a child.

The landscape itself is dominated, if you take the hills into account, by patchwork fields in different shades of green, this being mostly sheep country and not flat enough for crops on a major scale. The buildings tend to cling to the bottom of the valleys, of which we can count five here, at the southerly tip of the Pennines. Every hilltop is studded with electricity pylons, to and from which stretch the cables that take power to the dozen or so residential, retail and industrial zones we can see below us.

The old mills are elegant in grey stone with big windows, interesting shapes and decorative features. By contrast, the modern industrial units are ugly, low sprawls of corrugated steel, in pale blue and grey. Soulless, windowless boxes that visibly do nothing, apart from take up space. Financially, they probably keep our region going in just the same way as the old mills once did. Those are now mostly apartment blocks. Some of Alf's fellow students rent them. I hear they have been made trendy, with steel gantries and mezzanines.

'Jimmy Barrett were a nice lad. Went off to work in

Manchester, as I recall. Not sure what 'appened to him after that,' my dad was saying, apropos of apparently nothing, until I remember the farm with the grey slate roof. No fields around it now, only housing estate. I have to really struggle to pick out the old building again.

If all of this progress had not happened, Jimmy Barrett would have doubtless taken over the farm from his dad and thereby become the closest thing we have to aristocracy in West Yorkshire. But instead, the farm was engulfed by houses and perhaps the once rising star of Jimmy has been similarly engulfed, by Manchester co-workers.

I suspect Dad and I both feel the same sense of loss when people leave. And bewilderment, at the rate of change and the relative transience of modern society. I inhale and smell his pipe tobacco smoke. He is always soaked in the odour of it, so I have to look over his head to see it rising and realise he must have lit it silently, as I was pondering the new industrial units. I did not hear the rasp of a match, though. I find myself wondering, not for the first time, whether he ever really extinguishes it, or whether its embers perpetually glimmer in his pocket, threatening to set his trousers on fire, just needing a pat and a suck to bring it back to life.

I must be observing him suspiciously, because he frowns and says, *'Whaaat?'* in the same elongated tone of voice Alf uses, when I catch him helping himself to bus fare from my purse and here I am again, with the familiar feeling that I am merely the bridge between two generations of what is essentially the same person. Raised by one and raising the other. *Raised the other. Alf is grown up now,* I have to keep reminding myself.

'His old man were gored by his own bull,' he casually continues, to my utter confusion, as if I should know what he is talking about.

'Whose old man?'

'Barrett's!'

'Oh! Wow...' I am envisioning it in my mind's eye, the goring. Wondering how on earth it came about. My dad is about to satisfy my curiosity.

'Ol' Barrett liked his drink, and 'e liked t'landlady at 'Shears. One night he come 'ome, in 'is cups an t'bull did for 'im. Slammed him right up agin' t'field wall. 'E lingered on for about five days, but there were no 'ope for 'im.'

There is at least one old pub called The Shears in every previously sheep-farming West Yorkshire town. Also one called The Station, another making reference to either barges or barrels or both and there is always a Duke of York. I could write a list of necessary components for a standardised theoretical town in this heavily populated part of the world including business names and those three would be at the top.

'See that mill ovver theeya...' My dad is pointing slightly to the left, where there are three old mills in the middle distance and at least two more in the far. He clarifies: 'T'one on t'left...' so that I can identify a beige, rectangular, six-story, Victorian factory, with arched windows, trimmed in red brick. 'That were where me father worked.'

My dad's word "father" rhymes with "gather". Nobody in West Yorkshire speaks like this any more, apart from some of the very old people. I feel sad, to realise it will die with them and sad again, to remember the generation above them, whose dialect was almost unintelligible to me, who has never lived more than seven miles away from here.

'That mill,' My dad sucks on his pipe, biting down on it, which is his only remaining external tell of bitterness, nowadays. 'Give 'im t'emphysema 'at killed 'im.'

It is true. My paternal granddad died years before I was born, when my dad was still a very young man. I cannot resist asking the next question, even though I know it will trigger the retelling of a family event with which I have had a love-hate relationship, ever since I first heard it.

'Didn't he inherit his dad's dairy farm though?'

My dad never tires of answering this question, always as if I am asking it for the first time and he is telling me for the first time.

'Aye, 'e were t'eldest o' five lads. Din't want t'farm though. Preferred 'is job in t'mill. An' 'e were a Socialist. Din't agree wi' property ownership, so it passed ovver to 'is brother Samuel, instead.'

My dad brings local history – especially family history – alive for me in a way that nothing and nobody else can and the mental images he has invoked feel to be swirling around me, frantically, roaring in my ears. But this is only the chill March wind, rustling the birch trees on the hillside and shaking their leaves like the tide rattles the shingles on a stony beach, so that it often reminds me of the sea. But we are seventy miles from either coast and it is the cold that is making me shiver, not the imaginary ghosts.

The hillside opposite ours is covered in trees, at the base of which both a road and a railway line come into and out of visibility, as the trees allow. We cannot see the road traffic very well so far away, but a passenger train is clearly making its way through from right to left, east to west.

'Diesel trains, eh, Dad?' I prompt him, knowing it will lead him to another favourite subject.

'Nowt like t'steam trains,' he begins. ''appiest years o' my life, workin' that signal box. It's still theeya, on'y you can't see it for t'trees. An' I were born just theeya...' He points but it is needless. I know very well where my dad was born: in the house in which he also grew up, right underneath what is now a footbridge on the bypass. They demolished his birthplace for that, just as they dammed up the streams that once fed this hillside, to build the motorway that now roars three fields away behind us, *all for the greater good.*

And it is good, I remind my grumpy brain, *especially when we want to go on holiday or receive a quick Amazon delivery.*

'I know, Dad. Come on, let's go and get a cup o' tea.'

I hook my arm comfortably into my dad's and we slowly walk back to the house, my heels sinking into the soft ground, as we go past young daffodils, wagging their yellow heads in the wind.

7

The kitchen is peaceful and warm. I am still sleepy enough to be momentarily entranced by a chunk of sunlight, playing on the multifaceted plastic of an open bag of potatoes on the washing machine, as I make my way from the kettle to the fridge, stockinged feet padding gently on the stone floor. I bend and look, take out bacon and eggs and grab a punnet of mushrooms from the vegetable basket next to the fridge. I set them all out on the table, to cook.

A shimmer of contended anticipation steals over me. I will enjoy the quiet solitude of cooking and when the bacon aroma permeates the house, everyone will climb out of bed in search of breakfast. *Cook it and they will come.*

Oven on low, warming plates inserted, I heat butter in a pan and add the smooth, wet meat slices, which sizzle immediately. Eggs go on next, a different little pan for everyone. *I must remember that Amy likes hers flipped.*

Then, I break the mushrooms up, so they are ready to go into the bacon fat when I move the meat to the oven. I can hear movement from upstairs already, so I fill the kettle and reach for teabags, a teapot and a milk jug. Like my mother, I cannot tolerate a milk bottle on the table.

Before they come down, I want to use this time to think about the project that is increasingly on my mind. The history maps just will not go away and today, I am feeling determined and cautiously excited about the idea.

I want to recreate the house in which my dad was born, see his granddad's old farm as it used to be and the factory his dad worked in. Closing my eyes for a second, I visualise being able to walk the well-trodden path from their now-demolished home to work and school and to see the street my dad played in, as a child. In my absolutely ideal world, I want to somehow be able to walk that route, with my dad and the granddad I never knew. I am so curious about this man, about whom I have heard so much and after whom I apparently take. I would even love to see the streets I played in as a child – different ones, in the next-door town. I could drive to see those now, but they are not the same any more, either.

I am setting out the mugs, when Hugh comes in and hugs me, kissing the top of my head. I notice that he is even more tired than usual, due to the gale force winds that buffeted the house through the night, which woke us both up at about half past five. I went back to sleep, but he got up to do some work after that. Sometimes I think he seems to be perpetually drowning in work. I wish I could magic the pressure away, but at least I can feed and water him, which feels helpful in some way.

'Have you seen the boys, yet?' he asks, taking a seat at the table.

I frown.

'Boys? Did Adam stay over?' I do not know when we will stop calling them boys. Some time in their thirties, perhaps, or later. But they still behave as if they are teenagers and Adam has spent most Saturday nights at our house, ever since they were about eight years old, having become best friends as soon as they met. I cannot even remember how they first met. The only difference, nowadays, is that Alf no longer bothers to tell us when Adam is here.

'Did you not hear them coming in? They weren't exactly quiet. It was about two o'clock, I think.'

'Oh, they'll be hungover. I'll cook extra bacon. Blimey, how much sleep did you get?'

Hugh sighs and rubs his creased, pale forehead.

'Barely any. I'm struggling to think straight, for this work I've got to do. The wind was horrendous and I was just lying there, listening to that creaking sound, in the roof. Something's wrong up there. I want to go up into the loft today and see if I can see daylight.'

Hugh hates ladders, so if he is planning to climb one, then he really is worried. But he is an inveterate worrier, so it is hard for me to know whether to join him in being concerned, or not. I decide to wait and see whether he does manage to go up there and if so, whether he sees any daylight through the roof.

If he does, then I'll worry. The side of the house, where we think the damage is, rises three stories from the ground so we will need scaffolding, to resolve any problems up there and that will be expensive. I know exactly why Hugh is worrying about it and I sigh, as I add more bacon to the pan.

Amy comes next, shuffling in her extremely fluffy, unicorn slippers and looking sleepy, cosy and cuddly in one of the matching fluffy, unicorn onesies her grandmother keeps buying for her. She clutches a fluffy unicorn as well. If it were not for her height and her obviously older facial features, this child could still be three years old, first thing in the morning, at first glance.

I always want to wrap her in my arms when she is like this, but her preference is to be left alone in the mornings, so I restrain myself to just saying 'Hi,' and 'Breakfast? It's coming soon.'

She sits with her dad and lays her head on his shoulder, closing her eyes again. He smiles down at her. She is the natural antidote to his ever-fretting brain.

Kettle steam fills the air in that corner and it clicks itself off, so I lift it and carefully fill the teapot, thinking: *I bet the boys will want coffee instead.*

I fill the coffee machine and switch that on. Hugh and Amy both have their phones out, by the time Adam and Alf do emerge, just as I am plating up. They both look rough: tousle-haired, chalky-faced and visibly wincing at their state of semi-wakefulness. Adam grimaces at the bacon pan, but I know he will eat some and feel better for it.

'Hello, you two,' I say, quietly, smiling. 'Nice evening?' and they groan by way of response, taking their places at the table and both immediately laying their heads on their arms, making me feel glad I have not set it with cutlery and mats, because I do not think that would have stopped them. A whiff of stale booze and sweat follows them into the kitchen. They have come straight from their pits, bypassing the shower.

They really need coffee. While I am waiting for the machine, I put the bacon into the oven to keep warm and tip the mushroom pieces into the pan, then turn them with two silicone spatulas, watching them soak up the fat until there is none left. Some of the mushrooms are still dry, so I add more butter and turn around on instinct, just in time to see Adam raising a weary eyebrow at this. His mother, Maybelle, uses very little fat in her cooking, as Adam has told me with varying degrees of diplomacy, several times over the years.

The word *'Pfft!'* forms in my mind though, because hangovers need fat to soak up, just as the mushrooms do. *If Adam prefers to, he can go home for breakfast* – which I know he will not.

Hugh is not even trying to raise a conversation with them today, though ordinarily he might. I do not know if he is too tired to talk, or they are too hungover to respond. Possibly, both. But when I sit down, I am resolved to talk to them about my project. I need their advice and I have reached the stage where my thinking on it is going around in circles and I am not sure what to do next. I suspect these two bleary-eyed youths might provide some inspiration, if I can get them to take it seriously.

Serving up the food, I am trying to work out how to make it sound interesting and not something stupid a middle-aged mother would dream up, but I cannot think of any other way to say it.

'So, you know Google Earth?' No response. I give them coffee, sugar in Alf's, none in Adam's. Cream in both. Hugh audibly snorts and pours more tea for himself. At least I have Amy's attention, who seems to have woken up a little bit. *Try again.*

'Google Street View?'

The heaviest sigh in the world emanates from Alf's decumbent chest and head, which he lifts to look at me, with what I can only describe as almost desperate exasperation.

He says, '*Yes*, Mum,' breathing out the words, as if he has just run a marathon and I have asked him whether he is tired.

I have to press on, because he will be back at college tomorrow and probably out somewhere later and, well, I suspect the best time is now, because his defences are down. *Relatively down.*

'How would you go about creating a historical version of that?'

A frown. Some thought. A searching look towards Adam, who is frowning back at Alf. They both look at me. Adam speaks.

'Well, you already can go back a few years, to previous versions. There's a function...'

'No,' I cut in, feeling my enthusiasm start to surge. 'I already know about that. It's not what I mean. Imagine, if you could go back to the last century. The World Wars. The Victorian period, or the medieval age. Wouldn't that be cool?'

Bright smile of earnestness, from me. Brief snorts of laughter, from them.

'Ha! Yeah, it would be *cool*...' says Adam.

'...but it would never happen,' finishes Alf. And they underline it with a definitive nod to each other, as if that ends the discussion. *As if.*

'It *could* happen,' I persist, sitting down to join them with my food. 'You guys are actually building virtual medieval houses, this week!' These two are so inseparable, they applied for the same Graphic Arts course. 'Aren't they all being put together, to make a street or something?'

They face each other again. This time, quizzically.

'I don't think so,' Alf says slowly, when Adam has slowly shaken his head. 'We just each had to build one. Anderson didn't say anything about putting them together as a street.'

I feel sure Alf *did* talk about them being put together somehow, when we discussed it a few days ago, though I am struggling to remember exactly, now.

'Well they *should* be put together to make a street, or even a village.' I cut a piece of bacon, balance some mushroom on it and, adding a small square of egg white, lift it slowly to my mouth. 'It's not as if it couldn't be done, is it?' I ask rhetorically, just before the carefully loaded fork reaches its destination.

We all eat quietly for a few minutes, interspersed with slurps of coffee or tea. I love this kind of food, but keep wondering if I should cut down on fried food in general and bacon specifically, just to try and reduce the inflammation that makes my left hip so painful, sometimes. I assume it to be arthritis. It runs in the family.

The male representative of the youngest generation of the family finishes his mouthful of food and opens his mouth, to speak. It feels like a portentous moment. I wait, hardly daring to hope that he might be interested in my idea.

'Okay. From a technical point of view, in that it's possible to build virtual houses, then obviously: yes. It could be done. And yes, it would be a brilliant online facility.' I am watching and listening with interest, impressed by my son's effort to present a balanced argument – the benefits of which would not have occurred to him until quite recently – and also by his vocabulary. I do not think I have ever heard him speak in terms of *facilities* before, but I must remember he is twenty-one now, not fifteen. Those six years make a surprising amount of difference, even after a night on the town.

'But the sheer *size* of it: covering the whole world?' he continues. 'The only people who are going to do that are Google. And if they wanted to do it, they'd have done it already. It's not like they're waiting for you to think of the idea and suggest it to them. They're full of ideas like that. It's what they do.'

Are we all picturing the stereotypical playground Google office? Primary-coloured beanbags, slides and ball pools against a stark, white background? I certainly am, but Alf is still speaking.

'And the fact that they haven't done it, means they don't want to do it. They've already thought of it and decided not to.'

'Yep. Won't happen,' Adam-the-wingman confirms, through a mouthful of food. I try not to send a sneer in his direction, but it is hard to think of him as a guest, sometimes.

Anyway, I am ready for this argument of Alf's, having already had it with myself and reached a different conclusion.

'We don't have to persuade Google, because we don't have to cover the whole world, at least to start with. We just need one street – or, ideally, one village, to begin. One place. One time period. We could create a sample place and time – right now.'

'*Ha!*' Alf hardly lets me finish. 'Let us finish our breakfast, first!' Then, when I give him the exaggerated shrug, he continues: 'We've only just started doing houses and, bear in mind, these are just fantasy houses. If you're picking a point in history and a specific, real place, then you need to know what was there. You'd have to be a historian as well as a graphic artist and, let's face it, Mum...' He looks to Adam for a reciprocated smirk of appreciation and gets it. '...you're neither.'

He puts his cutlery down, as if his little speech needed any more percussion. Sits back. Observes me, with something approaching disapproval.

I do start to feel small and, despite the food, an empty

sensation of hopelessness again. But this time, Hugh speaks up. We all listen, curious to hear his position on the topic.

'She doesn't need to be either though, does she? She just needs to persuade them to do the work,' and I feel a familiar flood of love for him, his kindness and his perennial support for me.

Alf's face colours a little, as if he has been corrected, which I suppose, in a way, he has.

I can feel him bristling, needing to stick to his guns and am not surprised when he responds with a quick and hot: 'How's she going to do that, then?'

Hugh looks to me and smiles his warm, loving smile.

'I don't know,' he says through it, dancing eyes fixed on mine. 'But if she wants to do it, then I'm sure she'll find a way.'

I can hear Alf breathing hard, before he responds with uncharacteristic insight and determination.

'Well, she'd better not start trying to get our tutors involved. *Mum.* You're not going to do that, are you?'

8

I am struggling to take the next step in my History Maps project. To some extent, I know what I want it to achieve: a sample map of a specific, real street or village, from a certain time period yet to be defined, in which users can immerse themselves and navigate around as they can in Google Street View. I am feeling overwhelmed and out of my depth, even now that I have reduced it down to this size. I know that I need help, but I do not know who to trust or – more importantly – who might take me seriously.

Underlying all of my thoughts is a strong and nagging voice of doubt, constantly asking me, *Who do I think I am, to be even contemplating such a scheme?* And, *How ridiculous would it be, to spend time and energy in trying to take something forwards that can never succeed?*

I wish the idea would go away, or that someone else would undertake it instead of me.

I have just spent another hour searching the internet for similar projects, in the hope that something is being developed that saves me from feeling like I need to at least try, by someone who actually knows what they are doing. But the closest thing I can find is a three dimensional, "fly through" version of medieval London, undertaken by six students on a game design course, in 2013. The interactive version I thought I remembered from around that time, but am now wondering if I dreamed, has not surfaced. The other, the one I *can* find, is a non-interactive video which is, nevertheless, wonderful and exactly the kind of imagery I have in mind.

I am at my little work table – I suppose it could be called a desk – in the sitting room, trying to do yet more blue-sky thinking, whilst looking at actual blue skies, the shade of hyacinths, through the window. Small splodges of grey cloud race from west to east on a fast breeze, while more solid-looking white cloud forms a bank against the horizon, to the north. In the middle of it all, a large crow is lifted on a thermal and swoop-drops down, only to be lifted again.

Up and down it goes, like my confidence and enthusiasm. I am becoming irritated by my inability to commit and press on, equally matched by my inability to drop the whole thing and let it go.

I look at the items on the short list in front of me. College tutors; local history society; Facebook. A whole month of thinking about it and this is as far as I have got. Taking the pen, I carefully write underneath it, in speech marks, what I can remember of Rachel's inspiring words to me, because that was the moment when I decided to keep going.

'Pretend to yourself that you've been commissioned to do it by Google.'

But even as I write it, my inner voice of nagging doubt is sneering: *As if. As if.*

Underneath that and again, in speech marks, I set out what I can remember of Alf's words of yesterday morning, that stuck in my mind.

'If you're picking a point in time and a specific, real place, then you need to know what was there,' and I read it back to myself a few times. Historians are the best people to guess what was there and I am not one of those, as my son pointed out, so bluntly. If I *was* a historian, I possibly would not be feeling quite so desperate to see the past, on my screen. I imagine it would run, with reasonable accuracy, through my imagination instead and I would be able to tap into it, when I closed my eyes.

Alf has warned me off trying to get his tutor involved and I think I will probably respect his wishes. I could clearly see his real fear of the kind of public humiliation that would ensue, if his fellow students found out his mum had been in. But I could still, presumably, go and see someone in the History Department without that bothering Alf.

I am trying to envisage how that might go and the way I am imagining it is not good. If I went to see someone at this point in the proceedings, I think I would be laughed off the premises, because I have no progress to show.

The local history society seems less intimidating, perhaps because they are amateurs. I look again at the website of the closest one to our house. Eighty members and fortnightly meetings. *I'm just going to have to bite the bullet and at least turn up to a meeting.* I do not need to mention the project, until or unless it seems appropriate to do so at some point and I have been short of a regular social activity, ever since Amy and her friends decided they were too old for the kind of home education meetings where the parents sit around chatting while the children play. So this seems like a good plan.

The next meeting is on Thursday. I resolve to attend and mark it on the calendar. *It's in writing now, so I have to go.*

I guess the only thing on the list, that I can do right now, is Facebook. I can at least ask my four hundred-plus friends there if any of them can remember the interactive, medieval map of London, that I think I might have imagined.

A gulp of bitter green tea, a wriggle of tense shoulders and I start typing into a status box, first checking I am on "Friends Only".

'Can anyone remember an interactive London street map from about five years ago or more? You could navigate along the street and maybe look inside some of the buildings? I can't work out whether I dreamt it or not,' and I am just sitting back to watch for the answers to come in, when the synthetic "ding dong" of the doorbell chimes out.

Muttering out loud, '*Every* time!' I get up to go and answer it.

My heart sinks even further, when I see who is on the doorstep. It is Adam's mother, Maybelle, in her running gear. She is hopping from one leg to another, as if she cannot stop running to stand still and wait for me to come and answer. Darting a slim forearm past me, she pushes the door open wider and starts to move forwards into the house, still with the odd, alternate-hopping motion.

In slight bewilderment, I am starting to say, 'Hi, Maybelle...' but at the same time realising that if I fail to move, she is going to hop right into me. By reflex, I do move and Maybelle jogs down the hallway and into the kitchen.

Safely, behind her back, I vent a little of my frustration by showing the palms of my hands to heaven in a kind of '*What is going on?*' shrug, sigh dejectedly and follow her. By the time I get to the kitchen, she has helped herself to a glass and is filling it with cold water from the sink. She turns to face me, somehow managing to drink and grin at the same time.

Maybelle is not my favourite person, but she thinks we are best friends, by virtue of the fact that she lives close by and our sons are best friends with each other. I tolerate her, because she lives close by and our sons are best friends with each other. But I often wonder why she does not seek out other people, with whom she would have more in common than she does with me. Health nuts, efficient people, sporty types: the complete opposites of me.

I wonder for how long she has been jogging and also how long her knees and hips will last, before she needs replacement surgery. She is nearly my age, but she looks about thirty. *Because she lives on kale and organic guava berries,* I grump to myself, waiting for her to finish drinking and put the glass back in the sink.

It is only now that she speaks, breathlessly.

'Hi Zoe. How are you? Ooh, you look tired.' The tone of voice is critical, rather than caring. 'I've just finished my 5K.' I do not know what a 5K is, but nor do I wish to, so I do not ask. 'And I've just got a minute on my way home, before I meet my trainer, so I just had to come and ask you. What's all this about your new project? I didn't realise you *did* things. Apart from parenting, that is. Adam was telling me about it last night.'

The response, *'If he's told you about it then you already know, don't you?'* slips immediately onto my tongue.

I stifle that, in the interests of diplomacy and instead, tell her, 'It will probably come to nothing, but I just think it would be a good idea if people could go right back in time on Google Street View, to see how historians think things used to look,' and I do not have to wait more than a second, for her hyena laugh in return.

I am trying to stand casually, leaning by my arm on one of the work surfaces but my hand is gripping the wood, hopefully unnoticed by Maybelle. I am thinking I probably deserve her derision for any number of reasons, not least my pathetic use of *just* and, *'It will probably come to nothing.'* I subjugate myself and I know it, but being able to stop myself from doing it is quite another matter.

'Well, I suppose it's nice for you to have something to think about,' beams Maybelle, with mock kindness. 'I can't imagine who would use it, though! Who's got the time to go trawling Google Street View, looking for scenes from the medieval age? I suppose there'll be some stuffy historians who might like it, but I don't think it would interest many other people. *If* it ever got anywhere, which doesn't seem likely?'

I smile a false smile, knowing that Maybelle cannot tell the difference between that and the genuine variety, and agree.

'No, it doesn't seem very likely at all,' this being both the truth and also the news that I know Maybelle wants to hear. Sure enough, she is sufficiently crass as to give an audible exhale of relief, relaxing her shoulders and beaming beatifically, the status quo between us having been preserved. I think Maybelle only values her own life when she can compare it favourably with that of someone else, that "someone else" often being me.

'Anyway, I'm a bit busy…' I say, in the hope that she will leave soon, wishing I could just tell her to go. But, knowing this will cause a chain reaction for Adam in his friendship with Alf, I refrain from doing so through gritted teeth, for what feels like the millionth time.

'Oh, yeah!' Maybelle responds brightly, recommencing her alternate foot hop, bouncing from one spongy trainer sole to the other. 'I've gotta go too! I only dropped by to say hello.' She stops still for a minute and comes uncomfortably close enough for me to smell her minty toothpaste, grabbing my arm at the elbow, in a way she probably imagines denotes affection. Big smile. Teeth.

Then: 'I know how lonely you can get, Zoe,' followed by a cheery 'Bye now!' as she mercifully jogs down the hallway and back out of the front door, long pony-tail swinging and bouncing behind her.

I close my eyes and breathe deeply, revelling in the newly Maybelle-free space. Seeking a distraction from feelings that might fall somewhere between hurt and annoyance, I go back to my laptop in the sitting room. The sky is overcast now, the hyacinth blue only a memory and I think it will soon rain.

I look at the screen, which is where I left it, on the status update that Maybelle's visit has pushed out of my mind.

'Can anyone remember an interactive London street map from about five years ago or more? You could navigate along the street and maybe look inside some of the buildings? I can't work out whether I dreamt it or not.'

And I start reading the responses that have come in, since I posted it.

'I don't know, but someone should do that.'

'Not just for London. For everywhere! I want one for our area.'

'Hey Zoe, you should start this. Want some help? My cousin is a

historian.'

'*I did some archaeology last summer on my holiday. I bet archaeologists would love to get involved. How far back could it go, do you think?'*

'*God, that would be so wonderful.'*

And more, many more, in the same vein. I smile at the screen, eyes filling with tears, fireworks going off in my brain.

9

Tonight I am attending a meeting at the local history society for the first time. I am going on my own, despite offers of accompaniment from both Hugh and Amy, because if I am alone, then I will have to talk to some of the other attendees and they might feel more inclined to talk to me too. I am reversing my car into the parking space at the venue though, the better to make a quick getaway in the event of it being a disaster.

I really do not know what to expect, or how friendly and open this group will be to me, as a newcomer. It probably depends on the personalities involved and how confident and settled they are and the group's website gave no clues on this whatsoever. But there is no more time to wonder or worry, so I switch off the engine, pick up my phone and purse from the front passenger seat and go into the pub.

It is quite busy tonight and I know this pub from thirty years ago, but not since. Lots of eyes are on me, as I stand waiting at the bar. I suspect the regulars who sit and stand around the bar itself will know all of the other customers except me, because they seem curious about me. I meet their stares with a smile to hopefully disarm them, looking to see if I recognise anyone. There are one or two I feel I should know and might have at one time, but cannot name now.

One of these, a large, rotund man with several chins and slightly bulging eyes, can name me though. Just before he speaks, I remember him as a shouter. Lifting his foamy pint glass away from his mouth, raising his chins, he shouts.

''ey! It's li'l Zoe Wilson! Jack's lass! Wha' are *you* doin' in 'ere?'

His voice has attracted the attention of anyone not already focusing on me and I straighten my spine to my full five feet and eight inches, to prove him wrong, before I realise that I might have been about ten years old, when I last saw this man. I was 'l'il Zoe' then, so to him I will be 'l'il' forever, no matter how tall I grew afterwards.

He looks around the bar at his co-drinkers, nodding with pride and seeking acknowledgement for his memory feat, beer foam still gracing his huge moustache in large quantities. He receives various briefly raised eyebrows and accompanying half-nods, in return. Words are expensive and used as sparingly as possible in the mill towns of West Yorkshire. You do not speak when a facial, arm or shoulder gesture will suffice, especially if you are male and above the age of fifty.

I do not rush to respond. I know, from a lifetime's experience of this town, that what comes next is their proof of association with my dad, to be announced as a point of honour. It must be given in order of precedence, so the big man goes first.

'I saw yer dad jus' las' week. 'E were barn fer t'supermarket. Allus gus to Morrison's on a Tuesday, does ol' Jack.'

Another speaks, next. More grey and white hair, less body weight and a well-worn blue anorak. I do not think I know him, but most of the old timers around here have lived nearby and therefore known each other for all of their lives. So of course, he knows my dad.

'I see 'im near on every day. Lives up our road, dun't 'e?'

'Eeeh, 'e's a good 'un is Jack,' says another. 'Tecks 'is car to our lad's garage. Allus tips 'im.' Various nods and murmurs of assent ripple around the curved mahogany bar, some of them echoing into their glasses, as they simultaneously gulp beer.

'Ser what' yer doin' in 'ere?' repeats the big man with a direct look and I know why. Hardly anyone changes their habits in this town and people either go to the pub – usually every night, but otherwise at least twice a week – or they do not. Furthermore, each of the pub goers tends to choose just one pub as their local. Any deviation from this norm is therefore classed as a *happening*, around which there must be a series of events, leading to a reason, which must be known about and properly discussed, to ascertain its viability. If this is found wanting, the person must give a satisfactory account to anyone who asks, or thereafter suffer various degrees of shunning until they can manage to redeem themselves.

I meet his eye contact levelly, and respond clearly, but with a grin.

''istory society meetin'. Is it 'ere?' whilst mentally kicking myself for the obsequiousness of my momentarily enhanced Yorkshire accent. *There's no need for it: they know my dad and like him, so they're already on my side.* I also want to bring them up to date on my last name, but rapidly decide against it. I do not want to be stuck here for another twenty minutes or so, discussing my marriage, husband and his family history.

My response evidently serves as a suitable explanation. Big man nods, satisfied, and asks no further questions.

'Upstairs,' he tells me, waving his glass in the direction of another door, which must lead to the staircase. 'Get a glass an' teck it wi' yer. There's no bar up there,' he finishes, with real sadness.

I know that 'get a glass' means precisely 'buy half a pint of beer' and I sigh, thinking fast, because I do not want beer, but nor do I want the opprobrium of the tea-total label.

I realise I can dodge it by uttering a quick: 'I'll come back for one later,' and make for the other door, feeling relieved to have successfully run that first gauntlet and got through it, without much delay. I am now freshly daunted by the further gauntlet ahead of me, up the stairs, for which the bar crowd are only the gatekeepers.

The staircase is incongruously new and boxy, for this Victorian pub. As I ascend it, I remember the one it used to have, rising majestically from the centre of the main public lounge, with curved hardwood sweeping bannisters and twisted wrought iron spindles. In the old days, this place was a hotel offering overnight accommodation and the original, dominant staircase probably worked well, for that. I can see why they have opted to do away with it now though, leaving more floor space in the lounge and more privacy for the landlord and his family, in the flat upstairs. But the building is huge and houses two function rooms on its first floor, attendees of which must also share the family's newer and more concealed route to the top.

The sound of voices leads me along a passageway, to the door of one of these rooms. I take a deep breath and push it open, to find myself surprised by the scene that meets me on the other side.

It is a big room with high, corniced ceilings in three sections, coming to three chandeliers set in ornate plaster roses. The décor is pale, with the exception of the deep red carpet, which is bordered on three sides by matching, upholstered, wall-fixed seating in front of which, every few feet, is a solid oak table on a cast iron base, each one set about with other chairs. Five huge windows look out across the canal and river, or would, if it was daylight. The street lights of the town centre are currently visible, beyond.

Milling around the middle of the room, some standing, some sitting, are roughly a dozen people, many of whom are around my own age. I had expected them to be older and one or two of them are, but I often forget that I am now middle-aged and therefore of the demographic most likely to attend such a meeting. The old people I remember from childhood are long gone and their children, or even grandchildren, are now the old ones.

I blink and look more closely, to see that the focal point of the group appears to be an open laptop. In front of this sits a red-haired woman, frowning, as she looks at the screen.

A man leans over her and points at it, saying something like: 'It must have been there…' while most of the others look on, until one by one they begin to look questioningly towards me at the door, obviously wondering why their meeting is being interrupted. It seems like a strange meeting though, with seemingly no structure, that I can discern so far.

I clear my throat, it feeling suddenly dry. Step forwards.

'Um, hello.' Smile. I cannot work out which one of them to address, so I am trying to address them all at once, moving my eyes from one face to another to another, which feels embarrassingly awkward. 'Is this the local history society?'

'Yes?'

'Ah… I've come to… join…?' Even as I talk, I am doubting whether I really want to, but my words have triggered some welcoming movement and three of them advance towards me, smiling.

'Oh, good! Do come in. I'm Gail…' A plump, bespectacled woman is the one who speaks, placing a hand on her chest, to emphasise the point. She half-turns to the other two and gestures first to the older one, a crinkly-eyed septuagenarian in a soft, grey cardigan, saying: 'And this is Mary…' Mary and I exchange smiles and mumbled hellos. 'And this…' Gail gestures to a bigger, younger woman with a mop of curly black hair. '…is Jo.' Jo and I acknowledge each other in a friendly way.

Gail tells me the other names, but none of them stick in my mind, apart from Ava, which belongs to the red-haired laptop lady, and Nick, the man who was pointing at her screen. He still is pointing and the two of them are still engaged in their discussion, my arrival being dealt with.

It looks like an interesting conversation, in which I wish I could take part, but Gail is continuing: 'We're just having a chat about the church square. Do you know it? The cobbled area next to the parish church? By the bank?'

She starts walking back towards the group and I walk with

her.

'Yes, I know it.' It is an old part of town, of which I have always felt fond.

'Oh, good!' Gail answers, enthusiastically. 'I don't suppose you know what the tall building originally was? The one next to the Weaver's Arms, on the corner? That's one of the things we're trying to work out.'

I frown.

'Hmm. It's got a winch and hook above the first floor delivery door, hasn't it? Used to have, anyway...'

Nick startles me by responding, when I thought his attention was solely fixed on Ava and the debate around the laptop.

'Yes! Exactly! We've just been looking at that, on Google Street View. It's not there any more, but it obviously used to be.'

'Yes, I remember it. It was a printer's shop I think, when I was younger.'

'Right. We've got that. And a haberdashery, before that. But would a haberdashery need a first-floor delivery door? Seems a bit excessive for that trade, doesn't it?'

Nick looks a bit like a politician and I have a specific one in mind. Tall and very slim, in a neat, round-necked, expensive-looking jumper and clean, smart blue jeans. Cleanly defined cheekbones and a prominent, pointed nose. Dark hair above a big forehead with a slightly receding hairline. He is standing, but holding onto a chair-back, as if he is about to sit but has not quite got around to it, because of being distracted by the issue at hand.

He is looking at me when he asks the question and I get the feeling of being recruited onto his side of an argument I do not really understand yet, so I do not rush to reply.

Ava, the red-head beside him, jumps in, with: 'No, come on, Nick. Let's look at haberdashery again and try to think about why they might have needed it. We've got no evidence whatsoever that it was anything else before that,' and she starts to type on the machine's keyboard, running a Google search for the term, I imagine. 'This is what Wikipedia says: *"A person who sells small articles for sewing, such as buttons, ribbons and zips..."* '

'Exactly!' Nick interjects and it occurs to me that both he and Ava are the kind of people who tend to dominate conversations, not necessarily in a bad way, but everyone else seems content so far, to simply listen to them. 'You don't need a winch for those things, do you?'

'Well, it was a haberdashery back as far as 1841, we know that much from the street plan we've got from that year. How much older can the building be?' Ava again, gesticulating the question with palms up, long fingers splayed. She is wearing bangles, I notice and two giant rings, featuring some kind of semi-precious stones, roughly set in silver casings.

I move behind them to where I can see the laptop screen.

'Can you zoom in a bit?' I ask and Ava obliges, until nothing else but that building is in view and the features show more detail. 'It's definitely older than the others in that row, isn't it?' I can say, confidently.

'Yeah,' confirms Ava. 'We've got those down to about 1862. And here's what was there before...' She clicks an icon and calls up an old street map of the town, zooming in to the square. 'A baker, a grocer and an ironmonger. We just don't know what kind of buildings they were. Definitely a smaller footprint, though. Look. We superimposed this map onto a current one...'

A task bar item leads to this image, which I lean forwards to study. I am both excited and impressed by its graphic demonstration of the buildings' position from 1841 to now. It is very clear to see which ones have changed and how they have. I am peering at the area by the church and the discussion continues amongst the others.

I hear one of the older men suggesting that the original

haberdasher might have also stocked items in bulk, or bulkier items, so needed the warehouse doors and winch. One of the others wonders out loud whether the shop might have been not purpose-built for any specific trade and the doors and winch added, in case whoever did business there might have had need of them.

Jo, one of the three women who initially welcomed me to the meeting, asked if there was any way the group could find out who first owned the shop. If we could get hold of a name, we might be able to find his trade in the census data.

'The history of the buildings is so entwined with the history of the people,' Ava puts in. 'We can't research the one without researching the other.'

'So, it looks as if the haberdashers' might have been originally part of this row...?' I ask, pointing at a block of buildings that seem to have once been attached to it.

Nick confirms this.

'Yes, for some reason they replaced all of the others in the row and left that one. We ought to try to work out why that happened, actually.' Then, seeming to address the whole group, he picks up a pen and says, 'We need a list of jobs to do, don't we? Someone needs to try to find out who first owned that building. Does anyone want to volunteer?'

I do not volunteer, but someone else does. I watch and listen, as Nick works through the rest of his list, allocating tasks to people and sometimes electing to take them on himself and the thought steals over me, that this is perfect place for my pilot project. It is exactly the kind of work and they are exactly the kind of group I need. Hopefully, there will be a right time to introduce the idea to them, when I am more known and trusted by them.

For now, I just smile and feel very happy to be here.

10

For the next three days I am on a high, because of the local history society meeting and how well it went. It was such a surprise, after I had expected something much more formal, with a speaker addressing a passive audience. Instead, it was dynamic, natural and interesting. Compelling.

Today is Monday, it is just after seven in the morning and I am raving to Hugh about it, for the third time since the meeting, even though we have only just woken up.

He listens patiently, as I tell him my hopes for the group in the context of my History Maps project and how it could not have been more suitable, if I had taken out advertising for staff and employed people. His eyes are closed though, so I have started to wonder if he has gone back to sleep.

But then, he says, 'Do they know about your project?'

'No,' I have to admit. 'I wanted to get to know them first and let them get to know me. I can't just go in cold and try to get them to work for me… with me… on that.'

'What about…' Hugh chews and swallows at nothing, eyes still closed, and I realise we need coffee, to lubricate this conversation. '…the university? Are you going to let them get to know you first, too?'

I take a huge breath and blow it out, while I stretch out my body under reassuringly heavy duvets and grimace at the same time.

'No. Yes. No. Maybe I can manage without them. I'll go and put the kettle on, anyway. Coming down?' I plant a kiss on his biceps and sit up, swing my legs out of bed and push my feet into my waiting slippers.

Dressing gown on, I head for the bathroom wondering, for perhaps the thousandth time, how my bladder gets so full through the night, when I have drunk nothing in my sleep, or since I last went. I keep telling myself I will work that out, some day.

Downstairs, I greet the cat, who endures precisely two seconds of stroking before she runs away as usual. I switch the kettle on and open the back door.

It is the kind of weather that always makes me smile. Dry, soft air and the birds are singing. We are just past the equinox and spring is bursting through in the garden in the form of tiny flowers whose names I have forgotten and cannot remember having planted, though it must have been me because nobody else here plants anything.

There are some small purple ones, in a perennial pot by the door that especially catch my eye, as I pinch a tip of the large rosemary bush I keep here, ostensibly in another pot, but I know its roots broke through the bottom and into the ground several years ago. I rub it in my fingers and bring it to my nose, inhaling deeply. *Rosemary, for remembering.* The older I get, the more I feel I need it.

I am still on the door sill. The cat is still contemplating the outdoor air, as I start to feel its chill and hear the kettle coming to the boil. I want to close the door and come back in, but I know that as soon as I do, the cat will finally decide she wants to go outside after all. These are the only times I ever wish we had a dog instead, just because they do not do this crazy door thing that makes me want a straightforward animal, who knows what it wants.

Deciding to sacrifice warmth once again, on the altar of the cat, I opt to leave the door open and go to make the drinks anyway. As I am making the instant coffee, I am wishing I had used the coffee machine, instead. Hugh prefers instant and

I do not, but somehow the kettle always seems more of an automatic choice.

Hugh enters the room, strides across it and out of the door, to the garden. The cat follows him in leaps. He returns to the kitchen and closes the door behind him.

'Why don't I ever think to do that? She sits there at least ten minutes most days, desperate to be outside but refusing to move.'

'Yeah.' He has got the milk from the doorstep, one pint under his arm and another in his hand. I can almost taste the cream from its top in my coffee already and my mouth waters, in anticipation of it. 'Anyway…' He is adding it to the black liquid in our cups, generously giving me the cream, though I would have opened both bottles, so that we could both have it. 'We were talking about the university.' He hands me my coffee and I savour my first sip of creamy bitterness, immediately. 'I think you should go and see someone there. You need their input.'

Anxiety flutters under my breastbone and I drown it in coffee, before it can take a solid shape. Frown at Hugh, who is ever the voice of reason, which is not always fully welcome.

'I can't, anyway. I promised Alf I wouldn't embarrass him.' I am thinking of breakfast, wondering if we have time for bacon, before Hugh has to start work. Thinking of anything other than university, which is making me feel inexplicably nervous.

'Not graphic arts.' Hugh's insistent eye contact is unavoidable, over his coffee mug. 'Amazingly, my old history professor is still in post, though he must be about eighty, by now. Hmm.' He takes a drink. 'I don't know. Maybe sixty. Anyway, I think I can get you an appointment to see him, if he still remembers me.'

I look away in annoyance.

'I'll never be able to get an appointment because I'm nobody,' would have been my next objection and Hugh probably knows

this, hence the insistent suggestion. I know he is right, but I am feeling a lot of resistance to the thought of going there and asking them to take me seriously because, frankly, I do not expect them to do that. I do not even have a bachelor's degree, Alf's open day being the first time I have ever set foot inside a university.

'Hugh, I won't know what to say to him. I don't really...' *Gulp coffee.* I am no longer tasting it. '...feel like I belong there.'

He puts his cup down and steps towards me, placing a hand on each of my upper arms, firmly. His hands are huge and warm and safe.

'Zoe. You're very intelligent, your idea is brilliant and it needs to happen. You need to make it happen, and you can. I have every faith in you. You owe it to yourself to try. You know you'll never forgive yourself, if you don't. I know it seems scary, but you'll be okay, I promise. I remember Pritchard being quite a decent sort of chap.'

One of the major differences between Hugh and myself is that he uses phrases like 'decent sort of chap' and I do not. It sounds right coming from him, whereas it would sound pretentious if I said it.

When I pull the breath into my lungs, I can feel it in my throat and going down my oesophagus.

'Okay,' I breathe. 'Okay, I'll do it, you're right. Please try to get me an appointment.'

It is only then that he relaxes, but I do not. I am going to be on edge about this and trying to distract myself from thinking about it, right up until I am actually in the room with Professor Pritchard – whatever room that might be.

Ten days later, I am sitting in my car, fifteen minutes before the appointment, contemplating a laurel hedge and feeling nauseous. I know I have to pick up my laptop bag and leave the car and make my way to the correct room, though I do not yet know where this is in the building. But I want to prolong the inevitable, for as long as I possibly can. My breathing is a lot faster than it needs to be and I keep having to open my mouth, to take in more air.

The dashboard clock moves on a minute and I know I also have to make a move, now. I am good at this part, mechanically going through the motions, once I know the time has come. It is like getting out of a warm bath, into a colder bathroom: it just has to be done, without any further deliberation. Stepping out of the car and locking it up feels very like this. I join the pathway and make my way towards the main building, heels clacking on the tarmac.

The History Department is in the old part of the university, built in the mid-1800s in the neoclassical style, complete with imposing, Doric pillars across its frontage. Alf is in the IT Department, which is housed in a newer building down by the river, where a mixture of converted old mills and more recent warehousing has been co-opted for this fast-growing institution.

At least I feel quite safe from the risk of crossing paths with Alf, or anyone he knows here, there being anything up to half a mile and probably about a dozen departments between this place and them. I wonder, for a second, whether they are more correctly called "faculties" or if that is an American term. But Hugh and Alf always say "departments", so I decide that is what they must be.

I have reached a neatly-mown, grassy area and have to turn right and then left, to approach the main entrance. At the bottom of the wide, sandstone steps is a dark blue sign, sporting the words: "Faculty of Humanities" in grey letters. The heavy-ball, out-of-place feeling grows in my solar plexus, with this fresh evidence of the extent of my ignorance. *I am as alien to this establishment as it is to me.*

Looking at the students milling around in the spring sunshine and walking purposefully on their own, I notice that everyone is dressed casually in jeans and anoraks, or fleece jackets. Nobody but me is wearing heels, stockings and a business suit.

I have given a lot of thought to my choice of outfit and am now seeing that all of that was wasted. Instead of blending in, I now think I must look like some kind of sales representative and feel much more stupid and out of place than I would, if I had just worn jeans like everyone else. Also, my feet would be more comfortable, though I am enjoying a much needed automatic micro-boost of confidence, from each clack of my heels.

The students here are all easily young enough to be my children and I am not a student, so there is no need for me to feel quite so daunted as I reach the reception desk and ask for directions to Professor Pritchard's study. I have to ascend a wide oak staircase next, my left hand sliding up the smooth, wide bannister, as I go. The tactile connection grounds me a little and my journey to the room now has a flowing inevitability to it, like the tide up a beach or a babbling stream's sure, well-worn way down towards the sea.

Upstairs, I am tempted to keep clinging to the dado rail in the same way, but decorum prevents it. Instead, I focus on the directions I received downstairs. *Down the corridor, first left and then fourth door on the right.*

My heel sounds are softer now, on the soft, aged-oak parquet, but still regular and I wonder if my heart beats in time to them, as I try and fail to silence my seemingly endless, anxious and probably pointless internal questions.

Will there be somewhere to plug in my laptop if it fails? Will there be wi-fi? And the worst of all: *What on earth am I going to say, that won't sound ridiculous?* This is far more nerve-wracking than the local history society meeting.

When I get to his door, knock and am admitted, Professor Pritchard is nothing like I expect him to be at all.

11

I think I expected a beard and cardigan with corduroy trousers. Round-rimmed spectacles, messy grey hair and a distracted air. The kind of person who rubs his forehead in an endearing attempt to clear his thinking and focus, nevertheless emerging blinking and perplexed. An untidy room with desks full of papers, a roaring fire and invitingly distressed, chocolate-coloured, leather armchairs.

But Professor Pritchard has silver, well-trimmed hair and an upright posture, with a clean-shaven, unspectacled face – which is currently ignoring me.

He sits behind a silver, razor thin laptop, in an expensively Spartan room, with no paperwork in sight. I look towards the chimney breast and see no roaring, smouldering, or even empty fireplace. In its place is smoothly plastered, pale grey painted, blank wall and, where the leather armchairs were in my fantasy, is empty space on darker grey, luxurious carpet. The desk is huge and mostly empty and the room is peaceful, behind the heavy door. We could be in an executive office of Canary Wharf, or anywhere similar.

I have taken all of this in and the professor is still ignoring me, apparently reading something on his screen. I stand, reluctant to presume to sit down on the grey, generously-sized office chair opposite his own, until invited. I make myself breathe evenly and wait.

Presently he looks up, as if surprised to see me here and extends his pristinely grey-suited arm towards the chair. I sit down and he regards my face, saying nothing. I feel about thirty years younger than I am and as if I have broken some rule, like not smoking behind the bike sheds.

I make myself regard him back, feigning cool calmness like his own. I have to tell myself I am nearly fifty and only about ten or twelve years younger than this man, who is not my superior, because I am not one of his students. *I am too old to be psyched out by a steely stare and I will not let it happen.*

He clears his throat, artificially I think.

'So, Mrs...' He checks his screen, clicks his mouse, reads: '... Taylor? I think your husband is an ex-student of mine?' and he smiles, but it does not reach his eyes.

I am starting to wonder about Hugh's definition of *'quite a decent sort of chap'*.

'Yes. Hugh,' I confirm.

'I remember him.' Another smile, with no corresponding eye-crinkle. 'Bright boy. Hard-working. Has he done well? I thought he would.'

'Yes, thank you.'

'What's his field? History? I hope so. Too many of my students wander off into IT nowadays. One wonders why they bother to read anything else.'

'He's in IT.' I afford myself a smile and I know that mine does reach my eyes, because I can feel them twinkling.

The professor brays at this, genuinely amused, but quickly silenced.

'So. How can I help you today?'

Never have I felt to be more out of my depth with this project and quite so utterly ridiculous, to be contemplating it. This man actually means business, properly. He probably has hundreds of students under him and undoubtedly earns a six-figure sum.

Luckily, I have taken Hugh's advice and prepared something of a *précis* of the concept, on my tablet.

I now hand this over to him to read, saying, 'I'm here to seek your advice on this project and to ask if you want to be involved with it at all.'

He takes the tablet and sits back in his chair, crossing his elegantly trousered legs and reading at his leisure. I wait, nervously, wishing I had thought to send a copy to my phone, so that I could read with him and be more ready for his ensuing queries.

It is too uncomfortable for me to wait idly, watching him read and searching his impassive face for responses, so I take out my phone anyway and then wonder what to do with it. I can feel my heart beating faster and my palms sweating. I find a tissue in my bag and wipe them, slowing my breathing down to a more manageable rate.

The grey *décor* and the cool silence helps somewhat and I can hear Professor Pritchard's breathing, slow and even.

I open a fresh list in my notepad app, with the intention of adding whatever comes to mind, while I try to remember the contents of the *précis*.

First section: setting out the need for the History Maps project. The essential pooling of resources, knowledge and skills, to create visible images of the past in a super-accessible format, so that children can learn from it and older adults can remember, while everyone in the middle has their knowledge satisfied and can get involved in compiling data and ideas...

I sigh and check the professor's face. *Is he thinking, 'Pie in the sky!' as I so often do, reading all of that?* There is no way of knowing. His body is immobile, his face set, in blank inscrutability.

How to answer the challenge that it would all be too good to be true: an impossible dream, whilst also resisting the temptation to agree that yes, I too suspect that to be the case?

This is the key difficulty for me – having confidence in my concept and above all, in the ludicrous idea that I might be the right person to spearhead the project, when I know, better than anyone else, that I am not.

Hopefully, Professor Pritchard will like it so much, that he offers to take it on himself.

This thought makes me smile at least and relax a little bit.

I am in the middle of recalling the contents of section two, which is all about the process of how it would ideally work, with local history society amateurs working hand-in-hand with professional historians and graphic arts students, linking the universities with the communities around them in a shared endeavour of valuable creativity and so on, when the professor moves. Apparently, he has come to the end of his reading.

He hands the tablet back to me and sits back to contemplate my face once more, in the same direct and unsettling way as before. I look straight back into his eyes as before and await his verdict, allowing myself a mere, but pronounced, raised eyebrow of inquiry.

Two can play the silent game, I think to myself and I also remind myself to breathe. *He has to speak, eventually.*

When he does, it is on his outbreath, like a weary sigh.

'It's an interesting idea.' He lets his tone fall, at the end of the sentence, dismissively. 'But if I had a pound, for every such interesting idea I've received from students and other lay people, I would be a wealthy man.' And he smiles at what passes for his joke, though I am developing the distinct impression that he likes the position of power just as much, if not more so.

I listen on though, still giving him the benefit of the doubt.

'I think possibly the most *interesting* element of the whole thing, though...' He is giving me that direct piercing look again. '...is *you*.' He waits, now, to see my reaction to this. I am not reacting at all, so he continues. 'I'd like to know about your situation and experience, your qualifications. I think that this proposal of yours is lacking that important information.'

My first thought is to answer him straightforwardly: that I have no relevant qualifications or experience. But then it occurs to me that his question is a mistake based on a misunderstanding, possibly, of what it is I am requesting from him. So instead, I try to remedy that.

'This conversation isn't about *me*, Professor Pritchard. I am really quite incidental to the project itself, which I think is desperately needed. So many people will benefit from it, in so many different ways. It just needs to be taken forwards by someone...'

'So, take it to Google,' he interrupts me. 'You must know it would have to be hosted by them anyway, on their platform. I'm at a bit of a loss to know what you're doing here, quite frankly.' He has folded his arms, now. A bodily reinforcement of his words. 'Unless you're asking for my support in your approach to them, because you know they would refuse to see you on your own,' which bizarrely implies, I think, that I am up to something devious, trying to somehow trick him into becoming involved.

I am so shocked by this, that I am momentarily lost for words, so he keeps talking.

'I'm afraid I cannot commit to doing any such thing, but I do wish you the best of luck with it.' And he stands up, to signal the end of the conversation.

Finally, I manage to voice a clarification.

'Professor Pritchard, all I am asking for is your help, or advice...' My emphasis is heavy on those last two words. '...in compiling a sample street for the project. Somewhere in this town, perhaps. It could be a street very close to this building.' I am having to bend my neck to keep eye contact with him now and his reluctance to return it is obvious. 'Just one street, to demonstrate the approach.'

'My answer is an emphatic *no*, Mrs Taylor. The idea is very nice but not, unfortunately, remotely practical. Speaking for the university, our study schedules are set in stone, two or three years in advance and we simply would not have the flexibility to suddenly incorporate something like this...'

'It wouldn't *need* to be sudden at all...'

He steamrollers over my objection, as if I have not spoken.

'...and so, now, I must thank you for your time and wish you a good day. Please convey my regards to your husband.' He is striding over the carpet as he talks and now stands, holding the door open expectantly.

I have no choice but to use it. Gathering together my tablet, my unused laptop in its bag, my phone, handbag and what is left of my dignity, I stand and take my leave. But not before fruitlessly searching his impassive face, one last time, for some inkling of fellow feeling.

'No, thank *you*, Professor Pritchard,' I say eventually, even forcing a smile, though this one definitely does not reach my eyes. His door is closed behind me, luckily, some time before I reach the corner and look back to check. I manage to keep my composure until I reach the sanctity of my car, but now the tears have come. I cannot stop them or the loud sobs that come with them.

Stupid, stupid, stupid, stupid, stupid me. What on earth did I think *would happen? Of* course, *it's a stupid idea. So* ridiculous *of me, to come to a place like this, with nothing, no reputation, no position, no experience and no qualifications. Just me and my* stupid, *childlike fantasy: 'Wouldn't it be cool if we had some interactive, historical, online maps?' Of* course *it's not going to happen.*

I am still crying as I approach the car park exit, banging the steering wheel to emphasise the words of my thoughts, not even thinking about where to drive.

But then, a thought does come, like a visitation. A face in my mind. Someone calming and kind, a balm to my troubled and wounded, desperate soul, with a healing, genuinely caring smile. *Rachel.* Pulling over, I punch her number into my phone, to see if she is free to meet up for coffee.

12

I think it is about eight thirty in the morning, though I am not willing to tab out of my phone game, to find out for sure. I am consciously dissociating from the memory of yesterday's disastrous meeting at the university. Part of my brain is still squirming with humiliation and grief: amygdala bursting with the trauma of it. Meanwhile, my pre-frontal cortex has its metaphorical back turned, studiously ignoring that.

Ears plugged into Radio 4's "Today" programme, listening to some politician – I could not even say which one, exactly – being hauled over the coals – I could not even say for what, exactly. I am under two duvets and I still feel cold, especially around my neck. I reach around and tug them up a little, without missing a beat in my three-in-a-row game.

I am painfully aware, even consciously, that there will come a time when I will have to emerge and face my new reality, but for now, I choose to postpone that time.

I can hear Hugh and the children, moving around in the kitchen below me. He has brought me a cup of tea – worried, I know. He hates it when I shut down like this. But in some ways that makes things worse, as if there is an expectation that I should always be okay with absolutely everything. Never upset, never any different from my usual cheerful, presentable, approachable self.

All three of them would be happier if that was the case and they could blithely get on with their lives, without ever having to worry about me. I wish that for them too and usually, they can. Even today, I doubt my temporary disengagement from life has come to the children's attention. Alf fails to notice much in the mornings and Amy will have been told that I am just tired, if she asks. *Just tired.*

I am being unfair to them though, in my avoidant state of emergency. Of course, I am allowed to be sad and upset, even switched off and dissociated. Their unease is not remotely authoritarian and all of the pressure I feel, to be always "normal" for them, comes from within me. Not from them, at all.

Hugh will cover for me, this morning and just quietly worry about me. And I will worry about *him* worrying, because I know he already has another hundred or so things to worry about and I do not want to add to the heavy, long chain of stress that I imagine to be like that of Dickens' Jacob Marley. If it was worry beads, each one would be a football, tripping him up. Filled with sand, weighing him down.

Projection. The radio in my ears and the game at my fingers is supposed to silence even this sort of lazy, automatic thought pattern, which seeks to remove the grief from my own doorstep and place it onto Hugh's instead.

This is not about Hugh, it's about me. It is not even about me, it's about my pipe dream of an idea, that now seems to be worlds away from ever becoming real. And okay, it also is about me, to some extent: me and my wasted life and my non-existent career. My missing purpose and newly kindled passion, now firmly snuffed out. It's about my sense of self and my self-image, free-falling without a parachute again and me, having no idea where it might land.

Through the radio programme, the ultra-rational part of my brain makes itself heard. *It hasn't been a wasted life. You gave birth to the children and you are a good mother.*

Okay, not wasted then, replies the default mode network. *But that usefulness is coming to an end and needs to be replaced with something else that's meaningful.*

I turn up the volume on my earpiece, to drown out this

neural conversation that I do not want to be having and wonder if I can get away with staying in bed all day.

I see, rather than hear, the door opening again. To be more exact, I see the light change around me, a lessening of the gloom. I tense up, expecting it to be Hugh, tip-toeing in gently. Coming to be kind and loving in the face of my checked-out self-hatred, which is the first thing I need and the last thing I want. He stands quietly in the room, which is unusual. *Probably wondering what to say, or do.*

It is only when he eventually speaks, that I realise it is not Hugh.

'Mum...? Are you okay?' Even more unusually, it is Alf.

'Yes love, just feeling a bit under the weather,' I reply, going straight into mummy-mode and thinking: *does he need bus fare? We really should organise some driving lessons for him and a car of some sort. He's too old to be cadging bus fare, now.*

'Okay. I was just thinking...' I think it is likely that he has missed his bus and needs a lift into college. Inside my head, I groan. *Hugh will have started work already and I'm in no mood to get up and dressed to take him, but I will have to.* The thought of driving back to that place today fills me with dismay and I close my eyes, as if I can disappear that way.

'Yes?'

'Well, actually, I was talking it through with Ad and Ollie yesterday. Your idea about Google Maps isn't a bad one, really. The lads think we should help you with it.'

'What?' I open one eye, wondering if I really heard what he said. I feel the mattress shift a little and know that he has sat down on the edge of the bed.

'Ollie's really into the idea, actually,' he confesses, almost ruefully. 'Thinks we'd be mad not to jump on board with it.' I am trying to think which one of his fellow students Ollie is and wishing I had paid more attention to his college friends, not that I have met them all. I have heard Ollie's name mentioned before, though. I remember now. Always in slightly reverent tones, so I imagine him to be quite a confident, dynamic young man.

Whoever he is, he's rapidly going up in my estimation.

'Does he? What else did he say about it?'

I don't know why I'm asking, since it's a dead project without the History Department's involvement. And, Professor Pritchard could not have made it clearer yesterday, that will not be happening.

Rachel spent nearly an hour with me in Starbucks after that, trying to persuade me to keep the faith and persevere with it. But even Rachel failed in her endeavour, such was the blow to me of my meeting with him. She helped in some ways, at least managing to make me laugh a little, which was unexpected and against all the odds, but nothing more.

'Just that we should give it a go,' says Alf, with typical word sparsity.

I sit up in bed, intrigued and perplexed and suddenly irritated by the half-darkness in the room.

'Will you open the curtains, please?' I ask him, and also: 'Give it a go, how?' expecting one of his heavy sighs in response to this, but not knowing how better to phrase the question.

'So, there's a crowd of us on my course,' he begins instead, in a completely different tone to the one I usually hear from him. 'Around six of us, usually hanging out and getting work done, together. You know. Anyway, we've been trying to think of a project we can do together for our dissertations. We want it to be something we can work on together and Ollie says your idea would be perfect.'

I reach for my tea, slowly, mouth suddenly dry. The tea is cold, but I barely notice. I do not think I have ever heard Alf say the word 'perfect' about anything. Least of all, anything connected with me. *Perhaps I'm still asleep and dreaming.*

'So...' My voice is croaky. I swallow, drink more tea, swallow again. 'So, what exactly have you got in mind?'

'Like you said: a sample street. Just a few buildings. We pick a date. It has to be before photos were a thing. When was that?'

It is some years since I home educated him but my heart still does somersaults, when he asks me a question like that. It is the complete opposite of his sulky, late-teen '*My mother knows nothing,*' era.

I remember to be careful not to deliver a lecture on the history of photography and instead, I tell him: 'The local history society has a photo of the buildings in the church square from 1892. They think they know what was there in the 1860s and are trying to work out what might have been there, in the twenty years prior to that.'

'Are they? Great! Do you think me and the lads could go to the next meeting? If we can get some sketches off them, then we'll know where to start. I'll get Will to bring his art stuff and we can get some design work going.'

I say: 'Yes, okay love, that should be fine.' But I am thinking: *I don't know, I've only just met them myself. I was going to get to know them for a few weeks, before I mentioned my project thing, in case they think I'm just using them to get that done – which I kind of am. But I don't want them to think it. And anyway, I enjoyed the meeting so much I'd like to join the society either way and for them to become my new friends even if I don't bother with the History Maps which, since my meeting with Professor Pritchard and until two minutes ago, I wasn't going to.*

My thoughts pause for breath and Alf bends over and hugs me, a little awkwardly, saying, 'Thanks, Mum,' and even kissing my cheek. I think I might cry happy tears now, as opposed to the very sad ones of yesterday. Alf hardly ever displays affection for me, so whenever he does, it is all the sweeter.

'Get well soon,' he adds on his way back out of the room.

'I already am,' I tell his retreating back, as I reach for my handbag on the floor and fish out the phone number Ava gave me, at the last meeting.

I stab it slowly into my phone, double checking that I have got it right, before clicking "dial". I have to do this, before I change my mind and start to over-think it.

Just do it.

'Hello…?' Ava's voice answers, after three rings. She is obviously cautious about the unknown number, from my end.

'Hi. Ava? This is Zoe Taylor. I was at the local history society meeting a couple of weeks ago. You said I could ring you, if I wanted to know more about joining…?'

'Ah yes, I remember you, Zoe.'

I can hear the smile in her voice, can picture it on her face and I smile back, happily. *It's so nice to be liked.*

'I was just wondering… I mean, I would like to join. I read the information you gave me and I'm happy about all of that. But I was wondering, could I bring my son and some others to the next meeting? They're studying graphic arts at the university and they have a project in mind, about the church square area.'

'Oh? Tell me more.' She is still smiling.

I am thinking: *Maybe she just smiles all the time.* And then, correcting myself, as I recall her frowning at the haberdashery shop on her laptop screen. *Not quite.*

'Well, they've been working on creating three-dimensional images of buildings and they want to work together for their dissertation, to produce an online historical street. He says they want to choose a date, from just before the earliest photographs and try to develop something around that.'

I am not telling her it was my idea. I do not quite know why. *Because I feel like my association must somehow taint the idea after what the professor said, perhaps.*

'Oh, *wow*,' beams Ava's voice. 'That sounds *really exciting!* Of *course* they'd be welcome, I'm sure no-one will mind. I'd be really happy to meet them and hear about their idea.'

'Okay, good,' is my response. 'It *is* a brilliant idea.'

I am still smiling, too.

13

Now that I know where the pub's new staircase is, I realise we can use another door to get into it, enabling us to bypass the people who know my dad and will insist on stopping me to talk about him, at the bar. I can manage another conversation with them, myself, but the thought of brokering an exchange, bridging the divide between them and Alf's little crowd, is too much.

I can hear the hum of their voices from my right, as I lead the way through the side door to the staircase, hoping we are not spotted by a random glance from the bar around the corner, or person passing by on their way to or from somewhere.

Even though the stairs cause me a jab of hip pain, my heart still lifts to know I will soon be back in the company of the history society. There is a mid-point on the half-landing where the sound changes and I stop being able to hear the voices from downstairs and I suddenly can hear something from the meeting upstairs instead. Individual voices, though nothing of the content yet. It is difficult to hear anything very well, with five of us clomping up the treads.

I am much more comfortable and less trepidatious to enter the room than I was the first time. Alf and his friends follow me in and stand around, waiting to be introduced, so I do the honours.

'Hi, everyone, I don't know if you remember me from the last meeting, but my name is Zoe. I've brought my son and his uni friends, today. Ava said it would be okay.

'This is Alf... Ollie... Adam... and Will.' The four of them give little waves to the group, which immediately raises a warm chorus of welcome in return, that warms my heart and fills it with happy gratitude and optimism. 'They're planning a project for their graphic arts course, which will involve recreating part of a historical street, in a three-dimensional, virtual space. So, I thought of this group and the conversation we were having, about the church square.'

A small silence ensues, while the others absorb this information. Then Nick speaks up, striding towards them.

'Well, we'd be most happy to help. What an excellent idea! I can see it being mutually beneficial. It should be fascinating for us to see our ideas of what might have been there taking shape, before our eyes, on a screen!

'What time period have you chosen, or is that still up for grabs? I'd favour the medieval, myself...' he talks on, ignoring their indrawn breath when they try to respond. 'Because we've got photos back to the late 1800s, so we've got a fairly good idea of what was there throughout the nineteenth century, whereas we could really get our teeth into the medieval years. *No* clue what was there, then!'

I hear velvety, rich laughter. Ava is amused.

'Silly Nick!' she pronounces, to my surprise and his instantly rising colour. 'We'll be here another century ourselves, trying to solve that conundrum! Surely these young men have a deadline to meet, as they'd like to finish their course *before* they retire?'

Then everyone laughs. Me, with some relief because those were the exact thoughts that entered my mind at Nick's suggestion, but I did not know how to phrase them without offending him. It seems like Ava has offended him, because he is stalking back towards the chairs with an almost visible cloud of humiliation over his head. But she does not seem to care and is beckoning the four students to her table and offering them seats.

They go willingly and most of the rest of the group drifts over to join them, but I am worried about Nick. I do not want my family – the newbies – to be a cause of conflict, especially so early in our membership.

I go to sit next to him and thank him for his enthusiasm, adding: 'I think they're thinking of the early nineteenth century for a date, so that they can be almost sure that their content is correct, without having to do too much research.'

'Is historical research a part of their assignment brief?' asks Nick and I struggle to think of the best reply.

I have tried to get more information from Alf about what might be required from them, but typically, he has not wanted to discuss it with me in detail. So I have backed off, hoping he would be more willing to discuss it with this group of relative unknowns, rather than his mother.

I do not really want to confess this to Nick though, so I settle for replying, 'I'm not exactly sure, but I do know they can't use any photos and they do want it to be as accurate as possible.'

He seems intrigued.

'No photos?' he shoots straight back. 'That's going to be difficult, for the early 1800s. Most of the buildings in the church square that we have old photos of would have been there fifty years earlier. At least half of them are still there now. It seems like a bit of a cop-out to me, to choose such a relatively late date...' He considers me, with something that might be suspicion.

I wish I had got to know these people and built some trust with them before we sought their help. But I think if I had tried to delay it by a few weeks, then the students might have gone elsewhere, or chosen another project topic. *Serendipity brought us all together this evening and will hopefully smooth things over, through the course of it.*

Belatedly, I notice an opportunity to further my own scheme a little with Nick. I begin to speak, thinking as I go. Not really sure how much to say or how to say it, but going for it anyway.

'If their project goes well, we might be able to develop it further, to other parts of town and covering other dates, perhaps?' I focus on his bony nose and round spectacles, finding direct eye contact with him to be a little intimidating. 'We could recreate the past online, or as much of it as we can work out. It could become...'

He interrupts me now and I find myself feeling surprised, that I managed to get as far as I did. I am expecting it, having noticed the gleam in his eye through my peripheral vision and spotted the rise in his chest, from the intake of breath.

'It could become a learning and research resource! The repository for all of our findings and conclusions about what used to be here! *Yes.* We definitely need to encourage and develop this.' He has been addressing the air above and to the right of him, but now he turns to me and I can plainly see the zeal in his face. It makes me feel excited and relieved that he likes the idea, but also a tiny bit uneasy because I do not know what he will do with it. Trust works both ways and I know next to nothing about Nick, or any of the other society members.

His eyes now fall on the people around Ava's table, specifically the students there.

'Let's move closer and join in with their conversation,' he suggests, so we stand up and cross the room again, moving to the edge of the group.

'...so I don't know, we could definitely push it back to 1840, if we can go by guesswork, to some extent...' Jo is in the middle of saying, but Nick intervenes immediately.

'Guesswork? No! We can't use that. We must make a proper evaluation using every source we can uncover. We can't leave any stone unturned.'

'Okay...' Jo starts to say, doubtfully, while Ava heaves a dramatically big sigh and everyone else seems to look either confused or a bit worried.

'*Nick*,' says Ava, staring at him, with determined intent. 'They have a *deadline!*'

The random thought occurs to me – just from the way they are looking at each other, as if she has admonished him in this way a thousand times before – that they either are, or were, in a long-term relationship together. I am shaking my head slightly, as if that can dispel its gossipy thinking, when Nick responds.

'Okay! But we don't know what that is, yet. Perhaps the students can tell us?' He pauses and regards them inquiringly, waiting for them to speak. I feel mildly vexed, that he seems to have forgotten all four of their names already.

Alf, Will, Ollie and Adam look from one to the other, with some confusion, obviously not having expected this requirement for input. And especially not such a decision, at this point in the proceedings.

Ollie seems to self-elect as their spokesman, when nobody else speaks up. His voice is clear and sounds quite sure.

'We've got maybe three to six months, to finalise some of the details. But we'll have to make a start on the elements we're sure about in the next week or two.'

'Right,' speaks up an older man, whose name I cannot remember from the previous meeting. 'Well, what do you need from us? Where can we start?'

I warm to him already, without knowing anything else about him. He is not paying any attention to me, but I give him a smile anyway.

'Someone said you had an old street map…?' Ollie responds, looking around at the group. Ava motions that it is on her laptop.

'I'll send it to you, if you let me have your email addresses,' she quietly tells them all, smiling. Ava has a particular skill of addressing several people as if they are each the only one,

I notice. I also notice Alf smiling back with shining eyes, an expression I have not seen on his face since he was about nine years old and got his first computer.

'Thanks,' Ollie responds and then continues his reply to the older man, whose name I am making a mental note to ask for, later. 'Any old photos you have, obviously the older, the better...' He pauses for thought, which I am expecting to be filled by Nick, but then Ollie speaks again, before that happens. 'And anything else you can give us really. Sketches. Notes. Thoughts. Ideas.'

'Mainly the sketches,' puts in Will with a grin. I like his smile, all dimples and infectiousness. Even his square chin has a dimple in it. Most of the others in the group smile in response, I see.

Ollie again: 'We'll need to keep coming back to you, if that's okay, for clarification and as much detail as you can possibly supply. I think it's going to be fun.'

'Yeah,' both Alf and Adam grin to each other, this being the first words I have heard from them, since we left the car. For half a second, I wish they were not quite so close. I am sure Alf would have as much to say for himself as Ollie seems to have, if he did not have his best friend by his side the whole time.

'We'll do that,' says Nick decisively. 'Let's start now.'

Out comes the photo and the map and everyone supplies email addresses to receive copies. Ava volunteers to add both to the website and there is some talk about whether to add a page to the site about this project. But Nick says we must focus on the matter in hand and not become sidetracked by such issues. The rest of the meeting is taken up with explanations about what is known for sure and what is only suspected about the buildings of the church square, around the early 1800s.

Gail points out that we have enough information to be certain about at least four of the buildings and suggests that the students take one building each, to start work. She leans in to point these out on the photograph.

I feel absolutely elated. *We have begun.*

14

I have come home from shopping to find my kitchen full of people. Four people, to be exact, which at least makes it seem quite full. Alf's project group from college has taken over the table.

Ollie greets me in a friendly way. Will gives his cheerful, dimpled grin and a wave. Alf and Adam ignore me. I put my bags up on the counter and start to empty them, quietly putting the groceries away while I shamelessly listen to the conversation.

I am hoping to be able to resolve some of my own confusion, about what specifically their project is for.

Is it an assignment, or a dissertation? I am not sure of the exact definition of either of those titles. But I have been working on the vague idea that the first is issued by the tutor periodically throughout the course, whereas the terms of the second must be proposed by the student and usually happens towards the end of a course.

These four are nearing the end of their bachelor's degrees, so I think it must be a dissertation, but it seems unusual that they are working together rather than alone, from what Hugh has told me. And Alf did mention them having a brief rather than writing a proposal, so I am really in the dark about the details.

The other puzzle is the issue of photographs. I distinctly remember Alf telling me they were not allowed to use them, whereas Ollie mentioned them in the list of things they wanted, at the local history society meeting. This has been bugging me in the three days since and all of my requests for explanations from Alf have been rebuffed, so I am absolutely stumped by it.

They have put the coffee machine on, so I pour myself a cup, which empties it, so I busy myself with changing the filter and adding more water and coffee. As I work, the chat at the table goes on, with Ollie's voice being the one I hear the most.

'Yeah, I think we need to apportion the tasks properly, between the four of us and maybe break it down into specialisms to some extent?' he is saying, somehow managing to simultaneously type on his laptop.

'So, you're going to want some sketches from me.' This is Will. 'The thing is, I need to know what I'm sketching. I knocked some out yesterday, just outlines based on the photos and I went to have a look at the site itself...'

'That's something we should go and do together,' says Adam, who had thought all of this such a bad idea just a couple of weeks ago. 'There's a decent pub in the square.' He grins conspiratorially with my son and I turn away to check the coffee machine, while I roll my eyes.

'Have we decided on platforms?' asks Alf, and they talk about graphic interfaces for a few minutes, which means nothing to me.

By now, I am openly just listening, leaning on the counter with my coffee. They either have not noticed or they do not seem to mind, so I chance an enquiry.

'Can I just ask...?' Alf, sitting with his back to me, lifts his shoulders in a characteristic, weary sigh. Adam, whose face I can see focusing on that of my son, smirks. 'Are you working on a dissertation or an assignment?' I inquire, regardless.

Ollie and Will do not mind me asking, at least. I can tell from the open expression on both of their faces. It is Ollie who responds and he addresses me with respect, as an equal. *As if I am asking a legitimate and reasonable question, instead of just being someone's irritating mother.*

'It's a dissertation, actually. We need to work up a proposal, to put to our tutor. It's got to be one we think he'll approve of and we think he *will* approve of this because he's a history nerd, on the quiet.'

All four of them laugh at this in a knowing and jocular way. Only I am surprised.

'What?! How do you know?' and 'Wow, they're everywhere, aren't they?' I join in with the laughter a little, not really sure if it is all at the same joke.

'He's one of your local history society people!' exclaims Alf and now I am utterly baffled.

'What?! So he was at the meeting we all attended?!'

Why didn't they acknowledge him?

'No! Not that one! The bigger one, near the college! His is ten miles away from yours,' Alf elaborates. This clears up the question of why the tutor was not in our meeting, but still leaves a query over why he is one of *my* local history society people.

I decide to let that go and inquire instead why a history nerd is teaching information technology, to be told that he is even more of an IT nerd. I realise I am going to need the name of this man. I ask and am answered: David Crossley.

He sounds quite popular with his students and I want to meet him. In fact, I am starting to wonder why I have not, as Alf is in his third year now. And then I remember: university is not sixth form college and Alf never even wanted me to have much to do with that.

As my questions are being answered for once, I decide to keep asking them. The next one on my mental list is: *'Why are you doing your dissertation as a group? Is that allowed?'* – which *is a stupid question, really, because if they weren't allowed, they wouldn't be doing it. No wonder Alf usually sighs, every time I speak.*

I discard that one and ask, instead: 'What's the thing about the photographs? Alf, you said you couldn't use them, but then Ollie seemed to think they can be used?' And as soon as the words are out, I realise I probably could have phrased it more diplomatically.

Alf plants his elbow hard on the table and his head into his splayed hand. I cannot see his face, but I know his eyes are closed in a silent atheistic prayer for me to never reference him in public again.

I open the cupboard and reach for a pack of his favourite biscuits from its hiding place, behind the casserole dishes. Alf is twenty-one, but my old parenting strategies are still firmly in place. I am spilling them onto a plate and placing it in the centre of the table as Ollie replies, after a short laugh.

'It *is* a bit confusing, isn't it? Basically, we can propose anything for our dissertation that hasn't been covered in class before and we did buildings from photos in our last assignment, so we knew we had to pick a time period for this from before the photographic era. That doesn't stop us using photos for reference, though.'

I wonder, with a surge of optimism, whether Alf speaks like this to other people's parents in my absence. *Ollie probably still acts like a truculent fifteen year-old, at home.*

I chance one more question, the one I have been curious about ever since Alf first told me about their shared dissertation.

'So, what's attracted you to this topic?'

Ollie smiles his broad, open smile and looks around at his friends before responding to me with customary directness.

'Alf was raving on to us, about your History Maps project...'

Alf throws his half-eaten biscuit at Ollie. It hits him in the chest, before landing on the floor. I am so flattered, surprised and amused, that I do not even mind the prospect of crawling around to clear it up afterwards.

'I was *not* raving!' he protests and I do not know if he is more outraged than embarrassed. Adam is developing a fit of the giggles and this is when I first hear Will's infectiously bizarre honking laugh, which sets them all off again. I can see why these four have teamed up together and feel heart-warmed, to imagine them all being good friends for life. They have got that kind of chemistry between them and I know it is going to be nothing but good for my son.

Ollie is continuing, 'He was raving! Anyway, we all think it's a sound idea that we want to be part of and it will work for our dissertations. So we thought, why not do both? Working together is a good laugh and if we can get your pilot sample street out of it, then it's a win-win situation that ticks *all* the boxes. I reckon we can do it, don't you?'

My eyebrows are up in rapid accord and I am nodding and smiling, so delighted by his words, that no suitable contributory ones come into my head. So, after a pause, he keeps talking.

'We want you to be very involved in whatever we end up putting together,' he says, incredibly. I cannot believe Alf wants me to be involved in anything, but the evidence is fast stacking up to prove me wrong, against all previous signs and symptoms he has ever displayed in my presence. 'After all, it's your project and you're going to be taking it forward, when we've finished. Alf says you have some friends in PR…?'

'Oh yes! Ben and Rachel!' It seems strange, that this is the first time I have considered their involvement in a professional capacity. 'I wonder if they'd want to help on a *pro rata* basis, if we promise to keep them on if the thing takes off…'

'That's an *excellent* idea,' Ollie replies warmly. 'Let's concentrate on getting this initial thing done first. If it works out okay, they might give us some pointers on promoting it for you.'

'After all, it's your project.' 'Pointers on promoting it – for you'. I have mixed feelings on the stickiness this idea of mine seems

to have, to me. If someone like Ollie took natural ownership of it, as he so easily could, I probably would not put up much resistance and would feel quite relieved that it was just being done. Ninety percent of my urge to push on with it comes from the sensation of an itch that needs scratching. Annoyance, that it is not there in place and accessible for everyone already.

It is not really about me having something else to do in my life, other than home educating Amy, running the house and submitting the occasional article on a freelance basis for pin money. Although that is undeniably a small part of my motivation.

One more, bonus question springs to my lips and escapes before I can stop it.

'But, surely, you're not all into history? Why do you really want to do this? I don't get it.'

They know what I mean straight away, without me needing to explain any more clearly. That look between the four of them again. The mirth, never far from the surface of their interactions.

'*Assassin's Creed*, man!' explodes Will, after a two-second pause.

'Haha! *Yeah*,' adds Adam, actually slapping his thigh.

Ollie nods slowly, grinning, holding my gaze with dancing eyes.

'It's true,' he says, with mock solemnity. 'We're all wannabe Creed designers.'

I have seen this game enough in my sitting room on the consoles in its various iterations, over the last decade or so, to know what it is of which they speak. A series of glamorous, parkour-based, medieval city-scapes, mostly Italian, as far as I am aware.

They are right: it is a beautiful game. And finally, everything has fallen into place for me, now and I can properly enjoy that wonderful sense of knowing, for sure, where we are going and why – and what to do next.

15

We are in the function room at the pub again, with the local history society. It is a special meeting that has been convened to help the students with their dissertation, to examine the detail and develop an order of work.

We are about half an hour in and all is going well, so far. Each of the students has selected the building they are going to focus on first, the plan being to start work on the ones that are still there. The rest will be added in at stage two, when more research has been done into their most likely appearance, size and position.

Will has said he will do the Weaver's Arms pub, which the society knows to have been built in 1752, though this surprises me, as it does not look significantly different to other town buildings that are a hundred years younger. It is a sizeable, imposing building with a portico entrance and bay windows. We are looking at the Google Street View photo of it on Ava's laptop.

I wonder if the society owns a projector, because it is difficult for more than about three people to view her laptop screen simultaneously. It is being slowly passed around the table and when I get chance to look in detail, I try to imagine how the building must have looked in 1840.

There is no evidence of the windows having been moved, but I suspect the northern wing to have been a stable block, originally. In my mind's eye, I can picture the cobbles, running up to the front door and the area humming with people and trade.

'They used to hold the market in the church square,' says Nick, just on cue and my mental image is immediately enriched with traders, coming and going and making deals. It is only now that the penny drops, as the reason for its name dawns on me.

I try to imagine the sounds and smells of the area around the pub on market day. Beer, cooking food, chimney smoke and the open sewer with the added ingredients of blood and carcasses from the nearby butcher and the smell and sound of the horses.

Ollie opts for the bank, which is directly opposite the church, but Nick is peering at it and deems it to be too recent.

'I think that's 1880s...' he murmurs, which is then confirmed, by being cross-checked with the street map.

'I think the outdoor market might have used that space, before it was moved to the other end of town,' puts in Ava.

My mental image changes accordingly and puts more space, people, horses and carts between the market and the pub. In our modern times, that location is taken up by a main road, which mostly transports vehicles and hardly any foot traffic. I feel a passing but painful twinge of grief for our loss of face-to-face, visceral community.

Alf is in the process of volunteering to do the haberdashery when I hear the door opening, behind me. All eyes go to it and I turn around.

To my great surprise and apparently that of her son, the newcomer is Maybelle, Adam's mother.

The only assumption I can make is that there is some family crisis she needs Adam for and maybe his phone is switched off, so she has not been able to get hold of him. I expect her to go straight to him, urgently and I look towards him, to see him looking as shocked and puzzled as I am. But instead, she merely stands still by the door, taking in the scene and giving Adam no more attention than any of the rest of us.

In fact, her eyes stay on me, for the longest time and I cannot interpret their expression, but I smile questioningly.

Gail, knowing nothing about who she is or the family connection, approaches the newcomer in the same way as she had me, three meetings ago. But with less certainty, because this is not the usual meeting night.

I hear her hesitantly, kindly asking: 'Hello...? Can we help you?'

And then Maybelle's strident voice, ringing out.

'Yes, I'm here for the meeting.'

Adam looks straight to me and I to him, each of us wearing puzzled frowns, both evidently wondering why the other one invited his mother here.

Gail is equally puzzled, it seems.

'Oh! Ah... well, this isn't really a regular meeting, it's for a specific project. Could you come back on Thu...'

But Maybelle interrupts, snappily.

'I know, it's my son's project. I'm here for that, since it seems like *mothers* are involved, though nobody told *me*,' and she is staring straight at me, as she speaks.

This time, I recognise burning resentment in her glare. A shudder of repulsion goes through me, followed by a heart-dropping dread, that this situation will not be easily resolved.

Poor Gail does not know what to do or say. That Maybelle's words and focus are directed at me is obvious to everyone, but most of the others will not know the background of mine and Maybelle's so-called friendship. I am now wishing I had terminated this, quite definitely and permanently, several years ago. Instead, I have let it continue out of politeness – and because I thought our sons would benefit from it.

It is becoming rapidly clear that I was wrong. Looking over to them again, I can see they are not benefiting now. Adam and Alf are both pale-faced and regarding her, warily, as one might watch a rabid dog from such close quarters.

Maybelle strides across the room, all business suit and briefcase, her glossy dark hair, newly coiffed and her make-up, heavy and slick. She perches beside me and takes out an iPad and stylus, poising the one over the other, exactly like an executive's secretary waiting to take a letter. She is ignoring me now, as if our meeting here is quite normal and natural and she has taken her rightful place.

Back straight, attention on the students, lips pursed, she sits, in anticipation of things to continue as they were and even flicks her manicured hand at them, shrilling 'Carry on!' when they do not.

Sitting next to her I can feel the cold fury emanating from her, competing with the cloud of perfume in which she is enveloped. Although she is otherwise perfectly still, there is a tremble in her gold earrings and, checking her poised hand, I can see it manifested there, too. I try to think what to say to her, how to get rid of her, because that is really what I want to do, Maybelle having never shown the slightest smidgeon of interest in history before.

Of the group, Nick is the first to recover, being perhaps the last to pick up on signs of any potential problem in the air. He clears his throat and continues the conversation as if there has been no interruption, which I find I have enough spare emotion to feel impressed by.

'The haberdashery. Richard, did you find out who owned that?' He turns and addresses the man whose name I wanted to know at the last meeting. But now it does not matter so much, because the new arrival has changed everything.

'Maybelle, what are you doing here?' I ask *sotto voce.* I can no longer concentrate on the project and am starting to feel quite annoyed with her, for turning up out of the blue so passive-aggressively.

'What are *you* doing here?' is her instant response, as if we are ten-year-olds in the school playground. She does not look at me, continuing to watch the main discussion, still with stylus poised, even though she is yet to use it.

At least she has answered me quietly, instead of making a scene.

'Well...' I pull myself up short, wondering if I can say the next words, without triggering an explosion of the heavy, toxic conflict that now hangs in the air with her perfume cloud. Anger powers me on, though. 'It's actually my project. My idea.'

Now, she turns to me, looking down at me from her rigidly upright posture.

'Actually, I think you'll find it's *our sons'* dissertation project. And, unlike you, I don't feel the need to try and make that all about *me*. Now, could you please *be quiet,* so that I can pay attention?'

I am speechless with shock, but to my surprise, I am also suddenly amused by her sheer unconscious, hypocritical narcissism, if indeed that is what it is. I think it probably is, on balance. I breathe deeply and stifle a giggle. Adam is still glancing over regularly and I do not want him to think I am laughing at his mother. Nor do I want to risk her public outburst, if Maybelle detects any mocking response from me.

And so the meeting continues, in its quiet, studious, harmonious way, but with this added edge of foreboding and distraction, at least for me and probably also for Adam, who I notice is now not contributing much at all. This makes me feel sad and worried for him and myself and for the whole project.

Is Maybelle going to keep involving herself, in the coming weeks and months? Hopefully, she'll tire of it soon and become bored with the whole thing. I think that is the most positive outcome we can realistically wish for.

Ollie opts to work on the church and there does not seem to be a building left for Adam, who is not speaking up to take work on, his mother's unexpected presence having utterly thrown him. Ava gently suggests he work first on the stone-plinthed, timber lychgate. The appropriateness of this immediately and bitchily strikes me, because of the old superstition of it being a waiting place for ghouls, hanging persistently around the activities of the living.

Adam gloomily agrees and Nick rounds things up by listing the work still to be done.

'So, we still need to work out the most likely appearance of the baker's, grocer's and ironmonger's that are shown as being attached to the haberdashery on our 1841 street map. We know their footprint, but we need to do some detective work on the rest. Zoe and... er...' He motions to Maybelle, who eagerly supplies her name. 'Yes, Maybelle. Do you two want to go to the site and look for clues? You'll need to check for unexplained lintels and any incongruous stonework on the haberdashery. That might give us an idea of the height of their roofs.'

No, I do not want to do anything with her. Please don't make me. I try to beam this message into his head, with my obviously non-existent psychic power. Maybelle is answering for us both, though.

'Yes, I think we'd be happy to do that,' she says, as if checking for incongruous stonework is one of her normal, everyday activities. Nick nods and moves on and this is the moment that I fully realise: Maybelle is now part of the team, whether I like it or not.

I almost groan out loud, but closing my eyes momentarily suffices, with a deep sigh. I cannot believe this is happening, so smoothly and apparently unavoidably. It is so horrifically ludicrous, that I am struggling to organise my thoughts into words.

'Ava and I will check around for any literary references, published diaries and so on, to see if they are described anywhere. A sketch or painting would obviously be terrific, if anyone can find one, but we haven't had much success so far.'

As we leave the building, I can hear some of the angry

conversation that passes between Adam and his mother, behind me.

'Ridiculous… laughing stock… nothing to do with you,' Adam is quietly, but furiously, enunciating.

'It's as much to do with me as it is with *her.*' Maybelle's voice is clearer and louder. I can almost feel her spite jabbing me in the back as I walk, somewhere around my kidney area.

Adam is louder now, in response.

'That's *bullshit*. This whole thing is Zoe's idea, not yours. We need her involvement. We do not need yours. You're just doing this to humiliate me.'

No she's not, I answer in my head. *She's doing it to humiliate me, but it will probably backfire and we'll* all *suffer collateral damage.*

At the same time though, I am secretly doing an imaginary victory dance, for Adam's defence of me and my place in the project. This is some small compensation, at least. All the sweeter, for being completely unexpected.

16

'What are you drawing?' Maybelle asks me, managing to sound disdainful, even before she knows the answer.

I try not to let my hackles rise, remembering the resolution I reached this morning to remain peaceful and unprovoked, throughout this afternoon's site meeting.

'It's a sketch of the side elevation,' I answer with equanimity, still drawing. I am looking up at the top of the side wall of the haberdashers and noting, alternately. My hand is moving quite fast on the page, which I have almost filled with the outline of the building from this angle.

'Huh,' responds Maybelle, screwing up her nose. 'I'll take a photo. I think you'll find it's much easier and more accurate,' and she snaps one with her mobile phone.

I keep sketching, ignoring her. She sighs and I still ignore her. She shifts her weight from left to right and back again. I keep on sketching.

We are standing in the graveyard of the church, near the lychgate. It is Wednesday afternoon, the sky is blue and in the sun, there is warmth, even though we are still in April. A blackbird is serenading us against a background chorus of chaffinches, with percussion randomly supplied by a wood pigeon's '*Woo,*' in its stereotypically rhythmic sets of five.

I am tuning my ears into all of this, to enhance the sense of peacefulness that underlies my pleasant curiosity about the task in hand. I am resolved to not let Maybelle spoil it.

'Just explain to me, please,' she persists, drowning out the birdsong, 'In what way a sketch could possibly be of more use than a photograph. A photograph shows what's actually there. It's perfectly accurate. Your picture...' She leans across, frowning and squinting at my work. I can smell soap or fragrance on her extended neck, jarring in its floral artificiality. '... Well. What *is* that?' She looks from the page to me, her face an uncomfortable four inches from my own.

'It's more of a diagram than anything, really,' I finally explain, since I know she will not stop asking until I do. 'We've been asked to look for anything irregular in the stone work, so I'm marking those on my plan.'

'So, is it a sketch, a diagram or a plan? Make your mind up,' my companion orders.

I make my mind up, smiling.

'It's all three, or you could call it any of the above. Can you see that lintel, up at the top...?' I point and Maybelle squints in the direction, hand over her eyes to shield them from the sun. She does not answer me, so I further clarify: 'Just on the right hand side...?' Still, no response.

My arm is getting tired of pointing, when she answers.

'What's a lintel?' and I look at her face quickly, to see if she is being sarcastic. She is not.

She meets my glance without shame and frowns, at my answering frown.

Patiently, I explain that, 'It's a long, whole strip of wood or stone – usually stone around here, nowadays – that goes on top of the windows or doors, to bear the weight of the wall above.'

'Why?'

I frown again, quite sure this time that there must be some game play involved. But her countenance is still blank to mildly curious. Blinking.

'Because...' I am trying hard to resist slipping into the tone of voice I use when addressing five-year-olds. 'The wall and roof above is quite heavy and might fall down, without it.'

'Oh!' She seems genuinely surprised. Shocked, even. Arched eyebrows, wide eyes. I can see every globule of her mascara. 'Doesn't the window or door keep it up?'

I am taking a big breath, now.

Surely it's possible for me to develop a healthy and helpful attitude, towards this unexpected turn of events?

I have often commented to Hugh about Maybelle's lack of common sense, so it should not be such a surprise to me. I am undoubtedly being arrogant, or at least inconsiderate, to work on the assumption that everyone carries basic architectural facts in their heads.

I need to be kind. Another breath. *I need to respond kindly.*

'No, they're not strong enough and people keep opening them. Instead, the builders use lintels and they hold the building up. Look, I'll show you how it works.' And I flip the page in my sketchpad and very quickly draw a window in a wall, with the lintel clearly visible above it. Then I use arrows to show the downward pressure, explaining to her as I go. I include some stonework, to indicate the inherent weakness in the mortar joints and I take the arrows out to the side, when they reach the windows, to show how the weight is diverted and spread.

Then I stop and wait for her response, to see if she has understood.

'Hmm,' she says decisively, eyes on the page. Then on the building. Then on me. 'I'm afraid you're wrong.'

I cannot hold back a short laugh at this. It bursts from my nose and my mouth, before I remember to be kind.

Maybelle's Teflon-coated ego is undisturbed by my laughter, anyway and she follows through with: 'I ought to tell you why and you should listen. Because you are seriously mistaken and you're going to end up looking very stupid, in front of Nick and the others, not to mention *your own son,* if you don't pay attention.'

She is so rock solid certain of herself, that I am starting to wonder if I have missed something. I quickly think back over what I have said and glance again at my window sketch to check. But no, everything looks okay.

Eventually, I shake my head and shrug at her, asking, '*What?*'

The pillar-box red, glossy smear on Maybelle's mouth, is smirking. Her arms are folded and her high heeled, pointy-toed boot is tapping, pointedly. She slowly extracts a pillar-box red, glossy-nailed hand and points up towards the top of the haberdashery, to which she adds a twitchy motion of her head towards it, her gleaming eyes never leaving mine.

The mouth opens, exposing polished white teeth, between which pokes a little pink tongue to enunciate the first sound of: 'There is... no... *window.*'

I know the left side of my face has screwed up, in complete perplexity.

I can only ask, again, '*What?*'

The extended finger casually but elegantly draws an imaginary, rectangular window shape, in the air. This time she whispers, making exaggerated consonant shapes with her mouth.

'*No... window.*'

I am just bemused, by now. A young woman walks past, with a child in a pushchair and I feel embarrassed, that someone else might have heard us. I try to think what Maybelle might mean, because it is obvious, to anyone with working eyes, that the wall in question is fully devoid of aperture.

'Y-es?' I eventually stammer, brain full of confusion and now deaf to the birdsong, the occasional passing traffic, the noise of the breeze in the trees and the very ground under my feet. My determined resolution to remain impervious to Maybelle's presence has gone to the wind, to the extent that I cannot even remember ever making it.

Now it is her turn to sigh heavily. She turns towards the building and speaks very slowly to me, as if I am the one being obtuse.

'There are no windows, or even any doors, in that wall. So why would there be any of those lintel things?' And now she tilts her head and smiles brightly at me, widening her eyes and spreading her fingers to gesticulate the supposedly obvious question.

I cannot do anything but speak my thoughts, now. The shock of her ignorance has pushed all diplomatic faculties out of my mind and I could no longer call on them, even if I wanted to.

'Maybelle...' I begin, this being as good a place as any. 'That's the whole point of our site meeting this afternoon. Lintels in walls show us where the windows used to...'

She interrupts me with a peal of laughter, throwing back her head and shrieking with it. This successfully silences me, because I can no longer make myself heard.

'*You* are *so stupid*,' she then enunciates, punctuated with a jabbing finger towards – but not touching – my chest. 'You pretend you're clever, but you're *just not*. Going on about windows, when anyone can see that there aren't any. You don't really know what lintels are, any more than I do! You're a fraud, you and your so-called *smart idea*.

'Well, just because you've got Ollie convinced and he's bullied the other boys into going along with you both, don't imagine you have *me* fooled, Zoe Taylor. I know your game. You just can't let Alfie go! You can't let him grow up and it not be about you! You just have to keep meddling in his university studies and my poor son's work is going to suffer for it.

'I've got your number! And I'm going to be keeping my eye on you, from now on. A foot out of line, and I will *expose* you, and it will *not* be *pretty*. Now, I'm off to the pub to wait for you to finish your silly childish etchings, which will all be *wrong*, but of course you *won't listen* to the voice of reason. Stupid people never do. They can only learn by their own mistakes.'

I still have not closed my mouth, before she has swung her bag around onto her shoulder and clattered off across the gravestones, towards the Weavers' Arms. She slips a little and looks back at me, angrily, as if I might have pushed her. But I am frozen like a statue, twenty feet away, exactly where she left me. This seems to make her even more angry and she stomps, as well as a person can in stiletto-heeled boots, out of the graveyard and towards the pub.

I watch, until she has opened the door and gone into the building and then I stumble across to the lychgate and sit down on one of the side benches. It is better to be out of the sunshine for a minute and there is something calming and peaceful about the small space, under the tiled roof. The echoes of Maybelle's words are ricocheting around my head. She is obviously woefully mistaken, or grossly misunderstanding the lintels situation. *But is she right about me meddling in Alf's studies?*

I am breathing too quickly and my mouth is dry.

I need to calm down. Ideally, I'd go to the pub for a drink, but I cannot face Maybelle again. It's Hugh that I need, now, to enclose me in his arms... No. To look me in the face and tell me, honestly and truthfully, whether he thinks that might be what I'm doing.

17

I am heading into the university's Information Technology Department with Alf and Adam and the experience could not be more different than my previous visit, when I came to see Professor Pritchard.

This is a completely different building: a converted Victorian mill by the canal, no longer dark or satanic, but surface-blasted back to its original sandy yellow to match the new, purpose-built extension at the end.

I am keeping up with the boys' brisk pace, but while we are still outside, I keep glancing at the building to admire the conversion job with its starkly contrasting, tidy and gleaming, black-painted, iron wall ties and window frames. I would be curious to see their reaction if the spinners and weavers, who originally worked inside it could see it now.

The interior is equally impressive, with retained stone-flagged floors and glistening, black iron pillars. The roof has been glazed and its light falls down onto four young birch trees which grace the central atrium, from which other rooms and corridors lead. The trees seem to me excessive but beautiful, their tiny, bright green leaves made luminous, like emeralds, by the daylight from above.

I want to stand and look and take it all in, this vibrant hub full of young life, both human and birch. But Alf and Adam are moving so quickly I have to stride, to keep up with them. I feel purposeful and so much less out-of-place than previously. *Nobody is looking at me as if I shouldn't be here, anyway.*

We reach the IT suite that has been booked for this

lunchtime's meeting and a frisson of anticipation runs deliciously through me, as Adam opens the door. Sitting inside are: Ollie, casually sort of sprawled across a chair and table; Will, upright and sketching on paper, as he has been every time I have seen him so far; Nick and Ava, quietly talking between themselves and a fourth man I am yet to meet: David Crossley, the tutor with an interest in local history. A slim, good looking man, with silvering hair and neatly trimmed beard, he is smiling towards us as we enter the room. I view this as a very good sign of things to come.

He even stands as we approach and Ollie introduces me.

'David, this is Zoe, mother of Alf,' and we all laugh at his turn of phrase.

'Ah, so you're responsible for the existence of this young man?' jokes David in similar vein, grinning towards Alf, who is grinning back.

'Yes I am,' is my happy response, heart lifted by the upbeat atmosphere in which even Nick is smiling. Ava too, of course, who motions to a seat beside her whilst meeting my eyes with her own, sparkling green.

I go and sit and fuss with taking off my jacket and taking out my laptop, all the while exchanging small talk with Ava, about traffic and parking and the weather. She comments on the atrium and I am not surprised to also hear that she had similar thoughts, on the building conversion, to my own.

The tables at which we are sitting are mostly empty of computer equipment, apart from our own various laptops, but I can see plenty of achingly expensive hardware in the other part of the room. I realise, as I look at this, it is humming with electricity in the background. Someone has set our tables out in a horseshoe arrangement, so that we can work and converse, simultaneously.

I have a brief and quiet moment of surreality, when it occurs to me that we are all here in this room because of my persistence with an idea whose time, I am quite sure, has come. And then another moment of sheer indulgent bliss that Maybelle has not been invited. I do not know who issued the invitations, but I am feeling extremely grateful that they were only for the eight of us.

David begins the meeting by thanking us for coming and explaining its purpose.

'I hope it will be the first in a series of many,' he adds, and: 'I suggest we begin by going around the room, taking turns to introduce ourselves and describing what work we've been doing towards the project and how we envisage our input might develop, going forwards.'

I wince a little at *going forwards*', as it triggers my inbuilt prejudice against management-speak. But I decide not to hold it against David, who seems otherwise affable, focused and popular with his students here.

Nick is sitting to the extreme right of the horseshoe shape, so at David's suggestion, he is the first to introduce himself.

'Hi, I'm Nick Green. I think I know you all including yourself, David. We met...' he explains to the rest of us, '...at a local history society event a few years ago. Anyway, as you all know I'm acting chairman of our little branch - ' I did not know this, but it does make sense of a few things. ' - which is about half the size of the one David attends near the university. I think the project will be a good fit for my idea of how I see the future of local history societies, as more and more of our findings go online and become more accessible.

'I was thinking of doing something similar anyway, myself, before it was taken up as a dissertation project by the young men here and I'll obviously be very involved in making sure their submission is as accurate as possible. So far, my input has involved co-ordinating efforts at our end and checking for literary references of the buildings in question. I assume we'll get onto what we've discovered, as the meeting goes on.'

Characteristically, he does not smile as he concludes his little speech. Out of the corner of my eye I can see Ava, reaching out her hand to squeeze his. It surprises me to wonder if he is nervous about being here, or speaking in front of more than a few people.

Ava's turn, next. She keeps it short and sweet.

'Hi everyone, I'm Ava, Nick's partner in crime in more ways than one! I *love* this idea of Zoe's.' She turns to give me a wide, white, toothy smile. 'And I really can't wait to see it take shape. I think it's going to be a *thing*, you know? Internationally. It's exactly the online resource we all need. It's *so* exciting.' Everyone in the room is smiling when she finishes, so contagious is her enthusiasm and nobody seems to mind that she did not follow David's introduction request to the letter.

Now, it is my turn. I clear my throat a little and then tell them: 'I'm Zoe and it's *so good* to be here. I just want to do whatever I can to help develop the pilot project, which so far has included a site visit... er... I've got some notes from that to discuss later, if we find the time. In the future, I just want to stay engaged with this as much as possible and do whatever I can.' I smile and nod around the room, embarrassingly conscious that I said I would *'do whatever I can'* twice in quick succession as if I had no other phrases in my head, which at the time felt like the case. *Head case.*

Ollie, to the left of me, is already talking, sitting upright now.

'Hey everyone, I'm Ollie. Oliver Heartwell, if we're using Sunday names. Like the guys here, I'm in my final year on David's graphic design course...'

'Actually it's *John's* graphic design course...' puts in David, to the loud amusement of the students, and: 'John obviously isn't here,' to the rest of us. 'But he tutors graphic design, while I'm more on the IT side. I do mentor these four though,' he adds, confusingly. I had forgotten about John Anderson, Alf's official course tutor Now I am wondering why he is not here and whether he wants to be involved as well. But I do not want to interrupt, so I resist the temptation to ask.

Ollie goes on, to explain the allocation of the buildings and briefly outlines the progress he has made with the church. I am hoping to see something of this, today.

Will then explains that his passion is more on the arts side of graphic arts, '...along with Assassin's Creed...' he murmurs, which raises a deep and reverential: *'Yes!'* from the Adam and Alf corner. I spot my son's fist being drawn rapidly back into his ribs, in a tribal gesticulation of tribute, or something. I try not to smile at this, knowing it will infuriate him if I do.

Adam, when he speaks, is ten times more articulate and confident than I have ever seen or heard him be before.

'I wasn't into the idea, at first,' he confesses, looking straight at me and smiling. With some shock, I am struck by the thought that this is the first time he has behaved like a man, instead of a boy, in all his years of communicating with me. 'But Ollie convinced us and now I think it's an excellent plan of Zoe's.'

I return his smile, gladly. I do not really know Adam's dad, but I am thinking he must take after him, more than Maybelle. I am a little bit worried we might, as a group, be accidentally helping to drive a wedge between Adam and his mother and there is a warning bell, tinkling in my head, heralding all of the likely future problems that might result from it. But I am predominantly feeling warm and grateful towards Adam, just now – even proud of the man he has grown into, from the surly teenager he was, until so recently.

Alf speaks next and my pride grows with my smile, as he does.

'Hey, I'm Alf, son of Zoe. I've been working on the haberdashery, which is going pretty well, I think. Got the front elevation done, anyway, as it is now...' He picks up his iPad, to show us, but David extends a restraining hand.

'Let's look in more detail at the progress we've all made, after we've done the introductions please, Alf,' and I feel a moment of irritation at his silencing of my boy.

'As for me,' concludes David, 'I'm very much in support of this concept. There's no knowing how far it will go, but as an exercise, producing the pilot project as a group dissertation is perfect. I've talked it through with my colleague, John, who might come to some of our future meetings, as and when he can. And he agrees that it can only be good for the students and for our department, to be involved. We want to make our time and equipment available for the project and I want to take this opportunity to say that we welcome the collaboration with the local history society. Especially as I'm a bit of a history nerd myself.' He grins at this and we all laugh.

We spend the next hour or so looking at our progress to date and working hard as a team, to suggest improvements and next steps. The time flies for me. I am very happy and feel to be truly in my element. There seems to be no animosity or power play in the group, mainly because when Nick speaks up in his authoritative way, David gives ground and seems to respect his thoughts and opinions, even though he is interrupted more than once.

Maybelle has not entered my mind for the entire meeting, apart from that fleeting thought about Adam. Hugh did a very good job of convincing me she was wrong, as he fed me fresh oysters at the fish restaurant last night by way of therapy. Any lingering doubts I had, about me being included in Alf's university work, have now dissipated.

18

'I want to lodge a formal complaint.' Maybelle, *of course.* 'Against both the society here and the national body, if you have one. And against the university. I'll take it as high as I have to, if needs be.'

She is talking to Nick, standing over him, although "verbally assailing him with words" would be a better description.

Poor Nick cannot get a word in and is utterly vexed and confused. I can see his neck flushing a deep red colour and starting to swell against his collar. He rubs it with a nervous hand and peers up into Maybelle's face, the better to try and understand her.

'Pardon?' is all he can manage, for now.

Ava leans across him and wiggles her fingers, to try and deflect Maybelle's focus from his face. I have often noticed the way she protects him from difficult moments and situations like this.

'It's *deplorable* mismanagement,' Maybelle goes on, ignoring Ava's attempts. 'Absolutely disgusting and I will not be standing for it. There will be serious repercussions. I'd be very careful how you respond, if I were you. You'll be lucky to be allowed to carry on.'

I think I might be the only person in the room, with the possible exception of Adam, who knows what she is talking about. I glance across at my son, thoughtfully. *Yes, perhaps Alf knows too,* but the two of them are studiously ignoring Adam's mother and looking at their phones, instead.

Ollie is chatting to Gail and a few other people, over to the left of them and I am sitting next to Ava, also being ignored by Maybelle. I feel for Nick and Ava but I know that if I try to interject, it will make matters far worse. So I keep quiet.

We are upstairs at the pub, at the next routinely scheduled meeting of the local history society.

Ava is now openly waving at Maybelle, who still talks on to Nick.

'…and to hear about it by *accident,* as I did, made it all even worse. Do you imagine other people have no feelings? Have you got some kind of personality disorder?'

Ava stands up at this and raises her voice, so that it can be heard above all others, even that of Maybelle.

'Maybelle! Please! Focus on the matter in hand and try to desist from making personal remarks about people. We realise you're upset, but we have no idea what about! You have to explain to us, in a calm and rational way, so that we can understand.'

'*Huh!* It's no surprise that *you* would be pretending not to understand,' grumps my so-called friend, without even giving Ava any eye contact in return.

'I do *not* understand,' returns Ava, strongly. 'And I am asking you to explain. You can't come in here issuing threats and insults, without telling us what it is that's upset you so much!' She retains her standing posture and is a good four inches taller than Maybelle. Her hand on the chair back, she looks quite willing to intervene more physically, if Maybelle continues to berate her partner in this way.

'You *know* what it's about!' Maybelle persists, answering Ava, but with her eyes still on Nick.

'Please tell us,' appeals Nick. 'We do not know!'

'It's about your secret little conclave on Monday, of course!' she explodes. 'Did you imagine I'd never find out? Of course, I did. You couldn't keep me in the dark for long. I'm not stupid, like *some people*.' She glares over to me as she says this, making her low opinion of my intellect obvious to anyone who is watching her face, which I think quite a few people now are.

I look to my son and his friend again and see that they still quite determinedly are not. I do not blame them and am actually quite pleased they seem to have developed this selective deafness as a kind of self defence mechanism, if that is what it is. I am even wishing I was in a position to do the same thing myself.

'Our little…' Ava and Nick suddenly search each other's faces in shared speechlessness. I breathe deeply, in a silent, embarrassed sigh and wait for the situation to escalate.

I am suddenly remembering a similar scenario, from about ten years ago, when the boys were attending a tennis summer school and Maybelle thought Adam should be given preferential treatment over something, because… *I don't know. School grades or something, perhaps.* It had been a painful and almost equally embarrassing experience for all concerned, especially Adam, for whom I am feeling a lot of sympathy just now.

'…*What?!*' Ava looks back to Maybelle again, obviously wondering if she could possibly have heard correctly.

'Yes. You know,' responds Maybelle, finally gracing Ava with a direct look that is more of a scowl. 'Your little get-together? At the university, of all places? With *my son*?' She is shouting the last two words. Out of the corner of my eye I think I see Adam flinch and my heart goes out to him, in sadness and compassion.

'It was a private meeting of the core group of project workers,' Ava clarifies in clipped, cold tones. 'Invitation only. Space – and, therefore, numbers – were limited. The only people there were the eight of us who absolutely had to be.'

If only Maybelle could see what I can in Ava's face, she might be more careful. Ava's default benevolence is being replaced by a wary defensiveness, which could be permanent in all future dealings between the two of them. But Maybelle does not seem to notice or worry about such changes when she invokes them in others.

'Yes. So I heard. You and Nick, Professor Crossley...'

'He's not a prof...' Ava tries – and fails – to correct her. Maybelle just keeps talking over her, bulldozer-style.

'The four boys...' *Men*, I think to myself, not being able to resist the correction myself, even though I will not speak it just now. 'And one mother. *Her*.'

She points to me without looking towards me, arm outstretched. She could be seven years old, complaining to her school teacher: '*Miss, it was* her!'

Ava's eyes meet mine and I try to mouth the word *sorry* to her. But I cannot be sure she has seen it, before she regards Maybelle again.

What am I apologising for, anyway? I didn't tell Maybelle about the meeting. She's probably overheard the boys – men – *discussing it, or something. She might have been eavesdropping at doors or checking someone's phone messages, for all I know. Am I feeling responsible by association, somehow? If our sons weren't friends, then Maybelle would not be here... Oh. But then the project might not be happening.* On go my thoughts, rapidly, before Ava replies, running a hand through her red, wavy hair.

'Yes, of *course* Zoe attended. We could hardly manage without *her*, could we?' I think – I might be imagining it – but I *think* I can hear something of a smile in her voice. The possible injection of some humour into the situation might diffuse it a little. Or, it might antagonise it. There is no way of knowing, though I appreciate Ava's defence of me. Everyone in the room has stopped talking, or pretending to talk, between themselves and are all openly listening to the exchange at our table.

Maybelle is frowning, enough to bring her eyebrows down to the bridge of her nose.

'What?' she spits, short and shrill. 'What do you mean, *manage without her*? What do you think she does, that I can't do?'

Ava is openly smiling towards me, now. I half-smile ruefully back, not quite feeling the amusement, because I think Maybelle has a valid point. It taps perfectly well into my own imposter syndrome.

'I don't know you well enough to answer that question properly,' she says to Maybelle, still smiling, 'But I think there's one thing you did *not* do, that Zoe *did*, which was to conceive of this entire project and persevere with it until now, when it's starting to take shape. We all owe her a great debt of gratitude...'

Maybelle explodes at this lighting of the blue touch paper.

'What? *Gratitude*? Let me tell you something about *Zoe* here, which many of you may be surprised to hear.' She stops and checks around the room, to make sure absolutely everyone is paying attention. 'This woman, whose idea you're all slavishly following as if she's Albert Einstein or something, *does not even know what a lintel is*. Yes! Seriously!' she addresses the gathering, stunned silence. 'She was blabbering on about lintels, when we did our site meeting on the side wall of one of the buildings... *and there weren't any windows there!* She thinks every big bit of stone is called a lintel, whether it's on top of a window or not!

'I wouldn't have believed it, if I hadn't heard it with my own ears and I think you should all know what kind of a shady ignoramus you're inviting to your secret, private meetings.' Finally, she stops and waits for a response, probably imagining everyone to be suitably shocked by my extreme lack of technical expertise.

'Er, Maybelle...?' To my surprise, it is Gail, who finally steps forward and breaks the disconcerted hush. Gail, with whom I will always associate kindness. Gail, who was the first to welcome me here weeks ago, when I knew nobody and felt quite nervous. She becomes prominent and noticeable at such times, but somehow blends into the background at others. 'That's an easy mistake to make, about lintels, because they are of course originally there to support the weight above a window or door. But then, when the window or door are removed, the lintels are often left behind. So we can use them to work out where windows used to be.'

She smiles and walks towards Maybelle as if she is calming a fretful horse, which might cause damage to its surroundings and itself. I think it probably takes a similar quantity of courage. Amazingly, Maybelle is listening silently, sullenly, and not interrupting.

'I used to get really confused about them, too,' Gail quietly continues. 'But then, things started to make more sense. It's funny how we take that kind of information for granted, once we understand it. But before we do, it's all just nonsense, isn't it?'

Now standing by Maybelle's side, Gail physically reaches out and gently takes her arm.

'Do you want to come and help us try to work out how the market might have looked, before they put the bank on that site? Will is making some sketches for us and they're coming on really nicely.' She sounds a little like a nursery school teacher, coaxing a reluctant child away from an argument over a box of crayons. The tactic is the same. I wait, with baited breath, to see if it will work and it seems that the whole room is also on tenterhooks.

Maybelle, whose attention had been caught by Gail while she was speaking, now switches it to me, resisting Gail's gentle tugging of her arm. She stares at me with such cold hatred, that the pit of my stomach feels like a ball of ice. The irreverent computer gamer in me surfaces unexpectedly, with the bizarre words, thankfully not spoken out loud: *Wow, she's a frost mage!*

But I do not smirk. I hold her gaze with a rueful, hopefully compassionate grimace, which she does not return. Her look is almost ponderously calculating, as if she is wondering what to do with me. I can hear a wall clock ticking loudly, one I never knew was here. When I break our long eye contact to look for it, Maybelle actually growls, which makes me look back quickly to ineffectually check if she really made that noise. But already, her back is turned and she is going with Gail to the right hand corner of the room, where Richard, Will and Mary wait for them.

'Oh, my God,' Ava says quietly to Maybelle's retreating back, but really, to me. 'Come for a drink with us afterwards, Zoe. I want to know what's been going on, between you two.'

And we try to return our focus to the old journal entries they have found, about the pub and the square, but I can never quite regain my concentration properly. Instead, I am worrying about what Maybelle will do next, because I cannot imagine this situation ever being resolved.

19

The pub we are heading to, as we leave the meeting, is one of the oldest in Yorkshire and about twenty minutes' drive. As Nick and Ava are discussing where to meet and both quickly coming to the same decision, I am smiling to myself, because *where else would amateur historians want to meet?*

The Bridge at Ripponden has long been one of my own favourites. I have spent many hours observing the detail of the ancient timbers of its cruck frame, bent, warped, added to and changed over the nearly seven hundred years in which it has stood.

Ripponden is near a motorway junction on the M62, so I phone Rachel on my way out of the door, because I really want her and Ben to meet Nick and Ava and this might be the best opportunity for it. I doubt they are free and happen to have childcare at such short notice but, to my pleasant surprise, I find that they are and they do. Rachel's parents are staying with them and they are glad of the excuse to get out.

Getting into the car, I have that warm, bubbly feeling I get in my chest when things are progressing well, sitting on top of a heavy burn in my solar plexus, which I know is related to Maybelle's meltdown at the meeting. I really want to shift the latter and only feel the former, but I don't know how to even begin to do that.

We arrive before Ben and Rachel and soon, I am ensconced in a corner seat by a roaring fire, with Ava and a mug of beer before me. I am trying to explain my friendship with Maybelle.

'It was just the boys. They were always together, because both families home educated and live in the same street.' Ava looks blank, so I clarify. 'Home ed is great, but there's always a bit of a shortage of people doing it. It's a lot better nowadays, because it's becoming almost mainstream, but fifteen years ago we couldn't afford to turn friendships down. And, you know, Adam and Alf just clicked.'

'So you had to be friends with his mother?' I cannot quite tell if Ava is being sympathetic or challenging, but suspect the former. I am not even sure if Ava is a mother, so might have any relatable experience. I take a deep drink of malty beer, while I think about how deeply to go into it. I also suspect that while she is interested, Nick is probably not.

'I didn't really *have* to, but it just makes everything so much easier, if the parents are friends. Especially when you home educate.'

She observes my face for a minute, then says: 'Okay, yes, I can see that. It must have been difficult sometimes, though?' Her eyes flick from one of mine to the other, searchingly.

I want to be diplomatic, but it is hard to think how to be. I know what Ava wants: the lowdown on how we have come to this point. But the problem in trying to make that clear to her, is that it is by no means clear to *me*. I need to answer, though, so I start talking.

'I can't lie, it has been very difficult sometimes and as the boys got older, I tried to create more and more distance between us. Maybelle has... something wrong with her, I think...'

'Ha! You're not kidding!' Ava's instant, guttural validation feels good to me, because I sometimes wonder if I might be imagining things with Maybelle. If my perspective might be off, somehow. My frequent thought is that she cannot possibly be as bad as I think she is. *Nobody could. It wouldn't make sense to be that way and to be the cause of so many problems all the time, wherever she goes and whatever she does.*

And then I think, *I'm not with her all the time and maybe she's perfectly fine when not with me and I only bring out the worst in her.* But a mutual, long-time friend of ours is a psychologist and she once actually put a name to Maybelle's condition, unofficially, just between us.

'What do you think is wrong with her?' Ava is asking. 'I mean, it's obvious that she's madly jealous of you and she seems to need to be the centre of attention all the time. I feel really sorry for her son.'

'Yes, it's Adam who suffers the most, I think. As for whether she's jealous of me, I can't see why! Their family has a lot more money than ours and she does far more than I do. She often makes me feel quite lazy and ineffectual, with all of her activities, when all I'm doing now is the odd bit of writing and facilitating my daughter's home ed.'

Ava asks about Amy and I state her age and something about her interests in response, briefly. This would be the moment for her to tell me about any children of her own, but she does not, which seems to confirm my guess that she is childless. Then, we are back onto Maybelle again, about whom she seems determined to reach more understanding.

'It is weird, the way she behaves...' she ponders. 'I've never seen someone so angry about missing a meeting, before. It wasn't a meeting she needed to attend, for any other reason than you being there. It's as if she's scared of you being more important to us – or maybe to her son – than she is.'

I am nodding, slowly, replacing my beer on its little square mat and turning it, absent-mindedly. There is a hum of background conversation in the pub, but I am not really aware of it. It is not preventing me from thinking, but I am struggling with this subject matter, all the same.

'Yes, it's bewildering really. She's been difficult before, about Adam wanting to spend time at our house, which he always does seem to want to do. Maybe she has some deep insecurities, or something?'

Ava frowns.

'She doesn't seem remotely insecure. I'd describe her more as *over*-confident, if anything. And that's what's so *weird* about it. Jealous people usually keep it well-hidden. They're not shouting it from the rooftops, full of anger, like she was this evening. I've never seen anything like it!'

'I have,' I sigh. 'She's always been this way. Another friend of ours is a psychologist...' *I've said too much*, I realise as I am speaking. *It's not fair, to be sharing this unofficial diagnosis with someone else.*

Ava jumps on it, straight away.

'Wow, is she? What did she say about Maybelle? She must have had an opinion, professionally?'

'She did... although of course, Maybelle never sought her professional help, or anything. In fact, if anything, she seemed to want to avoid her as much as possible.'

'What does the psychologist think it is?'

I hesitate, but the green eyes will not let me off the hook. Ava's usual languorous pose has been transformed into a much more upright one. Her whole being is fixated on getting to the bottom of the situation.

Nick, on the other hand, is paying absolutely no heed to our conversation. He is sitting back, arms akimbo, looking with cheerful fascination at the roof and walls of this ancient place, even though it will be far from his first visit.

I was right to imagine his disinterest in Maybelle. *Maybe he's disinterested in people generally, because Maybelle does tend to evoke curiosity in most people, at some point or another. Curiosity, bafflement or repulsion, depending on the beholder.*

I look back into Ava's face, finally meeting her intense gaze.

'Just between the two of us...' I begin, reluctantly.

'Of *course*,' she confirms, and I do believe her.

'Narcissistic Personality Disorder.'

Ava sits back quickly at this and looks thoughtfully into

the room. Into space, really, her mind focused inwardly on its reaction to this news.

'Oh, right!' she eventually responds. 'Wow. I didn't realise it could look like that, but now you say the name, it does make sense of a few things. How interesting! What causes it, do they know? Is it genetic?'

'I think it can be, but it can also be caused by some serious trauma in very early childhood, which I think Maybelle did have. I did some reading around it a few years ago, when the psychologist told me what she thought it probably was,' I add for further clarification, in case Ava is wondering what kind of amateur psychobabbler I might be.

'So, I bet she has no idea she has this thing...' Ava ponders further, with characteristic perception.

'That's probably right. Apparently, they rarely do. She seems to be unhappy with most people most of the time, but her mental focus is very much outwards. There's a lot of projection of fault and blame onto other people, it seems. I've forgotten a lot of what I read, now, about how it works.'

'It's going straight into my Google search box, when I get home!' Ava exclaims and I smile and tell her I will probably look it up again too, since it has come back to my attention, now.

Rachel and Ben have arrived and I stand to go and greet them with hugs, at the door.

'So glad you could come,' I am saying, while Ben is looking over my shoulder around the room, possibly wondering if anyone he knows is here, or which ones are Ava and Nick.

Rachel and I smile at each other, fondly. It is good to see her face, which always manages to make me feel liked and as if everything will be okay. I forget this, between our meetings and remember again, every time I see her. *Rachel's roots seem to extend almost to the centre of the world, like the strongest, oldest tree. Maybe that's the beer thinking, though. I have downed my half-pint quite quickly.*

'We're sitting through here,' I murmur and lead the way, with that feeling that something momentous is about to take place: another vital piece fitting into the jigsaw puzzle of my now beloved project and in such a perfectly appropriate environment as this old pub. I am hoping hard that these four people click together socially, because it will make everything much easier if they do and the complete inverse if not. First impressions are everything, so there is a lot riding on the next few minutes.

I introduce the two couples to each other. Smiles all round, then Ben energetically jumps into the chair opposite Nick and looks eagerly into his face.

'Hi mate, are you a historian? Brilliant! We've got this farm, right, what year is it, Rach? 1782, yeah. *Really* ancient. But there's some more ruins across the yard and we don't know what those are. Do you wanna come and take a look? Come for dinner! They can come for dinner, can't they, Rach? You two and Zoe and Hugh, all six of us. That would be fab and we can pick your brains about these ruins. Well, you'll be on site. You'll be able to see for yourselves! When can you come? Are you free this Friday? Rachel does a *mean* shepherd's pie. You're not vegetarians, are you?' He looks anxiously from one to the other.

Ava throws back her head and laughs, uproariously and contagiously. I can feel the giggles rising, too, releasing the bubbly feeling in my chest I have felt so often, recently and it is a relief. I look towards Rachel and see that she is laughing too, looking towards her husband with much fondness.

Nick looks a little bit alarmed. I am wondering if he will have been hooked by the mention of local history, then started to think about the ruins at the farm and his mind will have plunged deeply into that, when he suddenly looked up, to see everyone unaccountably laughing, while he is being asked to remember whether he eats meat and all far too fast for him. I think I am getting to know Nick a little, now.

He looks to Ava for explanation or reassurance, as he so often does. She squeezes his hand, smiling broadly into his face.

'I think we're free on Friday, aren't we, love?' And then she turns to Rachel, her green eyes dancing with what I interpret as delight. 'We *do* eat meat. Can't wait to taste your shepherd's pie.'

20

Ben and Rachel's farm is the real deal. A genuine, unspoiled, little-altered slice of traditionally rural Yorkshire. The sun is shining, but the gentle breeze is bracing in its determination to bring to our noses the aroma of muck-spreading that I always associate with farmyards, even though its new owners have no animals yet. I do not know whether they are planning to get any but it is clear, from the smell alone, that their near neighbours have sheep. I can hear their distant bleats, from further around the hillside, carried on the wind with their pungent but comforting odour.

I have dressed for dinner, not for picking my way carefully, in heels, across the smooth, glistening flag stones, amidst longer grass that brushes my stockinged ankles. But I touch the barn wall appreciatively, imagined scenes of the long past flickering through my mind. The work, the early mornings, the animals, the smell, the sloshing buckets of warm milk, the cast iron rings I can still see, fixed to the walls where a roped beast would have been secured.

Beyond the barn, the view opens out. Fields and walls, woodland and the dips of valleys and cotton wool clouds, puffing by. I breathe deeply, to internalise the paradise, as if I might be able to take some of it away with me afterwards, like a party bag. I envy the comfortable sense of history, of the strong feeling of rightness that comes with an old venue of rural industry and strong family life. But not the isolation – both social and physical – that two miles of rough farm tracks engenders.

Most of the others have gone to look at the ruined buildings, but I stay by the barn, enjoying the kind of thoughts a broad vista always stimulates in me. It both stills and opens my mind and takes me out of myself at the same time. I feel simultaneously curious and settled, safe and inspired.

Hugh comes over to put his arm around me and I wonder if Ben's voluble enthusiasm is a bit much for him, as usual. What I find endearing, he finds annoying and sometimes *vice versa*. We smile at each other and I look across to the group of four and feel heartened by their instant and natural rapport. *This could be the start of a wonderful and long-lasting friendship group.* I hope my instincts are right about it, because the early signs are promising.

I can hear snatches of Ben's voice, above the background, occasional hum of the other three, floating across the yard on the wind.

'... doorway *there*... ...So, windows... do you think...? ...Yeah, cos that's what I said innit Rach? ...just across the way...' I can see him, gesticulating from the house, as if to indicate a direction of travel. My interest is lazily provoked, to the extent that I would probably go across and listen more closely, if I was not so comfortably ensconced in Hugh's embrace.

Rachel sets off back to the house, her slim welly boots striding across in easy bounds. Realising she is going to prepare the meal or set the table or something, I murmur something to Hugh about going to help and set off for the door, in her wake. I can hear him, following me and suspect he will find a comfortable chair in the living room, for a brief retreat from the effort of socialising.

An hour later, we are all sampling Rachel's famous shepherd's pie and it is indeed as delicious as its promise: tender, meaty and rich with buttery piles of mash melting into the gravy. Nobody speaks in their blissful savouring of this ambrosia, except to release involuntary '*Mmmmm*'s and other notes of enjoyment.

When Ben stops chewing, looks around the table and begins: 'So...' I am expecting the discussion about the ruins in the yard to continue and am surprised, when he continues: 'Where are we up to with the History Maps project?'

I keep eating, waiting for Nick or Ava to respond and when they do not, I look up, a forkful of pie on its way to my mouth. Everyone is looking at me and smiling or laughing. I am momentarily perplexed, until I realise my mouth is wide open, waiting to receive said pie, so I laugh myself, catching Hugh's eye and exchanging a glimmer of mirth.

Reluctantly, I put my fork down and bring Ben and Rachel up to date.

'Well, as you know, the four students have been developing their models of the buildings, around the church square, as they probably looked in 1841. We've got a street map from that year, which gave us a starting point. This is for their dissertation and will also give us a kind of prototype sample to hopefully use as some kind of basis for the next stage.'

'Right. How's that going?' asks Ben.

'Their buildings are coming along really well: Alf was showing me yesterday. We're just about up to the stage of dressing the street that connects them and I think we're going to have a society meeting, very soon, to help with that...?' I look to Ava for confirmation of this and she supplies it, without much of a hiatus in her own pie consumption.

'So, what date will it be ready to share online?' Ben is suddenly extremely focused on my words and I realise he is watching my face, intently. I think this is the first time I have seen him in professional listening mode and it is markedly different to his usual, relaxed and very chatty demeanour. I even feel slightly intimidated under his gaze, which is not an emotion I have ever experienced with Ben in all the years I have known him.

'Er, I'm not sure exactly. David Crossley, the tutor who has been overseeing it so far, says they shouldn't publish until their course results are issued, which is early July I think. The eighth?'

Ben nods and thoughtfully eats a mouthful of food. He looks across to Rachel, who nods as well and I get the feeling a decision has been made between them, without knowing what it is. I am about to find out.

'Rachel and I would like to handle the PR, if you're happy for us to do it, Zoe. We'll work *pro rata*, as long as our company can be mentioned on the press releases and so on. We want to be professional about it and do a proper job for you, though. I mean, the thing is...' We have to wait for him to eat, chew and swallow, before we hear what the thing is. 'This has to go viral. Am I right?' And he waves his now empty fork around the table at us, like a conductor's baton, as if we are the orchestra.

I turn to Hugh straight away, who is raising his eyebrows happily towards me. Ava is smiling her broad smile and Nick seems typically a little bit confused. Anything that does not deeply concern the minutiae of history always seems slightly beyond his comprehension. Rachel and Ben are watching me in anticipation and it is only then, that the need for my approval of their decision occurs to me.

'Wow! *Thank* you,' is how I phrase it. 'That would be wonderful. I didn't expect...' I think I might cry and start blinking fast to try and prevent it. I feel Hugh's warm, giant hand squeeze my knee in reassurance and I carry on. 'Yes, I think that's just what we need. Are you two happy for this to happen? Ava? Nick?'

Ava answers for them both in the affirmative and also reminds me of my personal ownership of the concept, which seems to be becoming a regular pattern between us.

And then we are all laughing and Rachel goes off to bring champagne from the fridge, which opens with the traditional pop, even though it is smothered in a napkin and we are sealing the deal, with glass clinks and bubbles.

Hugh shouts: 'Speech! Speech!' and I worry that what is left of the shepherd's pie on our plates might go cold so, laughing, I reply: 'Let's finish eating first!' which has the added benefit of giving me time to think of what to say.

A few minutes later, I am on my feet, urged up by Ava on one side and Hugh on the other, saying, 'Well, this *is* a momentous occasion, isn't it?' Happy grins and nods from around the table. Ben even whistles his agreement. 'Such a lovely surprise for me. I really didn't expect this evening to become the official launch of our official working group!'

The champagne has made me light headed, so that I have a little trouble enunciating the closely repeated consonants.

'I'm so looking forward to working with you guys.' This, to Rachel and Ben, but my eyes lock onto hers for a little longer than his, finding their usual grounding solace there. 'I feel like...' I am struggling to find the next words, but they are waiting to hear them, so I force something out, even though it might not be exactly right.

'I actually feel like this thing has a chance, now. I mean, it did before...' This last quickly to Ava and Nick, in case they think I am devaluing their input up until now. 'But we definitely will be needing some excellent PR, from some excellent PR people.'

Hugh and Ava both make low cheering noises to this and I notice even Nick smiling towards Ben and Rachel, who are laughingly enjoying the compliment.

'So let's drink to them. Ben and Rachel, and their kind contribution.'

I raise my glass, but Rachel interrupts me and forestalls the answering chorus. Not for the first time in our friendship, I find myself amazed to see her quiet voice eliciting immediate obedience, even in quite a noisy situation.

'No,' she says, shaking her head. She stands up and raises her own glass in a gesture towards me and then the other four in turn. 'To the History Maps project!'

'To the project!' agree most of the others with glass salutes and we all drink in mutual confirmation, though I am making a mental note to myself not to drink much more. Even though Hugh is driving home, I am now expecting more detailed discussion about the sample launch and what might be involved.

I am not wrong. This takes place through pudding and continues through coffee and mints in the sitting room, where Ben sits with his laptop open on his knee while we collectively make some further choices, after discussions he instigates.

I am so impressed by this professional version of Ben, it being so markedly different to the way I have always seen him before. He stays doggedly on track and in the two hours of this conversation, we seem to make more progress than we ever have before, due to his determined leading. It does not even feel like work and yet it is.

Rachel's input is no less effective, but compliments his own. She quietly refills coffee cups and gently elicits contributions from each of us, especially when it looks as if someone's participation – particularly Hugh's and Nick's – seems to be lapsing. It could have so easily become a three-way planning session between Ben, Ava and myself with the other three silently looking on, but Rachel's considerable skill prevents this from happening. It enriches the process immensely.

By the end, we have agreed a public launch date of July 15th, this to take place across social media and to be supported by a website and press releases. I need to double check with all four students that they are happy to have their work used in this way, even though we are all sure they will be. Their skills will be showcased to an extent they could never manage alone, which will enhance their employability, as Hugh uncharacteristically put it.

We also need to set out the legal position, this to be clarified by contracts, which we will visit a solicitor contact of Ben's to have drawn up. We finally take our leave at around one o'clock in the morning, after making plans for future meetings and email exchanges.

I climb into the car, feeling exhausted and elated in equal measure, as well as relieved, that Nick and Ava came in their own car, so I do not have to make any more conversation. Hugh's smile and mine in return conveys everything we need to say to each other.

It is still on my face, when I close my eyes to relax for the journey home.

21

We are back in our usual meeting place, the upstairs function room of the pub, having a "set dressing workshop", as Ava puts it. The invisible line that used to separate the local history society crowd from the group of four students no longer seems to exist. Everyone is mixed together and equally important, in the pooling of suggestions on how the church square would have looked in 1841.

The buildings are finished but they stand as islands on a pristinely empty, flat street which, ideally, would be populated by the people being sketched by Will. He is running a quiet kind of Identikit session in one corner, with his laptop and a graphics tablet, receiving descriptions from different people in turn, currently: Mary.

I can hear her conjuring up an 1840s woman, who might not have been unlike herself.

'Her back's bent with the weights she's had to carry every day, as well as the lack of enough good nutrition, poor thing. She's wearing a shawl. Probably some shade of brown homespun and a plain linen long skirt. And I should think she's got clogs on her feet. Something like...'

Will now, presumably, scrolls through a selection of clog images for her to choose from, because her index finger is running through them in the space between her eyes and the screen.

Eventually, she says, 'Yes, it would be those. Leather tops and a bit tatty. And her face looks sixty, even though she's only forty, out in all weathers. It plays havoc with the skin!' and she laughs her own sixty-something laugh, kind eyes crinkling, above her smooth apple-pink cheeks. Will laughs with her, rich and loud and my heart warms to hear them both together, the kind, older lady and the quiet, sensitive and considerate young man.

I am growing fonder of my son's three co-students, the more time I spend with them, which has been quite a lot recently, with all of the meetings and workshops we have had. If Will is the quiet one, then Ollie is the loud one, confident and stylish. He provides the social glue, bringing everyone together with his natural people skills that are not unlike Ava's. But hers are subtle and practised compared to his, that are much less polished. He is funny and charming, though can also be careless, which sometimes results in him accidentally blundering into problems.

He is currently at a table near the door, designing the open sewerage system with Richard and Nick. If I tune into it, I can hear Nick, earnestly trying to give specifications as to the width and depth of the channel, including how the cobbles would have been arranged. At the same time, Richard is enjoying describing the stench and constituency of the sewerage, to Ollie's rowdy hilarity. Nick's voice keeps being drowned out and he cannot see the joke, so is getting hot and bothered. My guess is that he is worrying about how much work still needs to be done and this apparently pointless sidetracking is incomprehensible and, therefore, frustrating for him.

My dear son Alf and his ever-present best friend, Adam, are working together with the help of Gail and Jo on an arrangement of stored crates and baskets by the market area. Jo is explaining to the boys what shape the baskets would have been and Alf seems to be searching for examples online.

I am glad I cannot hear or see what is happening there more clearly, because I am already feeling the parental urge to intervene and try to enhance the communication between them.

I just know Alf won't have explained what he's doing. Only Adam can see his screen and the other two, sitting opposite, will be having to guess. Ah, he's turning the screen around to face them now and they're peering and pointing at specific basket shapes. All is well.

At our table, Ava is attempting to wrangle something approaching a sensible and constructive conversation with David Crossley – with the added complication of Maybelle's involvement. This is why I am silently looking around the room and trying to stay out of it, since Maybelle's behaviour tends to be a lot less challenging when I keep my own mouth shut.

'She needs to be given a role,' Ava decided, at one of our post-mortem meetings in The Bridge, a few weeks ago. 'She's obviously going to cause more trouble if we try to get rid of her and she needs to feel important. I just can't think what role we could give her, that might keep her busy enough to minimise her attacks on you, Zo.' I love that she has started to call me Zo. Nobody else does it, and it makes this new and precious friendship feel even more special to me, though I am yet to refer to her as Ave.

'Hmm...' I remember thinking hard, trying to imagine Maybelle in a variety of roles and failing. *Not enough artistic talent to co-ordinate anything to do with the graphics... not enough historical knowledge to make decisions about content...* 'What skills has she got?' I ponder, out loud.

Ava, glancing quickly at my face, green eyes glinting, said something about her talent for public humiliation, which brought us both out in snorting giggles. This extra detail comes back to my mind now and generates a private smile to myself.

'How about putting her in charge of scheduling meetings and making sure all the right people are invited to them?' I finally suggested. 'It's probably what she'd be best at and the only thing that will stop her from feeling so left out.'

And so that is what we did, Ava presenting it as a flattering plea for her organisational skills. So far, it has worked successfully, give or take the occasional apparent memory lapse when it comes to inviting me to things. But luckily, I have not been dependent on Maybelle for news about upcoming events. So, to her frustration, it has not caused any problems for me.

Right now, our conversation with David Crossley is about how the university would like to be plugged in the press briefings.

'I should get you together with Ben and…' Ava is saying.

'I'll schedule a meeting for you with Rachel,' cuts in Maybelle. She does not like Ben, because he has no time for what he openly calls her shenanigans, whereas Rachel is characteristically more polite.

'Oh!' David seems confused. 'I thought the PR was being handled by Ben Heskel's company…?'

Maybelle huffs, irritatedly.

'Rachel is his wife and colleague,' she informs him crossly, as if he is a fool to not know this. 'You'll find her far more approachable.'

I cannot sit quietly in response to this and a noise, something like: 'Errr…' escapes from me, over which Ava hurriedly and diplomatically coughs, while she thinks of how to appease us both.

After a few seconds of coughing, she is ready with: 'But most people like him,' quickly followed by: 'Why not meet them both?' and a bright smile towards David.

'You could come to ours for dinner,' I suggest, mischievously. 'Ben and Rachel and Nick and Ava are often there these days, you could join in with one of those evenings,' and I sit back to watch the urge to kill rising in Maybelle. It is probably unwise, due to the high risk of a backlash, but there are times when I run out of diplomacy, long before Ava has exhausted her resources and I have to throw caution to the wind.

David brightens at this and opens his mouth to respond, presumably in the affirmative, but Maybelle is already verbally exploding.

'We have to keep everything official and above board!' she snaps, as if we were planning to rob a bank instead. 'Meetings must be *properly minuted*. This is a *serious business,* Zoe. You can't just plan things on the back of a beermat, any more,' and she takes up her iPad, to slide around its face with a scarlet, glossy-clawed digit, doubtlessly calling up the appointments spreadsheet, from which we all receive regular updates. 'Can you do next Tuesday at ten?' she asks David, who has returned to looking confused.

'Errr… no, I don't think so. I teach at the college full-time…' he begins, to which Maybelle exaggeratedly rolls her eyes. Sometimes, I can hardly believe her behaviour, even though it happens right in front of me.

'Okay,' she sighs her reluctance. 'I *suppose* I can make it an evening appointment.'

'Good luck with that,' comes from me without thinking. I know how busy Rachel is and how spontaneous she likes to remain, with the precious spare time she has available to her.

I should have stayed silent because it triggers an entirely predictable further reprimand from Maybelle, who shifts around to face me squarely in readiness, thereby turning her back completely on David. Ava closes her eyes wearily and puts her face in her hand. Maybelle draws a deep breath and begins, whilst I try my hardest not to smile.

'Zoe, I don't think you realise just how hard some of us are working, while you're sitting around enjoying the fun,' the diatribe begins.

I catch Ava's eye, opening widely with exaggerated shock and my mouth twitches, so that I have to make myself look away and back into Maybelle's face instead.

'It's very easy for you to sit there, making smart aleck comments, isn't it?' it continues. '...from your privileged position of having come up with *one idea*, just the one! So I would appreciate it, if you would now let those of us who *do* know what we're doing be allowed to continue, unimpeded by what passes for your snippets of wisdom. *If* you don't mind.'

Finally, she turns her back on me by pivoting the completely opposite way, thereby bodily excluding me from the conversation.

This frees me to look openly at Ava, whose face is now easily visible to Maybelle, while my own is not. I start shaking with silent laughter, because Ava is chewing her own fist in an attempt to silence her mirth. Eventually, she has to stand up and approach the table where Nick, Richard and Ollie are working on the sewerage, so that she can safely laugh out loud, though she dare not look back to meet my eyes, even then.

'Tuesday at six?' Maybelle has asked David, and her finger is poised to instantly and efficiently record his response. I cannot see him for her lilac-jacketed back, but there is a long silence and I get the feeling he is wiping his face in perplexity, wondering what on earth could be going on between we three women. I feel a stab of sympathy for him. I wish I could explain, without embroiling him further in the controversy. But I cannot, so I stand up myself and go to sit with Alf's group by the window, to see if I can make any contribution to the arrangement of crates, or whatever they may have now moved onto.

It is some time before I glance back in the direction of Maybelle and David and I feel a pang of regret, as I see them sitting in awkward silence together. At least, David looks awkward, but Maybelle seems oblivious to his discomfort and is engrossed in her iPad. If I could go to rescue him without triggering another outburst from her, then I would.

But I cannot. So I reluctantly have to leave him to his fate.

22

I think my instinctive maternal pride is feeling thwarted by the fact that it is Ollie and not my Alf who has control of the mouse, for the giant wall projection of our finished sample of the church square. *Of course, it would be Ollie,* the natural leader of the group of four students and I owe him my gratitude for persuading them all to take my idea on board and use it for their dissertations.

I do not need to scan the busy IT suite for my son. At some level of my consciousness, I usually know where to find him. Right now, he is in the back, left-hand corner, facing the screen but showing Adam something on his phone. Both of the boys are laughing, slid down in their chairs with their knees up, like recalcitrant little school boys at the back of the maths class.

I start working on feeling glad that he is happy instead of thwarted that he is not doing more. But my attention is soon distracted by Ben, who is physically shadowing Ollie as if he is marking the striker on a football pitch. He keeps trying to grab the mouse from under Ollie's hand, in his enthusiasm for the projected content on the wall.

'Oh *wow*,' he is saying, for about the tenth time. 'I can't *believe* it. It's *amazing,* innit Rach?'

The plan was for a quiet viewing, followed by an intensely constructive meeting to check for snags, to finalise the PR schedule for the launch and to try to answer any outstanding questions. But the plan did not account for Ben in happy puppy mode, seeing the whole project for the first time. Indeed, it is the first time most of us have seen it in full and I am also very excited. Thrilled, in fact.

'So, we can look around the corner into the market...' Ollie says, navigating around. It works very like Google's Street View, with greyed-out arrows in the street to click on and squares on the buildings, to look at them. It has got less of a cartoon-type look than I expected. Occasionally, someone asks for the tour to be paused, so that we can study a particular detail or angle and it is then that the realism of the scene becomes especially apparent.

'The only thing...' Ben starts, thoughtfully standing still and upright for the first time, instead of leaning forwards in constant motion and dodging around the back of Ollie. '... is the lack of *people.*' And it is only when he says it, that the emptiness of the square does become starkly obvious. It reminds me of Sunday afternoons, in 1980s town centres, where an actual piece of giant tumbleweed floating towards you would not have been a complete surprise.

'Yes, I thought we were having some, too,' adds Maybelle, who has been responding conversationally to Ben's comments more than anyone else, since the session began. 'I suppose it's because they're there in the modern day Google Street View, aren't they?'

'We wanted to put some in,' Will speaks up from his position, near the projector. The lights are low in the room and even so, I can see through the relative gloom that he has his trademark pencil in hand. Although the work is all done, Will is still sketching. It seems to be second nature to him and I am curious to know what could possibly be on his sketchpad, now that the pilot project is finished. 'We designed some great characters, but they just didn't look right, frozen in time like that, so we opted for a people-free scene in the end.'

'Aww, that's a shame,' Ben responds and we continue our tour around the market, until we reach the haberdashery and I feel that always sweetly unexpected swell of pride, warming me from the chest outwards. *Because my* son *did this, every last window and every last stone of it.* The haberdashery has a special place in my heart anyway, because it is the building the history society was discussing when I first met them and it has been the centrepiece of our project, ever since.

I glance across the room to my right where Hugh is sitting, with Amy. He has taken a day off work and she is missing her swimming lesson to be here for the momentous occasion. I hope Amy knows that this is Alf's contribution and is sharing in my pride in it. But I cannot see their faces very well in the dark and even more frustratingly, I cannot remember to what extent I have discussed those kind of details with her because I have been so busy, recently.

As I watch them, I see Hugh's head turn and lean downwards, towards her ear, so I think he is probably telling her now. Sure enough, she sits up a little bit more and then looks back towards her brother, smiling broadly at him. He does not see her, but I catch her eye and smile back, to be welcomed by her excited grin, before she turns back to watch the screen. It is one of those brief, to-be-forever-treasured exchanges, that make all the work seem suddenly extra worthwhile.

Ollie takes us to the front door of the haberdashery and is starting to move us past the window as he navigates towards the bakery next door, when Ben speaks up again.

'Can't we go inside?' and for some reason, the question is shocking, the room silent in response. Even Maybelle seems to be stuck for words. My first thought is to wonder why Ben does not know that we have only done the exteriors. My second is to realise, with some surprise, that this really is the first time he has properly seen any of it. My third thought is to actually ponder the question, for the first time, to myself. *Why* have *we only done the exteriors of the buildings?*

I am just reaching the point in my thought process where I am starting to draw comparisons with Google's current Street View tool, when I hear a voice from the corner and am slightly startled to identify it as Adam's. I suppose I must usually work on the assumption that neither he nor Alf are ever properly paying attention – quite unfairly, as they sometimes prove – but based on their general demeanour of distraction.

'Inside the buildings, you mean, mate?'

Ben performs one of his trademark exaggerated shrugs, hands fully splayed in the palm up position, arms outstretched at ninety degrees from his body, shoulders up. And, although I cannot see his face at the moment, I know his eyes will be wide and his mouth downturned in a sarcastic gesture that says *'Well, duh! What do you* think *I mean?'* without the use of any words. The lights are not too dimmed and everyone who can see him presumably gets the message.

I hear Adam sigh and I see Ollie and Will checking each others faces for answers, but finding none.

'It's a good question, actually...' begins Maybelle, before she tails off, having no better answer than the rest of us. *Yes it is,* I think, in silent response. *But do shut up, Maybelle.*

'Well, there's a limit to what can and, indeed, what *needs* to be done, for the dissertation...' begins David Crossley, amicably. He is usually so quiet that I forget he is in the room.

The man sitting next to him is John Anderson, the university's graphic arts tutor, who presumably does not share his colleague's hobby of amateur local history on the side, because this is the first of the shared project meetings he has attended. John is the main course tutor, whereas David teaches information technology. I assume, from their names, that the latter subject is more technical where the former is artistic, though I really do not know enough about it to be able to say for sure.

'And they've done more than enough, already. It's been very hard work,' John now adds, to various noises of appreciative assent from the room.

'We *could* go inside the buildings, though...' I hear myself pondering out loud. Alf's familiar, loud groan of protest reaches my ears from twenty feet beyond my left shoulder – the kind of groan only a son makes to his mother when she is suggesting more work for him. I quickly go on, to say: 'Not for this pilot though, obviously. If you say so,' I nod towards the tutors, sitting in front of me and a little to the right, 'Of course, the students have done enough. No, I'm thinking for the wider project, beyond that. Should we include the insides of the buildings?'

I look towards Ava and Rachel with my question, who are sitting together with Nick and Richard, to the left of the projector, along with Ben's empty chair.

'I don't know…' Ava replies thoughtfully, long, pale fingers slowly rubbing her pale, delicate chin. Rachel shakes her head, but I know she is gesturing uncertainty for the idea, not negativity. *It's a bit unfair of me to ask her, anyway, since she hasn't been involved in any of these decisions before.*

Maybelle's voice snaps, from about five feet behind my right shoulder.

'Well, the modern day Google Street View doesn't go inside buildings, does it?' It feels like a reprimand, as if she thinks I am too unintelligent to have worked this out for myself. I am sure this is what she *does* think and I am trying very hard, now, to not feel emotionally triggered by her superior attitude.

'We'll decide that after we've done the pilot, I guess,' I finish, needing to take the decision-making process well away from Maybelle's involvement, for my own sanity's sake. I am hoping she will let it drop.

Of course, she won't.

'Decide what? Whether the modern day Google Street View goes inside buildings? A quick check on your phone app will show you it doesn't, Zoe,' she persists. I grind my teeth spontaneously and force myself to keep calmly breathing and not to start yelling something I know I will later regret.

'Decide *what*, Zoe?' she asks again, when I fail to respond straight away. I have not even turned around to look at her, which I know will be annoying her and be partly responsible for her stabs at me, just now. *Not that she ever seems to need to search hard, for reasons to take stabs at me.*

'Never mind,' I insist clearly, with forced equanimity and lean forwards to catch Ollie's attention. 'Can we continue please, Ollie? I'm worried we might run out of time and there's still a lot to discuss.'

Maybelle's peremptory 'No!' is drowned out by the projector's hum and I can hear Hugh's loud compliment of the bakery, which all helps to move things along and smoothly past the obstacle of her objection.

Gail and Jo both add loud comments of approval, too. But the next interruption comes from Nick and is an entirely spontaneous sound of alarm.

'Oh!'

Someone else, I am not sure who, asks: 'What?'

'The... the... sewerage channel! It's really *far* too shallow. They just wouldn't have had it at that depth, because if they had, the sewerage would have been washing around their feet and really, this is just a few years before the first Board of Health was established in 1848, so they would have been well aware of the associated problems by then. I *did specify* that the channel should be a good *three* cobbles deep...' His voice is rising almost hysterically and I can hear and see Ava's quiet soothing of him. She is making the kind of noise a farmer might make to a cow that has got itself stuck in a fence and is becoming distressed. 'I *did say!*' Nick is continuing, his voice breaking with desperate emotion. 'Why did no-one listen? It has to be historically correct or there's no *point...*'

'It's okay, I'll change it,' Ollie says, quickly and clearly, so that there can be no mistaking him. 'It was my fault, for not listening. We were messing about, when I should have been paying attention to you, Nick. I'm sorry. Don't worry, I'll correct it in time and you can check it before it goes live.' The words *you can check it* receive special enunciation because Ollie knows, by now, that they are what Nick needs to hear, in order to be able to relax for a while.

Nick is obviously suitably mollified by them, though Ava is the one who silently mouths the '*Thank you,*' to Ollie, looking away from her partner, but leaving her calming hands on his arm. I feel grateful to Ollie, as well. This is not the first time I have been impressed by his intelligent maturity.

Indeed, I remind myself again, *if it wasn't for Ollie's enthusiasm about my idea, we wouldn't be here at all and the idea would still be just that.*

Glancing back towards Alf and Adam, I see that they have at least put down their phones and are watching the projected screen.

The tour eventually comes to an end and there is an unscheduled round of applause. Every face I can see is smiling, very happy with what we have all worked together to produce. John turns the lights up again and we move our chairs, to group around for the scheduled meeting about the actual launch, five days hence.

Ben characteristically flips, at this point, from what I fondly think of as his enthusiastic puppy mode, into his highly professional work persona. There is no more leaping around from him, no more '*Amazing!*'s, or 'Innit, Rach?'s. Instead, he is all frowns, correct dictum and definitive statements, about the interviews and the schedules. Whenever he mentions a schedule, Maybelle raises her hand and tries to interject, but he consistently ignores her and the smooth, controlled monologue flows on.

'We'll practice an interview,' murmurs Rachel from her chair that is now at my right hand side. And I suddenly realise that when they are talking about interviews, they might be intending for *me* to do them. With growing alarm, I think it through and realise that yes, they probably *are* intending this.

I have gone cold and lost the ability to concentrate, when Ava, from her chair on my left hand side, suddenly and bizarrely whispers to me: *'What star sign is he?'*

My answering bewilderment is enough of a distraction to take my panicking mind off the interviews.

'What? Ben? I don't know!' I whisper back, thinking: *Surely, he can hear us*? But he does not seem to have done, as there is no break in his verbal delivery.

Rachel has heard though, from my other side. She is obviously amused, and leans across me a little, to supply the information.

'Gemini.'

Ava wryly nods in confirmation, observing Ben again.

'Thought so.'

And I feel Rachel's body shake a little, with silent laughter.

23

'Can't Nick do the interviews?' I am asking Rachel, with a note of desperation. 'He knows a lot more historical detail than I do and he's really good at explaining it.'

'No,' she responds, patient but determined, grounding me as usual with those clear, blue eyes. 'He'll buckle under the pressure and anyway, it's *you* that people will want to hear from. They want the personal story, not the boring history facts.'

'They're not boring!' I protest, even though I know it is pointless as she will not yield and let me off the hook. 'Nick makes them sound so interesting!'

Rachel laughs and I cannot help joining in a little, when she says: 'Now you know *that's* not true,' even though I still protest that it *is*, in my sulkily reluctant mirth.

'Ava, then,' is my next ploy. 'Ava's great. Calm, confident, knowledgeable. Ask her to do it.'

'She'll refuse, because the History Maps project is *not her concept*. It's yours. You have to do it and you can do it. You're perfectly capable and when we've finished our practice, you'll be fine.'

'Alf and the other students should definitely be put forward for interviews before me,' I move next, cheerfully sacrificing my only son on the publicity pyre rather than myself. 'They've actually built the thing and Ollie is particularly articulate, isn't he? The rest of us only supplied the background research and stuff. They did the actual work.'

'It's *all* actual work and the original idea was *yours*. So *you* are the main face and voice of our publicity campaign, although the others will be doing some, too. It's a done deal, Zoe. There's no point arguing. There was never any question that it had to be mostly you. The only person who thinks there might be a question about it, is you!'

'But I'm *nobody,*' I protest, doggedly, but weakly. Defeated, but determined and honest to the last. 'A plain housewife in her forties, who plays at being a writer, with a bit of a hobby in local history. What's interesting about me? Nobody will want to hear anything I've got to say.'

'*That* is the entire *point,*' counters my dear friend and PR consultant, firmly. 'That's the human interest story, right there! Plain, ordinary, unassuming little you coming up with a wonderful idea and it actually starting to take shape, against all odds. Trust me, they'll love it. Not least because it's the truth, and that makes my job a lot easier than it sometimes can be.'

'Hmm,' I brood, glowering at her from under the shadow of my brow. 'I'm not *little.*'

Rachel laughs at this and sorts through some papers on the kitchen table, unperturbed.

'Anyway, it's not as if we've got you on the Today programme, yet,' she tells me. I cannot help fixating on the "yet" word and sense the top of the spiral of panic again. But the sound of Rachel's voice, continuing on peacefully, stops me from descending down it. 'It's only the local rags and small news channels. Most of it will be YouTube stuff, for the first day or two, until it gets going.'

'*Until it gets going?*' I echo back to her, instantly seeking clarification. 'How big do you think it's going to get?'

Rachel pauses and meets my eye again. I can see that she is weighing up her options, working out what to say to me.

'I think it's going to get very big. Ben and I have been working really hard, to give it the best start we can and there's no knowing for sure whether it will go truly viral, but we think it probably will. That means national media, Zoe. But don't worry. A little practice and you'll be fine. Is the website finished, yet? Is Nick happy about the final version of the project?'

Her questions successfully distract my thoughts from spinning off into scary, possible future scenarios and I focus on answering them, instead.

'Yes, Hugh roped the two tutors, David and John, into working with him with the website. They've both been a phenomenal help in so many ways. Then they gave up their Sunday to get this done.' I open the app on my phone and take it to the site, so that I can show her the current version. 'Ava is good on web design too, so she was there – without Nick, for once!'

Rachel laughs a little.

'Here, at your house? I wonder how he coped without her!'

I am laughing, too. I am so fond of Ava and Nick by now, that it seems a little disloyal.

But I know that Rachel feels equally affectionate towards them, so I add, mischievously, 'I don't know. She'll have left him with his head in a book and he probably didn't notice she was gone.'

My own panic now ably averted by Rachel's expert people-managing skill, which easily rivals that of Ava, I take the paper she is holding out to me and read it. It is a list of things I must personally do, before the launch date in three days' time. I read down it with a heavy sigh.

'Hairdresser?' I protest. I have trimmed my own ever since I got a parking ticket outside the last snooty salon I visited, twenty years ago, before vowing to never darken their doors again.

'I've booked you into mine for this afternoon,' Rachel responds, in a tone that brooks no argument.

'But, Amy...'

'...can go with you.'

'Make-up?' I am reading from the list, again.

'I'll do that. We might as well save on costs where we can, at this stage.'

That's okay. I trust Rachel with cosmetics. She'll make a much better job of it than I would myself.

'Clothes and shoes?'

'Yeah. We're going shopping before the salon appointment. Your clothes are lovely, Zoe, and they really suit you. But I think you should have something new for the publicity campaign.'

All I can do is smile at her diplomatic effort to save my humiliation. I know that my clothes are cheap and often scruffy, because I have been too busy with the children and not earning enough, or feeling myself important enough, to spend the time or the money on presenting myself more smartly. Rachel knows this too, all too well, since her own style went through a remarkable transformation when they set up the PR business.

'Ben and I are agreed that the costs should come from the PR budget,' she continues.

'We have a *PR budget?*' I am thinking rapidly, trying to balance the non-existent books in my head. Because so far, everyone's time has been given on a voluntary basis and, apart from the website hosting which Hugh picked up without much thought, there have been no other real costs for us to meet.

'Yes we do. Don't worry, it's not a loan. Let's call it an investment. We think it's worth the punt, because if and when the project takes off, it's going to do great things for our business, isn't it?'

'Wow, Rachel.' I study her beautiful, calm face, intently. 'You've got a lot of faith in it.'

'Yes. We all do, don't we?'

I am not sure I do. But I find it difficult to lift my perspective up from day-to-day activities and see the bigger picture – apart from that persevering initial vision, that this should be a universally available tool. I never imagined myself being so involved in creating it and am looking forward, with projected relief, to a time when someone else eventually agrees to take it off my hands, so that I can go back to my former life. And things can return to normal.

I am missing Amy and our quiet days together. We have still managed to do a lot and she has not missed any of her usual activities. But the sense of not being in a rush and not having much else on my mind, other than her, is now only a fond memory from months ago.

I am pulled back from my thoughts by a question from Rachel.

'Have you ever given an interview on the TV or radio?'

'Yes! I agreed to be interviewed by local radio about home ed, once. It was awful. My voice dried up, I couldn't breathe properly and my brain shut down, so I couldn't think what to say, even if I had been able to say it.' The memory is flooding back to me now and making my hands feel clammy again. I grab my cup of tea and drink it, swallowing hard to try to push the panicky feelings back down.

'Okay, that's really normal. It's what happens to most people their first few times. I promise you, it won't last. You can work through it and I've got some tips to help us to prepare for it this time, so it won't be as bad.' She pushes a laminated sheet towards me, containing a series of boldly printed statements, each in one of three alternating colours. 'We can easily predict their first few questions, so the answers are there.'

I read down, seeing: *'The idea came to me in the car, when I was driving my daughter to a lesson and she was asking about the old buildings. I wished she could just see on her phone how they used to be,'* in red. Followed by, *'Wouldn't it be great if it was universally available, like Google Street View?'* in green. And, *'I just went along to a meeting of my local history society and they loved the idea, so we started working on it,'* in blue.

Back to red again for, *'The students were looking for a good subject to collaborate on for their dissertation.'* Green for, *'Luckily, they've got the technical knowledge and the artistic skill to make it all work.'* And blue again for, *'The university tutors have both been very helpful.'* And so on.

I look from the paper up to the deep blue wells of Rachel's eyes.

'Do I just say the same thing, over and over again? What if their questions are different?'

'They won't be hugely different. And you'll quickly learn to vary your responses. This is just to get you through the nerves for your first few times. I'm going to help you to learn them parrot fashion and you'll have your crib sheet with you, too. To some extent, it doesn't really even matter what questions they ask. As long as you stay on message, make a good response and come across well, hardly anyone will notice if it's not exactly what you were asked.'

We spend the next hour role playing the interviews over and over, with Rachel teaching me the breathing and focusing techniques that will keep my voice steady and calm, even when I feel the panic rising. She keeps recording my responses and making me listen to them being played back and, although this is agonising for me at first, I do adapt to it. Eventually, I can hear an improvement in my tone and, more especially, the speed of my delivery, as I learn to slow it down and vary my intonation, even leaving little pauses in the right places.

The next stage is for Rachel to switch the questions around and to throw in a few different ones, to which I get used to responding and by the time we set off for town, I am almost bored of the subject. But she keeps asking me the questions all the way and playing back my responses to me, as I drive.

I am starting to feel a bit like a celebrity or top politician must feel: always working, even in transit between events. It is having the desired effect, though. I am no longer worried about the interviews and can focus again on working through my list of jobs, that keeps growing and growing as the launch day advances – with increasing rapidity.

24

The day of the launch passes in a blur for me, starting with an early alarm, followed by hair and make-up. And then a series of interviews in different studios, featuring, as Rachel predicted, much the same kind of questions as each other. The ones I like the best are those involving Ava and the four students. David Crossley features in a few, too, promoting the university and I am always careful to also mention Rachel and Ben's PR agency, at some point in my answers.

Rachel is also right about it getting easier. By the time I have done my first three interviews, I am feeling more used to it and less shaky. By about the fifth one, I start to actually enjoy it and feel relaxed enough to laugh, if someone says something funny.

In between, Rachel is there in the car before and after the recording, to touch up my make-up and to either prepare or debrief me. She makes it all smooth and easy. It is only about halfway through the first day that I realise we have never struggled to find our way to somewhere, or to find anywhere to park. Rachel knows the people and the places connected to her job. Her presence oils the wheels practically, as well as emotionally. In fact, I am finding myself spending much of the day just feeling floored with gratitude, that this wonderful woman is my friend.

As well as being used to preen and prepare me, the magical Rachel-fingers are busy on her iPad, checking the progress of the launch. The next day, we are doing the same sort of round of the same sort of interviews and features and it has spread a little more, then the next day it spreads even more. On day three, it suddenly takes off and she is now talking on her phone more than to me, our calendar for the few days after that filling up fast.

In these idle moments, I am tracking the project myself. I have treated myself to some Bluetooth ear pieces, though I keep losing them. But when one is in my ear, I can be listening to our interviews and then can just press the button to silence it, if someone wants to talk to me. Or if I need to pay attention to whatever is happening in the room, or the car.

Hearing my own recorded voice still makes me feel a little uncomfortable. But I am enjoying watching and listening to the four students' various appearances without me. And, at the same time, seeing the "History Maps" search term bring our project closer and closer to the top of Google's front page of results.

It is on the afternoon of day four when I click on something and hear Maybelle's voice, instead of Ava's, David's, my own, or that of any of the students. I turn the volume up and listen more intently, mildly surprised that Ben and Rachel have added her to the list of interviewees and thinking: *We must be being more successful than even I knew, if they are having to rope in members of what I guess I've been privately calling, 'the B team'.*

Maybelle is laughing coquettishly, at something the male host has said about her being clever, and replying: *'Oh, we used to talk about it together, all the time the boys were growing up. I can't honestly remember if it was my idea or hers, but it doesn't matter, does it? We just wanted the boys to be able to find answers to their endless questions about history, by using a tool like this, to actually see how the places they knew so well would have looked, back in the past. Zoe can put her name on it, if she likes. It doesn't matter to me. The only thing I care about is that it finally gets developed, after all those years of us discussing it together.'*

I press pause on the interview playback, pick my

metaphorical jaw up off the floor and swallow hard, thinking: *What...? What...?* For a bizarre minute, I actually try to remember whether we did have such conversations, but of course, we never did. Not only were the two boys supremely uninterested in history, but Maybelle was, too. In fact, I can think of several occasions in which she quickly became loudly and stroppily bored, whenever I stopped on our infrequent shared visits to castles and museums, to read, study or consider anything historical. After this had happened a few times I stopped inviting her along, offering to take both boys by myself instead to "give her some time off", an opportunity she always jumped at, without hesitation.

Rachel must have noticed a sudden difference in me, because she stops talking on the phone and watches me closely for a few seconds. Then, she tells the caller she will ring them back and ends their conversation.

She puts her hand on my arm, looking very wary and worried and urgently asks, 'Zoe! What's happened? What's wrong?' looking from my face to my phone screen for clues. But the interview I have just heard has no video, so there is no indication from that.

'It's just...' I manage, eventually. 'Something weird that Maybelle has just said. It's so strange and so completely untrue, that I'm pretty stunned, really.' I am feeling suddenly faint and nauseous, so I probably look pale, too.

'You've been talking to Maybelle?' Rachel looks perplexed and puzzled, obviously wondering when my phone rang and why she has not noticed me speaking to it.

'No! It's in one of her interviews...'

'One of *her*... She isn't doing any interviews! It's mainly you, but with the four students or sometimes David, or Ava. You know that!'

'Oh! Yes I did know that, but I've just heard part of an interview with her, so I thought I must have been mistaken.'

Rachel laughs, in a way I do not usually hear her laughing: short and harsh, ironic.

'We definitely would not have lined *her* up for anything. She didn't even ask, but if she had, we'd have said no. She doesn't even seem to have any interest in history, let alone any knowledge in it and she hasn't been very much involved in the project, has she?'

'Well, she's turned up to meetings and things. But mainly just to argue with me, it's seemed.'

'Right. That's what I thought. I'm just trying to work out how she's managed... Can you link it to me, please?'

I go back to my screen, copy the link and paste it into my ongoing Messenger chat with Rachel. Then, I press play again on my own version and keep listening to it myself, while Rachel finds it and starts playing it through her own headset. Not for the first time, I realise how lucky we are, to have a driver this week, leaving us both free to focus on whatever we have to, whilst travelling, like this. Something else that has coming out of the surprise PR budget.

'So, I'm just trying to build a picture of this in my mind,' the presenter is saying. *'There you are, the two of you, driving around the local area together with your sons in the back seat... and what is it that makes you suddenly wonder about the history of a place?'*

'Oh, it might be just a lentil out of place...' says Maybelle by way of response. I roll my eyes at this repeated mistake of hers, but the presenter is evidently – and understandably – confused.

'A what?'

'You know, a lentil. You see them sometimes, sitting there halfway up a wall, for no reason whatsoever. And then you know you're onto something.'

'Err...' says the flummoxed presenter. *'Onto what? A lentil, did you say?'*

'Yes, it's a funny name for them, isn't it? I was quite surprised

myself, back in the day, all of those years ago, when I first heard the term. And I mean, you spot one and straight away it tells you where the doors used to be. We used to see them all the time.'

'Halfway up the walls?' I think the interviewer is probably beginning to feel like he has fallen down a very strange rabbit hole. An unaccountable spread of hot shame fills my chest and makes my face flush. It is most uncomfortable, but I seem to be feeling in some way responsible for Maybelle's words, which are just getting worse and worse. It is bad enough to make me want to stop listening, but I am also strangely compelled to keep on.

'Oh, yes!' she chirrups happily back to him. *'They used to do that, you know. They'd always put their doors halfway up their walls. There's a good example of this on the building my son produced...'*

'Your son produced a... which?' This is a curve ball for the poor man, even by the standards of the current conversation. But she continues blithely on, regardless.

'Yes, you know, the haberdashery.'

I inhale so sharply it makes me cough. *Alf* did the haberdashery. *Adam* did the lychgate and a bit of the grocery, along with Will, who was sketching very precisely just ahead of Adam's rendering, to the extent that it became an interactive process between the two of them, with the outcome of Adam's infilling starting to inform Will's drawings. *How can she possibly not know this?*

I think back, feeling sure she was sometimes in the room, when this was happening. I make myself recall several incidents of seeing Alf working on the haberdashery, to check that it is not me who is mixed up. But yes, my own son definitely did that building and without – as far as I know – any input from Adam.

'Okaaay...' The presenter sounds unsure.

'Unbelievable, isn't it?' Maybelle squeals, continuing: *'You just*

don't expect it.But once you know it, you can't unsee it. A whole door, just halfway up a building! Like, on the second floor…? We don't know why, exactly, but we think they probably had lots of floods on the ground level, so had to build ramps up to the upstairs part, instead. It gets more interesting, the more you think about it. And that's why I'm so fascinated by history.'

'Right. Well, we're going to play some more music now…'

Rachel must be only about twenty seconds behind me, because I do not have long to wait, before she yanks her headset off and looks at me, wildly staring for a moment. Then she grabs her phone, presses it once and starts talking into it, the instant it is answered.

'Ben, that Maybelle woman somehow got herself an interview. Yep. It's on Piddy Pullman's YouTube channel. Just an audio, but honestly, it's dire. A total car crash. The woman is *insane.* How the hell did she get near…? You didn't…? No, I didn't think so. We've got to… yes.'

I can hear Ben's rapid fire voice, tinny over the call, frequently interrupting her, but not what words he is saying. I think I can guess most of the context though, from her responses.

'Yep… find her and stick like glue. I mean, someone's going to have to practically live with her… Yes… the legal position… you're right. Oh my God, it's a nightmare. Yeah, Zoe is with me now, she was the one who found it. Yeah, she will have, I'll get them.' Then, to me: 'Is she Adam's mother? Do you have her contact details? We've got to nail her down and make her promise to stop doing this…' And back to Ben: 'I'll send you the link, but honestly, it's horrendous. Really couldn't be worse.'

I find my phone's saved contact card for Maybelle and duly pass it onto Rachel, with one very strong thought in my mind.

Oh dear. I would not like to be her, when Ben or Rachel – or both of them – catch up with her.

25

'She's not answering her phone,' says Ben, pushing his hand through his hair exasperatedly, looking exhausted. 'I've tried all afternoon. We'll have to find some other way of getting hold of her.'

We are eating dinner at a Japanese restaurant, in which I am having fun with some chopsticks and a big bowl of noodle soup.

'You don't have to eat everything that's on your sticks,' Rachel advised me quietly, when I asked her where to start. And it is a revelation, to bite through some of the noodles and let the rest fall back into the dish. I am getting the liquid all over my chin but I do not care, it is so delicious.

I am not even feeling tired. In fact, I have not found the launch to be draining at all. It has been exhilarating and my brain is buzzing and happy to have found some chopsticks on which to focus. The noodles are satisfying and the soup is full of wonderful flavour: ginger, sharp onion and other salty but sweet and also sort of sour tastes I cannot quite define, but cannot get enough of.

'Zoe and I have both been trying, too. It's hopeless,' says Rachel despondently and I notice, out of the corner of my eye, that she is only toying with her food. I begin to realise why she is so model-thin, if stress affects her in this way. It does the complete opposite for me. 'She obviously knows we're furious. Have you got any ideas, Zoe?'

I look up, blinking, a chin full of noodles falling back into the dish with a splash. Hastily wipe my mouth with the napkin and try to refocus on the inimitable Maybelle. I do not usually like to go there, but for a few seconds I imagine myself in her shoes and try to think what she does, at times like this.

'Oh!' Something comes to me. 'She always jogs in the morning. Runs past our house at least twice a day, actually. The first time is always bang on ten past seven in the morning. But the second time is less predictable, I'm afraid.'

'Ohh, so early?' Rachel groans. 'Ben, we have to get home to see the kids. I feel like we haven't seen them all week and my mother says they're missing us. But we'd have to get up at about six in the morning, to get to Zoe's in time to catch her.'

'Yeah. We're not going to let that bloody woman ruin our family life. So Zoe, can we sleep at yours?' Ben says to me, *like it's nothing.* But I am immediately panicking about whether the house is clean and tidy and whether Hugh will mind. But then, I remember it is Ben and Rachel, two of the only people in the world who will not judge me for having a slightly untidy living room and Hugh will barely notice. All the same, I text to warn him, in the hope that he might tidy up a bit before we all get there. It is going to take us an hour or two to go via their farm and collect the children and everyone's overnight stuff.

And that is how the three of us manage to waylay Maybelle, on her early morning jog.

It is Sunday and everyone else in the house is still asleep. But we are drinking coffee around the front doorstep in the chilly morning sun, as I watch the top of the hedge for Maybelle's trademark, high pony-tail to come bouncing along.

Sure enough, it appears, right on time. Ben gulps his coffee and leaps through our gateway onto the pavement, literally ambushing her as she runs. By the time I have got there, the two of them are having a bizarrely comical face-off, with Maybelle darting alternately left and right, to try and get past Ben, but Ben darting to block her, every time.

Ben is trying to talk, but I cannot hear him over Maybelle's clear and repeated: 'Get out of my way, please!'

'Come inside, Maybelle,' says an authoritative voice from beside me, whilst still managing to sigh at the same time. It is Rachel and it is only the second time I have ever heard this tone from her, which brooks no disobedience. The first time was at a home education camp, when her son had been throwing mud at people from the stream with some other boys. *All* of the boys had stopped mud-throwing immediately and never taken it up again. Not just her own son.

Maybelle stops darting and looks rebelliously at Rachel, who has stood aside from the gate and is gesturing past it and up our front path and towards our open front door, with an extended arm. It would take a brave person to do anything other than follow the direction of the arm and Maybelle is not a brave person. She even stops bouncing from one foot to the other and quietly walks up the path, though her head is still held high, chin jutting proudly forwards. I fall into line after her behind Rachel and Ben, with a heavy heart, knowing that this is not going to be a straightforward conversation.

Once we are all in the kitchen and the doors in the hallway are closed to prevent us from waking the sleeping children, I busy myself with getting coffee for everyone. Ben starts the interrogation straight away, before Rachel has even sat down.

Maybelle has primly taken a seat at the table and is brushing imaginary crumbs from that onto the floor with her trademark, manicured fingers. She is looking down at her hands and only looks up to meet Ben's face when he starts talking.

'What was that all about yesterday, Maybelle? How did you get that interview? Why didn't you run it past me or Rachel, first? What were you thinking? Why did you try to pretend the project was your idea instead of Zoe's? What was that whole pile of crap about flooding on the ground floor when the church square sits about seventy-five feet above the river and why the *fuck* were you banging on about *lentils?* Have you got any idea how imbecilic it makes us all look?' He actually bangs his palm on the table, to add extra emphasis to '*fuck*' and '*lentils*'.

I do not really want to be here. Ben is a passionate man, full of infectious enthusiasm, which I love. But when all of that energy goes dark, which I have only seen once or twice in the past and from a much safer distance than this, he is unrestrainedly explosive. Rachel takes her seat now and accepts a top-up to her coffee mug from me, though her eyes remain also grimly focused on Maybelle's face.

If I was Maybelle, I would be full of apologies right now. But she meets Ben's anger with an expression full of defiance, instead.

'Are you going to give me chance to explain, or are you just going to keep firing questions at me? What is this, the Spanish Inquisition?'

Humour bubbles up in me unexpectedly as I hear the automatic Monty Python response in my head: '*Nobody expects the Spanish Inquisition!*' But I swallow it down and keep my face straight, as I am obviously the only one currently making that particular connection.

'Answer in any order!' snaps Ben. 'Let's start with the fucking *lentils*, why don't we?'

'Oh well, that's easy! You can ask your precious *Zoe* about those. She was the one who told me about them.'

Ben and Rachel look to me incredulously, so I have to respond in some way. But I can barely get the words out.

'I told you about *lentils?*' is all I can think to respond. In fairness, I am still flabbergasted that she has managed to mix the two words up and I cannot work out whether it was deliberate, or accidental. The last time she was cross with me about lintels, she at least seemed to not be confusing them with lentils.

'Yeees,' she answers slowly, with the voice she reserves for speaking to the very stupid. In her opinion, this seems to be usually just me. 'You remember? It was when we were in the church square together that day, working out how the other old buildings must have been fixed onto the haberdashery. Honestly Zoe, your memory is dreadful and I'm sure it's getting worse. It's not that long ago...'

At this point, Maybelle experiences the unusual sensation of being interrupted – by herself.

Rachel has her arm extended into the space above the middle of the table, phone in hand and the phone is replaying part of the interview from yesterday: *'I was quite surprised myself, back in the day all of those years ago when I first heard the term.'*

And now, something makes sense to me that I saw her doing, before we went to bed last night, sitting at the dining table with her laptop and phone, organising snippets of a sound file. I look at my friend Rachel with new appreciation, that she has had the foresight to prepare so well for this moment, when I barely had the foresight to fill up the coffee machine.

'*"All of those years ago"*, Maybelle? *"Not that long ago"*? Make your mind up. Which is it?' Ben is so insistent, I do not see how Maybelle can get herself out of this. *Surely, now, she'll crumple and admit she's not been factually honest.*

But nothing of the sort happens.

Instead, she juts her chin out even more and replies: 'Ben! You can't keep bullying your clients like this! How on earth does your company make any money? *I* seem to know some of the tricks of your trade better than *you* do!'

Her tactic is successful in pushing him back.

He physically slumps in his chair, saying, 'We don't tell lies and *you* are *not* our client,' with angry pronouncement.

'Yes, you *do*,' answers Maybelle straight away, totally

ignoring the second part of his sentence as if he has not spoken it. 'Everyone *knows* PR people tell lies all the time. You're just spin doctors! And I know, right now, we're all supposed to be spinning this line that Zoe is really clever and that it was all her idea, but...'

'Zoe,' Rachel cuts in strongly and Maybelle immediately shuts up. 'Please tell us all what a lentil is.'

'Err, it's a kind of bean...' I begin.

'I know, right?' Maybelle speaks up again, interrupting me. 'I *thought* it was a stupid name for a stone on top of a door, when it's quite obviously also the word for a kind of bean. My mother used to make...'

'Shut up, Maybelle,' orders Rachel, without even looking at her. Maybelle obeys and Rachel continues, 'Zoe, please tell us the name for the piece of stone that goes over a door or window aperture.'

'Yeah, that's a *lintel*.' I am surprised to even be being asked something we surely all know.

There is a silence for about two seconds, before Maybelle twists around in her chair to look at me and indignantly demand to know why, then, I had told her it was called a lentil?

I am so shocked at this that I laugh. I have known Maybelle for years and seen her embellish the truth many times. But I have never seen her cornered like this and I can barely believe my eyes and ears that she is still defending herself, by counter-attacking. *It's as if she's still a hundred percent sure that she is in the right, even though we have so much proof that she is not.*

'You think she said *lentil?*' Ben counters, his voice full of hostile contempt for Maybelle, which she does not seem to notice, although that in itself would have crushed me. 'Not only had you never heard of a lintel before, but you misheard it as lentil and you didn't think to look in a dictionary or run a Google search for the word to check, before you started telling people about it? I don't even know how you've managed to hear "lentil" for "lintel". They don't even sound the same, do they? Zoe, say "lentil" and "lintel".'

I sigh and obediently repeat: 'Lentil. Lintel.' He is right: they do sound quite different. But I am also puzzled, because I feel sure I have heard Maybelle referring to lintels as lintels, herself.

'Oh, well, you're making it sound really *clear* now Zoe, when usually *your* voice is so indistinct, that it's hard to tell what you're saying. If you don't bother to speak properly, how can you expect people to understand you? And you pretend to know about history!'

'But that's just it, Maybelle! Zoe *does* know about history! Zoe *did* know what a lintel was, when you hadn't even thought about it before!' I am forced to concede the truth of Ben's words. I did have to explain the term to her, that day in the church square. 'Zoe's been interested in history, for as long as I've known her. Nobody, who knows the two of you, would ever believe this project might have been *your* idea...' He is getting thoroughly exasperated, now. I think he and Rachel had a plan for the conversation, but it has not worked and he seems to be getting genuinely worried that Maybelle might successfully claim the credit for my idea.

I am not so worried, myself. Not only do I not really care who claims the credit, as long as the project is rolled out successfully, I also do not think anyone, who spends more than a couple of minutes chatting with her about it, will believe that she had anything to do with developing the concept. *Most* people know more about history than Maybelle does, even people who really do not care about it at all. Whereas, she seems to have something of a mental blind spot about it.

At this moment, the kitchen door opens and we all stop and look towards it to see who is coming in. I am hoping it is Hugh, so that I can go and be hugged. But I am surprised and a little horrified to see that it is Adam, who must have stayed over last night without my knowledge, yet again.

Of course, though, I think to myself. *It was Saturday night:*

their usual routine. You'd think I'd be used to it by now and I might have been, except for the upheaval caused by the launch. It is reassuring that this has not thrown Adam and Alf out of their normal patterns. But I wish I had thought through the prospect of Maybelle being confronted, while her son was in the house.

I look for an emotional prop and it is the pouring of coffee, as ever in this kitchen, so I am doing that, while Adam approaches the table, saying: 'Hello, Mum. Rachel, Ben. What's going on?'

All three answer him at once.

'Oh, *darling,* they're trying to accuse me of lying...' from Maybelle, 'Your mother did an unauthorised interview...' from Ben and 'Never mind, we're sorting it out. Don't worry, Adam,' from the ever-protective Rachel.

I am not sure how much of all of that Adam has actually heard, but he looks straight at his mother and asks: 'What have you done?' matter-of-factly and without much emotion. I do detect mild annoyance, though. And, perhaps, a little disgust that I would have hated to have heard in Alf's voice, if he was speaking to me.

'*I* haven't done *anything!* It's *these people* who are...' Maybelle protests shrilly.

But her son cuts in, speaking directly to Rachel this time. Her hand is still clutching her phone in the middle of the table, making it clear that she has been using it as a speaker for something recorded.

'Is it on your phone? Let's hear it.'

So, Rachel selects the whole file and presses play and Maybelle sits, sullenly looking at the table, while her own voice rings out from the phone.

We all listen in silence and there is a painful half-minute of further silence at the end of it, before Adam addresses his mother.

'Look at me,' he commands, which she does. Her big eyes are full of pain, as if she is the victim of we three, cruel aggressors. *This is going to melt his heart,* I am thinking. *No son could resist such a pleading look from his mother, such an obvious, visual cry for help.* I wonder what on earth is going through his mind, what he thinks of her performance and what he is going to say about it.

When they come, his words are clear and slow. There can be no mistaking them whatsoever and they send a chill throughout my own body, so I dread to imagine what they do to Maybelle's.

'If you *ever* do anything like that again, it will be the last you see or hear from me,' says Adam, clearly and very decisively.

And then, he turns his back on his mother and leaves the room.

Ben and Rachel and I wait for her reaction. I am full of sympathy and probably Rachel is, too, but I have no idea how Ben is feeling. If Maybelle bursts into tears, which she surely must, then I will of course hug and comfort her. *She's still a human being, after all and that was a dreadful thing for her to hear from her only child. No matter what she's done to deserve it.*

But yet again, I have underestimated her. She stands up, quickly, shoving her chair back, so that it makes a sharp grinding noise on the floor before it hits the wall, hard.

'*Now* look what you've done!' she shouts at us. There are some tears, but they are definitely tears of anger, not contrition. 'I hope you're all *satisfied!*' And she stamps from the house, banging the front door after her, easily loud enough to wake Hugh and Amy, as well as Ben and Rachel's two children.

We all exhale together, Ben with his face in his hands and Rachel with a hand in her hair.

'*Wow,*' says Rachel, eventually, voicing the feelings of us all, I think. 'Just... *wow.*'

26

I always do my best thinking either in the bath or when driving the car and I have had very little opportunity for either activity, in the past ten days of consistent, back-to-back publicity activities. But now, it is Monday afternoon, we have two free hours and there is – *glory of glories* – time for an actual bath in the hotel room *en suite,* instead of just the usual, rushed shower.

I fill it with hot water, have found some delicious musky-smelling foaming bath oil to add to it and I now have everything but my face and my knees warmly, relaxingly submerged.

The sensory deprivation caused by being unusually alone, with my ears underwater, my eyes closed, my relative weightlessness and my lack of access to my phone, is instantly liberating. It enables the creative part of my brain to fire up again, after what feels like weeks of necessary thinking on the hoof and I have a specific reason for having wanted – even needed – this to happen.

Increasingly, the questions I have been asked in interviews have been of the '*What next?*' variety. I have been struggling to answer these properly and I have realised this is because I have no clear idea myself of the answer and I have been hungry for an opportunity to work it out.

Last week's showdown with Maybelle is what has finally convinced me of the need for me to claim ownership of the History Maps concept. It showed me that if I fail to do it, someone like her will not – to possibly disastrous effect. It is my baby and I evidently need to raise it, at least to toddler-hood, before someone better qualified for the job comes along to take it out of my hands.

My thinking gets a little sidetracked by this analogy, as I follow it along the lines of parenting my actual children, which I did not even begin to delegate in Alf's case until he was fourteen and attending adult education college for three days a week to do some GCSEs. I have to sternly remind myself that the project is *not* a human baby and bring my mind back on task.

The '*What next?*' question can be answered vaguely, as I have been doing whenever I have been asked it, in terms of, '*Well, it would be nice, if...*' and, '*Wouldn't it be wonderful, if...*'

But claiming ownership of the project means I have to switch from dreaming into making things happen, just as I did many months ago when I found and attended the local history society meeting and pushed the idea with Alf and Adam, which so fortuitously sparked Ollie's interest. And the rest, as they say, is history – but so far, not much of it, in the grand scheme of things.

I need to flesh out some more of the detail in that grand scheme and make some proper decisions about, '*What next?*' before my foggy and feckless inaction dampens everyone's interest and wastes all of this dynamic momentum.

My end goal is still the same as it always has been: I hand off the concept to Google, which then brings together any interested amateur and professional local historians, artists and graphic arts students, to reconstruct as many virtual places and times as possible.

I see this as an ongoing, never ending, always evolving process, like Google Maps itself or Wikipedia, to which anyone can contribute. The thought of it actually happening on a worldwide basis is so exciting, it gives me the shivers even in the heat of this bath and I indulge in a few minutes of fantasy, as it all plays out in my head, at local meetings similar to the ones we have been having, everywhere. And the resource, the online tool working for everyone, whenever they might want it. No more lives spent wondering how things might have been: the best brains will have been pooled, to show the most likely images of how it really was.

But, how do we get from here to there? Our church square sample is only that: a tiny sample of what can be achieved and how it can be done. In my optimism, I have been fondly imagining someone at Google spotting this, after all of our hard publicity work and getting in touch to take it on. But it has not happened yet and I ought to face the possibility that it might not happen, at this – or indeed, any – stage. *What do I need to do, to both establish my ownership of the idea and push it forwards to the next step, so that it will come to Google's attention as a viable concept?*

With bath bubbles tickling my face, I realise Hugh has been telling me what I need to do, just about every time we have managed to talk together, which has been depressingly rare. But still, he has kept reminding me that I need to write something for the website. Something personal about what it means to me, how it came to me and where I see it going. I think this will help, but I also need to do more.

Thinking from the perspective of someone in another region, wanting to develop their own local version, I try to imagine what they might need to know and how I can develop an information package or toolkit, which will make it all so much easier for them.

Now wishing I was sitting at a table, with pen and paper or laptop, I start to mentally formulate a step-by-step guide for those people and thinking what order the steps need to be in. *Do they network the people first, or identify their target streets and year? Probably the former, but how?*

Belatedly, it occurs to me that I should have been using all of my recent interviews and appearances to promote this and I metaphorically kick myself, for not having thought this far ahead already and had something in place. *Why have I been so passive and careless about the whole thing, when it means so much to me? Well, that's a question for another day.* Right now, I am propelling myself out of the bath to go and find the table and laptop and to set it all down, before I can forget the details.

I am making good progress with this when my phone rings. Seeing Hugh's name and photo on the screen gives me a little heart lift and I answer it, happily. We spend a few minutes catching up with each other's news and conveying updates about the children, especially Amy, who sounds to be missing me as much as I am missing her.

Then I tell him about my thoughts of the day and he is blessedly silent while I speak. This respectful habit is one of the many things I love about him, especially after a fortnight of being interrupted and struggling to even try to *think*, in all of the competitive clamour.

When I have finished, he expresses his relief and enthusiasm which, as ever, is a balm to my fragile self esteem and he makes a couple of welcome suggestions about the toolkit, involving some possible ways of making it very user-friendly and clear. I can sense the more technically proficient parts of his mind starting to piece in the necessary background mechanism for all of this, with which he knows better than to clutter my own head. Our conversation moves onto the success of the publicity campaign and how well it is taking off.

'Viewing figures are through the roof, Zoe,' he tells me, in a tone that struggles to hide his surprise. He has had more confidence in the project than any of us and yet it is doing better than even he thought it would. But I remind him how much of this is down to the expertise of Ben and Rachel, so generously given.

'Hmm, not *so* generous,' comments Hugh sceptically, never having been a fan of Ben's. 'If it carries on taking off like this, it's going to put their company on the map like nothing else ever could. They know what they're doing. Speaking of which,

I had an unexpected visitor, this morning. You'll never guess who.'

I know he is going to actually make me guess, so I go through the mental process of eliminating all of the potential visitors who might have been expected and then all of the ones whose visits would not have been noteworthy, whether expected or not. I am not left with many likely contenders.

'Maybelle?' I ask, eventually. Hugh laughs and tells me to try again, but I have to confess to being stuck.

'Someone who rudely and stupidly turned down your kind invitation to become involved with the project early on and is now regretting it.'

I gasp, at this.

'Not...?'

'Professor Pritchard!' confirms Hugh, with a broad grin stretched across his face that I can hear in his voice, without having to see it.

'He came to visit you? Why? What did he say?'

Hugh laughs again, having obviously enjoyed the experience, though it might be my predictable reaction that he is enjoying, even more.

'He was quite nice and humble actually, by his standards. Said he was pleasantly surprised to observe the success of our pilot project.'

'God, he was horrible to me,' I remember, with a cold shudder. 'Really condescending and insulting. He treated me as if I was a stupid child.'

'I know, Zoe. I haven't forgotten. I made it really clear to him that it's not *our* pilot project – it's yours. It was your idea and you are the one who has made it happen.' Still silently doubting that it *is* all down to me, considering the extensive work everyone else has put into it compared with my own paltry contribution, I am keen to hear more, so I do not correct him. 'He was trying to get me to bring him on board and involve him from now on, but I refused and told him he'd have to approach you. I think he knows that he's going to have to eat humble pie.'

'I can't imagine working with him. Does he ever stop being arrogant? Do we even need him? Can we tell him no?'

There is a short silence, then my husband carefully reminds me that the decision is mine alone and not his to make.

'You can tell him whatever you like. Yes, he stops being arrogant, but only with people he respects and his criteria for respect is all warped and mixed in with hierarchy and qualifications, obviously. As for whether we need him, I dunno. That's your call too. We've got the university on board without him, haven't we?'

'Yeah, big time, but that's the Information Technology department. Thinking about moving the whole thing up a level, a good history department like his would be handy. His attitude would have to change, though, because we won't get very far if it's anything like before.'

'You could maybe take him on a trial basis,' responds Hugh, the smile back in his voice. 'Give it three meetings and see how he does. Agree to nothing, until he passes the basic courtesy test!'

'That's a good idea,' I tell him and I smile back.

And now, I am feeling strong, well-supported, optimistic and like everything is going to change, yet again.

And definitely in a good way.

27

I am meeting with Professor Pritchard today, but this time I do not have to crawl on my metaphorical belly up the cold, wide, stone staircase to his office, for he is taking me out for lunch. *What a difference a few months of hard work and a successful publicity campaign makes!*

My status has magically switched from *persona non grata* to *persona* very much *grata*, which I am finding quite irksome and am fighting the impulse to say, 'I'm still me! I haven't changed,' and to pedantically insist on the same treatment as before. But that would be ridiculously self-defeating, so I am not saying it and am forcing myself to be rational, instead.

Of course, I am still the same person – with some significant changes to my levels of confidence and self-esteem. I know a lot more than I did before in terms of bringing teams together and helping them to get things done. And I am more proficient, now, at putting ideas across, listening and engaging properly in discussions.

I am, in short, much more assertive than I was the last time I met him. All of this is not the reason for my ascent up his status ladder. The reason is the success of the project. This has made him realise he was wrong about both me and it and I do have some grudging respect for his willingness to admit it.

One other crucial change in me, since my first meeting with the professor, is that I am no longer intimidated by certain surroundings. Six months ago, the Japanese rooftop restaurant in which we are sitting today would have overwhelmed me with its luxurious perfection and the visibly confident affluence of its *clientèle.* But after a few weeks of hospitality suites and the kind of lifestyle provided by Rachel and Ben's seemingly endless PR budget, I am now taking it in my stride.

This is not to say I fail to appreciate it, ensconced in my ultra-comfortable chair, amidst a leafy green, surreal garden of delicious tranquillity. The busy, dirty streets of the city below are another world, above which we are elevated, in more ways than one.

It's a surprising choice for a doyen of history, though. I'd have expected somewhere more... well, historical, *instead of this epitome of modernity.*

As I sip my crisp white wine, the taste of which really does prove, beyond any remaining doubt, that more expensive wines are worth the money after all, I observe my lunch partner across the slatted oak table.

He could be wearing the exact same tailor-made suit from the last time we met, though I imagine he has a wardrobe full of identical ones, matched with the same heavy linen or silk shirts and an array of similar, achingly trendy and exclusive neck ties. He is a cookie-cutter version of any executive businessman in any UK city on a six-figure salary and I wonder, meeting his pale blue, unblinking gaze far more evenly than the last time, whether he still retains any passion for history at all.

So far, we have not eaten anything and yet he picks up his napkin and dabs his mouth with it delicately, as if he is blotting lipstick. Then, he speaks.

'It's good of you to come, Mrs Taylor. Can I call you Zoe? I'm Colin,' and at this, I have to drink to cover my quick grin, because Colin is one of the last forenames I would have expected him to have. I would not have been surprised by Ludovic, Tristram or Algernon, for example, but the name Colin evokes a much more down-to-earth persona than the one sitting opposite me just now.

I nod and use my own napkin to wipe away any last traces of mirth and after a pause, he continues.

'After our last meeting, it would have been quite reasonable for you to have refused.'

He seems to be waiting for an answer to this, but I do not know what to say, except, *'Yes it would,'* which I do not. Instead, I merely incline my head, to acknowledge the truth of his words. It is tempting to speed things up by asking what he wants now, but I have to wait and make him work for it, as a necessary part of the process of building respect.

We are therefore still no further, when the cheerful, smooth waiter cheerfully and smoothly brings our menus. We choose our food, place our order and then the conversation recommences.

'So. Zoe,' smiles Colin at me. 'You did it! You made your project happen. I was pleasantly surprised, to have it brought to my attention.'

I smile back and breathe deeply, reminding myself to stay cool and inspire respect, which is harder work than working. But with practice, I am getting better at it.

'Yes, I did.' Resisting the temptation to say, *'We did,'* even though it was not me alone, by any means.

'And... have you enjoyed the experience?'

'Yes, thank you. I received a lot of help, of course, from the IT Department of your university, amongst others.' A barbed comment, but true and important to make.

'Ah yes, your son...'

I can't let him get away with half sentences.

I am determined not to facilitate his part in this conversation, so I only answer, 'Yes. My son,' and the rest of Alf's part in the project – known to us both – hangs in the air, unsaid.

Professor Pritchard... *Colin...* takes a deep drink of wine and then a deep breath. I notice a frown puckering his brow and wonder if he is only now realising that I am by no means going to play handmaid, to his Fred. *The only way forward for him is to treat me with respect. A lunch invitation to a "fine dining" restaurant will not suffice.*

'Mrs…' *He's having the same problem as me, with the casual approach.* 'Zoe. I'm here to apologise, unreservedly. I made a mistake and misjudged you and your wonderful idea, when you came to see me. I fully admit, I did not predict that you would see it through and that the pilot project would be undertaken and launched by you and your team, so successfully. If I was wearing one, I would take my hat off to you. I would certainly like to add some congratulations to my apology.'

Don't answer straight away. Don't forgive him straight away. Deep breath. Sip of wine. Look at the view. I look back at his face and see him awaiting my verdict. And suddenly I am too annoyed, to partake in a politeness dance with this man, who brushed me off like a fleck of dust from his lapel only a few months ago, casually knocking my vulnerable, fledgling hope and confidence to the ground and not even bothering to check where it fell.

And so I say: 'What do you want, Colin?' and he is flustered. Opens his mouth. Closes it again. 'My project is moving on to its next stage,' I add, when he is clearly not going to answer my direct question. 'How do you envisage your part in it?'

I sit back and return to contemplating the view, to give him a chance to think. I am aware of his long, elegant fingers, nervously tapping out a tattoo under the table and in my peripheral vision, I see him brush a non-existent hair from his forehead.

'Well,' he eventually announces, thinking quickly done. 'I think we can help each other, exactly as you suggested in my office, in early April. I'd like you to consider a partnership with my History Department, to take you through to that next stage and even beyond. We can offer the kind of expert advice you need, to give people more confidence in the veracity of your historical data and profiles. In return, your project would naturally carry our name in its title. It would become the university History Maps project.'

I want to laugh, though it would not be helpful. Our starters arrive fortuitously at this moment and I can take some time to phrase my response, while we are introduced to our dishes with a flourish and we settle napkins in laps and begin to taste.

I cannot help exuding a 'Mmmm,' of appreciation, as I do. Raw swordfish with flakes of truffle: a delicacy beyond compare, that pushes all business thoughts from my mind, until I force them back again.

I smile into Colin's face and he returns my smile. Perhaps it has got his hopes up, but I am about to sweetly dash them, as efficiently as if I had picked them up off the table and dropped them over the rail, into the congested street a hundred feet below.

'That's a very kind offer,' I begin, still smiling. His echoing smile brightens even more. *Maybe he's just not accustomed to being politely let down.* 'But not one I'll be taking up. Thanks.'

I am hungrily contemplating my plate once more, when he says: 'Oh,' and: 'Can I ask why not?' and when I look at his face again, it is mired in perplexity. *I've got to keep eating, though: the food is too good to ignore.*

Another heavenly mouthful, a swallow and I tell him in a relaxed tone – for I am feeling relaxed – 'I don't need it, now. The last few months have shown me that this idea of mine is a popular one with many people. I'm not looking to make money or even prestige from it, unlikely though that may sound.' I can see, from his face, that it *does* sound unlikely. 'And nor are most of the team who worked together to make, distribute and present the pilot. We did it for our love of history and just because we want people to have free access to that.'

A brief expression of what I can only describe as emotional pain appears on Colin's face, before being carefully replaced by one of understanding concern. He is nodding like a fraudulent priest, addressing the poor and unsuspecting victims in his flock. Pious, almost wringing his hands in faux earnestness.

'Yes, of course,' he is saying three times over, as if I need placating. Which, with food and a view like this, I most certainly do not.

'I think there is *a place* for your Department on my current team,' I continue, between morsels of fish and threads of *hijiki* seaweed. 'We would value your expertise, freely given. And reward it, by including it in our list of contributors *only*. We'll be continuing to receive support from your university's IT Department...'

I stop for more food and he jumps in, with an elongated '*Yeees*, David Crossley and John Anderson...' as if he is a school master, referencing two of his most troubled and challenging pupils. Or an entomologist, examining two strange insects he has found, under a damp leaf.

'Indeed,' I confirm, cheerfully. 'David has been with us almost from the start, due to his own interest in history. Do you know, he is a member of a local history society, himself?'

'I had heard,' rejoins the professor, glumly.

I raise an eyebrow at his tone. *If he'd wanted to compete against the likes of David Crossley and other amateur historians, then he'd have done better to have begun the race before they did, back in early April, when he was given the first chance. As a latecomer now, he's forfeited the right to grumble and I will have no truck with it.*

'Yes. So he has that passion, you see, that impels people to want to be involved, without an obvious reward for their efforts. Apart from the end result in itself – which as I'm sure you can imagine...' *Can only imagine.* '... is sufficient reward in itself. The sense of achievement is wonderful.'

I smile to fondly remember it, recalling the bubbles of fizzy joy that filled my chest, the first time I saw it in full on the university projector screen, amongst other occasions along the way and since.

I am lost in reverie for a minute, the sun on my face and the divine tastes on my tongue, utterly content. Then, I catch him watching me warily, wondering what might be coming next and remember that I need to keep setting my stall out for him.

'You can join my committee,' I tell him, as if the idea has only just come to me which, in a way, it has. 'You already know my husband Hugh and your colleagues, John and David. You can meet my son and the other three graphic arts students, who rendered the pilot project. I don't know if they'll stay on board for long, but we're keeping them for as long as they have the time and the willingness.

'Ava Harris and Nick Green represent the history societies and Ben and Rachel Heskel do our public relations. We'll bring other people in, as and when we can, but for now, we need to keep things fairly small. There's a legal structure,' I add for his open mouth which, I assume, was about to frame a question about that. 'Which establishes my overall ownership of the project, with contributory input from the other *volunteers.*' I feel the need to further emphasise the last word, in case he still has not got the message.

He has got the message. He heaves a sigh, nods and finally presents me with a gracious, conceding smile.

'First among equals, eh?' he offers, raising his glass to me and drinking deeply from it, before raising it again.

Hugh would have smugly given me the Latin version of the phrase and I'm sure Colin could also. But he has benignly chosen not to, in case I don't know it.

I sigh myself, in private acknowledgement of that. *Of course, I don't know it. But never mind. Pritchard has to take or leave my offer, now. And I don't care either way.*

I reconsider that for a minute, to check whether I do care and I realise that the gravitas he will bring to our team means that on balance, I *do* want him on board. *But it has to be on my terms, or he'll crush me again and I can't allow that.*

'So, you'll join us?' I ask, out of interest.

Then I wait for his smiling confirmation, before I raise my own glass to him, in return.

28

In the version of our project that I dreamed about last night, David Crossley and Ben were both in prison, whilst Colin Pritchard had ordained himself king of the hill fort city we all inhabited. He lounged on a stone throne at its summit. My subconscious mind was obviously trying to make its own kind of sense of the week's activities, in which I have had to choose between three venues, for the upcoming meeting of what I am now calling my steering group.

"King" Colin offered the waking equivalent of his throne room: the grandest of two seminar chambers in the university's History Department, while David said he would be more than happy to let us use the IT suite in his department again. I was struggling to choose between the two because, although the seminar chamber has the perfect seating arrangement, with tactile ancient oak tables in a hollow square and suitably historical setting, it lacks the range of equipment in the modern IT suite conversion.

I have found Pritchard's naked determination to host the meeting on his own territory to be extra off-putting, when it came to trying to make the best decision for this and probably all of our meetings in the foreseeable future. David Crossley has been his usual laid-back, informal self, but his loftier counterpart obviously struggles to contain his urge to be running the whole show. Given my personal history with this man and the extent to which he can trigger my self-confidence issues, I knew I would probably have to decline his offer despite the inspiring venue.

I was settling on the IT suite, when Ben and Rachel took me to see a conference room in the Dean Clough complex, in Halifax. This is a converted set of Victorian mills in which my maternal granddad worked as a loom supervisor, before that trade moved off to the Far East and the site was artfully restored for multiple post-modern uses.

I always love visiting the place. Walking through the cobbled streets which link the buildings, I can see the flat-capped or shawled workers in my mind's eye and hear their conversations in my imagination.

The modernisers have left the old iron, cart rails in situ. They appear from one set of wooden doors and disappear into another across the yard. This is how the yarn or cloth, in one or other of its various stages of production, would be shifted to the next building of purpose, to be further improved. I always bend down to touch the worn metal strips and pay silent homage to the thousands of lifetimes of poorly paid graft spent in the place, now just a *chic* backdrop for our knowledge-based economy – however authentic the props.

But again, it is Ben's unveiled eagerness to be the host, that has made me feel uneasy about *his* chosen venue, even though it has retained its cast iron support pillars, one of which I could lean on from my chair and try to absorb our local history by osmosis, as we worked.

There is a natural rivalry building between Ben and Colin and I can see myself being squashed between two egos, if I am not careful. Like two bulls in a field. Given their head, they could easily trash the whole thing. If I chose Dean Clough, I would be signalling my alignment with the idea of Ben as leader. But I think my choice of either university room would probably be fashioned into a weapon by Colin and brandished by him, whenever possible.

A chat over coffee with Ava has eventually provided the clarity I needed to resolve my dilemma and successfully silence my over-thinking. With her customary pragmatism, she pointed out the fourth option. A location paid for by me which, for economy's sake, would have to be somewhere cheap.

And even *I* can run to a mid-week evening's hire of the old function room above the pub, where our history society has always met. Input from both the university and the PR company are vitally important, but I want the local history societies to be the lynchpins of the project teams, just as ours was. And we do not need an expensive room in which to discuss and make plans, for now. Only an accessible location, with internet and electricity. *After all, there are only fourteen of us.*

The fourteenth member of the new steering group has been my other dilemma. We needed someone, because I am superstitious about the number thirteen, which came about when Colin Pritchard joined us. Obviously, Maybelle was never in the running. But I have been feeling bad about the angry way we ambushed her that morning when she was jogging past our house and I am sure Adam's warning will have chilled her to the core, so that she will be much better behaved in future.

I am also forced to concede that her natural bossiness and formidable organisational skills did make her a good appointments co-ordinator. Although she has no sense of history, she has been involved in the project all along and seems to have an emotional commitment to it, but I still was unsure whether she would agree when I phoned to ask her to stay on with us.

She jumped at the chance, much to Rachel's consternation. A few months – maybe even weeks – ago, I would have automatically deferred to Rachel's judgement. But now that I am focusing on owning the project and being more assertive, I know that I can no longer do that.

So, Hugh, Amy and I arrived an hour early, for the first of the new meetings. We planned to make a hollow square of the tables, but it transpired that eight rectangular tables makes a kind of elongated square and not a perfect one. I have now taken my place at the far end of it, facing the door, as near to the middle of that end as possible, given the table legs in the way. I watch the rest of my steering committee file in as they arrive.

Hugh is on my left, looking after Amy, who sits on the other side of him. He plans to also pay as much attention to the meeting as he can.

Ava is sitting to my right, which feels nice, as she and Nick together present the least challenge to my leadership position. From the technical history perspective alone, I know Nick would love to take charge and often did, through the pilot project. But he lacks the ability to see the bigger picture and can only focus on minutiae, whereas Ava is one of the most refreshingly unambitious people I know. She just seems to want the project to do well and for Nick to be happy – luckily, two mutually compatible aims, for now.

David Crossley arrives next and sits down on the long side to my left near to Hugh, who immediately begins chatting with him, reinforcing my positive opinion of that man. Hugh will not voluntarily strike up a conversation with many people and the ones he does are invariably good sorts.

Will and Ollie come in soon after and sit down with their tutor. I wait for Will to settle himself by taking out his ubiquitous sketchpad and it does not take long. Ollie gives me a broad smile, from diagonally across the gap and asks how I am doing. I return it and answer briefly, but happily, for he is on my ever-growing list of favourite people.

Alf and Adam turn up, with Maybelle behind them, who makes a dash for the furthest remaining seat away from Ben and Rachel, who have positioned themselves on my right, after Ava and Nick. Maybelle therefore ends up in between the four students although I notice Adam taking the chair next to Ben's, leaving my own son to sit next to her.

When Colin Pritchard arrives, he chooses the seat directly opposite my own, nods to the other attendees and then fixes his attention disconcertingly on my face, until Maybelle leans past Alf and Adam, to try to engage him in conversation. I wish I had better hearing, because I would love to hear the words that pass between those two.

John Anderson bustles in almost too late and waves across to his friend and colleague, David. But he interestingly opts for the chair next to Rachel, instead of the remaining one by Colin Pritchard. And we are complete.

I know that either Ben and Rachel's company or one of the university departments would have gladly printed the meeting agenda and accompanying documents. But in my new spirit of self-reliance, I have done them myself on our home printer, even though it took two hours, a whole cartridge and almost a ream of paper. The agenda is at the top of the neat pile of papers in front of each attendee, along with what I have written so far of the toolkit, for other regional teams of History Map creators.

I am recording the meeting myself, but I have also asked Maybelle to take notes and draw up some minutes, because it finally occurred to me in our phone call, to ask what she had done for a living, before Adam was born. It turned out that she had been a personal assistant for a business executive, which made sense of a lot of things about her, which I am feeling almost ashamed not to have previously known. The reason for her automatic, almost comical, iPad-and-stylus stance in meetings is suddenly apparent, amongst other things.

The first and main agenda item is for us to look at the toolkit. An uncomfortable sensation of shyness comes over me as they all sit and peruse my work in silence. I have set out a list of considerations for new teams in new areas: the need to choose a suitable site and the criteria they should consider for it; the deliberation of historical dates on which to base their selections and the order of work entailed in the process.

David is the first to comment that his department could develop an app or other technical version of this tool, to which John adds that perhaps something similar could be done from a graphic arts perspective. This leads to Will and Ollie volunteering to work with their tutors on developing both of those functions, even though they have now finished their degree courses. I cannot help looking across to Alf and Adam and being unsurprised and chagrined to see them looking at something on Adam's phone together, probably unrelated to the meeting discussion.

Colin holds the floor for a while, on what he considers to be his department's most appropriate role going forwards, this being mainly in gravitas and networking between the History Departments of various universities.

Ben keeps jumping up to interrupt him with thoughts on the different ways we can spread the word and keep the PR ball rolling. I get the feeling that Colin would be saying a lot more if it was not for Ben's frequent, animated interjections. I have been hoping Colin might want to try to incorporate something of our projects in his coursework, somehow. But I can still remember him snottily informing me at our first meeting that '*things don't work like that*'.

I cannot help smiling a little, to see his involuntary cringe every time Ben cheerfully refers to him as '*Mate*'.

I am very keen to make sure the history societies are not overlooked, so keep bringing Ava into the conversation by asking her to contribute ideas about how best we can create a network between them. She mentions the British Association for Local History, which our local group has not yet joined, but could. David Crossley rolls his eyes at this and I make a mental note, to try to find out why.

Moving down the agenda, the next item is about our own next project. Do we want to do another local, historical scene? There is much enthusiasm for this where I anticipated groans and my heart lifts to picture us, happily beavering away at one or several more projects like the pilot one we have just done. We make a note to have another meeting for this purpose alone and to keep it separate from the steering group, even though it will most likely end up involving much the same people, amongst, hopefully, many others.

Eventually we come to "any other business" and I look around curiously, wondering what might come up. The only hand I see raised is that of Maybelle, still elegantly holding its stylus, so I motion to her to speak, in blissful ignorance of what is to come.

'I don't know about anyone else,' she says, somehow batting huge, false eyelashes, in the opposite directions of both David and Colin. 'But I think you would benefit from some proper, clerical help, Zoe, from someone such as myself, who is qualified to offer it. Obviously, it would be a voluntary post, like all the others at this stage, but I'd like to put myself forward for the role.'

I know my eyes close for more than three seconds, as I realise what a hole I have dug for myself with my kind forgiveness, as the whole room silently awaits my answer. I open them to see the shocked and distressed faces of my dear friends Ben, Rachel and Ava. Even Adam looks aghast and Hugh has uttered a quiet expletive.

In focusing my thoughts on trying to stay in charge of competing powerhouses like Colin and Ben, I have overlooked Maybelle and now she has me cornered. For how can I refuse such a publicly made, apparently generous offer? With a sinking feeling in my stomach I realise I cannot, without seeming churlish. There is no reason that is easy to explain.

The only thing left for me to do is to force a smile, clear my throat and tell her: 'Oh, thank you so much. How kind.'

We put the tables away and people mill around chatting for a while before adjourning to The Weaver's, in the square, for a drink. Hugh finds time to hug me sympathetically and I want to cry, but blink back the tears and keep smiling. Rachel is watching me with concern. I manage to avoid her approach for a quiet chat by asking Nick whether he thinks we should roll back the church square another fifty or a hundred years or move onto another site for our next stage. This plunges us into an intensely long and detailed conversation, as I predicted it would, leaving no scope for debate about anything else with me, this evening.

All the time, though, I have the same thought repeatedly running through my head.

I may have won one battle, but now it looks like I might lose the whole war.

29

It was the TED Talk that brought us to Google's attention, in the end.

I was wrong about the TED Talk, expecting it to be one of the most nerve-wracking experiences of my life. Instead, it turned out to be one of the most enjoyable, such was the smooth, rehearsed process, which has now been refined to perfection. I loved the Teleprompter, to the extent that I now wish I had one for everything, instead of struggling with notes. Of course, Rachel's ever-soothing but highly professional presence made it all even easier.

I was also wrong, about Google. I have always imagined, whenever I let myself dream, that the summons to see them – if it ever came – would come from California and that I would have to fly transatlantic, for my first time ever, to visit the office with the play slides and the bean bags. But instead, to my great relief because I was not relishing that long flight, it has come from their new London headquarters, along with two first-class train tickets to King's Cross station. And this – Google Maps tells me – opens right onto the forecourt of their own building.

Except, there is a kind of accidental History Maps-themed occurrence, with this. When I go to Google's Street View, there is a panorama shot, taken on the concourse, looking out from the station. But where the Google building should be, there are only boarded screens, of the sort used by builders, to shield a construction site. This is the Google construction site, from last year. On my laptop, I can see cranes behind the brightly painted boards and the developing concrete shell of the new build, but no building, so at this point the entrance is a mystery to me. I have watched some YouTube tours of the building, now that it is open, but they do not give me that "on the ground" experience I would get from Google Street View.

On the day before our meeting with Google, I learn with dismay that neither Rachel nor Ben will be able to accompany me, because of a family funeral. Ava cannot come either, because she has to work and the same is true for Hugh, who will also have Amy at home to look after. The only person available is Maybelle, who cannot seem to decide whether to be annoyed or delighted by the prospect.

'I suppose it will have to be me, then,' she tells me with a smirk, which promptly disappears. 'Though you'll have to be quiet on the train, Zoe. They always give me a headache.'

And so, next morning, we catch the six-thirty train in Yorkshire, for a ten-thirty appointment at Google. The first-class compartment is luxurious, as ever. I love the huge windows, the wide aisles and the comfortable seats. Maybelle is grumpy with her planned headache, so I watch the counties go by, telling myself that today is the day I have been hoping for. I really want to feel excited and delighted, but the pilot launch has inured me to big days to some extent. I try to propel my mind back to the months before the launch, when the History Maps project was just an idea in which nobody seemed interested.

How would I have felt then, if I could see myself now? This does bring the surge of pleasure to my chest and the smile to my face.

It also brings a snort, from Maybelle.

'What are *you* grinning about? I suppose you're feeling full of yourself today, but please try to remember that we're supposed to be *working*, and that *some* of us like to take such things *seriously.*'

But even Maybelle cannot wipe the smile away, now that it has arrived, so I am still smiling when I ask how her head is feeling. I am told that it is okay, so far, but will not be for much longer if I keep talking.

Breakfast comes. I have ordered the hot bacon baguette and I sink my teeth into it gratefully, but Maybelle only has coffee and expresses her disgust in my food, both facially and verbally. This does not prevent me from enjoying it.

We are somewhere in between Grantham and Peterborough, heading through a tiny medieval village that has been dwarfed by a new housing estate and some long, metal, industrial sheds, when Maybelle seems to suddenly decide she wants conversation after all. Albeit of the one-way variety.

'I've got to talk to you about today's meeting,' she begins. 'I don't know what you're expecting, but I think it's going to be very important for our project. It's wonderful, really, that we've got this far, against all the odds. I don't know about you, but I'm feeling quite grateful to the people who have made it happen. The thing is, this is quite a crucial stage and we don't want to blow it.'

I open my mouth to agree, but close it again as she continues, 'So, I think you should let *me* do all of the talking.'

This makes me laugh. But, being Maybelle, she is not joking.

'Honestly Zoe, we should do everything we can, to minimise the chance for any problems.'

I try again for some words and this time, am permitted to speak them.

'And do you think we'll risk more problems, if I do the speaking?'

In response, I get what she probably imagines to be a diplomatic silence. Maybelle hates to be laughed at, but my body is shaking in silent mirth, which puts an end to it. She turns in her seat to face me, so that I can gain the full benefit of her words.

'*This* is *exactly* what I mean. You refuse to take anything seriously and you are *so* selfish. So many people have put their all into this project of ours and you never think of them, only yourself, having a good laugh and jetting around the place, telling everyone how clever you are.

'In actual fact,' she continues. 'This project would never have got off the ground without Adam and the other boys and without the university *so* kindly giving us their time and facilities. Or even without your *so-clever* friends, Ben and Rachel. I myself have invested many hours of my own time. And you, Zoe? You're just joking around, *having a laugh.* It's just an excuse for a permanent holiday for you, isn't it?'

I think this might be the point in which I make the decision to take on a new assistant, given that the current one apparently despises me. She talks on, as I am thinking through the various problems her hatred of me engenders, from the damaging public relations, to the way it affects my own, sometimes fragile, self-esteem.

This journey is a perfect example. It should be an enjoyable experience and would be, if the person accompanying me was a true friend, who wanted both the project and me to do well. Maybelle does seem to want the former, but ideally without the latter. I think if she could shove me out of the train door with impunity, she cheerfully would.

I cast my mind back back just a few weeks, to the various similar trips I have made with Rachel in the publicity campaign, with sad longing. Rachel's company is always such a salve to me and even though she was there to further her own business as well as to represent me, her care, attention and unfailing support cushioned me through everything. Maybelle is right about that: I could not have got this far, without people like Rachel.

As soon as I open the door in my mind, labelled: "Maybelle is right," her words start getting to me.

'And really, you *could* have made more of an effort with your appearance. When was the last time you had your hair done? Really, Zoe, we're not going shopping for cabbages in Halifax market. We're actually going to meet some *important people.* In *London.* You really need to try harder. You're not going to be able to get away with being so lazy in those sorts of environments.' And I let out an involuntary sigh.

'It's no good sighing,' she comments, in response. 'You've got yourself into this mess and now I'm going to have to get you out of it, as usual.'

This does generate a splutter, from me.

'*Pardon? What* mess? Everything is going really well. You've only just said so yourself! We've been invited to talk to *Google,* for goodness sake. How much better could things be?'

She looks at me with annoyance and snaps, 'I do *know* what we've been invited to do. I'm not *stupid,* you know. You can stop that attitude, right now.' I sigh again. '*And* the sighing. You can stop that, too.'

I want to take a stand and ask her to back down, but I know she will not and the more I resist and object to her behaviour, the worse it will get. Instead, I excuse myself and go to the toilet. When I get back, her eyes are closed and I am very careful not to disturb her, but I spend the remainder of the journey trying to work out the best way of making sure that this is the last time I subject myself to this sort of treatment.

At King's Cross station, we emerge, blinking, onto the tree-dotted plaza, which I *can* recognise from my Google Street View forays. But now, to our right, instead of the construction boards, is the vast, glass-fronted edifice of Google London, with the famous logo, displayed in white, above the door.

Maybelle's attack has had its desired effect, though and instead of feeling excited, I am feeling shabby and wishing I had not sacrificed my smart heels, for the comfort of flat boots and my tailored suit, for jeans and a big sweater. Maybelle looks like the executive I am supposed to be, because, of course, she is dressed as if for a main role in Dynasty, complete with shoulder pads and perfectly coiffed hair.

I have stopped walking, to take everything in, but Maybelle keeps going, heels efficiently clack-clacking on the new, Italian stone pavement. I am almost tempted to just give up and let her take over, thinking she probably would do a better job of it.

Realising I am not by her side, she stops, to look back and tut at me, exaggeratedly looking at her watch and rolling her eyes.

So I sigh and trudge on behind her, wondering what on earth Google will think of us, when we get inside.

30

Approaching the Google building is like being presented with a strangely-shaped gift, with excitingly mysterious contents. I do not know what to expect, on so many levels, from my curiosity about the building's interior, to my feeling of bewilderment about the summons to the meeting in the first place. Even though it is what I have hoped for all along.

They asked me to set out my concept for the project and send it to them in advance, which was a pleasurable task, because it gave me a sense of completion, or perhaps of the successful handing on of a baton in a relay race. The puzzle for me was in the reason why they needed to meet me in person, but I have decided it is probably because they want me to sign documents, to transfer my ownership of the project to them.

This was all part of the plan from the start, if it was ever going to be lucky enough to get this far. But it gives me mixed feelings of contentment and sadness.

I imagine I will feel the same way when Alf moves out of the family home, that my work as his mother will be pretty much done and I will be both proud and regretful that he will not need me any more. *Does a bird feel that way, when its young fly the nest? All of that work: the home-making, the endless feeding, the rushing about bringing things and worrying and keeping them safe. Only to watch them fly free in the end. Gone.*

My thoughts have propelled me through the glass rotary doors and inside the building, without me even realising. It is Maybelle who announces our arrival and snaps at me to find my ID in my purse when they ask for it. I am busy looking around, awe-struck.

The whole place is flooded with natural light from the roof through an internal courtyard of glass walls, set in a complex steel frame. I look up and it goes up for about a dozen floors, against which a series of glass lifts glide up and down.

Someone comes to meet us, a young woman, with a silky curtain of brown hair, somehow managing to be both enthusiastic and very relaxed. I am surprised and relieved to see that she is wearing an outfit not dissimilar to my own. In fact, when I look around, I realise that it is actually Maybelle who looks out-of-place, with her tailored business suit and high heels. Everyone else is dressed casually, for comfort and relaxation.

Our guide introduces herself to us as Katie and takes us through glass turnstiles, towards the glass lifts. I notice that she selects the floor number on the outside of the lift, to summon it and for a few seconds, I wonder why. Then, it occurs to me that the entire lift system is an intelligent one, which will use the advanced notification of users' destinations to organise its movements and stops, with maximum efficiency.

Inside the lift and shooting upwards, the whole place is bringing somewhere else to mind and before we stop, I have remembered what it is. The Ministry of Magic, from the Harry Potter films. This place is lighter and airier, but the sensation of being somehow both outside and in, and the air of slight unreality, is the same.

I wish Amy and Alf were here to see it and I position my phone to take a picture for them, but Katie puts up a gentle, restraining arm and asks me not to. She points to the giant cartoon characters which decorate the glass walls of the huge light well, up which we are fast travelling. I spot a blue owl, a pink cat and a yellow ghost amongst others, but I fail to recognise them, although I feel like I should.

'It's pixel art, made out of Post-it notes,' announces Katie with real delight. I look again, still puzzled, not really grasping her explanation.

Many of the rooms we pass seem like public spaces or open plan offices and I am speculating furiously about what our meeting space will be like, wondering if we will sit by one of the huge external windows, to take in the view as we speak. Or perch on the edge of one of the vast, horseshoe-shaped sofas, instead.

The last environment I am expecting is the long room we are shown into, with dark, flocked walls on either side of a rectangular, glossy white table. At the far end is a giant screen, surrounded by upholstered décor, in deep-buttoned rust red.

Katie is holding out a seat for me halfway down the length of the table with a smile and I realise my mouth is open, in surprise. I close it, with an answering grin. Sitting down, I am still assessing my surroundings, from the white roof with tiny spotlights, like stars, to the incongruously pale blue carpet beneath my feet.

Katie leaves us, closing the door behind herself and the sudden silence tells me that the room is soundproof, which perhaps explains the thickly upholstered walls. Maybelle is busying herself, with setting out her various devices and gadgets on the table in front of her. Phone, laptop, iPad. I am just starting to wonder why she imagines she might need any of these, let alone all three, when she hisses at me to remember that *she* is to do all of the talking in the meeting, not me.

'*No*,' I manage to tell her, emphatically. Then: 'Anyway, I think we'll both be mainly listening,' and I calm my mounting anxiety, by reminding myself that it is going to be a legal formality and that they have to make sure I know what I am agreeing to, in signing their contracts. I have noticed a camera, underneath the giant screen at the end, which suggests to me that by the end of it, they might have evidence that I was not coerced into any agreements. Maybe Maybelle has noticed the same, hence her whisper.

I glance at her face, which is looking pale beneath its make-up, her mouth set even more tightly than usual. And I wonder why, trying, with familiar difficulty, to see things from her perspective. *Maybe it's just the stress of having to spend the whole day in my company, but it seems like more than that.*

The door soon opens and four people enter and sit down with us. They introduce themselves, casually and warmly, so I have no trouble returning their smiles. I listen carefully, in case I need to remember their names, for future reference.

Den is an athletic man, with salt-and-pepper hair and a bizarrely shy, brown-eyed face. When he speaks, I am surprised to hear an American accent which, to my untrained ear, might be Californian but I am not sure. I get glimpses of dazzling white teeth when he tells us his name, but am much more surprised to see a leather necklace in the V of his open buttoned shirt, bound with copper rings.

Rajesh is a beautiful man, with deeply set, dark brown eyes and an infectious grin. I expect an Indian accent and instead he speaks in a kind of transatlantic drawl, but I need to hear more from him, to be sure about that.

Pippa exudes a confident, easy glamour I can only dream of exuding, myself. She has a straight posture, long, blonde hair, a peaches-and-cream complexion and she moves like a ballerina. As a child, I had a tiny doll called Pippa, who would have grown up to be this lady if she had been human.

Finally, we meet the red-bearded Karl, whose north European accent is barely perceptible, but definitely there, I decide.

What surprises me about all four of the people now sitting across the table from us, is their age. Most of the faces we have passed on our way to this room have seemed no older than forty and most have looked to be in their twenties. But these four are closer to my age, I think. And Den might be even older than I am.

I am also surprised that they address me by name, without being told which one of us is me. But I only need to think that through for a second, to remember the number of PR interviews and appearances I have made in recent months, not to mention the TED Talk. I am still not accustomed to being recognised on sight, though.

When we were talking, last night, Hugh concurred with Ben's guess that only one of the people we meet today would have any ranking at all within the organisation and that at least fifty percent of those in our meeting would be interns. But while Katie, who showed us to the room, might have been an intern, I think all of these four must be too old for that.

Ben told me to expect at least one person to be 'bouncing around the room', which made me laugh, coming from him. Nobody here today is bouncing – not yet, anyway. And I have to say no-one looks likely to become bouncy either. I am trying to guess which one of them might be the one with any real power, but there is no indication whatsoever, that I can discern. I imagine it will become apparent as we get under way.

Pippa thanks us for attending and Maybelle interjects, rather rudely and unnecessarily, I think, to thank them for inviting us. Pippa allows the interruption, looking down at her tablet, which, Hugh explained last night, would probably be one of the new Pixels. It is white-framed and therefore almost invisible against this table. In fact, I am only really noticing it now that she is paying it some attention.

Maybelle finishes speaking and Pippa looks back up at her, unsmiling.

'You must be...' she looks down again, reading. 'Maybelle?'

Maybelle flushes, displeased at being asked.

'Yes,' she says, angrily, though only I would know it. 'Maybelle Shaw. Zoe and I conceived of the History Maps project together, when we were home educating our sons.'

I know my mouth has fallen open, as I turn to stare at her.

Instinctively, I have known, ever since she started instructing me not to speak and then filled her portion of the table up with her devices, that she was going to try to usurp me again, but I did not expect it to be this blatant, or this early on in the proceedings.

My surprise has evidently been noted.

'Did you?' asks Rajesh quickly. 'That's not what Zoe said on the TED Talk, or anywhere else.'

'No, we did not,' is my firm response, feeling a strong need to nip this in the bud before we get any further. 'The concept is entirely my own.'

'Prove it,' says Maybelle quietly and I stare at her, aghast all over again.

How can she be choosing this moment, *to have this argument?* I can hardly believe my ears and feel like prodding her, hard, in the ribs, but restrain myself.

'I don't need to prove it, Maybelle. You know nothing about history and you care even less,' is what I am forced to say, cringing with embarrassment that we are conducting ourselves like this in front of these people, who we want to take us seriously. And bemoaning my gullibility, for being tricked by Maybelle, yet again.

If I had imagined that she was going to do this, wild horses could not have dragged me into the building with her. And yet, going by her past form, I should have known.

Her sullen: 'Not true,' is drowned out by Rajesh, saying: 'Okay, so this is Zoe's concept, as we thought.'

His eyes have never left my face to look at Maybelle, throughout the exchange. I feel, rather than hear, Maybelle's angry sigh and I hope this is the last of any trouble from her, today.

I am feeling so embarrassed and ashamed, that I just want to go home, now. But I owe it to the project and to everyone who has worked on it, to see this meeting out and to pass it onto the right people, as best as I can, so that it stands the best chance of becoming the universal resource it was always meant to be.

For the first time, I begin to feel some relief at the thought of handing it off and being free of all of the power struggles and the need to be constantly assertive. I am not sure I will ever speak to Maybelle again, though for Alf and Adam's sake, I will probably be polite. But I do not think I will ever deliberately seek her out, or choose to spend one more second in her company than I have to.

I am so flooded with thoughts and feelings prompted by her blatant lie, that I barely take in the next part of the meeting, which involves our hosts going through my concept and explaining what they like about it and what they would like to change. Den echoes Ben's early sentiment that it would be good to be able to see inside the historical buildings.

And Pippa tells Karl that she agrees with him that it would be, 'Good in VR', though it takes me a few minutes to realise she means Virtual Reality. This blows my mind and finally stops me brooding on Maybelle's antics.

Den is intent on finding out from me how the different groups of volunteers interact on a local project. How does the university formality meld with the amateur history societies?

I explain that the universities do not necessarily have to be fully formal in their approach and that the history societies are often peopled by professionals in their own fields and can therefore hold their own with the students and even the professors.

As I am talking, I bring to mind a recent exchange, between Nick and Colin, on whether stone was routinely transported over large distances in the middle ages. Nick proved it was, by demonstrating from pictures and maps that certain elements of key sample structures could not possibly be vernacular.

Pippa follows on with a close set of questions about how the university IT departments work with the history ones. So I describe how it has worked in our local case and also how I see it working in other instances, when the history department would be in at the beginning.

'Okay, so, here's our proposal,' says Karl, eventually, when I have almost forgotten what we are here for. 'We want to take your concept on. Are we right in thinking you want to sign it over to us?' I nod my head and try to smile. 'But on one condition. We want you as well.'

I am confused. *In what way do they want me as well?* I am soon to find out.

'We want to pay you to co-ordinate the Google History Maps project for us. You'll basically carry on doing what you're doing, but in a slightly more formalised way and we'll want to keep in regular contact with you. We'd like you to continue being the face and voice of History Maps, since you've done such a great job so far.'

'It's your baby, isn't it?' adds Rajesh with a huge, sympathetic smile into my eyes, which are filling with tears.

'It's my baby too,' puts in Maybelle. 'It's everyone's baby. About forty people have worked on this project so far...'

Everything else passes in something of a blur, though they are determined to ensure I understand exactly what I am signing.

At the end of it all, we are met by Katie again and taken up to the eleventh floor café for lunch, which I barely taste, such is my shock.

I have signed the ownership of my concept over to Google and in return, have signed up for their job. While I was signing, I saw that they were also pushing papers towards Maybelle.

They have employed her, to be my Personal Assistant.

31

My new job is both similar and different to what I was doing before. I am still working with Ava, Nick and the others in my home town, but now I am also travelling to give seminars and workshops, to both universities and local history societies, as well. It is a lot of hard work and not very glamorous. And, if my feet ever look like floating off the ground, there is always Maybelle to bring me back down to earth again, with a well-placed, acerbic put-down or telling-off.

No matter how much I do, she remains convinced that I view life as a lark or a holiday and generally swan about enjoying myself, while other people – mostly, herself – get the important things done.

I can spend two long days, painstakingly bringing together an IT Department and History Department who have never spoken to each other and reassuring the amateur historians in the same town that they have a vital part to play and Maybelle will call this, *'Sitting down, to have a nice chat.'* Whilst her scurrying around, booking train tickets and meeting rooms and printing things is considered to be hard graft.

I am determined to ignore her frequent attempts at sabotage and to focus on getting the job done. But at the same time, I cannot help being fascinated by the nature and direction of her attacks. She takes her Personal Assistant role seriously and admittedly works hard at it, so I think she still wants the History Maps concept to succeed. But her personal animosity towards me is always there and often unveiled. She treats me with utter contempt most of the time, tutting and sighing audibly when I speak and trying her best to undermine people's confidence in me, wherever we go.

I yearn for Rachel's quiet, supportive professionalism, but I am not seeing much of her or Ben, now. Their company was given the predicted boost, from being so publicly associated with our pilot project.

And now they are busy with new clients, from whom they can take their pick and really, as Ben said, *'Design and build our business like an architect with a new structure, exactly how we want it.'*

They are interviewing staff and training and supervising them, as well as spending every spare minute in meetings, still taking a hands-on approach, themselves. They have hired a nanny for the children, a formerly unschooled young woman who understands, from her own childhood, how learning can be optimised by following a child's curiosity.

My own child is much-missed by me and I get home to her and to Hugh whenever I can, but it is not enough. I feel very torn, between wanting to scale back my hours and spend more time with them – and Alf, too, when he is free and wanting to see us – and wanting to work harder to get the job done more quickly. Then, I could stop working for money again and focus on Amy, full-time.

Amy does not want a nanny and is probably too old to need one, given that Hugh works from home and her learning is self-motivated, without needing much input from us. But I miss being there to help her find answers to the constant questions she always has. Hugh reminds me that she can find them on her own, now and he thinks that a bit of educational independence is probably what she needs. I know he breaks off from work many times a day, to help her and makes sure she still gets lots of time with her friends. But it is a lot for him to do and... *I miss her.* We Skype every day, *but it isn't the same.*

I have quickly learned that I have to carve out some time off, though, to prevent burn-out, much to Maybelle's derision and disgust. Getting home, kicking off my shoes, becoming lost in the view from the garden, spending precious hours with the family, including my old dad, are things I will never take for granted again. Even though I am starting to feel, worryingly, more like a visitor than a resident.

Hugh is talking about going part-time, which would be good for both him and Amy. But privately, I fear this will lock me into my new role indefinitely. It pays well, but we still have the mortgage to cover.

When we are travelling, I only have Maybelle to chat to.

But she dismisses my pining for Amy as, *'Pathetic,'* and reminds me that, *'Some people don't have children to miss, let alone an important job to pretend to do.'*

She also chides me, for interrupting her own work and makes it clear that she would generally prefer to have teeth extracted, than to have a conversation with me.

So I throw myself into work, into improving and refining the package we deliver. And into cringing at my own use of such clichés, which have become so commonplace, I sometimes hardly recognise myself in the words I am saying. Every town, every local project, teaches me more about how to do my job more effectively.

We start by finding the key people, although it is often the case that they find us, as Google expertly manages the publicity and application process. The amateur historians are often the keenest at the start, but sometimes, the first contact comes from the university.

I especially love to begin with the graphic artists, those who feel inspired to replicate the work done in our pilot project by Ollie, Will, Adam and my son Alf. Sometimes, one or other of those four can be persuaded to accompany me to meetings or seminars. This always injects the event with extra pizzazz, the young students being quite star-struck by the graduate.

Each of the four brings a different flavour of input, though it is pot-luck which one we get, if any, as they are all busy with their new jobs and lives, post-university.

Will, now becoming established as a free-lance cartoonist, inspires their creativity with his quick pencil on paper, showing within an hour or so, how the whole thing could look. He listens carefully and quietly to their answers to his careful questions and sketches as they talk, like he always did. By the end of it, the participant is more sure of their ideas *and* they can see some manifestation of them on his sketch-pad.

Ollie has been head-hunted by Google himself, though not specifically to work on the History Maps, as myself and Maybelle remain the only two on the payroll for that. He is involved on the design side, somehow, though I am not sure exactly what he does. But when I phone and ask sweetly, he is often happy to take half a day out of the office to come and help us if we are anywhere near London.

He brings his customary energy and charisma into the room, charging everyone's enthusiasm and making the whole process more enjoyable and believable. This is great, because confidence is often a problem, especially amongst the amateur historians, who cannot imagine being taken seriously by the universities. Ollie has a natural talent for bringing together self-conscious, disparate folks and making them feel united.

Alf and Adam are still based in the North. They have set up a web design company together, which already has half a dozen good clients, although they both want to go back to university to undertake a Master's degree in game design. I can imagine them managing to do both, between them: keeping the business going whilst doing their studies. They never seem to fall out, or to spend much time apart, but have to come one at a time to help with our events, because someone has to man the office.

When we get Alf, I am so happy and proud. He has a gentle way of helping and directing people, especially the younger students, who are still struggling with the basics of graphic design. Adam is a bit more collaborative and can talk to anyone. He is good at interjecting, with just the right question or comment at the right time.

I am not allowed to employ any of the four, but my budget does allow for consultancy rates, which I make sure they all get. And we can go out for dinner together, too, although there usually is no time for anything other than a snatched lunch, on the hoof. I am losing weight, slowly but surely and without trying, by virtue of hardly ever being in my own kitchen. And having a full brain and schedule that no longer has space for indulging in seconds, or snacks.

As for my clothes, I have settled into something of a uniform of jeans or leggings and smock-tops. Maybelle sneers derisively at me, whatever I wear, so I have stopped worrying about what I look like. I am too busy for that, anyway and I need to be comfortable on my feet and be able to move around a room, easily.

Today, Colin Pritchard has joined us, because we needed his help in bringing a university's History Department on board. He is taking his counterpart out to dinner at a restaurant of his usual, classy extravagance and I am really not in the mood for it. I want to Skype with Hugh and Amy and have a bath or a swim, depending on which I can find, in or around the hotel.

It would usually be okay for me to leave Colin to speak the language of history professors without my help. But this man's wife is attending, so Colin is politely insistent that I should. When Maybelle jumps in with a breathy offer to take my place and Colin readily agrees, I feel relieved, but slightly worried. I cannot put my finger on why, but this is Maybelle, so I do not need to justify any anxiety.

I do my Skyping and my soaking and then sit down in my hotel room, to think and take some notes. We are on the outskirts of Nottingham and I am struggling to see the history in the place, as the buildings are all red brick and I cannot date them at a glance, as easily as I can our Yorkshire stone. I start touring the area on Google's Street View, trying to take myself back in time in my imagination. But I find it quite difficult, in areas where there is no visible remainder of the Medieval or even the Georgian period and we really have to rely on old maps and old memories.

The local history society will have some recollections of their own and their grandparents', I hope, as well as photos and maps. I feel out of place, though, not knowing this area or much about it and am glad that my only job is to kick-start their own work and to check back on it regularly, instead of trying to do some of it myself.

Navigating my way around Google Street View by laptop mouse, I come across some streets of late-Victorian houses, with half-timbers in some of their gable ends and charming sandstone contrasts, picking out their lintels and front door arches.

Most have been modernised and have car parks, instead of front gardens. But every now and again, I see grass, with sometimes a swing and even children and parents, enjoying their small space, together. Then, my mind forgets history and goes back to longing for Amy, Hugh and even Alf. Or it remembers my own living history in my own childhood, when cars were few and green gardens, plentiful.

I can hear noise from the corridor outside my room and go to open my door, to find Maybelle, in an electric blue sheath dress, high silvery heels and the arms of Professor Colin Pritchard, both looking the worse for wear. She is giggling and pulling his tie, coquettishly, while he sways and tries to kiss her.

He would have succeeded, if she had not spotted me and raised a drunken bare arm, yelling, '*Oi!*' as if she has forgotten my name, which she might well have.

I sigh. *This is so predictable*: they are always flirting with each other and we never hear or see anything from Maybelle's husband, who, I gather, is always working away nowadays. I do not even know whether Colin has a wife and I cannot find it in me to care, either way. But I had wanted a peaceful evening and now this looks unlikely.

'Take tomorrow off!' Maybelle instructs me, as if she is the boss and I am the assistant. 'You're always whinging about seeing your little *brat*...' She and Colin collapse in giggles at this, followed by loud attempts at shushing each other, in case there is a chance I have not noticed. 'So go and see her! I'll be you. No-one will notice, in fact... they'll prefer it!'

This is followed by gales of laughter, in which Maybelle doubles up and staggers, Colin grabbing her, to either stabilise her, or steady himself, I cannot tell which. But I have had enough of it.

'*No*,' I tell her decisively and shut the door on them both. I lean against it, feeling a wave of loneliness and sadness, missing home now, more than ever.

Checking the time, I see it is only ten-thirty.

Perhaps Hugh will still be up. I'll call him, to see.

32

There is a building, in the West Yorkshire town of Milnsbridge, that I have passed by sometimes and wondered about. I am standing in front of it now with David Crossley, whose local group is making it the centrepoint of their History Maps project. A quiet, affable man, David is highlighting various previously unnoticed aspects of the building to me, with his IT tutor's eye for detail.

'The three-part window, in the box gable end, is known as Diocletian, I'm sure you know. And the recessed triangle of stone, that sits within the gable end, is of course the tympanum. It's a classically Georgian style, isn't it?'

I pull my spectacles down from the top of my head and apply them to my eyes, to take a better look.

'Yes. I don't often retain that degree of architectural terminology in my head, though.' I am out of practice, having spent more time recently engaged in the diplomacy surrounding fledgling local projects, than in the history itself. This is a welcome change.

'But I ran the building through a Google search and noticed, in one old image, that the tympanum window had a spectacular Rococo cartouche, whereas this one is plain. It must be around the other side?' *I haven't forgotten all of the terms, evidently.*

'Right, yes,' David replies enthusiastically. 'Because, of course, we're looking at the original *back* of the building, even though it now acts as the front. I think it's the change in surroundings, rather than the building itself, that's made the most difference between now and the eighteenth century, when that picture was painted.'

The building, Milnsbridge House, looks at first glance like one of the dark, satanic mills for which this part of Yorkshire is famous. It sits surrounded by tight streets and terraced, Victorian mill housing with a derelict building site, complete with graffitied hoardings, to what is now the front. Its main entryway has even been replaced with a huge, wooden, sliding mill door.

Above this is an original, triangular pediment which looks, from this distance, to be *surbaissé.* Unadorned, though bold in definition. But you have to look twice, to notice it. The building's stone is nearly black from centuries of factory smog, as would all the buildings around here be, if they were never sandblasted back to their original, honey colour. There was a craze of doing that in the 1980s, but it obviously passed by Milnsbridge House.

You have to be at the other side of the street and look up, to see beyond its semi-derelict, old mill appearance. This is when it stops making sense, to the careless glance, because the stones beneath the grime are not cut and set in rough courses, like the mills are. *This* is finely dressed, smooth-surfaced ashlar, of the type that graced only the better Georgian buildings.

The back – now the front – is quite sparse in adornments, so we pick our way carefully around what remains of last week's snow to the side, noting the centre window's topping of a moulded cornice on fluted consoles, camouflaged, as they are now, by blackness, like the surrounding wall.

The east side is more ornate, with that stunning cartouche at the top, its curling, splayed scrolls ostentatiously embellishing the circular oculus and I think this is what has caught my eye in the past and jarred in my mind, as being out of place for a mill.

I smile and frown simultaneously, to see a set of first-floor loading doors with a winch, just like the ones on the haberdashery of our pilot project, the very first building of the History Maps. The smile is with warm recognition that I feel, like comfort in my belly, because of the association with our beloved haberdashery. The frown is from my heavy sadness, about the utilitarian vandalism wreaked on this once glorious structure by the monster that was industrialisation.

David is listing the various mouldings, friezes and pediments for me. But I pull out my phone and find on it the painting that so shocked me yesterday, when I first saw it. It is of Milnsbridge House, but in a barely discernible form.

A cream-coloured, sturdy but elegant, three-storey manor house sits imposingly on an open green landscape, with rolling hills behind it, mature woodland to either side and a generous sward of grass in the foreground. The meadow looks like it would have been even more extensive than the painting allows.

Swans glide on large ponds and three people can be seen walking a dog: two women, in brightly coloured, floor-length dresses and dark jackets and a tall man, festooned with top hat and tails. Some rolling clouds, of the same colour as the building, set against a cornflower sky, finish the composition of a site which would not look out of place in the National Trust catalogue.

To look, from the picture to the actual building and back again, renews the shock, every time. David stops his technical descriptions when he notices what I am doing and touches my shoulder, sympathetically.

'It's absolutely tragic, isn't it?'

I nod, not really able to verbalise my thoughts on it yet. But he continues, explaining it perfectly.

'The Victorians didn't give much thought to the preservation of our Georgian heritage, it seems. They probably had no idea how important it would be, to us. They just wanted to do the practical thing, get the machines working and the people in to keep them working, hence all the houses. I think much of the Georgian era is probably completely lost to us, as with the medieval and every other stage before that.'

He sighs deeply and continues, 'The march of time. There's not much we can do about it, except to try to piece together what's left and make intelligent guesses to fill in the gaps.'

I look into his kind, crinkled eyes and nearly cry with gratitude, that he put it so well and that he understands, so perfectly, what it is that we are doing. It was quite amazing good fortune, that brought the four students under his wing and I wonder, not for the first time, how much influence David might have had in Ollie's initial enthusiasm for my concept.

'Have you seen enough?' he asks me. 'Or do you want to take some photos?'

I am tempted to suggest a revisit, with Nick and Ava, who have a camera that would pick out every scroll and modillion, but I am learning to compartmentalise my mind, between the various regional projects with which I am involved. I am here today as an interested friend, but also in my capacity as co-ordinator of the History Maps and I am painfully aware that if I throw myself and "my people" deeply into every local project, we will burn out within weeks. Nick and Ava have more than enough to do in their own – *our* own – local society area, for that.

'Let's go,' I smile at him. 'Thanks for showing it to me properly. It looks as if they've made some improvements to it, since I last drove by, anyway, which is heartening.' The windows on the east side have benefited from a clean and a new lick of paint, in an authentic shade of green-grey.

'Maybe the blue plaque helped them to attract some funding,' answers David, with what might be a hint of cynicism or irony, as we make our way back to our cars.

It is *quite ironic, especially as the funding might have come from one of those multinational, charitable foundations that have often sprung from the same Victorian industrialists who caused the problem in the first place.* But then, my thinking always comes full circle: *without the industrialists, I would have no car, no phone and no Google. And,* I concede, reluctantly, *there'd now be no funding, to fix what is left of the old buildings they wrecked.*

'Are you joining us, this evening?' I ask him, unable to remember whether he responded to the invitation. 'Apart from Ollie, who's down in London and Maybelle and Colin, who are both ill, we'll all be there.' By "all", I mean the steering group, of course.

David's eyes narrow and his eyebrows rise.

'Maybelle and Colin are both ill, are they?' And I realise he has probably suspected what I saw evidence of in Nottingham, last week. My heart sinks, to think of it and if I was alone, I would be rolling my own eyes to heaven. *Their affair will probably be an embarrassing complication we can all do without.* I can still hear Maybelle's drunken giggling, echoing through my mind: part empress, part wild teenager, part psychopath. *I really want to think happier thoughts.*

'I wouldn't miss it for the world,' finishes David, taking his car keys from his pocket. 'Do I need to bring anything?'

'No, just yourself,' I smile, in response. I am looking forward to this evening.

When I get home, I find that Hugh and Alf have been working to resolve one of my key anxieties about the meal, to which we have invited everyone. They have moved everything superfluous out of the dining room and brought another table in, so that we can quite comfortably seat ten, after all. I hug them both, so happy to be home, and go to find Amy.

She is not in the sitting room, but Adam is, his favourite game of Assassin's Creed on the big TV screen. This makes me smile. *Time moves on, but some things stay the same.*

'Hi, Adam! How are you?' I ask him, planning to only exchange a few pleasantries, before I resume my search for

Amy upstairs and let him get back to his game.

But something in the tone of his voice, when he responds, makes me go into the room properly and sit down, on the chair opposite his.

'I'm fine, thanks, Zoe,' is what I have heard him say, but I have known him for long enough to know that is not strictly true. He might be fine, physically, but he has something on his mind and if he is letting me see that, then it must be something important.

'What's wrong?' I ask him, directly.

His eyes move back to the screen and back to me.

Whatever it is, he obviously doesn't know how to say it so, hazarding a guess, I offer: 'How is your mum? Not too ill, I hope.'

I can tell by his eyes that I have guessed correctly. *This* is *about Maybelle.*

He takes a deep pull of air into his lungs and blows it out, like candles on a birthday cake, minus the delight. *He might be making a wish, though.*

'I don't think she's really ill,' he says, eventually. Heavily. He looks at me and stretches his mouth to denote uncertainty, unhappiness.

'Okay...' I prompt, waiting patiently.

'I... I think she's with Professor Pritchard.' This flows out in a rush, as if it has been pent up behind a dam, which is now open. He seems relieved, to have said the words, but sad and ashamed to have had to say them.

'Oh love, I'm sorry,' I tell him, with equal sadness and a bucket of heartfelt sympathy. 'I had an idea they might be together. It must be really awkward for you.'

'Yeah...' he responds. But then looks at me directly again, in a way that makes me suddenly worried.

'There's more?' I ask, knowing the answer.

He takes another one of his deep breaths in and blows it out.

'Yeah. I heard them talking about you. She's... not... you know, my mother isn't a very kind person.'

Now, it is my turn to heave a sigh.

'I know, love.' I feel so dejected for him, that he has to try to be Maybelle's polite, peacemaking interface with the outside world.

'She was trying to persuade Pritchard to go to London with her. I think they might have gone today. I... I think she's arranged a meeting at the Google office. Um. About you, Zoe.'

Adam puts his head in his hands. I put my head in mine.

33

Hugh has cooked chicken in a creamy, wine sauce, which sits warming in the slow cooker. The rice is ready in the rice cooker and needs only to be switched on. Amy has set the table and got the knives and forks the right way round, a sure sign of nascent maturity, for her. There are wine glasses – I know the white wine will be chilling in the fridge – salad and bread set out on the table, which consists of the two tables pushed together, to make one. This has all happened without any input from me. And while until fairly recently it might have made me feel redundant, today I am just relieved and grateful.

The house feels warm and welcoming and the smell of the herbs in the sauce fills the air. If it was not for Adam's bombshell I would be basking in contentment, but instead I am anxious, now, wondering what his mother is up to. *Causing trouble for me, for sure – but how?*

I go and sit in the kitchen where Hugh is setting out pudding dishes – *such forethought!* - and try, yet again, to put myself inside her head, to imagine the detail of her plot. Our guests will be arriving any minute and I do not want to ruin Hugh's evening by telling him my news, so I am trying to both process it and to simultaneously act as if it is not happening.

On the one hand, Maybelle has been trying to assert shared ownership of the concept, ever since it started to look potentially successful. On the other, she has kept up her usual stream of ongoing complaints about my choices and activities throughout her tenure as my personal assistant, just as she did when we were developing the pilot. *Just as she has, ever since I first met her, come to think of it. So which will it be? She part owns the concept, or I can't do my job properly? Knowing Maybelle, it'll be both.*

I let out a harsh breath, angry with myself for adding her to the steering committee, just because I felt guilty about our early morning ambush of her, after she had given the dodgy interview.

Hugh has heard and turns around sharply to look at me, concern in his eyes. I smile brightly and go to kiss his cheek.

'Everything looks and smells wonderful, love.'

But I can see from his face that my distraction ploy has not worked. Luckily, the doorbell rings.

'Saved by the bell…' he mutters, to my departing back, as I go and answer it.

Half an hour later, dinner is underway and, although the heavy sensation of foreboding has not fully left me, the conversation is sufficiently distracting as to keep taking my conscious mind away from Maybelle's antics.

As is often the case in groups of more than a few, there are two different topics being discussed at the same time and I am trying to keep track of both. At the top end, John Anderson and Will are telling David about a tuition session they ran for a graphic arts course last week, based on the rendering of buildings and streets. I already know, from the participators' feedback, that this went very well. The three of them are working to develop a coding template, which will cut out a lot of the time-consuming, repetitive elements of building rendering.

While they are talking, it occurs to me that we really need to add some video tuition from these three into the package for new developers. I make a mental note to ask Colin how much progress there has been in getting History Maps incorporated into the syllabi for the graphic arts courses.

Ask Colin. This reminds me of his likely treachery with Maybelle and I feel the burn of tension across my shoulders and close my eyes, momentarily. When I open them, Hugh is watching me with that direct, probing look he has, so I smile brightly, in response. His returning smile is not bright, but sad and rueful. *He'll worry, now, until I've told him what has happened and then, he'll worry some more.*

At the bottom of the table, Nick and Ava are discussing our next local phase with Rachel and Hugh. From a national perspective, we are trying to encourage everyone to centre their current History Maps to the time period just after the last war: 1948. This will hopefully encourage engagement with the very elderly, who will have memories of the way things were.

There are photographs and accurate maps of the era too, which, my marketing guru at Google agreed, would be a good starting point for the generation of maximum interest and input for the national launch. The graphic artists will be mostly recreating buildings from photographs instead of from guesswork. But this will not be for dissertations, so creative originality will not be necessary.

Ben has a seat in the middle of the table and is doing what I am doing: trying to listen to both conversations at once. In Ben's case, this means getting actively involved in both and it amuses me to watch him switching his posture from left to right every few minutes, for fear he might miss an opportunity to interject.

Turning to the two tutors and Will, he listens for a few minutes and then says, 'That sounds *brilliant*, guys. I want to come to some of these sessions myself! You should get them on Youtube!' and I twitch my lip at his mirroring of my own idea. Ben and I are often both riding the same Zeitgeist wave – and he usually verbalises it before I do.

Turning to the right, he listens for a while and then says: '*Brilliant* plan. I wish you could do our farm. That'd be great, wouldn't it Rach?' Then, he is back to the other side again.

Alf and Adam are doing their usual thing, sitting back and sharing their phone screens in their own private conversation. But this time, they are very sweetly including Amy, who looks delighted to be involved. I do not know what the three of them are so interested in, but I suspect it to be a game.

1948. My dad would have been ten years old. He does remember that time and speaks of it often, describing people and places in great detail. In my mind's eye, I can see his now-demolished, childhood home, he has depicted it to me so often. A black-stoned, inner terrace with lace curtains and exactly three feet of stone yard to the pavement, boundaried by a waist high, flat-topped, black stone wall. Like the stones of Milnsbridge House they would not have started out black, but a beige, sandy colour, gradually darkening in the relentless smoke of the town's many chimneys.

My dad speaks of this house with such fondness and such a glorious sense of belonging, that I suddenly want him to be able to see it again and another idea begins to grow. A few seconds ago, I was mentally rolling my eyes at Ben, for wanting our next phase to centre around his farm, but now, suddenly, I want it to be about my dad's childhood. The street, the path he took with his own dad every morning, to school and work respectively.

I am not sure it is right for me to request this, but Ava suddenly turns to me and asks, 'Have you got any ideas for which town centre location we should do next, Zoe?'

And, without giving it much more thought, I tell them about my dad's childhood on Easterly Street.

When I have finished, Ava says, '*Yes!*' and turns to Nick, eyes shining.

'It does sound like an ideal spot,' agrees Nick. 'We'd have a wealth of data. Would your dad come and help us, do you think?' he asks me.

'I'd love to meet him,' grins Ava. I grin back and I know we are both envisaging this happening and working well. So many people share my urge to recreate the past, but Ava and I frequently both experience an instantaneous mutual connection, in that respect.

I catch Hugh's eye. He is smiling, too, but not really with his eyes, because he is still wondering why I am not quite my usual self. None of the others can tell: I am behaving exactly as normal, I think. But he knows me better than anyone else in the room and I cannot fool him.

I glance over at Adam and wonder how he would feel, if I told this intimate group of people, with whom we both feel so comfortable now, what his mother is up to. I catch the three of them laughing over the game, or whatever it is that they are sharing, and I realise he would probably feel ashamed and more than a little betrayed by me.

He can't help being Maybelle's son and he has redeemed his position several times, now. As well as making it clear, for the past ten years or so, that he's more comfortable with us than with his own family. I do feel maternally protective of him and his wellbeing, I decide. *I'm going to have to be very careful.*

Ben grabs my attention, with a question about the Google London office and I enjoy spending a few minutes describing it to him.

He is such an engaged listener, albeit one who interjects with exclamations like, '*Wow!* Do you hear that, Rach?' and more questions: 'So how do the lifts work together like that, then? They must be all computerised. In fact, the whole *building* must be computerised...'

He reminds me of Tigger, in the Pooh Bear books. Catching Rachel also observing him fondly, the thought occurs to me that she, then, would be Christopher Robin.

Although I am on edge about Maybelle, I am still more relaxed than usual in this group and it suddenly dawns on me why that is. *Maybelle is not here!* Nobody is carping at me, snapping at me, shooting angry sideways glances at me or talking down to me. *She's undoubtedly directing most of her energy against me, right at this moment, in London, but the absence of it in my face is so restful, all the same.*

The evening passes in the same conviviality. But as soon as the front door has closed on the last departing guest, Hugh turns around in the hallway and grabs me by the shoulders, looking searchingly into my face.

'What's *happened?*' he asks urgently. 'You've had some bad news, I can tell. And you tried to keep it from me so that it didn't spoil my evening, but it did anyway, because I can see right through you.'

I cannot help smiling at this, even as my eyes are filling with tears of relief at being able to finally offload my secret.

'Adam told me that Maybelle has gone to London with Colin, for a meeting with Google. About me.'

Hugh loosens my shoulders and puts his hands on his head – in exasperation, I think.

'I *knew!* I knew it was Maybelle! Firstly, because it always is, secondly because she and Colin being ill at the same time is just too suspicious. And thirdly, because I saw you watching Adam when you were thinking about it. Argh! *Will no-one rid me of this turbulent woman?!*'

I smile through tears again, warning him: 'Be careful what you wish for! If anything did happen to her, it would be on your conscience...'

'No, it wouldn't,' he reassures me, sweeping me into a giant bear hug. 'Come on Zoe, let's stack the dishwasher and go to bed with a whisky nightcap, while we chew this whole thing over.'

And that is exactly what we do.

227

34

Today, I have to go and collect my dad and take him to a meeting at the local history society, so that he can meet everyone and share his 1948 memories with them. Before I leave the house though, I try Maybelle's number, one last time.

I have been trying to get hold of her for three days, now. Mainly because I need to know what I am supposed to be doing. Maybelle, very annoyingly, keeps my schedule mostly to herself and imparts snippets of it to me on a strict "need to know" basis.

I am also anxious, with a sort of dreadful curiosity, to know what happened when she went to London. I have left messages on her home answerphone and her mobile voicemail, emails, in case she lost her phone and a couple of text messages for good measure, all asking her to contact me. All, to no avail.

I have decided now that if I do not hear from her by the end of tomorrow, I will reluctantly have to discuss the situation with Google, myself. I do not want to have to do it, because I think it will give them an even worse impression of us, if we *both* appear to be snitching on each other. But I cannot do my job properly without the scheduling information she holds.

I am also missing her formidable organisational skills. She finds things I have lost, does a good job of arranging transport and hospitality and remembers things I have forgotten. Without her personal assistance, I have to admit that I am struggling in all of those respects, even though she does it all in a manner that is alternately complaining, criticising and condescending. In addition to this, she does all of the expense-submitting on our behalf. I do not even know how that system works and have resorted to just paying for things, keeping receipts and hoping for the best.

I have not really slept properly, since the weekend. My eyes feel gritty and my body aches. My stomach is perpetually churning and there is a burn of anxiety at the back of my neck and between my shoulders. I just need her to get in touch, or to come and see me and to explain everything honestly to me, even if it is bad news. I also need her to come and do her job again.

Usually, when I dial, I hear her voicemail message: 'I can't take your call. Leave a message,' in the snappy tone she always uses, when she wants to convey busyness and importance. But this time it rings and then stops, so I know that she has checked the caller, noticed it is me and then switched off her phone. *She isn't even pretending to not be avoiding me, she is* blatantly *avoiding me.*

For what feels like the millionth time, I wonder what is going through her head. But then, I get my coat and set off to my dad's house, because it is time for my visit and because he will comfort me just by his presence.

For the last forty years my dad has lived in his now ex-council house that he remembers being built, in the 1950s. He knows how much concrete is under the floor because he saw it being poured, a subject that comes up every time an electrician or plumber considers routing something under there. The garden is huge and beautiful, keeping him busy and healthy.

I am welcomed with a hug and an offer of tea, even though I have only come to collect him, so I end up in the middle of his huge, living-room sofa, stroking his cat and answering his questions about the project. I have come early, anyway, guessing this would happen.

'So… 'ow 'ave you got this London job?' he asks, in obvious confusion. This is something of a surprise to me, after all of the publicity, but social media is not really a part of my dad's life. His mobile phone, like that of many of his peers, is not a Smart one. And, although he has a computer, I think he uses it mainly for emails.

'They wanted the History Maps project, so they hired me to co-ordinate it,' I tell him simply.

'Right...' he answers. 'So tell me again, what exactly is the History Maps project?'

'Okay. You know Google Maps?' He nods. 'Well, it's the same thing. It's going to be part of that platform, but you'll be able to select a year and look at how each place probably was, back then. To the best of our knowledge now, anyway.'

'What, you're going to do that for every place on Google Maps? For every year? That's going to take forever, love! 'ow many people are working on it?'

''undreds, Dad! Soon, 'opefully, thousands.' I happily sink into our dialect with him.

'And are you in charge of all those people?'

'Not in charge, no. I'm just 'elpin' out and kinda pullin' it together.'

'Yeah but still, love, 'ow are you gonna do every year?'

'We're not, dad, we're starting with just a few. It'll grow organically after that, like a wiki.'

'Like a what, love?'

'You know, like Wikipedia. Anyone can contribute and it just gets bigger and bigger.'

'Oh! Right...' I suspect he still does not really get it.

'When it goes live on the site, there'll be over a hundred areas in the country who've all produced something for at least one date. So you'll be able to look at a part of Edgbaston as it was in 1948, for example. But that team – it's the local 'istory societies and the universities wekkin' together – they'll do another date after that. Then another and another, until eventually you'll have several time periods to look at, for that area. And the more we do, the more people will want to come onboard an' 'elp with it, so then the more we'll get done.'

'Eeh, love, that's gonna be good. Yes, I can see why you're doin' it, now. Do you want another biscuit? Oh. Looks like the cat wants to go out again.'

Arriving at the pub with him feels like being with a celebrity.

He insists on going through the main bar area, ('I just want a chat wi' Paul Pickersgill, if e's in, about that part for me car…')

And people quickly recognise him and call across: 'Eyyy! It's Jack Wilson! 'ow do, Jack?'

He plunges into the room in search of Paul and I am left standing there for a few minutes. But I no longer have celebrity status myself as his daughter, now that the man himself is here, so I am alone and undisturbed. Time to try Maybelle again, but with no luck.

I am just beginning to wonder whether I have lost my dad to the world of spare car parts, closely related to that of spare gardening tools, when he emerges from the fray, smiling. He now has a pint of foamy beer in one hand and a forever-to-be-unexplained, white plastic carrier bag in the other.

'Come on, lovey,' he urges. 'They'll be waiting for us upstairs!' and he bounds off up the stairs like a fifty year-old, while I trudge up them behind him like an eighty year-old, still checking my phone for signs of Maybelle.

By the time I have reached the top and got into the meeting room, my dad is already involved in the meeting, sitting with Ava and the others and pointing out things on her laptop. He reaches into his pocket for some old photographs he has brought with him and starts pointing, from them to the screen, obviously demonstrating which specific places they depict.

My dad is always so comfortable with people. He already knew Gail and Mary, and within about ten minutes he starts asking after Nick's antecedence and trying to place Ava's family locally, as well.

This, I silently observe, *is how the older generations kept their sense of belonging: by keeping track of all the families and putting people in their right place, within them. We've lost more than buildings, to the past. We've lost an entire way of thinking and being.* I smile to see him settling in, anyway. *I should have known I wouldn't need to make any introductions.*

Will and Adam are here, sitting at the next table together, each in their signature poses: Will, busy at his sketchpad and Adam, reading something on his phone. He looks like half of a whole unit, without Alf by his side. I sit down, opposite them and ask Adam the question I really did not want to have to ask, but feel to have little choice.

'Have you seen your mum, Adam? Or heard from her? I've been trying to get hold of her for days, now.'

'Well, Zoe...' he begins, looking awkward and worried. Then he looks towards the door with horror and the colour drains from his face. I turn around to look and there is Maybelle, with Colin in tow behind.

Colin! At an amateur history society meeting! He is looking extremely uncomfortable and keeps easing the collar away from his neck as if he is more used to wearing T-shirts, in a most uncharacteristic way.

I jump to my feet impulsively and approach her, saying, 'Maybelle, where have you been? I've been trying...'

But she silences me with a royal wave of the hand and walks past me to the table, shrilling, 'Not now, Zoe! The world doesn't revolve around you, remember!'

She plants a kiss on top of Adam's head saying, 'Hello darling. Mwah.' But he irritatedly jerks it away.

Undeterred, she grabs Colin's hand.

'Come in, darling. Come and meet my people. I feel so at home here, it's so *good* to come back to Yorkshire isn't it?' And he follows her into the room, uncertain of his movements, for the first time since I met him.

As for Maybelle, I am starting to wonder whether she is on drugs, she is so flamboyant. Her entrance has completely silenced the contented hum of the room and everyone is just watching her, probably waiting to see what she will do next. Some look worried and others, the ones who do not know her so well, are just curious.

Maybelle gets to the table and sees my dad surrounded by the others, a new face, to her, as she has never met him before.

'Oh, hellooo!' she says to him loudly, as if he might be deaf. 'Are you new here? I'm Maybelle. You've probably heard of me.'

My dad considers her for a few seconds and then speaks.

'Tha'art nobbut a lass, to me,' he says in his broadest dialect, reserved only for the very obnoxious. 'Si' thi', ah don't ken thee from Adam.'

It means: *'You are nothing but a girl to me. Do you see, I don't know you from Adam,'* and it is not particularly offensive. But Maybelle looks over to Adam, bewilderedly, having absolutely no idea what he has just said to her.

Ava is the first to laugh, followed by Mary's quiet chuckle and then Jo and Richard join in and it spreads, like ripples on a pond, until the whole group is roaring with laughter. It breaks the tension, like the fast rain of a pent-up storm and we should, theoretically, be able to just proceed with the meeting as before, now.

But Maybelle is furious. I can see Adam put his hands to his face at the sight of her, now and I feel like doing the same, because she is clenching her fists and actually stamping her feet. I suddenly remember that mocking laughter and public humiliation – however gentle and kindly-meant – are like kryptonite, to a narcissist.

'Shut up, you cretins!' she screeches. 'Shut *up! Imbeciles,* the lot of you! And *you!*' She advances upon my old dad, with her gleaming red, taloned index finger, extended in threat or accusation. 'How *dare* you come to *my* local meeting from nowhere and try to mock me like this? Don't you know who I *am?*'

'Well, *no, lass,*' answers my dad, evenly, the room having fallen silent once more, now. 'That's rather t'point, in't it?'

And everyone laughs. *Again.*

'*Colin!*' snaps Maybelle. '*Do* something!' And to the room, desperately: 'My partner is an eminent professor of History, at the university...' She pronounces it univ*aar*sity and there are tears in her voice, but the laughter does not abate. 'Oh! You're all *horrible!* Especially *you,* you old corpse,' to my dad. 'Which grave did they dig *you* up from?'

And then, the laughter stops. Even Colin looks shocked, by what she has just said. Suddenly, I am angry too, white hot fury stealing over me. I step forwards and grab her shoulder, so that she is facing me.

'That's my *dad,*' I tell her, tight-lipped.

She only looks surprised for a minute, then I see the familiar light of triumph in her eyes.

'Oh! Ho ho! Well!' She sounds manic now, fake-delighted. 'I should have known *that,* shouldn't I? Now you come to mention it, the resemblance is undeniable.' She sneers from me to my dad and back again.

I sigh deeply. *This is not getting us anywhere.*

'Maybelle, I need to talk to you. It's important. Let's go and sit over here. Please.'

She allows herself to be led to the far corner and slowly, people go back to what they were doing before, though I notice a lot of curious glances shooting over in our direction. Colin sits down, uneasily, near to Will and Adam and nods an awkward greeting to them. They nod an awkward greeting back. I feel sorry for all three of them.

'What's happened in London?' I ask her, straight away.

'Wouldn't *you* like to know?' smirks Maybelle, eyes sparkling with hatred and victorious glee.

'Well… yes! Yes, I would.'

'Well, you'll have to wait and see, won't you? Patience is a virtue, Zoe, though it's not one with which you're familiar, I know.' She starts speculatively rubbing the outside of her arms, apparently instantly recovered from her upset of just minutes ago.

'Right. I'll have to ask Rajesh, then.'

'You do that.' *She looks like the cat that's got the cream. Smug and gleaming.*

'It's not just that,' I persevere. 'Where have you been all week? You can't just go AWOL. I need…'

'"*I need, I need!*"' Maybelle mocks me in a whiny voice, waggling her head from side to side and pulling an exaggerated, sulky face. 'Everything is always about what *you need*, Zoe Taylor. Does it ever occur to you that some of us might need a break from *you,* from time to time? Some of us might need to think about other things than your selfish, over-bloated self.'

I look at her contemplatively, wondering what on earth to say next. And yes, a part of me wondering if what she is saying might be true, even just a little bit. *My body could be realistically – if unkindly – described as bloated and I can certainly be selfish.*

'You really hate me, don't you?' I venture eventually, from a place of now calm curiosity.

'Oh, Zoe. "*Me me me me,*" again. Anyone would think you'd make the most of an opportunity like this, especially when you might not have it much longer…' Still rubbing her arms. Slowly. Luxuriously. Utterly bizarrely.

'What?! What do you *mean?' I need to know what on earth she has said in London.*

Her exultant eyes know it and only now, it becomes clear to me that she is not going to voluntarily give me anything I want. I could kick myself, for being so gullible.

I stand up, pushing the chair aside, needing to get away from her. But also, needing to assert myself in some way, to rescue the situation as best as I can, now that my wits are about me again.

'Please, email my schedule to me and turn up to work tomorrow. I'll wait until ten o'clock. And if you haven't done that and turned up by then, I'm phoning Rajesh, to ask for a new PA.' My words are cold and dispassionate, which is how I feel, now.

Maybelle merely raises her eyebrows and gives the appearance of suppressing laughter.

'I *might* do,' she retorts. '*If* you've still got a job, by then.'

35

By nine-thirty the next morning, I am ready for Maybelle to arrive – or not. I am sitting at my desk trying to work out from emails what my schedule for this week should be. And I am worrying that I must be missing something and should be somewhere else, or at least on a train to somewhere else.

And the other part of my brain is thinking: *What's the point, if they're going to sack me anyway?* That self-sabotaging "me" has been convinced all along that I have never been up to the job and has felt to have been winging it from the start, always generating a background feeling of unease, which only goes away when I get lost in my work. *Imposter syndrome, I guess it's called.*

Maybelle's talent for honing in on my weaknesses, like an Exocet missile, is exceptional. I do not know how she knows where to attack, but for years she has been an occasional witness of my responses to various triggers and must have been quietly squirrelling all of this information away for future reference. I feel like I have been scanned by something on Star Trek, my innermost thoughts and being laid out bare on a mountain side, to be picked through like bones by the alien vulture, Maybelle.

I feel, I realise with a sharp intake of breath, entirely vulnerable to her and utterly at her mercy.

This makes me scrabble around in my mind for compensatory factors and points of safety and strength. I know my job, to the extent that I can see what needs to be done and I can and do successfully convey this to other people, whenever required. I might not be able to organise my time or documentation very well, but I can inspire and reassure people, depending on what they need.

And I love it. And I can't imagine Maybelle being able to do any of that. She can't tell the difference between a Victorian brick and a new one and – more to the point – she's not sufficiently motivated to learn how. She simply has no interest in the project, which begs one or two questions. Why has she stayed on board with it? And who does she imagine would replace me, if she did manage to get me sacked?

I force myself to consider this, because, surely, anyone at Google could do it just as well as I can. They are all dynamic, intelligent people, although one of the essential criteria is a passion for history and I would hazard a guess that is not shared by many Google employees. It needs more than a passing interest: the person would have to possess the skill of being able to spot the clues in a building of its history. In putting two maps together and working out what happened in between them. And in knowing where to look in archives and seeking people out for memories.

The people: they make this project. Whoever runs it after me will have to be able to inspire people, get them interested and make sure they know that their contribution is wanted and needed.

David Crossley, for example, would be brilliant on the history side, but less strong when it comes to engaging people. He is a lovely man, peaceful and friendly, but will sit quietly listening, rather than intervening and taking an active role in group conversations. I wonder what he is like as a tutor. And then, who else would do my job well, if not David. Suddenly, the likely candidate is there in my mind.

Of course. Why has it only just dawned on me? The replacement for me, who Maybelle at least probably has in mind... is Colin Pritchard.

Professor Pritchard has vast technical knowledge of history

and how we discover more about it. He will have better ideas than mine, about how to organise and display this whole thing. And he has flair and charisma – or he used to have, before the days of his affair with Maybelle. Since then, he has seemed a bit lost, but I have not seen much of him since Nottingham, so those might have been off-days.

Above all else, Pritchard has the attribute I most lack: self-confidence. It comes from his gender, his expensive suits, his high salary, his title and position and his decades in the field. *How can I rival that, with my housewife-based curriculum vitae?*

Ironically, I was originally hoping he would volunteer to head the project, when I first went to see him in his office last year and was sent away with a flea in my ear. *So why would I mind now, if he did?* We would lose my salary, which would mean more stress for Hugh, though I would get to see more of him and Amy. But it is still not about the money, for me. Before the project took off, it was about making it happen. Nowadays it still is that, but I never predicted the extent to which I would so thoroughly enjoy the job I have been given to do.

I love explaining it to people and showing them how it works. I love watching the interactions between middle aged and elderly amateur historians and university students that we have brought about, in which both parties are enriched and seem to come away feeling more grounded, heard and accepted. I love their joyful, incredulous faces, when they see their part of the project working for the first time and I myself love to see the whole thing taking off and taking shape. These are the things I will desperately miss, if Colin takes over. And I am not sure if even Colin could pull it all together properly, in spite of his extra kudos and bearing. I do not know whether he would be sufficiently approachable.

Still, when did that ever stop the men in grey suits? They breeze through life, getting the job done, not really caring what the rank and file thinks of them. Earning their high salaries, zooming about impatiently in their brand new Audis, feeling – and being, in the grand scheme of things – more important than the rest of us. Could I entrust my baby, my precious fledgling project, to someone like that? Well, I'll have no choice, since I signed it over to Google. It's up to them.

And, looking at the clock, I realise I will have to call them soon to discover my fate, as Maybelle, predictably, has not arrived.

Right on cue, the doorbell rings. I am absolutely not expecting it to be her and I am wondering whether one of us has ordered a parcel, as I go to answer it. When I open the door and see her standing there, I am shocked.

But I do not have the luxury of gaping at her for long, as she pushes past me and barrels down the hallway into the sitting room, the words: 'Come on! Let's get on with it!' cast in her wake.

'I didn't expect to see you,' I comment, as I sit back down at my desk. 'You still haven't sent my schedule through, so I assumed you'd be resigning.'

'Huh!' she exclaims. '*Me*, resigning? Oh no, dear, that won't be me. I'm a professional – unlike *you*, Zoe. Fancy, not knowing your own schedule!'

I can see that this is going to be as difficult as ever.

'Maybelle, knowing and organising my schedule is supposed to be *your* job.'

'Hmm. And co-ordinating the project *was* supposed to be yours. I take it Rajesh hasn't called you, yet?'

'No. I was just about to call him, when you turned up in the nick of time, as if you'd been waiting outside for the clock to strike ten.'

'Oh! Well, he's going to call you today, at some point. I'd have thought he'd have done it by now.' She looks about her in disgust at our furniture, books, pictures and ornaments. 'We're really going to have to tell them we need an office in the future for this project. Not that that's anything for *you* to worry about.'

My heart plummets, lower than it has for a long time. I try to hide it from her, but of course, I cannot. My eyes fill with tears and I wipe them away, annoyed with myself for the lack of control.

'Oh, *poor Zoe!*' Maybelle mocks, sing-song. 'She's finally going to discover that the whole world really doesn't revolve around her. You had to realise it, sooner or later.' She looks at me directly, unblinking. I try to return the direct look, but we both know I cannot. Instead, I busy myself looking for a tissue and then, finding one, concentrate on blowing my nose and trying to pretend I have a cold.

'Why do you do this, Maybelle?' I ask, eventually. 'I don't understand why you seem to want to run me down all the time. I don't even understand your interest in the project, come to that. You don't even like history, let alone me.'

She performs an exaggerated eye roll to this and slumps her shoulders, in dramatic exasperation.

'Ugh! *Yet again* I have to say, *the world does not revolve around you!* I've got *far* better things to do with my time, than to *run you down*, as you put it. Honestly Zoe, get over yourself. We've got work to do.'

But I am determined to push for a little more, to see how far I can get. *I might as well, if I'm losing my job anyway.*

'Did something horrible happen to you as a child, Maybelle? Something traumatic, that you never got to process properly? I've heard that can cause lifelong feelings of upset and anger, without the person ever realising where it's come from...'

'Sorry, but that comes over to me as amateur psychobabble and it doesn't impress me.'

'Um... it wasn't meant to *impress* you. It was meant to help you!'

'I think you'll find that *I'm* not the one needing help, Zoe. Try looking in a mirror sometime. Meanwhile,' she heaves a heavy sigh and takes her iPad out of her bag, '*Could* we get down to business?'

And we conduct the rest of our meeting as if the Sword of Damocles is not hanging over my head, both pretending everything is normal, punctuated by Maybelle's snide asides, as usual. But I must not have abandoned all hope, because I am careful to take a snapshot of my schedule, when she leaves her iPad open on it, to go to the bathroom.

On her return, she clicks away from it and looks at me accusingly, which I ignore. I feel some welcome relief, though, amid the worry and the gloom.

If I stay, at least I will know what I am supposed to be doing, in the next few weeks.

It is almost evening by the time Rajesh calls me. I have been through so many stages of fear, anger and finally acceptance, through the day, that I feel exhausted, but ready to hear whatever he has to tell me.

I take a deep breath. And press "answer".

36

I hear a click and then Rajesh's rich, drawling voice.

'Zoe? Hi, how's it going?'

I am not sure whether this is his transatlantic way of asking how I am, or if he is actually wanting information about the project, so I hedge my bets by responding: 'Okay, thanks...'

'Good, good. Okay, so, first of all, Zoe, I need to tell you about a meeting I had with Maybelle, at her request.'

'Okay...' *This is it, straight away. So little preamble.*

'So, she asked for the meeting, so that she could share with me some concerns she's been having. These seem to fall into two distinct categories. Firstly, she's worried about your performance. She raised issues about your organisational skills and your effectiveness in the role. I have to say, Zoe...' *This is definitely it.* '...I don't share those concerns at all. In fact, I don't think it reflects well on her that she made them, especially as it's supposed to be part of her job to help you to be more organised.'

'Oh! Okay.' *There's surely going to be more bad news.* This conversation seems to bear the weight of many more words before it is over.

'As for your effectiveness, we've been receiving feedback from the teams you've visited around the country and there have been no complaints about you, from any of them at all. Some of the people you've addressed in your seminars have posted videos online of you in action...' This is news to me.

'All of which I've watched and I want to tell you that I'm very impressed by your approach.'

He wants to tell me? Does that mean he wants to, but can't for some reason? No, Zoe, don't be paranoid. He is actually telling me that he's impressed.

He continues, without giving me space to thank him for his kind words.

'In fact, I think it's due to the success of what you've been doing – as well as the teams themselves, of course – that we're ready to talk about setting a launch date now. But I'll tell you about the other category of Maybelle's concerns first.'

A launch date! And it includes me! It is only now, that I start to believe my job might be at least currently secure, though there is obviously more Maybelle-related trouble to come.

'So, I don't know if you remember, but when we met you for the first time she raised a question about your ownership of the concept?'

'Um...' My mouth is going dry, now. 'Yes, I do remember...'

'So, it was just that again.' *Just* that? 'She's pushing the point, somewhat, that you and she came up with it together. When you were homeschooling your two boys.'

I cannot help releasing a nervous laugh, even though it is not funny.

'Rajesh, we *didn't* come up with it together. Maybelle has no interest in history...'

Rajesh laughs himself, at this point.

'Ah, yeah, I kinda worked that out, from talking with her...'

'She rarely attended the history outings I'd make with both the boys, because they bored her so much.'

'Okay. Zoe, I want you to know that I definitely believe you on this.' This is what I needed to hear, but did not realise it until I heard it. Tears of gratitude and relief splash down my face and, when I softly thank him, I think he must be able to hear them. My whole body feels relaxed and euphoric, like a hot air balloon, that has been untethered from the ground.

'But...' The balloon is being re-tethered. *I must stay grounded. I'm not out of trouble yet.* 'It would be better if you had some way of proving it, to put paid to her claim, once and for all. Otherwise, it could become a legal issue which – although I think we would win...' His use of the word *'we'* gives me a warm swell of happiness. '...we really don't want the hassle. If it can be avoided. So, can you think of anything you could provide by way of proof, that this is your concept and yours alone?'

'Well, I talked to lots of people about it...'

'Okay, what kind of people?'

'Well, my husband and various friends... the local history society...'

'And Maybelle wasn't involved in any of those conversations?'

'Not the early ones, no. She got involved a few weeks later, when things started happening. You know, when it started to become an actual project.'

'Okay. This is good...' The way he says *good* indicates that it is not quite good enough. 'Testimonies from people like that will all help, if you can start to gather them. But what would be really useful would be a testimony from someone who could be called eminent. Did you happen to discuss it with anyone in academia, for example, before Maybelle became involved?'

'Well, yes! I went to see Professor Pritchard about it at the university!'

Before Rajesh answers, my spirits slump, as I realise for myself the likelihood of this actually helping my case.

'Colin Pritchard?' asks Rajesh.

'Yes,' I confirm sadly, already knowing what he is going to say next.

'Ah. Yeah. He was with Maybelle in our meeting. I got the impression they're a couple, now?'

'Yes, they do seem to be,' I am forced to agree.

'So...'

'Yes. He's not likely to want to help me.'

'I mean, I don't know, it depends on the depth of friendship you guys share, I guess...'

'It's not deep enough.'

'Okay, okay. Leave it with me. You gather what testimonials you can and try not to worry about any of this. A person only has to spend five minutes, with both you and Maybelle, to know where this idea came from. In my personal opinion, it's likely that she'd fall on her face in a court room. But obviously, we want to try to avoid that if we can. If not, so be it.'

'Okay! I'll get as many as I can.' I am still worried that the only person who could provide sufficiently convincing proof of my concept ownership is Colin, *of all people.*

'So... that all leads me onto my next question. Do you still want Maybelle to be your personal assistant, now that she's raised these complaints about you?'

This is a choice I was *not* expecting to be presented with today and not one I find instinctively easy to make. It would be so simple, to just ask Rajesh to sack her, which is effectively what she has done to me. But I am not a vindictive person, so I would need more of a reason than reciprocation. I am also still flooded with relief and happiness, which is imbuing me with a spirit of benign generosity and forgiveness.

But Maybelle has tried, is still trying and will continue to try, to stab me in the back. This much, I know. She wants to make me feel and look stupid, get me sacked and claim ownership of the project for herself. Though I am not seeing these as the serious threats I was, before this conversation.

I have to also consider that she is good at her job and she does know me well. She knows, for example, that if she tells me the night before that we have a train to catch on the following morning, I will need to be told again in the morning, an hour before we are due to leave, or we will miss the train.

She knows I am likely to forget my phone or laptop charger and, quite often, both. So she brings a spare one of each. I get fully berated, often in public, each time she has to pull such a thing out of her bag to give to me, but the point is, she always has them. And umbrellas, in case of rain. And the right train tickets. And she is usually ready to supply me with the names and positions of the key people I am about to meet, though she sometimes maliciously hoards this information and smiles, to watch me trying to manage without it.

I have learned how to keep her malice to a minimum, though. Never be too ebullient or confident, which Maybelle interprets as smugness that must be punished. Try to never receive compliments in her hearing and never be tempted to confide in her, because the information she gleans from this will always be used against me.

If I follow those rules, all the time, without fail, will it be safe for me to keep working with her?

'Zoe?' I must have been thinking in silence, for a couple of minutes.

'Sorry, Rajesh, I was thinking it through. Um, can I say yes, for now? And review it in a few months?'

'Yes, of course. Her contract isn't time specific, so we can let her go any time with a month's notice. I must say I'm surprised, though, Zoe. Is she very good at her job?'

'She is, actually. Surprisingly good in some ways and less good in others. I just think that if we're talking about planning a launch day for the near future, it's probably not a good time for me to be getting used to a new assistant.'

'Yeah, that's a good point. So, we'll leave her in post for now and see how that goes.' Something about the tone of his voice, in those last few words, tells me that he is not optimistic it will go well. I am pleased, though. It feels good to know there will be some light at the end, if the tunnel of working with

Maybelle becomes particularly dark.

'Now, onto the launch,' says Rajesh. 'I'm thinking, we should incorporate Daydream in some way.'

This is followed by another long silence from me, as I try to work out what he means.

'You know? Our VR platform?'

"VR" rings a bell in my mind and I know that I *should* know what it is, but right now, I cannot think.

'Virtual Reality…?' I can hear the laugh in his tone and I return it.

'Ohhh! Yes! *Wow!* That will be… quite something! But I mean… have you got enough space for that?'

I am imagining everyone walking around through the various maps. They will effectively *be* the little yellow Google Street View man. I can picture us all, bumping into each other, as we all try to explore our own individual versions of the map. Or maybe there is some way of us being visible to each other on the network, to prevent that from happening.

Rajesh is laughing out loud, now, so much that he can hardly talk for it, which makes me laugh, too.

'No, Zoe! That's not how it works! I'll have a set sent to you and you'll see. You stand still and use a handset, to navigate. It kinda feels like walking around and everyone moves their feet instinctively. But you have to learn to stand or sit still and use the handset instead.'

'Wow.'

A whole fireworks display is going off in my brain, as I start to consider the ramifications of this.

And then, suddenly, I realise: *my dad will be able to visit his old street, again.*

37

I have bought a poster-sized map of the UK and stuck it onto a cork board. I am in the process of sticking pins into all of our current project areas, when Maybelle strolls into the sitting room, having evidently stopped bothering with the doorbell.

I have some pins in my mouth and probably look something like a dressmaker at work, alternately bending forwards, to see the detail and stepping back, to observe the overall effect. I can see already that we are thin on the ground in Wales and Scotland and there are large, pin-less areas in Norfolk and Gloucestershire. Also, our relatively nearby Cumbria is looking sparse, which surprises me.

'What on *earth* are you doing now?' Maybelle exclaims, throwing her handbag on the sofa and coming closer to peer at the map, before stepping back herself for the bigger picture. 'Zoe, you do know that we have these amazing new inventions called *computers,* now? Why must you insist on doing everything on *paper?* You're the only person I know who still does.'

'You and I both grew up in the age of paper, Maybelle,' I respond equably, after I have removed the pins from my mouth. 'It just works better with my brain.'

'Huh! Speak for yourself,' she responds, even though I know for a fact that she is only a year younger than I am. 'Anyway, why are you still working? Didn't Rajesh give you your marching orders? A month's notice, I suppose...'

I give a short laugh to this and proceed to pop the bubble of her wishful thinking, which I can imagine doing, neatly, with one of my map pins.

'Actually, no! He's very happy with my work. In fact, we need to start gearing up for the national launch of Google History Maps. Hence the map.'

'Oh *God,* I suppose you managed to charm him, somehow. Your talents are wasted in this role. You should have been a prostitute.'

I laugh out loud, before remembering the dangers of ebullience in Maybelle's company. I open my mouth, to tell her about the videos Rajesh has been watching and the feedback he has received.

But then I stop myself in time and content myself with an ambiguous shrug and a: 'Yeah, maybe.'

Feeling the time pressure of the launch, which is likely to take place within the next six months, I follow on with some speculations about the empty areas of the map.

'I suppose they are some of the least populated areas…'

'Well, *duh!*' contributes Maybelle, unhelpfully.

I stop peering at the map and turn, to look at her.

'I'm just wondering if we can get any new projects going, at this late stage. Another publicity drive might do it.'

'Isn't that all Google's department, now?'

'I'd need their agreement and their help, of course. But we haven't been very proactive yet, in generating new local schemes, have we? We've been *re*active: waiting for people to contact us and show an interest, which they did a lot, just after our local project launch went viral.'

'I can't imagine you ever being anything other than *re*active…' mutters Maybelle, automatically I think, lest she misses an opportunity to snipe.

'Hmm. I'm going to go and see Rachel and get her views on the matter.'

'"*I'm gonna go and see Rachel!*"' mimics my assistant, in the high-pitched, whiny tone she always uses to impersonate me. 'Can you not do anything without running it past *Rachel* first?'

I open my mouth, to list the many things I have been doing, since I last saw Rachel and then close it again. Instead, I scribble a note for myself to check my own – secretly photographed – version of my schedule and fit in a slot for a Rachel lunch. The very thought of it makes me smile. *In terms of nourishing friendship input, it will be the oasis in my current desert.*

I hear the door go again and go through, to see who has arrived. It is my dad, slightly bewilderedly holding a package from the delivery man he must have accidentally met on the driveway.

''Ello, lovey. You've got a parcel to open. It's not your birthday, is it?'

I can never tell when he is joking, so I just say, 'No, Dad. Come on in, we're in the sitting room.'

My dad ignores Maybelle and makes straight for the map.

'Oh! It's a pin map!' he pronounces, in great delight. 'I like a good pin map. What's it showin'?'

I start to tell him, but Maybelle interrupts, before I can get a word out.

'Oh! It's the *unintelligible* one. I can't tell a word he's saying, Zoe. You'll have to interpret.'

I see the light of mischief in my dad's eye, before he speaks.

'Tha's got yon clarht-eead eya. Shi mun git a'gate: shi's allus martherin' abart summat. 'Supwier?'

I am not going to translate this for Maybelle, but in English it means: *'You have the stupid woman here. She must go away: she is always complaining about something. What is wrong with her?'* My dad's dialect is not usually this broad, but obviously their previous meeting has set a pattern, for this and all of their future encounters, out of which my dad will wring maximum enjoyment.

To Maybelle, I say: 'My dad says hello,' and to my dad, leading him determinedly *off* the subject of Maybelle in case she ever does understand anything he says, I respond: 'It's a map to show the current History Maps projects that are underway around the country.'

'By! Thi's a lot! Tha's been wekkin' 'ard, lass,' says my dad, still in broad dialect.

I sigh a little. *This is going to be hard work, because he'll keep it up, for as long as Maybelle's in the room.*

'We have been working hard, but all of these pins aren't down to us. We haven't worked directly with all of them. Some of them have just been following the videos we made, on Youtube.'

'By 'eck, it's reight tekkin off!'

'What's he *saying?*' asks Maybelle plaintively.

'That was an easy one!' I tell her. 'He's saying it's doing well!'

'Tha' mun git thi' lug 'oils fettled, lass. Tha'art diff as a po-ast!' He is telling her that she is deaf and must get her ears syringed.

Maybelle must at least have detected an insult, because she puerilely sticks her tongue out at him, in response and says: 'Shut up, you nasty old man!' My dad laughs and I sigh again and raise my eyes to heaven.

I want to offer him a cup of tea, but I am worried about leaving them alone, while I go to make it. I ought to be able to ask Maybelle to make it as she is supposed to be my assistant, but I know there is no chance she would ever agree to do that.

'Oppen thi paarcel then, lovey!' my dad chivvies me, proffering said package in my direction.

Thinking: *Oh, well, at least this'll distract them from their bickering...* I pick up the letter-opener from the mantelpiece and start to attack the tape. It is a big package and the reason for this soon becomes apparent: it contains both the Virtual Reality set *and* a box containing what looks like a new Google

Pixel phone.

A handwritten note from Rajesh falls out of it, saying: '*Zoe, you'll need this phone to work the VR set. I don't think it will work with yours. I've set it up for you, so that you should just be able to switch them both on and put the phone into the headset, then you're good to go! See you soon. Rajesh x.*'

I read the note and cannot help smiling to myself, that familiar glow of happiness, gently warming my chest. Almost as soon as I have put it down on the table, Maybelle snatches it up and out of the corner of my eye, I can see her devouring the words with gleaming eyes, her mouth set tight. She replaces it and I can nearly hear the *click* of our metaphorical reckoning-sheet, shifting at least one position against me. The warm glow is replaced by a weight of foreboding. But my dad has already grabbed the Daydream set, such is his enthusiasm for new technology.

'Dad, I need to...' I start, before reasoning that he probably is not going to do any damage to it and anyway, I need to read the instructions, before I am going to try to do anything with it myself. I fish them out of the box and begin reading.

'Aren't we going to get a cup of tea?' asks Maybelle. 'I mean, I could watch you two monkeying around with your new toys all day, but I might die of thirst before any actual *work* happens around here.'

I take the leaflet into the kitchen, fill the kettle and switch it on, grabbing cups and tea bags, while I try to read at the same time. But the kettle has not even boiled, before I am being called back into the sitting room, by Maybelle.

My dad is in the middle of the room with the VR set on his head and the handsets clasped in his grip. Both his profile and his gait resemble nothing more than a spaceman. As I am standing there with my mouth agape, he crashes into the coffee table with one of his big strides, only just managing to remain upright.

'*Dad!* Dad, take it off!' I start tugging at the headset, but he snatches his head away and pushes it up onto his forehead, revealing his grinning face and bright, excited eyes. This is what I always privately term his mad professor face.

'Eeh *lovey.* It's a *crackin'* bit o' kit, this is! Ye can see *everythin'!'*

It is only when I ask if I can look too, that he agrees to part with it and I take up the handset and slip the Daydream onto my head, surprised at how light and comfortable it feels.

I just about hear Maybelle's sharp reminder about '...the *tea...*' and then I am transported into another world, albeit one that is just a few virtual feet away.

It is the outside of our house. *Our driveway!* I turn around in a three hundred and sixty degree arc, to check that everything is as it should be and realise it is the same image that comes up on Google Street View, when I look on my phone or computer: I think it was taken last year, because the cars are our previous ones, not the ones we have now.

I want to move and I take an impulsive step with my feet, until I remember Rajesh's laughing words, hearing his voice in my mind: *'You stand still and use a handset to navigate! It kinda feels like walking around and everyone moves their feet instinctively, but you have to learn to stand or sit still and use the handset.'* So I tentatively press a button and see a white arrow, extending into the tarmac. Using that, I work out how to click on it and shift my position forwards, correspondingly. A few more clicks and I am halfway down our street. But then, I feel a sharp tap on my shoulder.

Reluctantly, slowly, I remove the apparatus from my head and blink to adjust my eyes to the room again. Maybelle's irate visage fills my field of vision and her sharp voice fills my ears and my consciousness.

'Zoe! Zoe! I've been shouting you for ages!'

She can't have been, is my unspoken response. *I've only had the thing on my head for about three seconds.*

'I'm... going... out... for... *lunch*,' she informs me, slowly, as if I am slow of understanding. 'Let me know when you've finished messing about.'

And she is gone, with a slam of the door. Dad and I look at each other in silence for an instant and then, we both grin.

'My turn!' he says, grabbing the set. I press the controller into his hand and tell him *not* to move his feet.

Maybelle is right, though. The day is lost.

38

After much calendar juggling, Rachel and I end up meeting mid-morning, in Starbucks. We are both too busy to manage lunch, or even dinner, at short notice. As I go in, I can see she is here already, having chosen the exact seats I would have chosen: the orange leather barrel chairs. By far, the most comfortable in the whole place.

She has a new hairstyle: a sweep of her natural, platinum blonde, coursing from left to right and shimmering in the sun. It suits her and I tell her so, after I have ordered my chai latté and sat down to join her.

She grins her acknowledgement of the compliment and returns one for me.

'You're looking very different, too. Slimmer and more... alive. Racing around the countryside with Maybelle, of all people, seems to suit you!'

All I can do is smile ruefully and tell her it keeps me on my toes.

Rachel sits forward and plants her elbows on the table, propping her face up in the palms of her hands. She is smiling, mischievously.

'First question. I've got to ask it. What has that woman been up to? There's always something.'

At this point, I am called to go and collect my drink, which gives me chance to consider my response. I really do not want this conversation to be dominated by Maybelle, as so many others invariably have been.

So when I return, sipping the cinnamony concoction, I just say, 'Oh, you know, the usual routine. Insult, put-down, try to get me sacked. None of it is working, though. It seems like Rajesh at Google is on my side, no matter what she does. He's fab.'

Rachel takes a swallow of her own drink and sits up.

'I know!' she smiles. 'He got in touch with us, to see if we want to come on board for the national launch PR.'

This is a complete surprise to me and a joyful one. I have so many questions, I do not know where to start.

'*Wow!* No! *Wow!* Oh, I hope you decide you will. What capacity does he want you in?'

She is smiling even more broadly, now, either at my reaction, or at whatever is coming next.

'He wants me to do what I did last time,' she responds in her usual gentle, low tones, which are music to my ear. 'I don't know how he knew what I did...'

'I told him,' I put in. 'I mean, he'd worked out a lot of it, or someone else had told him already. But I filled in the gaps. It was months ago, though! I never imagined it would lead to this.'

'I just assumed they'd expect Maybelle to do that sort of thing. But he said they need more of a PR specialist, to help you through the launch.'

I am taking a drink, when I hear this and I nearly choke.

'*Maybelle?!* Ha! She'd have me turning up to the wrong venue, with my face on back-to-front!'

Rachel giggles, a tinkling peal of harmonious notes.

'So, anyway, if I can carve out the time, which I think I can, I'm going to do it. I'm so happy to know we're going to be working together again soon. You have to bring me up to date, though! What's been happening?'

I really cannot wait to tell her.

'Workshops and seminars! Everywhere. Well, nearly everywhere and that's something I want to pick your brains about. Oh, but Rachel, I've been having *so much fun!* I never imagined I'd enjoy it this much! Not the travel, obviously, or the way things are with Maybelle but, you know, she gets us where we need to be with the right print-outs and software. She can do that side of her job, perfectly well.'

'Wow, your face lit up, when you were talking about the work you do! What exactly happens at these seminars and workshops? How do they go?'

Explaining it all to her feels like she has allowed me to unwrap an amazing gift on her behalf, for our mutual pleasure.

'The seminars are to set out how it all works. They get to ask questions, we get to explain stuff, show examples and so on. We use projectors, print-outs, or, if they're a tech-savvy group, we'll just share the documents to their devices.'

'We?'

'Ah! Yes, sometimes it's just me. But if I'm lucky, one of the boys is free to join us for the seminar part. Or David comes. Or Colin.'

My face must have soured at Colin's name, because Rachel raises her eyebrows, by way of a question.

I feel dejected, just saying it. Somehow, Maybelle always manages to take the edge off everything that should be fun.

'Colin and Maybelle are together, now. They're a couple.'

Rachel is not one for big reactions and merely widens her eyes in surprise and then grimaces.

'Wow,' and 'That must make things a bit difficult for you,' are her only comments.

It is tempting to take the chance for some self-indulgent complaining about it all and to wallow in the warm bath of Rachel's nourishing sympathy, but I am learning not to waste my precious time on Maybelle's antics, so I just say: 'Yeah,' and then get back on track.

'So, most of them just need a little help after the seminar, in getting started. We don't want to do it all for them. Well, we can't, we don't have the resources and that's not what it's all about, of course. But we usually run a couple of workshops and we do a bit of liaison work, between the universities and the amateurs. Otherwise, in some cases, they'd never speak to each other.'

'The amateurs too lacking in confidence and the universities too snooty?'

I grin.

'Yeah, that pretty much sums it up, whenever there is a problem. Although I wouldn't say so to them, of course. Sometimes we hit lucky with a cross-over, as we did in David, and then that's the bridge we need to get them together. Other times, we arrange meetings, but both sides can take some persuading. Colin's been a big help with that, actually. Apparently, he's pretty influential in his field.'

'Right. And the lure of Maybelle gets him there, more often than he would be otherwise, I imagine...' speculates Rachel, accurately, as usual.

'Yep. But I try to focus on the positives,' I laugh.

'So which part do you enjoy the most?' she asks, and I take a drink and a moment to appreciate her generosity of character. She is so rooted and peaceful, that she can take such a deep interest in things outside of herself, without rancour or impatience. I think I will always aspire to be more like Rachel.

'The seminars, the workshops or the liaison work, you mean? Hmm. Definitely not the liaison work, although that's nice, when it finally comes together. The seminars are fun, but kind of routine now, depending on who's presenting it with me, if anyone. I'm not so keen on the ones I do on my own, although they tend to go okay. It's just so much better when there's someone else for, say, the technical questions, or the historical detail, or to talk about the art work.

'It's great when Will's there, or David and of course it's wonderful when Alf or even Adam can come, though they can really only get to the northern ones, because they're all so busy. Ollie is London-based now, of course, and he tries to come to anything we're doing in the south-east. You can imagine how much easier it is, to have him around!'

Rachel is nodding, her kindly eyes sparkling.

'It sounds like it's the workshops that you like the best, then…?'

My enthusiasm bubbles over now, and I say, 'YES!' a little too loudly, before looking around to see if anyone heard. We are both grinning. 'I *love* the workshops. By the time we do one, they already know from the seminar what the process is, and the liaison work has brought some students and maybe a couple of interested tutors in and the ideas just flow. There's always at least one graphic artist and, you know, they love putting pen to paper or stylus to tablet, depending on how they work. Some of the conversations… well, I wish I'd recorded them all.

'But it generates a proper feeling of *community,* you know? That thing we've been missing in our society for so long. Old people and young people, working together, to create something they both want. Ah, I could happily witness that, every day for the rest of my life.'

'Wow, so it's more than the street scenes you're creating, then, isn't it?'

'Well, yes. I mean, it's not me doing it, it's the project. And the people. They do all the work.'

'You build the fire and put the match to it.'

'Yes! To some extent, I guess. Well, me and whoever is helping. I just hope we don't accidentally burn the place down!' We both collapse into giggles.

'So. What happens next?' Rachel asks eventually, when we've settled down. 'Are you on track for the launch?'

'Yeah...' My uncertainty comes across in my voice.

'But?'

'Oh, it's the dark patches on the map that are worrying me. Here, I took a photo.' I find the snapshot of my giant pin map on my phone and pass it over to her, adding, 'We don't seem to have been able to reach many people in places like Wales, East Anglia, Scotland, although most of the cities have a project. But hundreds of the towns just don't and I'm struggling to work out why and what we can do about it, if anything. Even Cumbria has nothing, and that place is *steeped* in history.'

'Well, they all are,' inputs Rachel, pragmatically.

'Yeah, but it's just that Cumbria is so close to Yorkshire. I think that's what's bugging me about it. Why has nobody from there got in touch with us? Do they not *have* local history societies? Actually, they don't, really. Not as many as elsewhere.'

'When you think about it, though, how much has actually changed in those places in the last few hundred years?'

'Well, not much, I guess. Do you think that might be the explanation? They haven't really lost anything, so they don't need to get excited about reclaiming it?'

'Yes, probably that and population density. How many people does it take to make a project?'

I can answer that straight away, without even having to think about it.

'About thirty. I mean, the more the better, obviously, but they struggle with fewer than thirty. Ideally, at least ten of those come from the university and the other twenty are from the local history society. Or get drawn in by the project from elsewhere, when it starts.'

'Right, so, in the towns and cities that are participating, what's the background population size?'

'I see where you're going. It's bigger.'

'And there has to be a university?'

'It certainly helps. Some of the universities send students out to all of their local projects, but it has to be within easy travelling distance.'

'Yeah. You need a different colour of pin for each university and some shaded areas, to indicate population density, on this map. Then, you'd have your answer, I think.'

It all clicks into place in my mind, now. *I need a meeting with Rachel every day, not every few months!* I am also wondering why Maybelle and I could not have worked this out, when we were standing in front of the map, the other day. It seems so obvious, now.

'I've got to go,' says Rachel, grabbing her bag. 'But, before I do, one more quick question. This is the UK launch, but what happens after that? Presumably, it's going to be a global thing.'

My pulse quickens at the thought of it. I take a deep breath, to calm down, but cannot help grinning.

'Yep. I won't be heading those, though. I think there'll still be a lot for me to do in this country, as it keeps evolving. There will always be new projects. Google is going to find someone from each participating country, to do my job there.'

'Ah! I wondered whether you'd be going international, too.'

The very thought of all the long haul flights makes me feel overwhelmed and tired.

'No,' I tell her, with a grimace. 'The UK is quite enough, for me.'

She kisses the top of my head and takes her leave, a gentle summery waft of perfume following in her wake.

I sit for a few minutes, basking in the knowledge that before long, we will be working together again.

39

From the viewing platform of the castle at Scarborough, I can see the entirety of the south beach and harbour and the majority of the town buildings. A red-bricked, ridge-roofed Victorian structure dominates the ones around it and is still labelled, in letters clearly visible from this position, PUBLIC market. The rest of that part of town seems to cluster around it: a clear sign of how things used to be.

If it was all rebuilt now, I ponder, *they'd cluster around the seafront, where the tourists want to be.* The new supermarkets are well out of town. Out of sight and mind, until people jump in their cars to go and use them. *We've successfully separated our shopping from our living and our holidaying and it's probably cars – progress – technology, that allows for this. And, as with everything else, there are both benefits and drawbacks.*

I wonder what the people of Scarborough are doing, now, with their old public market building and I make a mental note to find out.

I can hear the mixed roars of the sea and the damp, warm, salty wind coming off it, punctuated by the almost supernatural shrieks of the many seagulls, confident and lithe. I cannot hear the town, which, Wikipedia informs me, now has a population of more than sixty thousand people.

Earlier today, we were twenty miles further up the east coast at Whitby Abbey, which sits similarly above its own town, whose many dwellings and shops gather around the harbour below. As at Scarborough, the two are together and yet separate and reading about their respective social and economic histories bears this out. In Whitby, the monks were permitted by the king to tax the townsfolk quite heavily, so there was resulting animosity between the two. At Scarborough, the castle housed a garrison and eventually a prison, with both towns taking opposite sides in the Civil War.

And now, today, on this glorious working holiday – as the sea air is encouraging me to view it – there is still disparity between the two ancient, windswept headland buildings and their vibrant, burgeoning towns below. *It's still the same essential argument,* I realise, as I pick out the white lighthouse, the church and the spa theatre and pavilion, *between the haves and the have-nots. Between those above and those below. Between the people with the power, the position and the money and the multitude of ordinary residents who earn a living, are taxed and have to spend everything else on bills.*

From this, I know from personal experience, there is often nothing remaining, to cover even the hundred pounds annual subscription to English Heritage required for each family to enjoy its local landmarks on a regular basis. This thought makes me even more excited than usual about Google History Maps and the depth of freely shared and easy-to-access information it will contain.

Apart from enjoying the ruins and learning about the history, I have spent much of the day encouraging the local history societies to talk to the university and vice versa. It does not help that the campus at Scarborough is an annexe of Coventry University and runs no history courses. And Whitby is without university, so we are liaising with the one at York, instead. This, at least, has a very strong, pro-collaboration History Department which is excited about working on History Maps projects anywhere. But the local people in both seaside towns live more than forty miles away and are struggling to see the York students and professors as locals, in any sense.

English Heritage has assigned a volunteer to work with me today, a retired man called Philip, whose knowledge of local history seems to know no bounds. He is also fluent in both French and Italian, I have discovered, after seeing him effortlessly interact with school groups from both of those countries. Philip is someone who bridges the charity and the local history society, as he is active in both groups and the much-needed links between the organisations seem to be thin on the ground here. So to me, he is gold dust in various ways today, as well as being engagingly enthusiastic about our project.

As usual, I have endless questions, but Philip seems happy to keep the answers coming and remains unperturbed. I am delighted to hear from him that the Public Market in Scarborough was recently refurbished and still operates as a market, featuring artisan crafters.

'Some of them are descended from the original traders. We haven't lost as much heritage as you might think,' he comments, as if he was reading my mind as I looked out over the town.

As we talk, I cannot help reaching out a hand to touch the ancient, pitted stones and trying to visualise how things were at various times, how life was in this place. Thousands of people will have lived and worked here over the centuries, each accepting their own time as modern, by the standards of the day. Most of them were probably unquestioning and merely going about their business, but we cannot know that for sure. In all of my yearnings to explore history, this is what I really want to find out, but probably never will be able to.

I am just starting to think about our next meeting, due to be held in the church hall in the early evening, when my phone rings and Rajesh's name appears on the screen. I apologise to Philip and take the call. As usual, there is no preamble, but as ever, a feeling of warmth and welcome for me in Rajesh's voice.

'Zoe, are you in York today?'

'No Rajesh, but I was there yesterday. I'm in Scarborough just now, up at the castle. Is everything okay?'

'I think so. Is Maybelle with you?'

I start to wonder whether I should be trying to make excuses for her absence. But then, I remember that she is currently threatening to sue us over the concept ownership, so probably does not deserve that courtesy just now.

'No. She was with me yesterday but she doesn't like castles, so she's opted out of today's field trips.'

'She... doesn't like *castles?!*'

I laugh.

'Or old buildings of any sort, really!'

'Oh, my Lord!' he drawls. 'Who doesn't like *castles?*' And we both laugh, while I make a mental note to try to arrange a castle visit with Rajesh, sometime soon. *Arundel, perhaps, or Hever, would be close enough to London for him. Both intact and unslighted, unlike many of our northern former strongholds.*

'I have news about her claim. A letter from her solicitor, asserting the claim and demanding that we recognise it. Basically, challenging the contract we drew up with you, as we expected. Did you get the testimonies we talked about?'

'Most of them, yes. I need to remind one or two people. David Crossley in particular has written a good one. I'll send copies to you, when I'm with my laptop again. Probably later this evening.'

'Well, no rush. I imagine you're busy.'

'Yes. We've got a meeting tonight with the locals here in Scarborough and then it's back to York again tomorrow.'

'Don't forget downtime! You're near a beach. Have you had your feet in the sea?'

'This morning,' I confess. 'And it was blissful. Also, I had fish and chips for breakfast.'

I smile at his rich, deep laughter and we end the call. It leaves me feeling happy to have spoken with him, but uneasy about Maybelle, who grumped and snarked her way through yesterday's seminar in York, as if nothing else was going on. I was supplied with my usual half-hourly reminders that the world does not revolve around me, which litter our interactions so pervasively now, that I barely hear them any more. But she was as efficient as ever, having pre-booked the room and checked the equipment in advance, so that everything went quite smoothly.

Philip has moved away a little, to give me privacy for my call. I return to him now and try to put thoughts of Maybelle out of my mind. But as we chat together, she keeps sneaking back into it as I wonder, not for the first time, how she justifies her actions to herself.

Has she really convinced herself that she had some part in the concept development, or is this legal challenge just another one of her endless micro attacks on me? I suspect the latter, *but why does she feel the need to make them?* And underneath those ruminations are the questions that are bothering me even more: *what chance does she stand of succeeding in her quest to claim shared ownership, and if she does then how will it affect the project and my work in it?*

I can hear her voice in my head, now. The big sigh.

I can see her eyes rolling upwards and the weary: 'Zoe. The world does *not* revolve around *you*,' and I sigh myself, only for Philip to catch my eye inquiringly and realise he has asked me a question of his own, which I have failed to hear.

He asks again if I have had enough and would like to take a break – and what I am doing for dinner. I have no plans and would enjoy some more of his company, so we arrange to meet in the dining room of my hotel, soon. I think food will help to ground me, although what I crave even more than that, suddenly, is home and Hugh and Amy's quiet company. Alf and even Adam would be more than welcome, too.

I decide to walk back to the hotel and instead of history-seeking through the streets and houses, I fantasise about spending a happy evening with Hugh, Nick, Ava, Rachel and Ben in our own dining room or Rachel's kitchen. For a few minutes, I recall the feeling of being socially embraced by these five people, with whom I share mutual trust.

And then, the spectre of Maybelle appears like the bad fairy at a pantomime, to imaginary boos and hisses from the audience in my head. So I shake it involuntarily and decide instead to focus on the buildings, past which I am walking.

The evening meeting is well attended, with some faces I recognise from the university, English Heritage and the local history society. And many I do not: local residents, I assume, who have heard about the project and want to join in.

I am in a bit of a flap, without someone to help me with the organisation. But have remembered all of my devices, chargers and batteries and managed to produce something of an agenda for my own use, even though I have no spare copies for anyone else. There is no overhead projector in the church hall, but I can digitally share some documents and images and I use these, to punctuate my introductory speech.

Then I invite questions from the floor. The first is from a young, bespectacled woman near the front.

'Why 1948? Scarborough changed the most in Victorian times, so surely the early 1800s would be more interesting?'

I smile at her, but she does not smile back, so I feel a familiar but brief heaviness in my stomach. I push it down and answer her.

'If you all decide that you want to begin in a different year for Scarborough, then that's fine. But we think 1948 is a good year to start, because there are people who will remember how things were, then, who tend to enjoy being involved and sharing their memories. Also, it's easier to find photos and generally be more certain about the buildings and streets. One of the key jobs at the beginning of a town's History Maps project is bringing people together and encouraging as much engagement as possible.'

I see bespectacled lady shake her head at my response, but I have learned not to get bogged down in individual debates at such meetings. So I look across the room towards a raised hand in the back left corner and motion to its owner.

'Yes, you please, in the blue jacket?'

'Thanks, Zoe. Len Harness, from The Guardian.' The heavy feeling in my stomach becomes harder, like stone, and I swallow. 'I'm just curious to know, what have you done with Maybelle Shaw, this evening? And is there any truth in her claim that you stole her idea for the History Maps project?'

40

His questions hang in the air for a few seconds and time slows right down for me, so that they feel like minutes and I find I have the luxury of looking around and seeing people's stunned or bewildered faces.

Some will not have heard of Maybelle, or even really know who I am, whereas others might be more clued-in. Someone nudges their neighbour, in exaggerated slow motion by my perception and I even have time to think: *this is the effect of adrenalin and cortisol, triggered by the shock. A million years ago, this would be the flight-or-fight mode I would need to deal with a predator. Nowadays, my predator is a journalist from The Guardian.*

I have to reply and it has to be good. Keeping the meeting going, as well as it can, has to be my top priority, so: containment. Also, he will be writing a story, so I need to try to manage this as well as I can. *Rachel. If only she was here, I don't think this man would have got through the door.* If he had, and managed to ask his question, she would have worked her Rachel-magic on him in a way I cannot even begin to understand, let alone replicate.

But tonight, I have no Rachel. I do not even have a David, or an Ava, or an Ollie. There is just me and I have to reply, even though my mouth feels dry and there is nausea rising quickly in my throat. My heart is racing, to the extent that I can hear it and surely everyone else can. And my shoulders and stomach are clenching tight.

The room is silent, as if everyone has been holding their breath with me, until I answer. I have to force myself to start breathing and meet the journalist's eyes, as steadily as I can.

When I speak, I expect my voice to be hoarse and I am surprised to hear that it is strong and clear.

'Welcome, Mr Harness. I'm sorry to say, I think there must have been some confusion. Maybelle is my personal assistant and quite definitely not the co-creator of the History Maps concept. She's enjoying a well-deserved day off, today. If you want to discuss this further with me, can we talk at the end of the meeting? Tonight, we're all here to talk about Scarborough.' And I smile.

He nods, temporarily satisfied. I move onto the next raised hand and try my hardest to focus on the rest of the questions, while my brain just wants to obsess on him and his agenda – and Maybelle and hers.

Afterwards, he is at the back of the little queue of people who want a personal chat with me. Outwardly, I am focusing on each one individually, as they approach. But inwardly, his presence is burning a hole in my awareness, which I am needing to use precious, tired brain power to contain.

Someone wants to personally thank me and offer their skills. Someone else is also a member of the Whitby group, and do I know about that one? Someone just wants my autograph and a selfie. And lastly, there is an ex-history student, who might add strength to the very tenuous bridge between these people and York University.

Then, it is Mr Harness.

He extends a hand for me to shake and apologises, quite gracefully, for ambushing the meeting with his questions.

'I just wanted to be sure that you'd see me and I couldn't think of any other way of doing it. I'm preparing a story which is looking quite big and obviously I'd appreciate your input. If we could do an interview...?'

I smile, reluctantly, nodding slowly. *I'm going to have to give him something to mitigate this, as Ben and Rachel would put it.* I cannot think what to offer. *Buy time*, is the only strategy I can come up with. *Buy time and phone Rachel.*

'Okay. Well, it's obviously too late, tonight. I'm really tired, I don't know about you. I'm back in York, tomorrow afternoon. How about tomorrow morning?'

'That would be great. I'm off back to London tomorrow, too. Wasn't sure I'd be able to catch you...' He grins engagingly, as if we are on the same side and I feel a surge of optimism, because *maybe – just maybe – we can be.* But Rachel's oft-repeated advice to never trust a journalist comes ringing to my ears.

I am just starting to think of a possible meeting place, when he asks which hotel I am staying at and, when I reply, he tells me he is there too.

'We could do it over breakfast?'

This gives me a further flutter of panic, because I will have little time to prepare and I know I need to be very careful what I say to this man.

'After breakfast.' I offer my most winning but assertive smile. 'About nine, in the hotel lounge.'

He nods and takes his leave, but not before offering me a lift back to the hotel in his car. Luckily, I have already arranged for Philip to drive me back there, so I can happily and gracefully decline his offer. Even without the arrangement with Philip, I would have walked home, rather than accept it.

Back in the hotel room, I am calling Rachel as I kick off my shoes.

She answers quickly and I plunge straight in with: 'Rachel, there was a journalist at the public meeting this evening...'

'Who? Did you get his name?' is her first question.

'Um... Len Harkness, I think he said?'

'Harness? Len Harness. Guardian.'

'Yes, that's him.'

'Ohh, I know him, but not very well. Hold on a sec... Ben? How well do you know Len Harness? Yeah, me neither. He's doing a story on the History Maps. Yeah, it's bound to be that... Zoe? Is it about the Maybelle thing?'

'Yes!' I answer, unable to keep the surprise out of my tone. *How does Rachel know so much, without having to be told anything?* It is relieved surprise, though.

'Ah, I don't think we can get it easily pulled. We don't have much influence with him. We might be able to go higher, though, if it's going to be very damaging. What happened, exactly?'

I am blinking back tears as I tell her, remembering that feeling of wanting the ground to open up and swallow me whole. The public humiliation of being caught out. *How had I looked? Shocked? Flushed? Guilty?* Philip politely avoided mentioning it, so I have no way of knowing.

'Okay, that's not too bad. Sounds like you handled it well. Right. You go and relax, while Ben and I have a chat and work out a strategy for tomorrow morning. I'll call you back in about half an hour, okay? Try to stay calm, Zoe. It will all be fine.' And hearing her voice saying those words makes me believe it will, at least mostly.

I cannot even try to stay calm, but I am tired. The mini bar is tempting in the absence of a strong coffee, but both of those ways lie madness. So I call Hugh instead and moan on to him for a while, before remembering to ask him how he is and how things are there. I spoke with Amy before dinner, but of course, she does not have Hugh's perspective.

He finishes the job of making me feel better, stronger and more confident that Rachel has begun, so that by the time she calls me back, I am more like my new usual self instead of the old, pre-History Maps one. But I really want to be at home and be physically held by him. That will be tomorrow night, after York.

'Right, Zoe,' says Rachel. 'Here's what we've come up with. I'll talk it through with you first and then email the salient points. I'm actually thinking I might come over and be there with you in the morning. But it would be a very early start and I'd have to rearrange a few things here, first.'

'Oh, don't, there's no need…'

'Well, I might. Let's see how this goes. So, first, it can only be Maybelle who has alerted the Guardian to her ridiculous claim. "Stolen the idea," is straight from her. It can't be anyone else and it's actually slanderous. If they print it, it will be libellous.'

'Oh! Yes, I suppose it will. That won't stop them, though, will it?'

'Well, they won't expect you to sue, but Google is a whole different and less tasty prospect for them, isn't it?'

'Right. So, I need to make it clear to him that the accusation is actually against Google and not just me.'

'Exactly,' confirms Rachel. 'Then, he'll tread much more carefully, as he should. As for challenging the claim itself, Ben and I think it's about time you started setting out the case for the defence, as it were.'

'What, with Len Harness?'

'Well, the idea is to stop it going to court. Because, although she's highly unlikely to win, the hearings would be time consuming and really stressful for you. Not to mention, potentially bad PR.'

'If he gets his story printed, it's not exactly going to be great PR though, is it?' I point out the obvious, grimly.

'Well, that depends. I think you can turn it around. We all know her claim is ridiculous and we all know why. Why not tell him?'

This shocks me a little, so that I take a few seconds to respond.

'Um, wouldn't *that* be slander? Libel?'

I hear her delicious, tinkly laugh in my ear.

'Not if it's true! Ask him to interview *her* and quiz her on her historical knowledge! Describe her reaction, every time she sets foot in a castle, or anywhere older than half a century! I've seen it with my own eyes and heard it with my own ears. Most of us have. You could even tell him about the lentils.'

And reluctantly, finally, I laugh too, a little. *How gloriously liberating it would be to do this.* And yet, somehow, it feels wicked. *Maybelle's kind of wicked.*

'I'd need to call Rajesh and run it past him first.'

'Do that. I'm going to call Adam,' says Rachel, shocking me all over again.

'*Adam?* Why? What's it got to do with him?'

'He made his position quite clear, when we confronted her over the lentils, didn't he? It's not just your reputation and Google's she'd trash, if she managed to get her way. It's everyone's who's been involved from the beginning. Ours, too. David's, everyone's at the local history society and all four of the boys', including Adam. He'll want to know what she's up to and he'll want to stop her.'

'No, Rachel. It's too stressful for him.' My eyes are filling with tears. Adam is still ten years old in my mind, or even younger.

'He'd be furious not to be told and he's probably the only person who can stop this going any further. Think about it, Zoe. He can verify that she wasn't involved in the original concept when they were both children, because he was there. Alf too of course, but Adam's voice carries more weight, because she's his mother.'

'No. We can't drag him into this…'

'He's *in* it, up to his eyes! The success of their business is based on the dissertation they did and how famous it's become. And she's his mother! He *knows* what she's like. Better than anyone. Look. I'm not going to use any persuasive tactics on him. I'll just tell him the facts and let him make his own mind up. Now, get some sleep and we'll talk again in the morning before breakfast. Okay?'

41

I manage to follow Rachel's instruction to get some sleep for only about three hours through the night, with those snatched uneasily and by accident, in and amongst the tossing and turning.

The problem is that I feel extremely uneasy with her plan for me to use the interview to turn the tables on Maybelle.

It's just not me. It does not sit well with me. It's not the kind of thing I do and it doesn't feel right, doesn't taste *right. But we all have to do things we prefer not to do sometimes, for the greater good. I really hate that phrase, "the greater good". That's not me, either.*

The phrase I do like, which keeps coming to mind, is the Castaneda one, about whether the path has a heart. I am picturing myself at a fork in a woodland path, undecided as to which way to choose. One is the way recommended by Rachel: fighting back and giving Maybelle a taste of her own medicine. The other: *does it just involve me being a perpetual victim, forever at her mercy?* Dimming my phone light, I run a Google search for the Castaneda phrase and find it.

'*Does this path have a heart? If it does, the path is good; if it does not, it is of no use. Both paths lead nowhere; but one has a heart, the other does not. One makes for a joyful journey; as long as you follow it, you are one with it. The other will make you curse your life.*'

Behaving like Maybelle will, undoubtedly, make me curse my life. I am not sure the other way will be joyful either, though, because I have to assume that her attempts to bring me down will ratchet up, as much and as quickly as they can. She has had several setbacks along the way, but these only seem to renew her perseverance and, meanwhile, *what is it doing to me?* I cannot answer this straight away, except to say that I am becoming accustomed to it and I suspect that might not be good news.

Our never-ending conflict affects so many other people and especially the project itself, which is the most important element in this for me, because without it, I could walk away from Maybelle without a backward glance and never see her again. But we are on the brink of a key stage of success and I cannot walk away. I need to consider how the two different paths might affect the project.

I imagine the headlines: *HISTORY MAPS – CONCEPT THEFT?* or *WHOSE IDEA WAS IT REALLY?* and force myself to follow it through and envisage how this would play out. On the one hand, it raises awareness of the project, which, at first glance, looks like a positive outcome.

But does the project absolutely need raised awareness at this stage? No. It needs work and engagement at the local level. Our posters and flyers, along with Facebook and local news stations, have been taking care of that.

I think any kind of controversy at this stage will put some people off becoming involved. The kind of people who would want to help create a History Map probably tend not to enjoy this kind of controversy.

I really just want it all to go away, but Len Harness wants his story and is unlikely to stop until he gets it, or one of equal value.

What else can I offer him? Nothing with the same click-bait power, for sure. What can I offer him that would be good for the project? The only thing that comes to mind is exclusive access to the History Maps development process. *He can shadow me for a few days and see the whole thing, if he likes. We can supply him with stock photos, or he can bring a photographer and take his own, or both. But first, I need to strongly dissuade him from running the concept theft story, by setting out the legal position.*

I look at my phone, to check the time. It is four-thirty in the morning. *So first, I need some sleep.*

I am woken by the phone ringing, at seven o'clock. I am still partly dreaming when Rachel starts speaking to me, a stressful dream in which I am being chased towards a cliff edge by a monster. I rub my eyes and try to blink it away.

'... sleep?' She is finishing saying something, but I have to ask her to repeat it.

'I was just asking whether you managed to get any sleep, but you're still so sleepy it sounds like you need to order some coffee and get in the shower, before we speak properly,' she clarifies.

'Sorry,' I mumble. 'I was awake until four-thirty, trying to work it all out.'

'Okay, I'll phone back soon. Don't go back to sleep!'

'I won't,' I tell her and propel myself instantly onto my feet, before I do. I use the hotel phone to order coffee and splash cold water onto my face, patting it dry with a towel.

I dial Rajesh's number, wanting to speak with him before Rachel calls back. I know he keeps early hours, which is why I could not call him last night, when I really wanted to.

I tell him what happened and Rachel's advice, then my night time thoughts, concluding with the offer of an exclusive on the project.

'Yeah, that's good thinking, Zoe. I like it. And I agree with you, that we should keep the Maybelle thing out of it, at all costs. If he wants confirmation that we will sue for libel, you can give him my number and I'll put him onto our legal team. That should convince him. I think he'll go for your offer. It's a great opportunity for him, though I assume Ben and Rachel will want to okay it first, if only to make sure the guy can write.'

'I'm due to speak with Rachel in a minute, so I'll run it past her then.' I hear a knock and go to fetch my coffee, holding my phone awkwardly between neck and shoulder, while I swap the drink for a tip, but Rajesh is just wishing me luck with the interview, before he hangs up. Almost as soon as he does, the screen lights up with Rachel's name and it rings again.

'Hi, Zoe, so what does Rajesh think?' she asks, with her customary insight.

'Hmm. He agrees with me,' I begin, taking a sip of bitter coffee. She does not respond, waiting, so I continue. 'I'm not going to hit back at Maybelle.' I have to sound very definite, to forestall her arguments. 'I'm going to put the project first and convince him to back off from the Maybelle angle.'

'Okay... How?'

'I'm thinking of offering him exclusive access to the development, pre-launch.'

'Wow, that's a bit of a gamble, Zoe. He could just use that to slate you instead.'

'Why would he do that?'

I hear her heavy sigh and know I am about to have a layer of naivety carefully removed.

'To raise the value of his copy. Scandal sells, Zoe. I think you know that.'

'Yeah. But I'm planning to appeal to his better nature and offer him a really good deal. Plus, also explaining the legal ramifications of his proposed libel, in glorious technicolour. Rajesh has given me full backing on that, including permission to pass on his number, for a direct contact with their legal team.'

'Ah, that *will* make a difference. I also have some good news for you: Adam says he would testify in court that the concept was yours, which makes your case a lot stronger, doesn't it? He also says you can share that information with Len Harness. So yes, I can see your point and think you have a good chance of getting this turned around. But Zoe, she's just going to take it to more journos until someone eventually uses it against you, don't you think?'

'Probably. Yes. And that's the big problem, isn't it? As ever. What to do about Maybelle.' The coffee is waking me up, but all the zing in the world is not going to make this an easy question to answer effectively.

'I don't know. We'd need a whole team of psychologists to sort that one out and even then, I don't fancy their chances. How do you manage to keep working with her?'

'It's okay, for the most part. I guess I'm getting pretty immune to her low level antics now...'

'I bet you're not, really. It will be affecting your self esteem at some level. It really worries me, Zoe, but I suppose we've got other things to discuss right now. Let's have lunch as soon as we can to talk about that, though?'

This is the first time I have smiled all morning, albeit wanly. I am feeling more settled, now that my immediate path is chosen. Even if I cannot hear its heart beating yet, at least it does not feel queasy, with a bad conscience and a heavy sense of foreboding.

'I'd love to. So tell me about Len Harness. Is he good? Do we want him shadowing us through the launch prep?'

'Actually, yes I think so, though I'd want to talk to him first. Can you make that a conditional offer? He'll know who we are and that we should be able to come to a good arrangement for him. But bear in mind we only have the one exclusive to offer and if she sets anyone else on you, we obviously can't use it again.'

'I know. Do you think it's something I *should* be offering him?'

'Yeah, I actually think it's a good idea. I was wondering about setting something similar up with someone and he might have been on the list to be approached for it. He would be a useful person to have onside, *if* we can develop some trust with him. Go with your gut, though. If it doesn't feel right, don't make the offer. Personally, I think the promise of legal action will be enough on its own.'

I am opening the curtains and wincing at the early sunlight, but then instantly calmed and uplifted by the stretch of sunlit, sparking sea.

I take a long, slow breath and tell Rachel: 'I wish I was still wandering around Scarborough castle, not knowing about any of this.'

I hear her sympathetic smile and it calms me some more.

'I know. But it will soon be sorted and then it's back home to Hugh and Amy, isn't it?'

'York, first. I've got a meeting and a workshop there. And *then* home. I'll be exhausted, though! I really needed more sleep.'

'Yeah, I can imagine. Coffee is your friend!'

Today, it will have to be. I throw prudence to the wind and order another one from room service, before I get into the shower, to start this day properly.

42

I am on the train from Scarborough to York, watching fields and hedges rush by, interspersed by the occasional solitary tree and then copses of shady darkness. Then old, stone walls. A red-bricked village, with a level crossing and glossy white gates. Then fields again.

I am so tired, that the motion of the train is lulling me almost to sleep. But I am still sipping coffee, because I have the York meeting and workshop to run, before I can go home and rest.

Maybelle is supposed to meet me at the university – or, rather, she is supposed to be there assisting me. But as usual, we have had no contact with each other and I do not know whether she is planning to actually turn up.

Closing my eyes for a few perilous minutes, my forehead leaning on the gently vibrating window, I fervently hope she is not and relax into a soothing reverie. This invokes a quiet, stress-free space, in which I do not have to keep looking over my shoulder, to check if I am being stabbed in the back.

Sleep threatens, so that I have to sit up, blinking and drink more coffee as we pass through Seamer station, under its almost ubiquitous, Victorian, iron framed, glass roofs.

I should use the time to prepare for the afternoon's sessions, I think to myself, reluctantly. I pull my notepad and a pen from my bag, to start working. *At least it will keep me awake, unlike staring out of the window.*

In York station, my eyes always go to the roof: a bending spine of iron, stretching along the whole length and sprouting vaulted arcs, like the ribs of a giant carapace, with chitinous plates of glass. The cacophony of engines and people and station announcements is immense, but somehow rises and is lost in the vastness of its cavernous arches. The whole effect is that of a cathedral for trains.

But I cannot stand and stare, because I have to go and find a taxi to take me to the university.

We drive north-east on the Station Road, which always seems heavy with traffic, but still not unpleasant, thanks to its wide, green verges and lining of trees. My eye is drawn to the statue of Victorian industrialist George Leeman, as the traffic slows, just as we are passing it. He looks down on us from his stone, ivy-ensconced perch, a sardonic eyebrow raised and I fleetingly, but searchingly, wonder what kind of man he really was and I wish there was some way of travelling back in time, to find out.

Now, we are moving again and surrounded by buses of both the touring coach and double decker varieties. Rounding the bend, we pass a homeless person, sitting on the pavement and between him and the rumble of the diesel engines, I am brought sharply and reluctantly back to the present time.

A slight bend to the right and we are driving next to the city walls and at the height of them, so that it feels like we are on top of them, punctuated as they are by modern day, strolling tourists and ancient, square, musket loops. This is a strange and jarring juxtaposition for my tired brain to try to process, so I close my eyes for a few seconds, only opening them again when I feel sleep sneaking upon me again, to fend it off again. We are crossing the River Ouse, now, on first a stone-crenelated bridge and then a Victorian, wrought-iron one, equally elegant and unashamedly of their respective eras, comfortably sitting side by side.

Now, we are plunging into the city proper. Past the old, red-bricked River House on our right. Once the imposing Yorkshire Club, its listed status has ensured that it retains some semblance of its previous dignity. But now it incongruously – and rather embarrassingly – houses a pizza chain and an estate agents' office.

Forwards, past newer red brick on the right and a pedestrian entrance to the Museum Gardens on the left, so I know we are nearly there, now. Both these and our destination, the King's Manor, were once part of St Mary's abbey, the former being its grounds and the latter the abbot's house. But by car, we must drive on and turn left before the Catholic church, with the twin square towers of the gothic Minster clearly visible, beyond.

Into St Leonard's Place and we glide past the pristine crescent of grand, town houses on the left, with their shared, black, intricately wrought-iron balcony that supplies them with a kind of lacy foil finish, which emphasises the white sweep of the building. On the right is the sandy-coloured, ornate Theatre Royal, once a medieval hospital and still retaining part of that incarnation, although it is now the Victorian gothic frontage that is visible from the road.

More stark white after that, with the De Grey ballroom, mirroring the décor of the crescent terraces and the taxi finally drops me by Exhibition Square, where I am greeted by the tinkling, flowered fountains in front of the statue of nude-painter Etty which always makes me smile, for some reason. His shy but enduring adoration of the fairer sex, perhaps.

King's Manor sits in the gardens to the right, beyond wrought-iron railings, so I go and make myself known there, happy to hear that we have the Huntingdon Room again. I check the time on my phone. Twenty minutes early: I can inspect the plaster dragon frieze in there more closely, if I am the first to arrive.

I was fascinated by it, the first time I saw it and wished, then, that I had more time for it, with fewer interruptions. Such curious detail and I *think* four hundred and forty years old, like the room, though am not completely sure about that. I want to take photos of it, this time, so that I can pour over them at home and enjoy the luxury of trying to ponder the meaning, behind the images.

And so, I am looking down at my phone as I barrel into the room, accessing its camera setting, in eager anticipation of capturing these. But I am not the first to arrive after all and am brought up short, by a noise, from someone else already inside.

Maybelle.

And my heart sinks, because somehow, I have completely forgotten that she is supposed to be here today.

'Oh, you made it then,' she states the obvious, with clear disappointment.

Maybelle is wearing a crisp, cornflower blue, linen suit, which emphasises her slim figure and makes her look cool, relaxed and professional. I am wearing my old jeans, as usual and some tunic top so insignificant, I cannot even remember which one it is and have to look down at myself, to recall it.

I am hot and, suddenly, at the sight of her, drained of all remaining energy. I slump into a nearby chair and wearily agree that yes, I did make it.

'Hmm,' she comments, archly, whilst continuing to place, in front of each chair, a sheet of paper, which I can only assume to be the meeting's agenda, though she has not consulted me about this. 'I didn't think you would.'

'Why not?' I ask, absent-mindedly, because I have picked up one of the agendas and am by now reading it, with interest. I can see items on both the Scarborough and Whitby projects, but am alarmed to spot mentions of both Hartlepool and Middlesbrough, about fifty miles to the north of Whitby.

'Oh, I thought you might have been distracted by something...' she is replying, with a smirk in her tone and, I see when I look up at her, inspecting my face rather too closely for comfort.

'What's this on the agenda?' I ask, now having something more important to worry about than her smirking and peering. 'Hartlepool and Middlesbrough? What have they got to do with York?'

'Well, if you check your geography once in a while, Zoe, you might notice that Middlesbrough is only fifty miles up the A19 from York and Hartlepool just ten miles further. They're obviously going to be covered by York university, aren't they?' and she actually adds a: *'Duh.'*

I exhale, heavily, as if I can get rid of my Maybelle-induced stress this way, but to no avail.

'No. Durham,' is as much of an argument as I can be bothered to make.

'What?' she asks, shortly, full of impatient irritation at my daring to question her assumptions.

'They're both on the doorstep of Durham University,' I clarify, in the vain hope that this, then, might suffice. It does not.

'Well, who cares about Durham?' asks my assistant, in one swoop dismissing the entire institution. 'York is far older and more important. They should come under York.'

I have got my head in my hands, now, deeply regretting my decision to keep her on, after Rajesh offered me the chance of escape from her.

'Durham University is the third oldest in the country, established in the early part of the nineteenth century,' I tell her, from the crook of my elbow on the table. 'York University isn't even sixty years old, yet. And anyway, those two towns are right next to Durham. *And* they're already being covered by Durham, as they should be.'

'Actually, I think you'll find you've got that the wrong way around, *Miss Smarty Pants*. Everyone knows Durham is just an old mining town, whereas York is very old and historical.' I peep up just in time to see her waving her hand vaguely towards the window, as if the history is floating around in the air, just outside of it.

'Google is your friend, Maybelle,' I answer, flat out refusing to continue with this idiocy.

She looks momentarily confused and then straightens up, as if I have challenged her more than I actually have.

'Yes! Yes, Google *is* my friend,' she tells me, decisively, with a strange kind of complacent smile on her shiny lipsticked mouth. 'Far more than they are yours, I think you'll find. Didn't my friend Len look you up last night…? He'll soon put things right. You've got a whole load of trouble coming for you, Zoe, as I've been *trying* to tell you for months.'

Suddenly, I realise something about the journalist's ambush at the Scarborough meeting that has not occurred to me, until now. I have gone physically cold and momentarily cannot find the words I need, to ask the confirmatory question.

Eventually, I manage to get out: 'You told him where I'd be.'

'Well, of course I did. How else was he supposed to find you?' She is now busying herself with collecting up the agendas, again, which is the closest she ever comes to admitting to being in the wrong about anything.

'No, but you chose that meeting on purpose, didn't you?' I am watching her closely, now, whereas she is moving around the room about her task and noticeably avoiding meeting my gaze. 'Because you knew I'd be on my own there, which is quite rare. Normally, there's someone else to assist and support me, but you knew that nobody else could make it to the east coast, this week. So you thought he'd ruin the meeting.'

'I don't know what you're talking about and I'm far too busy to be bothered by…'

'He didn't.'

'What?' She stops and looks at me, now, not hiding her surprise quickly enough.

'He didn't ruin it. The meeting went very well. As did the

one I had with Len, this morning. *How* good a friend was he of yours?'

'That's none of your business,' she snaps, now pale, beneath her make-up.

'Well, he's *my* friend now,' I tell her, picking up my phone and standing up to find the wall dragons, before the other meeting attendees arrive.

'What… *what do you mean?*' asks Maybelle, urgently, incredulously. Uncertainly, for once.

'Just what I said,' is my only response, as I set a spiky dragon squarely in my viewfinder and snap the shutter.

43

We are just a few weeks away from the public launch of the first Google UK History Maps and, although it feels a little self-indulgent when there is so much else left to do, I am having a meeting of my original, volunteer steering committee, followed by a dinner. From the very beginning, they all believed in the concept and have worked to support it – with the possible exception of Maybelle and Colin – and I want them to know how important they still are, to it and to me.

Maybelle has booked the room in the executive suite of a local converted mill. But I have drawn up my own agenda, her east coast mistake having undermined any remaining trust I had in her to do that properly.

It is Saturday, so that nobody has had to book a day off work and we are setting the room up, when Len wanders in with Kumar, his camera man. The exclusive access deal, that was hammered out with Ben and Rachel's approval, involves me sharing my business calendar with him, along with an almost open invitation for him to attend anything we do. A chat on the phone last night clarified this as being one of the more useful events for him to cover. I know it might be a little awkward, because we have become such a comfortable and intimate group, but I think Len will fit in quite well. Rachel has been particularly keen on him attending, to supply the proper background to his story.

The only potential problem, I suddenly realise as I hear her high pitched voice from the door, is that I forgot to tell Maybelle. And it is becoming increasingly obvious that she has never met Len, despite having given him the lead in the first place.

'I don't care who you think you are, you're not invited and you're not coming in. Now, go away, please. I'm far too busy to be bothered by this sort of thing…' are the words that float towards me as I move closer to the door, to hear more detail.

'I *am* invited. I'm a journalist…' is all I can hear from Len, back outside in the corridor, to where she has physically shooed them, her arms flapping as though he and Kumar are a swarm of flies in need of dispersal.

'Then you're *especially* unwelcome,' she snaps, as she tries to close the door on them and would, if Len did not have his foot in it.

'Maybelle, it's okay…' I advance, trying to lead her away from the door. She will not move towards my coaxing. I get a lung full of her perfume and try to hold my breath whilst adding, 'I do know them…'

'Zoe.' She rounds on me, whilst still pulling the door on Len's foot. 'You might want to fill your social life with all kinds of reprobates and miscreants. But I, for one, plan to keep this enterprise free of them. You're not just some sort of cowboy outfit any more. You're working for *Google* now and *that* means you're *supposed*…' Len gives another shove at the door and she breaks off, to renew her efforts at keeping it closed on his foot. '…to be doing things *properly.* We'll call the police, if you don't go away!' she calls to the men outside the room.

I can hear Len giving up, angrily, muttering, '*Stupid cow.*' I assume he is going to wait there with Kumar, until I have managed to convince her that they can come in.

'Maybelle, it's *Len Harness,*' I tell her very clearly, thinking that this will do the trick. But she merely blinks at me and performs her exaggerated shrug.

'I don't care if it's the *Queen of Sheba*. If he hasn't got an invite, then he's not coming in.' And she folds her arms, decisively, like a very stern nightclub doorman.

'He has got an invite.'

'*No,* he *hasn't.*'

'*Yes,* he *has,*' I insist, no choice but to give the pantomime skit retort.

'How?' Her hands are on her hips, now, so that she is physically, as well as verbally, challenging me.

'Because... I gave him one!' I am sure some other words would be more convincing. But when I am under pressure, like this, they never come to me.

She frowns and then sighs and tells me, wearily, 'You have to stop doing this kind of thing,' as if I have done it before, which I have not. 'I know you like showing off for the journalists, but today's meeting isn't about you, Zoe. It's about all of the people who have helped us...'

'Len's got exclusive access.'

Maybelle frowns, again.

'*What?* Do you even know what that is?'

I think it is this final insult which opens my verbal floodgates and renders me capable of useful speech, once more.

'Maybelle, this is all *your* doing! Len is the journalist you sent to Scarborough, to hijack my public meeting.'

'Oh!' *Do I see her cheeks redden?* She processes the new information for one click, blinks, and recalibrates. 'Well, that was Scarborough and this is Halifax. And that meeting was public, but this one is private. And what do you *mean,* exclusive access?'

'He gets to attend whatever he wants, within reason, between now and the UK launch. It's a level of access no other journalist can have. Exclusive.' I speak slowly, puzzled that she does not understand the term, when only a few seconds ago, she was condescendingly assuming I did not understand it.

'I know what *that* means, of course!' Her voice is rising almost to shouting pitch, now. 'But how has he got it? What's happened and why wasn't I told?' She stops for one blink, as the penny drops.

'Oh. Wait a minute. I think I might know the answer. You offered him the deal, to persuade him to sit on the story I gave him.' My silence is all the response she needs, to continue, 'Well, of all the sneaky things to do!' And she looks me up and down, sneering, as if I am already on my way to the stocks to have rotten tomatoes thrown at me.

'*I'm* sneaky?' I feel compelled to respond. '*You're* the one who went behind my back, with this stupid, ridiculous ownership claim and who set me up for public humiliation at the Scarborough meeting!' As soon as I have spoken, I regret it, because I have done the two things I know I must never do in her company: lose my temper and tell her what I really think. Either one will be exploited by her and, with both together, I have handed her so much leverage that it might as well be a crow bar.

She is smiling, now. Triumphant.

'Stupid and ridiculous, is it? Well, *prove it.*'

I say nothing, reluctant to compound my mistake.

'You can't, can you?' she persists, examining my face this way and that. 'It's only your word against mine and it *is* going to go to court. And I *will* win.'

I call to mind some of her gaffes. Her mistaken attacking of Nick, when she was angry about missing a meeting invitation. The infamous lentils. And her more recent dismissing of Durham, both town and university, in the *blasé* assumption that York, being older, must therefore have the oldest institutions. I remember some of her more minor, frequent blunders. Her open disdain for old buildings, calling them dirty, musty, smelly and boring.

I imagine all of this being laid out in embarrassing detail before a judge and finally, I quietly, but surely, say: 'I don't think so.'

'Yes I *will!*' she retorts, her voice shrill. 'I've watched you hijacking the boys' dissertation and pretending it was yours! I've watched you prancing about like a precious princess, as if the world is at your feet, as if you're *so important...*' She is almost spitting the words, her face contorted with hatred for me. 'Well, it can't last forever, Zoe Taylor. It's down to people like me, to make sure people like *you* are put in their place. And I'm not the only one. There's plenty of us,' she adds darkly.

Out of the corner of my eye I see movement by the door and so I look. And, seeing my eyes go that way, Maybelle looks too. Colin is standing there, looking from one to the other of us, with what I can only describe as an unpleasant expression on his face.

Of course, because he is one of the "plenty", I think to myself. *And the one who will do the most damage, probably.*

Maybelle's demeanour undergoes a miraculous change on sight of him. Her features brighten and a bright smile appears, showing sparkling teeth.

'Colin! *Darling!* You arrived in good time! Did you find the coffee? It's all laid out in the next room. Come on, let's get you some.' And she leads him out, ignoring Len and Kumar, who wander in past them, looking puzzled and bewildered.

'Is *that...?*' Len indicates, towards the empty door.

'Maybelle Shaw,' I confirm. 'My assistant. And your erstwhile client.'

He laughs, dryly.

'She was never my client, thank goodness! I had no idea how things were between you two, but I can see now why you offered me the exclusive. She's like a pitbull, isn't she? Doesn't let go!' And he shows his teeth, miming a dog with a bone.

Against the odds, he makes me laugh, which relieves some tension. And one by one – and sometimes in twos and threes – the others arrive. Nick and Ava, who I have not seen for weeks. Rachel and Ben, who I have seen more recently and we are all happy to be reunited. Adam, followed by Will and even Ollie, up from London. Alf comes in with Hugh and they are closely followed by John and David.

We are all chatting so much and so happily, I barely notice the return of Maybelle and Colin. Or that Kumar is taking pictures and Len watching, smiling – and taking notes.

The sudden sight of him doing so is what prompts me to begin the meeting proper.

'Everyone, if you haven't met him before, this is Len Harness, a journalist who is shadowing me until the launch. I hope we can all make him welcome.' I smile around at them all, knowing that they will, with the exception of Maybelle. 'And Kumar Devi, his photographer.'

Rachel and Ben exchange a few words with them, along 'Nice to meet you properly,' lines. And I switch on the overhead projector, which is showing my first slide: the pin map of the country. It now has a few more gaps filled and some shaded areas to show university reach and population density, as per Rachel's suggestion. This has indeed enabled us to better understand and start to remedy some of the previously blank spots.

'Ladies and gentleman,' I announce, a proud and wondering tear flickering in my eye. 'Our projects. All *three hundred and fifty-eight* of them.'

There is a round of applause, interspersed with a few: '*Wow!*'s and other comments of delight.

And it might have been a trick of the room's acoustics, but I also somehow hear Maybelle's voice in the mix, clearly saying: '*Huh! You'd think she'd done them all by herself!*'

44

I feel like a stranger, to my child. Every time I come home, she is taller and more serious and capable, but I think what upsets me the most is that she needs me less.

She is always happy to see me. Comes for a big hug and tells me what she has been doing, but she no longer wants the bedtime stories reading to her, which carried on long after she could read for herself.

I suppose it's natural that they'd stop, now she's twelve. Which nearly-teenager would still allow themselves to be read to?

She does her own hair, now and chooses her own clothes, without any input. And when she needs something or thinks of something to say or to ask, she shouts, *'Dad!'* instead of, *'Mum!'*. Then sees me in the kitchen and says something like, 'Oh! Mum. I forgot you were here today.'

It is times like that, I want to give it all up and go back to being a full-time, home educating mum. But I would be an unsatisfied one, with an unquenched, burning passion to realise my ever-growing idea, the monster that has taken over my life.

Most of the time, I love it and when I am very busy, I can go for whole half-hours without giving Amy a thought, knowing that Hugh has enough time for her now. He has been able to cut his hours back, thanks to my earnings.

It is when I go home, or call or Skype home that it really hurts. And even that is bitter sweet, because it is heart warming, to see how close she and Hugh are now and how comfortable and easy they are together.

I always suspected Hugh would be the better parent of us both: he's far more attentive than I ever was.

But today, he has gone out and it is just Amy and me, at home.

I have offered to take her somewhere, bake with her, do some sewing or drawing or anything else she might want us to do together.

But she hugs me, nearly my height now, and kisses my cheek saying: 'No offence Mum, but I just want to play Minecraft. I promised Hannah we could, today.'

'Oh, is Hannah coming round?' I ask, trying to remember whose child she is. And wondering whether Hugh has made arrangements with the parent, or whether I need to do it.

But Amy just laughs and says, 'No, silly Mummy! She's in America! I have to play with her now, because she'll be going to bed soon!' And she opens her laptop, uncoiling the cable on an oversized microphone that I have never even seen before, even though Amy has probably used it for our Skype sessions since she got it. Whenever that was.

A noisy conversation ensues through the game, which sounds like a lot of fun. I empty the dishwasher, enjoying listening to it in the background. And as I start to put things away, I find a new set of mugs that I have never seen before. And the pans stored all the wrong way round, from the way they used to be, *when I lived here,* I nearly find myself thinking, before correcting it, because I still do, if only technically. Even though I feel a little bit more like a guest and less like a permanent resident, every time I come home.

And everything is so *clean,* far cleaner than I kept it, before we could afford to pay cleaners. *Perhaps that's why it no longer quite feels like home.*

The thud of mail, hitting the doormat, is a welcome interruption to the wave of displacement currently engulfing me. I pull myself together and go to pick it up, standing in the hallway to flick through the envelopes, which seem to be mostly bills and business stuff for Hugh. But then there is something official-looking for me, which gives me an instant twinge of unease.

I go through to the study and put Hugh's post on his desk. Then I sit in his chair to open mine, all the time trying to speculate what it might be – and also trying not to.

It's probably junk. No, it doesn't look like junk. It looks important, in a scary way. But how can it be scary? I've done nothing wrong and I've even managed to pay down my overdraft. It'll be the doctor, wanting to get me into whatever cancer screening programme they're running now... No.

I open out the bundle of sheets of crisp, white paper and see the familiar lion and unicorn of the royal coat of arms, at the top of the uppermost sheet. *Dieu et mon droit.* The court's right to act on behalf of the Queen. In this case, the county court, in Huddersfield.

I am still speculating, even as I read down the page. *It can only be about Maybelle and her challenging of my contract with Google. But surely, she's suing them, not me? Perhaps I'm being subpoenaed as a witness, but there's no need for that, because I would have done it anyway. I can't believe she's actually going ahead with it, though.*

The letter is headed NOTICE OF ISSUE and it cites me as the defendant, not merely a witness. I sit down and gulp, the chill hand of dread stealing over me. I force myself to read on.

Maybelle is bringing action against me, for what she calls my personal, fraudulent misrepresentation, in the matter of the History Maps project. She is seeking an unspecified amount of money from me – presumably, to be decided by the judge, if she wins – of more than two hundred thousand pounds, says the form.

How could we pay that? is my first thought. We have been more comfortable since I joined Google's payroll, but we still do not have hundreds of thousands in spare cash sitting in a bank account, or anywhere else. *We'd have to sell the house* is my next thought, even though there would still not be enough money left to pay to Maybelle, once the mortgage was settled.

I am shaking and very cold and I feel nauseous. Then, I know I am actually going to vomit and run to the bathroom, where this morning's breakfast leaves my stomach and is heaved into the pan. Now, I am cold and sweating and hyperventilating, sipping water and looking at my pale, panicking face in the cabinet mirror.

I hardly recognise myself. My hair is sticking to the side of my face and I just want to cry, but do not seem to have the energy to do so. I flush the loo and go carefully back to the sitting room, avoiding Amy in the kitchen who, I can hear, is still happily playing.

I cannot think clearly or logically at all, even though I know I have to.

Why is she doing this? As far as I knew, she was suing Google and not me. So what's happened, to change her mind?

I close my eyes and her face swims into my mind, disgusted and disdainful... *angry? Yes. Furious, I think. In the meeting room, last week, when I told her that I'd given Len the exclusive.*

'Well, of all the sneaky things to do,' she had sneered. But I did not think much of it, because Colin arrived soon afterwards and she was simpering after him, completely transformed. *But she remembers*, I realise. *She doesn't forget a slight, just because her mood or demeanour has changed. She pretends she's fine and you have no idea she's still fuming. And then, she strikes.*

Can I win this? It's wrong. I did not misrepresent myself to Google or to Maybelle. But as she said, it's her word against mine.

Has she cooked up some kind of fake evidence that we came up with the idea together and it wasn't just me? Can she do that? Would it work?

I am panicking so much, I do not know what to do with myself. Sitting down feels wrong, so I am pacing up and down and trying to make myself breathe more slowly. *I'm probably in shock. I need someone… Hugh? Rachel?*

I probably need a lawyer, but I cannot think who to see.

Ben would know.

But how much is that *going to cost?*

Another wave of panic. *Do I have to pay her costs too, if I lose?*

Of course I do.

This could completely finish us.

I picture myself, being taken to prison, thrown in a cell, crying – and my cheeks are actually wet, now, but I am telling myself off, for being over dramatic.

I can't actually go to prison for this. Can I?

'I've done nothing wrong,' I say, out loud, to the empty room. My voice sounds strange. Tight and high-pitched.

At that moment, Hugh comes in. I have been so distraught, that I failed to hear the front door and I have no idea for how long he has been in the house. But as soon as he sees my face he rushes over, to hold me.

'What on earth has happened now?' he asks. And only a small part of my brain notices the *'now'* and worries that, from his perspective, my life might seem to be full of unnecessary drama, these days.

I thrust the bundle of papers into his hands and he starts to read. I notice him going pale, too. And then, a creeping red flush around his neck, which he rubs, absent-mindedly. When he looks at me, I can see that he is furious and, even though he is never angry with me, I always expect that he will be and feel the faint echo of that small child's dread of having upset the grown-ups.

'What a *bitch!*' is his first response. 'What the hell is she playing at? Our sons are in business together! We've practically brought hers up! *And* you've given her a job and made sure she's kept it, despite her own best efforts to repeatedly get the sack. Why is she doing this? I just don't understand her, or why she hates you so much. But you must realise that's the case, now, Zoe. It seems like she'll stop at nothing to bring you down.'

'What am I going to do?' I ask him in a quiet voice, sitting down suddenly on the sofa. Somehow, his reaction seems to have diffused some of my own nervous energy.

'Well, fight it of course! We've got no choice about that. Everyone knows her claim is bullshit. It's *asinine,* that she's brought it. Unbelievable. I mean, God knows how much she's paid, in court fees alone. I'll find out.' He starts to type on his phone, presumably running a Google search, to find the court fees. 'Ten thousand pounds!' he exclaims a minute later, and sits down, heavily, on the sofa next to me, mouth agape.

He turns to face me and contemplates me for a few seconds, before asking: 'Are you going to have to keep working with her, with this hanging over your head? As if nothing is happening? With the launch so close and everything?'

This has not occurred to me. But his question forces me to consider it, now.

'How would it look to the court, if I got her dismissed or moved, now? I've no idea.'

'Possibly not good. I don't know,' he concedes. 'We need some very good legal advice, for sure.'

'I'll talk to Rajesh,' I say, wearily, picking my phone up from the coffee table. 'And Rachel, I guess.'

It is only then, that I meet his eyes and burst into tears and he hugs me and strokes my back, while I properly sob into his chest.

And we sit here, clutching each other, as though we are alone together on a life raft, in the middle of a stormy sea.

45

It is now just a few weeks before the UK launch and I am trying to pretend, to myself and everyone else, that all is well. That I am not lying awake every night, in fear of losing our family home. That I am not clutching a perpetual ball of dread in the pit of my stomach, which persists even when I am consciously distracted by something, like the immense amount of work there still is to do. And that I do not keep finding myself staring at Maybelle, in a grisly kind of fascinated disbelief, as she bustles bossily about her business, the epitome of righteous innocence.

We have hired an office suite in the Dean Clough converted mill complex for a few weeks, which is at least a comfort, due to being both drenched in local history – my maternal grandpa worked here for most of his life – and close to home. Coming here every day has been good for me, because it reminds me of him. The steeply cobbled lane he walked down and back up to get home, every day for sixty years, is still here and largely unaltered. It has gained some new lighting and probably a lot more greenery than it had, then, when he left school and began his full-time employment nearly a hundred years ago, at the grand old age of thirteen. His only significant break from that was when he was away, fighting in World War II.

I retrace his steps, sometimes and remember his life, trying to embody some of his no-nonsense, Yorkshire grit. *What would Grandpa have done if he had found himself in the situation that I am in, with Maybelle?* The answer does not help me particularly, because I think he would have been far less gullible than I have been and consequently, would never have exposed himself to such a threat.

I've been so stupid.

But there is not much time, even for self-recrimination, because whatever happens – court case or not – two hundred of our now three hundred and sixty-two projects will go live on Google UK's new History Maps site. In just under three weeks. We have all been working frantically, to ensure so many of them will be ready in time, though Rajesh is professionally and reassuringly chilled out about it.

'It's okay if some of them come a little later, Zoe. We'll just do what we can. It's all we can do.'

This attitude from my immediate boss helps a lot. But I am still stretching myself literally thin, living on strong coffee and take-outs and even more, living on my phone and my laptop. My eyes are gritty and my body often jittery or dog tired, depending on where I am in the caffeine cycle.

We have drafted Alf and Adam in to help and many of Google's in-house graphic artists have been seconded to the effort. I am reluctant to admit it, but Colin has been a godsend, in regular contact with several dozen colleagues in various universities around the country and making things happen that I could not.

Even Maybelle has been little trouble, apart from the litigation bombshell that haunts my waking dreams. Every now and again, she makes an acerbic aside about people stealing ideas or lacking integrity. But these are ignored by the rest of us.

There has been no time for anyone to respond to any of her usual antics, so as far as I can tell, these are at a minimum. Unless she is secretly cooking up more problems, which would no longer surprise me in the least. She is still simpering over Colin, wearing ever lower-cut blouses, redder lipstick, higher heels, more perfume and shorter skirts. But he has been ignoring her, too, as far as I can tell in this time of hands on deck and noses to grindstones. He seems as embarrassed by her behaviour as the rest of us and sometimes I catch her watching us and, as if she has realised this, she tones it down a little. For a while.

I responded to her legal claim forms in the allotted time. We are waiting for a date for the first directions hearing, which is where the judge decides whether the case is to be fast-tracked or multi-tracked. My solicitor tells me it will be the latter because of the potential sums involved, his mention of which made me want to vomit again. Either way, the project launch will happen first, so I am trying very hard to keep the other, more existential threat at the back of my mind. At least, that way, I can keep food down and my brain functioning, to some extent.

Today is Rachel's first day with us and Len is here too, with Kumar, to whose camera lens we are all just about oblivious, by now, I think. Len's newspaper is running a series on us, with which Rachel and Ben have been heavily involved, behind the scenes, hammering out the kind of win-win compromises that work for everyone.

Ben is as happy as a playful puppy to be sometimes working here in Dean Clough, one of his favourite locations. He comes to join us as often as his other work allows, but spends as much time ranging around the entire complex, making new friends and refamiliarising himself with old ones like the consummate politician I can well imagine him one day becoming. He has been pushing for us to meet here for almost as long as he has been involved in the project. It is quite a surprise for me to realise I must now feel secure enough in my own position to agree to it. I am glad about both the secure feeling and the venue choice. It suits me perfectly, too.

Right now, Rachel is moving my hair in a certain way, for a photograph I am barely aware is being taken. I am waiting for Rajesh's face to appear on my laptop screen. He is going to be attending the meeting via Google Meet, Google's video conferencing software.

As I wait, I am flicking through the various regional projects. Most are ready and looking good. A few need a final push and I know Rajesh is going to ask me for the details of those, so that he can bid for more staff to help with them. It is delicate, though: the amateurs and volunteers working on those projects in their own local areas will not take kindly to the London-based professionals, swooping in and taking over. I do not want it to happen, either, especially in those projects where the key people seem a little sensitive to that kind of input. But in a few cases they seem quiet unaware of the time pressure involved at the moment, despite our best efforts to try to step up the pace a little.

'Hello!' His voice emanates from my speaker and I click to the Google Meet screen to see his face, putting the laptop in the centre of the table, so that Rachel, Colin, Maybelle and myself can all see him too and he, us. Rachel sits down, as does Maybelle, Colin being there already.

Rajesh sounds bold, confident, happy-to-see-you. But the rest of us respond with typical British understatement, mumbling our greetings and making – certainly in Colin's case, I notice – only brief eye contact.

'How's it going?' he asks. 'Zoe?'

'Pretty good. Leicester is ready, now. That wasn't on the list I sent to you last night, but I've spoken to their lead this morning and had a look at it. It's fine. They've added the extra elements I asked them for.'

'Ah, that's great news! And all without our help?'

'Largely, yes. The De Montfort University has an excellent graphic design course and most of the students have been involved. I think Colin and David have put in a lot of liaison work, there...'

'Yes...' Colin leans forwards to speak, loudly and clearly. No matter how *avant-garde* he likes to think he is, he still cannot quite grasp the range of a modern microphone. 'David more than I, on the whole. He travelled down there with Zoe and made the personal connection, whereas I was too busy for that at the time.'

'You've done a lot for them online and by phone though, haven't you darling?' puts in Maybelle, smiling her glossy smile at him.

Colin looks at her blankly. Blinks.

'Not as much as David, no. I helped a little with the History Department, but the graphics side is very much his area of expertise.'

'Oh, I think you're being too modest,' persists Maybelle.

There is a pause. A few seconds of awkward silence in the room and on the screen, before Colin issues a definitive 'No.'

And he looks away from her and back to the screen, quite markedly refusing to return her smile.

I am watching Maybelle for her reaction, wondering if their relationship has hit a rocky patch and her nostrils are indeed twitching, mouth twisting in the tell tale shape of sourness and suppressed fury.

But instead of looking at Colin, her eyes are on Rachel.

I glance quickly towards Rachel, just in time to see her wiping her mouth to cover a grin, even though her eyes are determinedly back on Rajesh's face on the screen. I feel that familiar tightness in my solar plexus, whenever I see Maybelle looking like that, now that I know what it means. The main focus for her ire is always me, but I can see that Rachel is probably second in the queue, just now.

Keen to move us quickly past the incident, I glance at my list and discuss a few other areas with Rajesh. And together, we apportion the resources he can make available to the places they might be most needed. This reassures my panicking mind somewhat, especially as the launch date is approaching with frightening rapidity.

'Right,' he continues, that section finished. 'How about PR? Rachel, are there any points on that to raise?'

'No, we're doing well, Rajesh. Len's series is due to begin next week, which is looking good. We still need to fine-tune Zoe's diary for launch week…'

'You'll need *me* for that,' puts in Maybelle, quietly.

'…but it's…' Rachel is going on. But then she stops, abruptly, having belatedly noticed Maybelle's interjection. She turns to face her. *'Pardon?'*

Maybelle smirks a little and I spot the gleam of triumph in her eye, which triggers a deep inhalation of foreboding in me and a tight burn, in the back of my neck and shoulders. I do not know for how much longer I can keep this going. The micro-tensions are really getting to me, now, on top of everything else. And with Maybelle they cannot even really be classed as "micro". It is ongoing, every day, all of the time. My very being is saturated with the toxicity of it.

'I *said*,' she begins, flexing her talons as she contemplates her prey, 'That you'll have to come to *me* for that.'

Rachel fixes an answering frown on her own face and asks, 'For what, sorry?'

I am trying to think of ways to intervene, because now we are into yet another awkward pause. *Surely, Rajesh will soon reach the end of his tether with this atmosphere?*

Maybelle laughs, shortly, as if the answer is obvious and Rachel is therefore stupid.

'For Zoe's diary, of course! Of which *I* am the keeper. Not you.'

Rachel meets my eyes and her meaningful expression says many things.

'This woman is impossible.' And, *'How are we going to get through the next three weeks like this?'* And, *'How do you cope with her?'* And possibly, *'Can we plan the perfect murder?'*

I cannot help smiling at the quick warmth that the precious, silent, shared intimacy floods me with. And then, as I feel

Maybelle's glare sweep around to me like nothing other than the Eye of Sauron, I turn my smile into a fake but hearty laugh.

'Now, ladies,' I joke, albeit feebly, 'No arguing over my diary!' And everyone else weakly laughs, along with me.

Except Maybelle, who sits, stony faced and furious.

46

It is launch day. The Odeon BFI IMAX cinema on London's South Bank has been hired to stage it, for the benefit of key contributors and the media. It would be an understatement to say that I am nervous.

Rachel is waiting in London, with Ben and an expensive dress for me, which has required two fittings. But this has felt almost normal, in a week that has included hair-styling, facials and manicures, throughout all of which I have had to keep connected with work, mostly via my phone.

I am at the bottom of the stairs at home, now, waiting for Amy and Hugh, because we need to be at the train station very soon. Adam and Alf are going to fetch my dad and then will meet us there, as will most of the rest of our local team. Travelling down to London together is going to form part of our celebration.

I take a breath to call upstairs with a time-check, just as my phone rings, so I answer that instead. It is my solicitor. Any excitement I was feeling about the day immediately dissipates at the sound of his cautious voice.

'We've received the date for disclosure, now. Disclosure is where, in a nutshell, each side must show their evidence to the court and to each other, in advance of the hearing.'

'Okay...' My mind is racing, looking for the bad news revelation it has come to expect from such calls. I glance upstairs, hoping Hugh will appear and stand by my side, for when it hits.

'So, we've received theirs, already. It appears to hinge around a statement from Professor Colin Pritchard, about a meeting you and he had, in April of last year. I'll send it onto you. But in it, he says at that meeting, you mentioned that the History Maps initial concept *was* a joint idea, although you didn't give him any names.'

I think back, rapidly, trying to remember that meeting. *Did I say such a thing? Why would I?*

'That's not true. I'd have had no reason to mention anyone else, when it was my idea alone. I mean, he knew Hugh, so we discussed *him* briefly I think, but nobody else, as far as I can remember. I'd sent him an outline of the project, in advance...'

'Oh, do you still have your copy of that? It might help. As well as copies of any emails or other messages you two might have exchanged, at the time.'

'He didn't reply, but I'll find it and forward it onto you, along with my covering email. Will... will the court believe him? It will be my word against his, won't it?'

'In the absence of any other sufficiently compelling evidence, then yes, it will. As for whether the judge will believe him, we can't know for sure. The testimonials you've gathered should help, especially the one from Adam Shaw. But Professor Pritchard's eminence might well go against us, I'm afraid.'

All the way to the station, I am in a kind of low level shock all over again, to the extent that Hugh keeps shooting concerned glances at me and making extra efforts to distract Amy. He manages to pull me to one side on the platform, when she is chatting to Ava, to quietly ask what is wrong with me.

I only have time to murmur: 'Solicitor stuff about the case,' and he grips my hand tightly, as David Crossley comes to greet us, expecting to share in our presumed joy. We have to put fixed smiles on our faces. I glance at Hugh's and hope that mine is more convincing.

My internal pressure ramps up a notch as I see Colin's car

pulling up and Maybelle, climbing out, right in front of Len's, out of which jumps Kumar as soon as it stops, snapping pictures already. It is one of those times when I realise I have stopped breathing and have to force myself to *breathe out, then in,* a few times.

Hugh lets go of my hand, to attend to Amy and Ava comes, to squeeze my arm and ask if I am okay. I tell her I am, but her question triggers a spring of tears which I blink away, determinedly.

The train ride should be a happy occasion and I think, for everyone except Hugh and myself, it is. There is lots of milling about, happy chatting with each other and some reminiscing, as well as excited chatter about the evening's presentation and what it might contain.

Even I have not seen the final version. I asked to, but Rajesh kept telling me it was not completely ready. Something about this is nagging me, for not being quite right, but the bigger problem of the court case drowns it out.

In the space between two carriages, on my way back to Hugh, I come face to face with Maybelle.

One of us should move, to let the other pass. But we do not. Instead, we stare at each other. Her, with pure, unadulterated disgust. And me, with... a strange mixture of curiosity, fear and anger.

I feel compelled, one last time, to ask the question: 'Maybelle, why are you trying to ruin me?' - not expecting any kind of truthful answer at all, but knowing it will probably be the last chance I get to ask it.

She raises her eyebrows and draws in breath to answer.

'Well, you gave me no choice,' she replies, as if it is obvious. 'You *made* me do it.'

I am incredulous.

'*What?* How?'

She blinks and her expression hardens.

'Where do you want me to start? We home educated our children together and yet now, somehow, *you're* in charge of *me*. That's not right. You're always on about it being everyone's project, but when it comes to sharing the spoils and the fame and the glory, you're not interested, are you? And when I send a journalist to actually investigate you, you offer him a load of whining stories and glossy photos of *yourself*, to get him to back off. What else was I supposed to do, to prove to you that the world does *not* revolve around you and that you *can't* just have everything you desire, on a plate?'

My mouth is open, trying to think of an answer. But I end up merely gulping her perfume-drenched air, as she shoulders past me and carries on into the carriage I was leaving.

I look up and see Colin, who, I did not realise, must have been accompanying her. I do not know how much he heard and I cannot read his expression as he stands there contemplating me too, for a second.

That's probably disgust as well, is my thought about his facial expression. I push past him and go to find Hugh.

The worst part of the launch, which is being billed as a *première*, is the red carpet entrance. I am supposed to be glowing, brim full of happiness and delight, focused enough to issue wise and insightful soundbites, while the flash bulbs are making me feel like I might develop a migraine and I can barely balance on the precariously high sandals Rachel has given me to wear.

I am leaning on Hugh, in more ways than one. Physically, he is holding me up, which is fine, until they shout that they want pictures just of me. When we get inside, I have to stand against a promotion wall while they shoot even more of them. It is immensely stressful.

Inside, there are about a hundred people to say hello to. I keep seeing the faces of people from around the country, some of whom I might have spent weeks at a time working with. But tonight, I cannot remember their names. Normally, I could, but just now, I can barely breathe for anxiety, let alone think.

Hugh and Rachel gradually steer me to my seat, in a row with Rajesh, who is sitting with people from Google. I recognise Pippa and Karl, from my initial meeting with them. I have not seen them since, but Rajesh references them enough for me to be able to recall their names.

My place is next to Amy, with my dad on my left. Hugh sits to the other side of Amy, to my right. I look along the row and behind me and there is everyone I know and love. The entire steering group and some other members of the local group. The stalwarts, Gail, Mary, Jo and Richard.

Ollie has given me a huge hug, which was so full of care and support that I nearly broke down, then and there. Adam and Alf are sitting with him and Will immediately behind us. I do not know where Maybelle and Colin are and I am not looking for them.

Somehow, in this moment, I feel a sense of calm. Seeing everyone here together, as I sit between my dad and Amy, for a brief moment I do not care what else happens. Yes, losing the house will be distressing if it happens and of course, I do not want that. But the fact that we have brought this event to pass makes it seem, for now, almost worth it. For the first time, I get the feeling that we will probably be okay, even if Maybelle wins her case – *within a given definition of "okay".*

The lights drop and the screen lights up. To my shock, it is filled with my face and a voice-over, describing who I am and how I developed the idea. All I can think is what Maybelle will make of it and what the repercussions will be. I had no idea they were going to use Kumar's images in the presentation, but I can see from the background that this was taken at Dean Clough. I do not really hear the rest of the words, I am so embarrassed and uncomfortable.

There are comments from Ava and Gail, about the first time they met me and heard about my idea, then we are on Easterly Street, where my dad grew up.

I turn to see his face and there are tears in his eyes, glistening in the reflected light of the screen. He gives my hand a squeeze. Then, amazingly, I hear my dad's voice, booming out from the sound system.

'This is whe-ar ah grew up...' and he gives a full rendition of the houses and buildings, who lived in them and what they did. Much as he has so many times before, standing with me in our garden, looking down at the town.

Now, it is my eyes that are wet. I cannot believe they have done it and, as I look around, certain people are grinning towards me, so that I can pick out who conspired to give me this wonderful surprise. *Ava, Nick, Rachel, Rajesh. Their gift to me.*

As it finishes and moves on, to cover some of the other projects, with the original narrator, I am openly crying with gratitude and – yes, delight. Amy hugs me, my dad is rubbing the back of my hand and Hugh leans across to pat my knee, broadly smiling, himself. *He must have known about it, too*, I think.

I turn around, to look for Alf's reaction and some movement catches my eye from the aisle. Two figures, ascending the stairs, towards the exit.

Maybelle and Colin.

47

I just wish I could properly enjoy the rest of the *première.* I try, but the most success I have is vicariously, when little cheers go up from different sections of the audience, when their own project is on the screen. Whoever has put this together has somehow managed, in a very short space of time, to fit in at least a few seconds of every single one of them.

Afterwards, Rajesh pulls me to one side and gently scolds me, for looking so tired. I praise and thank him for the presentation, especially the section with my dad. Then, he asks what is happening now, with the court case. I briefly tell him what the solicitor said, which makes him frown.

'It's all *wrong,* Zoe. I can't believe they're doing this. But listen, whatever happens, you've still got a lot of work to do on this with us, right? We have to move into Phase Two, next. Keep bringing new projects online and keep adding to the existing ones, but also we need to do a lot to improve the VR interface. I want it to be less stilted, more flowing. I want you to meet with our tech guys on that, to see what can be done. It needs to be even more of an immersive experience.'

'That sounds exciting.' I have not given much thought to the next phase of work, having been too absorbed in this one and, latterly, in being sued, to look ahead. But my heart lifts, to hear him set it out now and I know that, whatever does happen, I want to continue with History Maps, if possible.

There is a party to attend, with lots of food, drink and conversation, but I am glad to get back to the hotel, as soon as we politely can. It feels strange and good to have Hugh and

Amy in my hotel room, for once, instead of having to video call them, although Hugh does not sleep any better than I do. We find ourselves awake, more than once, quietly discussing our predicament, so as not to disturb Amy. I feel miserable, that my ongoing strife with Maybelle is now leaking into every aspect of my life, to the extent that it is robbing Hugh of precious sleep as well as me. Our very real fear, now, is that it might rob us of far more than that.

On Monday morning my heart sinks, to receive another call from my solicitor. I am in the kitchen, supposedly enjoying a week off work, but really just pacing about, unsettled and feeling sick with nerves.

'Zoe, we have good news,' he begins, in a markedly different tone of voice to his usual, cautious gloom. My spirits do not lift, though. Whatever the good news might be, I cannot imagine it making a big difference to anything.

He continues, when I fail to respond, speaking slowly and quite dramatically.

'The case... is being... dropped.'

'What?' Instead of feeling elated, I am just wondering: *What new trick is this?*

'Professor Pritchard has withdrawn his statement, thereby dismantling their evidence. There's no point in them proceeding, because you would now obviously win, so Mrs Shaw has formally dropped her claim.'

'Okay...' I still cannot believe it might be over and am waiting for the catch, for the *'But...'*

'It's all over, Zoe,' he clarifies, probably sensing my disbelief. 'You're not going to court. You won't have to pay her any money.'

I blindly reach for a chair and sit on it, heavily. I do not know what to think, how to be, whether to accept this news. *Do I still need to be tense and fearful?* I still am, somehow. *It doesn't make any sense.*

'Um. Okay. Well, thanks,' is all I can muster by way of response.

I am still sitting there, staring into space, when Hugh comes in and switches the kettle on, then turns to look at me.

He contemplates me for a minute, in an extremely worried way and finally says, 'Zoe...? I hardly dare ask what's wrong. Have you had more news?'

'Yes,' I say quietly. 'It's... She's... Uh...' I cannot find the words.

'*What?*' asks Hugh, a note of anguish in his voice. He rushes over and kneels down at my feet, taking both of my hands in his. 'Whatever it is, we'll face it together. You know that, don't you? We'll get through it.'

Only now do I understand that he thinks it must be bad news, so I make an extra effort to put him out of his misery.

'*No.* Hugh, it's over. She's stopped it. She's dropped her claim.'

His eyes search my face, then widen, then he stands up and pulls me up and hugs me hard, saying: 'Is it true? She's not doing anything?' and when I nod, he slowly smiles and starts listing the consequences. 'We won't lose the house. I won't have to increase my hours again. Zoe, we'll get to *sleep at night.* We'll be able to breathe, to relax and enjoy life again. Oh God, I wish we'd known this was going to happen before the weekend, so that you could have properly enjoyed the *première.* You'd put so much work into that and this business completely spoiled it for both of us, but especially for you. It was supposed to be your night.'

'Yes. Never mind. I just can't take it in now and I need to know why it's happened.'

'Does that matter? It's happened! It's wonderful news! Let's just enjoy it. Let's *go* somewhere today with Amy. A day out, with no stress and no work, for either of us. Do you want to?'

I cannot make the emotional leap from frantic, gnawing worry to delighted relief, that he has made. Not until I fully understand why this has happened. I do not think I will feel properly safe, until then.

So I say, 'Maybe, but not just yet, okay? I'm going to call Colin and try to find out why he's withdrawn his statement.'

So Hugh goes off, to plan an outing and after a few minutes of more quiet sitting and thinking, I find Colin in my contacts list and touch the green phone icon, listening for the ringing tone. He answers quite quickly and seems to have been expecting my call.

I do not waste any time on small talk, going straight to: 'Why have you withdrawn your statement?'

There is a pause, and then he tells me, 'Because it was wrong of me to make it and I've been feeling increasingly uneasy about it, as time has gone on.' I make no response, so he continues. 'Yet again, I find myself in a position of needing to apologise to you, Zoe. It's no excuse, but I seemed to be sort of bewitched by Maybelle, for a time, which is now over.'

'Why?' I ask, quietly.

'Why is it over? Lots of reasons, but overhearing her conversation with you on the train was the last straw. She made it crystal clear to you then, that she'd had no part in developing the concept, which I knew in my heart, but had somehow been convinced by her was not the case. She sort of... talked me into believing that you *must* have mentioned her at our first meeting, even though I really knew you had not. I don't know if that makes any sense to you?'

I think about Maybelle and how she operates.

'Yes, it does,' I tell him, simply.

'And when she insisted we leave the cinema, just because they'd featured a voice-over from your dad, I finally realised that the whole thing must be based on jealousy and was absolutely unreasonable. We've split up,' he adds, bleakly. 'Not before time. It was madness, for me to take up with her in the first place. *Not* my usual type,' he finishes, and I can hear the weak smile in his voice.

I take a few seconds to absorb this, and then say, 'Okay. Well, thanks for clearing it up for me and for withdrawing your statement. I appreciate your honesty.'

'That's very kind of you, Zoe,' he responds. But I suspect we both know our acquaintance is likely to be strained, for a while. Trust takes time to repair.

So now, the knot of dread in my solar plexus starts to loosen and I start to feel a little lighter, less coiled. I look around the kitchen and instead of mentally packing it all up for a move, as I have been doing for these past weeks, I see stability.

It feels like ours again. Properly and permanently *ours.*

I flex my neck muscles, noticing that the ever present burn between my shoulders has gone and I breathe properly, slowly, deeply, for what feels like the first time in a long time. A smile grows on my face, without me really noticing it. I start to wonder what kind of outing Hugh has planned for the three of us and go to his study, to find out.

He grins at me, from behind his laptop.

'They've put the presentation on YouTube! You can watch it again, and properly enjoy it this time.'

My smile grows.

We end up at Bolton Abbey, in Wharfedale, a Gothic skeleton of an edifice, mostly ruined by the Dissolution, which sits in a valley, ensconced by visible miles of rolling, green hills. The only noises we can hear there are bleating sheep, the gurgling river and Amy's giggles, as she jumps across the stepping stones. I take photos of her from the adjacent, ancient, stone-arched bridge, trying to catch her in mid leap. Hugh is following her across the stones, worrying that she might fall in. His arms are outstretched, ready to grab her if she does, but this just makes her feel like she is being chased and enhances both her joy and her speed across the water.

We find a clear stretch of soft grass around the bend of the river, right by its low banks and we sit down.

I start to unwrap the picnic, while Amy paddles and Hugh takes pictures through the archway of the gable end of the building, which sits majestically, incongruously, past the other shore. We talk idly, about how it must have looked in its heyday and what functions it performed, how the town grew around it and people depended on it for medicine, healing, education and emergency food supplies.

'They were the local governments of the day, really, weren't they?' I find myself pondering out loud.

And then I realise that this is the first time in ages that I have managed to properly lose myself in history.

And that now, finally, I feel safe again.

ABOUT THE AUTHOR

Gill Kilner

lives on a windy Yorkshire hilltop with her family and some cats.

Printed in Great Britain
by Amazon